CORPORATE
ANNIHILATION

MUSTAFA KULLE

Corporate Annihilation
Copyright © Mustafa Kulle, 2022

Hardcover· 978-1-3999-2340-8
Paperback: 978-1-3999-2341-5
Ebook: 978-1-3999-2342-2

This book is dedicated to my family who I love so much.

Chapter 1

The doors of the subway train opened. The commuters poured out of the claustrophobic metal carriages like liberated prisoners. Among them was Daniel Crawley; as he stepped out onto the platform he looked up for the "Way Out" sign, spotted it, and followed the arrows. Like many of the other commuters, he was in a suit, carrying a briefcase, while others had bags over their shoulders. Nobody was empty handed, everyone had either a smartphone, a paper cup of coffee, or a newspaper in hand. There was a constant sound of shoes pattering the concrete ground. The sound of the train echoed along the platform as it departed, it bounced around the concrete walls and girders with adverts plastered on them. Daniel Crawley kept his eyes on the dirty pipes and cables attached to the ceiling, they were dark brown at the edges with black gunk on the screws that held them in place. He brushed passed the stream of commuters along the way, he held his briefcase tight, and then he spotted the stairs. With a touch of a card he passed the barriers and then ascended the stairs out to the daylight.

His eyes adjusted to the sunlight as he made his way up the stairs and onto the pavement. He smiled at the clear spring morning and let out a sigh of relief to be outdoors again. He relaxed his shoulders. He tightened the grip on his briefcase for a moment. He looked around and once again he found himself among commuters making their way to work. He blended in to the bustling city around him. Coast City was alive. The sound of pattering feet continued, but this time there was the sounds of cars, trucks, and buses on the roads, with their engines and horns. On top of that was the sound of people talking on their phones. He looked at his watch, 8:46 am. And there, amid the noise and haste, he spotted a portable coffee stall where a young lady stood, possibly a graduate or a student, and walked towards it. A black street cleaner whistled a tune as he swept the dirt along the gutter with a broom, he smiled and tipped his hat at Daniel.

"Good day, sir."

"Good day to you too," Daniel replied. He smiled back. The black street cleaner continued to whistle and sweep along. Daniel approached the coffee stall.

"Good morning sir," the young woman greeted him with a smile, "How can I help you?" He smiled back and read her name tag.

"Good morning, Edwina. I'd like a cappuccino please."

"Coming up."

As he waited he looked around at the passing commuters on the pavements, and the vehicles on the roads. All of their sounds came together to form a cacophony of noise. But then he focused his hearing on the tune that was being whistled by the street cleaner as he made his way along the gutter, major notes of a familiar melody he had heard before, Spring by Vivaldi. There was a gentle morning breeze. He brushed his light brown hair to the side with his free hand.

"Here you go, sir," said the barista. He paid and took the cup. "I've never seen you before. You new here?" she asked.

"Yes. I have job interview," Daniel replied.

"Oh? Where?" she asked.

"Helix Inc," he said.

"Wow!" She looked up in amazement. He followed her line of sight and his eyes widened. There, among the tall skyscrapers that shone in the sunlight, was Helix Tower. The tallest of them all. The imposing structure stood out with its modernised version of Art Deco made of glass and steel. The sunlight gave various tints of blue. And right in the middle was its logo, a dark blue spiral with the words, Helix Inc. next to it.

"Wow," he gasped quietly. "I've never seen it this close before. It's a lot bigger than I thought."

"You're very lucky, sir," said the barista, "What's the job?"

"Oh yes," he snapped out of his daze. "The job is project management. An intermediate role. Nothing too prestigious."

"I wish you the best of luck," said the barista.

"Thank you," said Daniel.

He walked along the pavement taking one sip at a time. By the time he got to the revolving doors at the bottom of the tower he finished his cappuccino, and then he took in a deep breath. At that moment he heard a familiar whistling sound, he looked around for a bin for his paper cup.

"I'll take that, sir." It was the street cleaner, he reached out his hand.

"Thank you," said Daniel as he gave him the empty cup. He relaxed his shoulders and went through the revolving doors.

The lounge was huge, two storeys tall. Ahead of him were escalators behind security walls made of glass in between steel barriers where a security guard stood. Next to him was the reception desk. He looked around amazed at the interior design. Every surface was white, shiny, and clean. The interior looked like an ancient Greek temple. Every hard surface was white marble with various shades of the blue for the cracked patterns. The Corinthian columns went from the floor to the ceiling, in every corner there were large whitish-pearl pots with an assortment of plants, from kentia palm plants to sword plants. The couches were made of dark bluish-grey fabric. On the walls, in between the columns were dark blue banners bearing the white Helix Inc. logo while other walls had Renaissance paintings of ancient Greek Gods in gold frames.

At the reception desk was a young brunette in a dark blue suit who sat in front of a computer. He walked over to her.

"Good morning," said the receptionist. She greeted him with a smile. "Welcome to Helix Inc. How can I help you?"

"Good morning, I have come for an interview," he replied.

"Your name please?"

"Crawley. Daniel Crawley," he replied. She typed away at the keyboard.

"Yes, here you are. You'll be seeing Julia Esposito. I'll let her know you're here–"

"Daniel Crawley?" A lady's voice called out as she approached. Another brunette in a dark blue suit. She smiled.

"Yes," he replied.

"Hi, I'm Julia Esposito. Head of HR. Welcome to Helix Inc."

"Pleased to meet you." They shook hands.

"I recognised you from your profile picture," she said. "Can I get you anything? Coffee?" she asked.

"No, thank you. I'm good," he replied.

"Great. Let's go up."

Chapter 2

At the top floor, Gerald Helix stood by his gigantic mahogany desk in his office, alone as he spoke on the phone. He was a tall gentleman in his seventies, in a black suit to go with his shiny black shoes. His grey hair was brushed back.

"Are all taxes paid?... Excellent... Thank you. Good day." He put the phone down.

Then he stood by the floor-to-ceiling window facing east, so that he could look into the direction of the sun. The modern, consistent and carefully planned architecture greeted the sun with illuminated surfaces and shiny windows. There were some gems that stood out such as Art Deco towers that were built in the 1930s and in the 1940s. And then there were the two spires on top of the towers of St Luke's Cathedral next to Coast City central park. He looked down at the bustling city below, from his viewpoint people and vehicles moved along the streets and roads like active blood cells in healthy veins. He breathed in with delight the smell of freshly shampooed olive green carpet. His office looked more like a boardroom than a private office, filled with opulent decorations such as a gold lamp on his desk with a dark olive green lamp shade made of glass. Next to that was his black telephone, and black laptop bearing the Helix Inc. logo engraved onto them. Next to that complete with a little stand that held two small flags, of the United States of America, and the other dark blue with a white Helix Inc. logo on it. A small photo frame stood next to his gold plaque that read 'Gerald Helix - CEO'.

He turned to his right, walked towards the ivory coloured walls with floral patterns where pictures were hanging in golden frames. He placed his hands behind his back, held his head high, and took his time to look at each one. One was a photo of himself enjoying a cigar and a glass of whiskey with the President. Another was a photo of him awarding graduates their diplomas at Coast City University. Another was a picture of him proposing a toast at a charity ball he funded, behind him was the Helix Inc. banner next to the banner that displayed the logo of the faculty of medicine at Coast City University. Another photo showed a picture of him cutting a red ribbon to celebrate the opening of a new clinic next to the Coast City General hospital. All photos were monochrome, everyone around him looked happy. There was a proud look in his eyes. And then he moved on to look at two elegant oil paintings. At the bottom of the gold frames there were small labels that said, "To express our most sincerest of gratitude, this is our gift to you on behalf of all art students in the faculty of Arts at Coast City University." One was a painting of Saint Luke the physician, with his curly brown hair and big brown beard. In one hand he was holding a scroll, and in the other he was holding a staff with two snakes intertwined at the top. And the other painting was a depiction of Mary and baby Jesus. Both had gold painted halos behind their heads. Gerald closed his eyes, recited a prayer to himself, crossed himself with his fingertips, and then he whispered "Amen".

He opened his eyes and went back to his desk. He stopped at the sight of the photograph on his desk. The smile was wiped from his face. It was a picture of his four children. His hands began to shake. He quickly reached into the pocket of his suit and took out an inhaler. He inhaled it. Next, he took out a glass from one of his drawers and filled it with water from his own water cooler next to his desk. He took in a deep breath and sighed.

The phone on his desk rang. He picked it up.

"Yes?" said Gerald.

"There's Police Commissioner Banks on the other line," said his secretary.

"Put him through... Hello?"

"Mr Helix, this is Banks. It's about your son Eric."

"Oh no," he whispered. "What's he done now?"

"He's been in another car accident. He was racing around the city last night."

"Is he alright?"

"Yes, he is. There's something else too."

"What?"

"He was drunk."

"God dammit," Gerald growled. "Was anybody hurt?"

"No. He crashed into a truck. The whole front of the car is crushed though. He survived."

"Where is he now?"

"He's in police custody."

"I'll take care of everything. Leave it to me." Gerald put the phone down.

He sighed. He bowed his head as he slouched. His hands were hanging from his shoulders. The look of pride was gone.

The phone rang. He picked it up.

"It's your friend Barry Brooks," said his secretary.

"Oh yes. Put him through...Hello?"

"How you doin' Gerry?" asked the elderly businessman.

"I'm well. Taking one last look at the city before I retire tomorrow. How are things with you? And Brooks Inc.?"

"Not good," Barry replied.

"What's wrong?"

"It's about your daughter, Jodie."

"What about her?"

"Haven't you heard? She's been having an affair with my son and he was due to get married tomorrow."

"But Barry, she already has a boyfriend, she's been dating some guy for over a month now."

"You know her as well as I do, Gerry, it's always one man after another with her. Of all the men in this city she picked my son to get back at her boyfriend over some petty dispute. Their sex videos are all over the internet!"

"Good God!" Gerald exclaimed.

"There's something else too. The girl he was due to marry, after learning about this...she couldn't take it. Last night... she...she threw herself out the window. She's dead."

"Oh my god," Gerald whispered.

"So I'm calling to let you know, the wedding is off, instead we have a funeral to go to."

"I am so sorry to hear that, Barry."

"It's not your fault, Gerry. Don't beat yourself up."

"Alright, I'll be there. Bye," said Gerald.

He put the phone down. He placed his hands on his desk to hold himself up. He leaned on his desk. His midriff felt heavy as if he was doing a press-up with a heavy weight on his back. He sighed.

The phone on his desk rang. He picked it up.

"It's the Mayor," said the secretary.

"Put him through...Hello?"

"Mr Helix. It's about your daughter, Penelope. This morning she organised a protest. It escalated into a riot."

"What?" he exclaimed.

"Penelope and her friends have vandalised the statue of Jeffery Irons. She's all over the news right now."

"Oh no!" he whispered as he picked up a remote control and turned on the biggest screen in the office.

The news channel showed live footage of the city centre. In the middle was a pedestal with the black statue of Jeffery

Irons himself in a military uniform during the Civil War, standing tall and proud. But the statue was covered with graffiti of different coloured spray paint. Banners with slogans made of cardboard were stuck onto him with duct tape. Some of the pieces of cardboard had the words "Nazi!", "White Supremacist", and "Slave Owner" written in black markers. On the pedestal stood Penelope with a megaphone shouting obscenities. Meanwhile her university friends sprayed more graffiti on the walls nearby, on cars that tried to drive past, and some passers-by who gave disapproving looks. The protestors ranged from students to pensioners with different banners and colours of their own agendas. Communists held red banners with yellow sickles and hammers. Many of them dressed in red and yellow waving communist flags while some carried pictures of Stalin and Che Guevara. They chanted slogans like "Shut the corporations down! Workers' Rights! Viva la revolution!"

Another group of protestors were Vegans, some were dressed in green while others were semi-nude with fake blood smeared on themselves. They held banners that read "Meat is Murder!" while they chanted "Go Vegan, Go Meat-free!"

Another group of protestors were Feminists, some were dressed in various shades of pink while others were semi-nude with slogans written on their bodies with black markers. They held banners that read "Kill the Patriarchy! Equality for Women!" while many others chanted "Girl Power!"

Another group of protestors were Environmentalists, dressed in various shades of green, some were covered in leaves, while a few were dressed like trees. The rest had painted their faces green. They held banners that read "Climate Change = Crime! No nuclear power!" while they chanted slogans like "Save the Trees! Cut Carbon Now!"

Members of these groups ran around shouting at people that refused to join them and shoved their banners in people's faces.

Gerald Helix froze at such a sight. His jaw dropped. He began to sweat.

"Mr Helix? You still there?"

"Uh...yes, I...," Gerald swallowed, "I'm still here. I'll handle this. Bye."

He put the phone down and collapsed onto this leather chair. He wiped his forehead with the back of hand. He tilted his head as he gasped for air, and then loosened his tie. He tried to steady his breathing when all of a sudden the phone rang again. He cringed.

He picked up the phone.

"Yes?" said Gerald.

"It's Jo Williams, the Dean at Coast City University," said his secretary.

"Huh? Yeah, sure. Put him through...Hello?"

"Good Morning Mr Helix, I am sorry to bother you but I'm calling to ask about your son, Toby. Is he alright?"

"He's fine," said Gerald.

"I assume he's in good health?"

"Of course he is. Why?"

"Well... he hasn't showed up since the academic year started."

"What do you mean? That doesn't make any sense, I asked him about the course the other day and he said he said he was doing good."

"He's been absent for months, sir. We've been trying to get hold of him but we can't reach him. We thought we'd call you to see if he's alright."

"Oh Lord," he whispered, "Everything's fine. Thank you for letting me know. Have a good day."

"Good day to you sir."

He slowly put the phone down and began to stare into the space ahead of him. There was a long moment of silence. All of a sudden there was a loud bang that echoed across the office. He slammed both fists onto the desk like an elderly martial artist attempting to break the hard wood with this hands. But the wooden desk was unfazed. His bones took the damage instead. He had hit the desk too hard. He felt the pain in his hands travel through his wrists up to his forearms. He trembled as he closed his eyes tightly and gritted his teeth. Then he gave in. All strength was gone. The echo of sirens of police cars and ambulances that came from the city below disturbed the silence. He crossed his arms on his desk, leaned forward, and then buried his head into his arms.

A few moments later, there was a knock at the door. Gerald lifted his head, buttoned his shirt and readjusted his tie. He sat up straight. "Come in," he called.

In walked his secretary, Gosia, who pushed in a small trolley. She was a well-dressed Polish girl with blue eyes. She wore a white blouse under a black blazer, and the length of her black skirt went below the knee. Her flat shoes made her movement almost silent. Her long light-brown hair was tied in a bun that held a pen. Under her blouse was a gold chain with a small golden crucifix. She had a constant smile.

She pushed the trolley along as she approached him. She stopped and stood tall next to the trolley, hands crossed in front of her body, like a servant addressing her king. The sirens outside subsided as though her presence brought peace to the office.

"Mr Helix, your medication," she said.

"You're right. I almost forgot."

She picked up the glass on the desk, filled it with water at the cooler, and placed it back on the desk. She opened one of the small drawers on the trolley and took out some small boxes containing pills that came in a variety colours and sizes. Still seated, Gerald took one pill at a time after each sip of water. She looked at him with admiration and pity at the same time, the same way a daughter would look at her aging father. She knew he was having a hard time. She read him like a book.

"Sir?" she asked. "I heard everything. Are you alright?"

He fell silent and put his glass down. Like a prism, the light that passed through the cut glass emitted spectrums of colours onto his desk. The expensive glass was thick and solid, but the light that passed through the jagged patterns revealed the troubles he held inside.

She noticed that too. It was a moment they shared. He took in a deep breath and slowly exhaled. He kept his eyes on the scattered spectrums on his desk reflected from his glass.

"Why are you here?" he asked. To that Gosia looked puzzled.

"Sir?" she asked.

"Of all the companies to work for, of all the places you can go, the people you can work with, why me?"

She paused for a moment to think.

"Mr Helix, you gave me a job when I needed it the most. I was a homeless orphan when I came to you. I worked my way up and the fact the I am your Personal Assistant makes me proud. I respect you, sir. And, I love my job." She paused. "Every other employer I worked for treated me like I'm something on the bottom of their shoe, a mere number on a spreadsheet. But you treat me with respect, and dignity. Everything I have is thanks to you. I have a home, and a good job. None of this would have happened without you. I am proud to work for you, sir."

He looked up at her. Her eyes meant it.

"Thank you," he replied. "Your gratitude means a lot to me." A weak smile appeared on his face.

"Mr Helix, you have given so much happiness to others, you deserve happiness yourself," she replied.

There was long moment of silence. He picked up the glass and gulped the down the remaining water.

"Ger– I mean, Mr Helix," said Gosia, "I strongly suggest you take the rest of the morning off. I can cancel the meetings. I'll call one of the Helix Hotels. They'll have a vacancy for you. You'll feel better by lunchtime."

"Very well," he replied. "Do it. I need a moment alone."

"Yes sir," she nodded. She then pushed the trolley out of the office.

Gerald leaned back on his chair. He sighed. He pressed a small red button under his desk. The ivory panels on the west side of the office moved apart to reveal scarlet red curtains hanging on golden rings. They slowly split open as if they were in a theatre, and revealed a huge life-sized painting with a golden frame. It was the portrait of his wife, Katherine Helix, young, beautiful, dressed in an ivory gown. She had an affectionate smile, accompanied by brown eyes. She had a gentle tan, and dark brown hair, long and straight at the top and curled at the ends. In her hands she held four large roses that represented their children, two of them pink for the girls, two of them white for the boys. She looked like a queen without a crown or a tiara. If not, an angel.

She had been the most loving wife any man could want.

Gerald got up and stepped forward towards her. His blue eyes looked into hers. He began to cry. He wheezed as he slouched again. He cried uncontrollably as tears rolled down his cheeks, and dripped on to the floor.

"I'm so sorry. I failed you," he cried. He gasped for air. "Everything I did, I did it for you, and for our children. Please, tell me... Where did I go wrong?"

He swallowed.

"When you got cancer I tried everything to help find a cure... but I couldn't do it. There isn't one." He shook his head. "All the money I had. I couldn't save you. I'm so sorry."

He sniffed, he took out a handkerchief, wiped his nose, folded it and then put it back in his pocket.

"But know this." He tightened his fists. "As God is my witness... I love you. I still do. And I always will. I wanted to give our children the best of everything and now... I don't know what to do anymore. I wish I could hear your voice again."

Tears filled his eyes again. He could barely hold himself up. The old CEO lost all strength, he broke down and cried again. He walked away from the painting back to his desk. He pressed the red button again. The red curtains slowly closed. And then the wall panels followed, and sealed shut. He wiped his tears with his hands. And then he left the office.

Chapter 3

Lunchtime had passed. Gerald marched back into his office. He stood tall with tight fists. He had a constant frown. His lips were firm. His eyes were on fire. His head was held high as he looked ahead. Both feet firmly planted to the floor.

"Gosia!" he called. The Polish brunette walked in.

"Yes sir." she answered.

"Send a message out to Eric, Jodie, Penelope, and Toby. Tell them to come and see me in my office right now. Tell them it's urgent. Send the bodyguards and drag them here if need be."

"Yes sir." She took out a tiny notepad from her blazer pocket, pulled out the pen from the bun in her hair, and jotted down everything he said.

"Get me the best Business Consultant you can find. Get me two. No. Three. A second opinion is not enough. I need to be certain. Get me three lawyers too."

"Yes sir. Anything else?"

"Yes. And Gosia..." He paused as he turned to look at her. Her blue eyes looked into his, "I need to get in touch with some old friends," said Gerald.

***

That evening, Gerald Helix stood tall in his office, hands behind his back as he looked out of the window down upon the city. The sun had set. The sky was a painting of dark blue mixed with dark purple brush strokes. The clouds blended the colours beautifully. Against such a backdrop were the buildings, black blocks with white lights dotted all over them. Far below, he watched the traffic. Red lights trailed in one direction and white lights trailed going the other way. Street lights emitted beams of white light, so bright with a tint of blue. He observed people making their way home after a hard day's work, all they needed was some rest to get ready for tomorrow.

But not Gerald. His frown remained. His face was stern. He held his head up. But there was something else. He was in his iconic dark blue suit and trousers, his best white shirt, his best blackish-silver tie, and his best shiny black shoes. All of them products of Helix Inc. He had a new haircut, his grey hair was perfectly styled, brushed back. And to top all this off, he had a silver pin on his suit, a silver belt buckle, and silver cufflinks that had the Helix Inc. logo engraved on them. He was complete. Perfect. He looked like decorated soldier, his mood and look wouldn't be out of place if he was in a military uniform. He stood tall, shoulders back, and kept his head up.

His phone rang. He picked it up.

"Yes?" said Gerald.

"They're here," said Gosia.

"Send them in," he commanded. He put the phone down.

He heard the mechanism of the elevator echo along the corridor beyond the double doors. The elevator doors opened. He heard the footsteps of his four children step out and walk towards the office. They opened the double doors without knocking. Gerald closed his eyes with annoyance. Without turning to look, he knew it was them just by listening to the sound of their footsteps on the floor. One was a fine pair of shoes for men, the other one was the sound of high heeled shoes. The other two were the pattering of thuds. One was a pair of boots and the other was a pair of trainers worn by someone heavy. When he turned to face them he noticed they left the doors open. He let out a puff through his nose, and shook his head a little, annoyed. And there stood before him were him were his children.

Eric, twenty-seven years old, was a tall charismatic narcissist. He had brown eyes like his mother. Built and muscular with a tan. His brown hair had the uppercut hairstyle. He too wore an expensive suit with an expensive pair of shiny black shoes. To go with that, he had plenty of jewellery. His watch, the rings on his fingers, the necklace around his neck, cufflinks, even his earring. All gold. He would accept nothing else. He had a square jaw and a broad chin with a slight stubble. He loosened the top two buttons of his white shirt to show off his chest. That made Gerald Helix frown. He looked like the sort of man you'd find on the front cover of a men's magazine. Women desired him.

Jodie, twenty-four years old, was a tall blonde, with blue eyes similar to her father's. Like her mother, her long hair was straight at the top and curled at the bottom. She too was well dressed. She wore a black dress that was cut diagonally at the lower half so that when she stood one leg was covered and the other was completely bare. The dress was tight around her hips and waist to show off her figure, and there was a long V-cut from the top showing off her cleavage and her large breasts. Her outfit made Gerald Helix sneer at her with disapproval. Her long blonde hair shined like gold. She also wore jewellery to go with her outfit; pearl necklace, pearl bracelet, pearl watch, and pearl earrings that curled downwards from her ears. She came complete with high-heeled black shoes. She had a beautiful face. She looked as if he walked out straight of a Women's fashion magazine. Men desired her.

Penelope, twenty-one years old, was a short petite little girl. She had brown eyes like her mother. But unlike her sister, she was poorly dressed. She wore ripped jeans with holes in various places. She wore a crop top which was a patchwork of random materials and different colours, which she obviously stitched herself. On the front there was the word "Diversity" spray-painted in white with a stencil. It must have been uncomfortable since it gave her an itch in different places. She had silver piercings all over face; on her eyebrows, lips, nose, and on her ears. She had a thick black leather dog collar with silver spikes for a necklace. Her hair was shaved at the sides to go with the pink and purple Mohawk on the top of her head. She wore big glasses that had thick black frames. She wore big black boots with thick soles to give her extra height that came with silver spikes. She recently had a new tattoo done on the side of her neck, a big black sickle and hammer. The sight of it made Gerald's lip curl with disgust.

Toby, eighteen years old, was short, fat, and unlike his brother, he was also poorly dressed. He had blue eyes similar to his father's. He had curly brown hair. His black t-shirt bearing a blue hedgehog was so tight it revealed his fat belly, it was covered with crumbs and stains left over from the foods he had eaten earlier. There were still some crumbs in his beard. He probably hadn't noticed. He wore glasses with small frames. His extra-extra large jeans had holes in them. To top it all off, he had large white trainers with their laces undone. He bit his nails while he stood looking around the place. Gerald Helix rolled his eyes at the sight of him.

"What's this all about Pops?" Eric said.

"Yeah, what's this all about?" Jodie repeated.

"This better be good!" said Penelope.

"Uum yeah, errr, I don't really want to be here," Toby moaned.

"Sit down," said Gerald. He gestured towards the four leather chairs in front of his desk.

"Huh! You can't tell me what to do!" Penelope burst out in her high-pitched voice. It was so loud everyone winced.

"How rebellious." Jodie chuckled.

"Oh geez, tell us what you want already will ya?" Eric complained.

"Do I have to?" Toby moaned.

"Sit down!" Gerald yelled.

The four siblings obeyed.

"Ooh he's pissed," Eric whispered. He chuckled.

The four of them sat down. Jodie crossed her legs so that both of her naked legs were on display which was what her dress was designed to do. She and Penelope sat in the middle, while the two men sat at opposite ends. The two women sniffed. Then they both looked at Toby with disgust and pushed their chairs away from him with their feet towards Eric. At least Eric was wearing a Helix aftershave.

"You stink!" Penelope ranted at Toby.

"When d'you last take a bath, dipshit?" asked Jodie.

"Um... yesterday," Toby replied.

"Bullshit!" Penelope shouted.

"Ya see?" Eric said as he spread out his arms. "Women can't resist me."

"Uch," Jodie let out.

"Shut up you!" Penelope shouted.

"Get over yourself, asshole!" Toby whined.

"Quiet!" Gerald commanded.

The office fell silent again. Gerald walked over and stood behind his desk to face his children directly. "First, I want to make it absolutely clear that I am very disappointed in you all," Gerald began. He took a deep breath through his nose and then he exhaled.

"Eric, this is the last time I bail you out," Gerald began calmly. "No more racing, joy riding, or drink driving. You could have been killed. Hell, you could have killed someone. There won't be a next time! Understand?! You're on your own!" Gerald's voice escalated to a bellow.

Eric rolled his eyes and sighed with irritation like a teenage boy. Gerald collected himself.

"And Jodie, look at yourself," Gerald began calmly again. "What you did was disgusting! The son of my lifelong friend was about to get married, and you ruined the lives of his entire family with YOUR shenanigans! I've lost count of your sex scandals as it is. Enough is enough! You are making us all look bad!" Gerald bellowed. Jodie hung her head in shame, or fake guilt. Then she began to twirl her hair with her fingers and look away. "You could be anything you wanted," he continued," I made sure you had everything you wanted. Of all the things in this world, you decided to become a WHORE that worked for FREE! Have you no self-respect?!"

"You can't tell HER what to do with HER body!" Penelope shouted at the top of her voice. The other three siblings cringed. "You sexist misogynist pig! It's HER body! She has every right to do whatever she—"

"Shut up!" Gerald shouted at her as he slammed his desk with his hand. They all jumped. Penelope froze in shock. She trembled while the other three siblings smirked at her, enjoying the show.

"Never speak to me like that again. I am your father. You will respect me whether you like it or not. Don't forget that I am the reason you are here at all. So don't you dare give that hippie talk!" He paused to glare into her eyes. She couldn't look at him, she turned her head away as if there was a bright light coming from the fire in his eyes.

"That stunt you pulled off today was unacceptable," he growled through his teeth. "You insulted everybody who lives in this city. The statue you defiled was the man who built this city from a small town with the help of men who fought on both sides of the Civil War. My great grandfather was one of them. He was close friends with Jeffery Irons. He brought everyone together to build this city."

He paused for moment.

"They believed in freedom, prosperity, and peace. These are the values that this city was built upon. And these are the values I worked hard to preserve. THIS IS YOUR BACK-GROUND, PENELOPE!" His loud voice echoed across the office. She began to shake, her jaw trembled, and tears filled her eyes. She sat in a fetal position as she cowered, arms crossed on her knees. She looked like she was about to cry.

Gerald paused for a moment more before lowering his voice again. "Since you have no respect for your horrible self, then at least have the decency to show respect to others. Otherwise you and your 'ideals' can go to hell."

Toby chuckled.

"And as for you, Toby."

"Uh oh." He covered his face with his chubby paws.

"You told me you wanted to be a game developer, so I enlisted you on to the best course that Coast City University had to offer. And you threw it back in my face. Why?" said Gerald.

"Buh-because...uh...there's no point," Toby replied.

"What do you mean there's no point?"

"I...I mean...errr, there's no point going to university because I can learn everything for free on the internet."

"Is that so? Then what have you learned for the last six months?"

"Errrrrrr."

"Shut up! It's obvious. You gained even more weight and got even more dumber playing video games the whole time no doubt. I don't want to hear any more excuses from you. And the same goes for all of you." He turned his head to look at his other three children.

He resumed his original posture, stood up straight, and took a deep breath and exhaled.

"Look," said Gerald, "You are my children. I want what's best for you. I worked really hard to give you the best life possible, yet all you do is take everything for granted. It has become clear that you have not learned what I've been trying to teach you all these years. To make something of yourselves. Contribute. Give back to the world around you. So I am giving you all one last chance."

He took out a remote control and pressed a button. At the back of the office, in the north-west corner of the of the room, a large steel cabinet opened up. The four siblings turned to look behind them. The doors of the cabinet hissed as they opened, it was airtight. The metal panels opened up like a giant oyster. Inside there were four shiny black leather briefcases. They had solid gold handles, gold locks, and gold hinges. Each one had a different coloured tag tied to the handle of each briefcase: green, blue, yellow, and red.

"I have split Helix Inc. into four separate companies," said Gerald. "And you are in charge of the one I give you."

"Eric, the one with the red tag is yours. Helix Motors is your responsibility. I thought this was fitting since you love cars so such. You are to build and develop new cars, make better vehicles for this city."

"Jodie, the one with the yellow tag is yours. Helix Gen is

right down your street as I have included Helix Fashion, Helix Cosmetics, and Helix Hotels. See what you can do with it."

"Penelope, I'm giving you the one with the green tag. Since you're such an attention seeker, I have created Helix Press, you have access to the media and the press. As a little extra, I have included all the charities that I have created. See if you can use your influence to raise awareness for the right causes for a change."

"And finally, for you Toby, the one with the blue tag is yours. This is your speciality. Helix Tech is where you will work your magic. Technology is an ever-changing arms race. Here you will specialise in all electrical goods, from computers to phones, ecommerce, and telecommunications. Even the military. And yes, video games are included too. Whatever the market wants, you must adapt."

"Now, take your cases and go," he commanded, like a military leader inspiring his army. "Make something of yourselves. Make this city greater. And then, the world," he said with optimism as he spread his arms out.

There was a long silence as the four siblings turned to face their father. They didn't look impressed.

"Well?" said Gerald.

"Nah, I'm alright, Pops," said Eric.

"Thanks, but no thanks," said Jodie.

"No. I can't," said Penelope.

"I... I don't want it," said Toby.

Gerald allowed his arms to drop to his sides. He sighed with disappointment. For him, all hope was gone.

"How dare you," he growled, "I give you the opportunity of a lifetime. And all you can do is spit in my face? Such insolence. Such lack of gratitude. Look at yourselves, you're acting like spoilt brats!" said Gerald.

"What's your problem, Pops?" Eric moaned.

"I don't have to take what you give me," Jodie hissed.

"You can't make me, asshole," Penelope yelled.

"Look, I'm not interested, okay?" Toby whined.

"Silence!" Gerald bellowed as he slammed both fists onto his desk. At that moment he was a bull. He hunched. His eyes went red. His nostrils expanded and contract as he breathed through his nose. His closed mouth concealed his gritted teeth. After a long moment of silence, he stood up straight and calmed himself down.

"Very well," said Gerald, "Have it your way!"

He took out his phone, made a few taps on the screen, and then put it back in his suit pocket.

"What did you do?" Jodie asked. She raised an eyebrow.

"It's done," said Gerald, "You no longer have access to my bank account. You're all on your own now."

"He's lying!" exclaimed Eric.

"No! He really means it!" Jodie said with alarm, and a look of horror on her face.

"You can't do that!" Penelope complained.

"Ooh man!" Toby moaned.

"Since you can all do so well without me, then go ahead and prove it," said Gerald, "Your chance is right there. In those cases." He pointed at them. "It's either that or flipping burgers for life."

"Ewww!" said Eric.

"Yuck!" said Jodie

"That's slavery!" Penelope shouted.

"No way!" said Toby.

Gerald stood quiet for a moment, he pumped out his chest and let it all out one last time. "Get out! All of you! Out of my sight. Before I call security."

"Screw you man!" said Eric.

"Fuck you asshole!" Jodie hissed.

"Drop dead you misogynist pig!" Penelope shouted at him.

"You're a fuckin' lunatic," Toby whined.

The four siblings got up and marched over to the doors. But as they left, one by one, they turned their heads to face him hoping he would change his mind. But instead, each one had an uneasy look on their face. Gerald Helix had a frightening glare. The look made the siblings shudder, so they hurried as they made their way to the doors. They closed the doors with haste not wanting to see him. Then they hurried over to the elevator, and when the doors closed, they all let of a sigh of mutual relief.

The next day, it all over the news: Gerald Helix had vanished without a trace.

Chapter 4

That day, the sky's canvas was nothing but greys and no colour. The gloomy sky made everything look grey: the buildings, the vehicles, and the people too. But the citizens of Coast City were no different. That day the commuters walked at a slower pace and everyone had the look of sadness. The street cleaner wasn't whistling. The young barista at the portable coffee stall wasn't smiling. A newsagent stood outside his newsstand with a pile of newspapers under one arm and one in his hand waving it around. His kiosk was packed.

"Read all about it. Read all about it," he called out. There was sadness in his voice. "Gerald Helix Missing," he read out the headlines of the newspapers in his newsstand. "Helix CEO Gone." One by one, people bought a copy of the newspaper he had. "Here you go sir," after a quick exchange for a quarter. The newspapers had a picture of Gerald Helix in his suit smiling. But the word at the top of the headlines read "Missing".

One man was reading a folded newspaper as he walked along the pavement while he carried a briefcase in the other when all of a sudden someone walked into to him, almost knocking him off balance.

"Oh! I'm terribly sor–" said the gent.

"Move fucker!" the other man boomed. Unlike the rest of the crowd he had his head up and his suit jacket held over his shoulder.

"Wha– Eric Helix?"

"Yeah, whatever," Eric walked on.

One man in a suit among the crowd who saw the collision had the look of disgust at Eric. He decided to follow him. He took out his phone and began to film him.

"Hey Eric?" asked the man in a suit. "What happened to your father? Is he alright?"

Eric ignored him.

"Mr Helix?"

"He's fine. Now get away from me," said Eric.

Eric approached a group of cars parked along a pavement. He stood next to his red Helix Muscle car, took out his car key and then pressed a button. Nothing happened.

"What the–" He pressed the button again. He pressed several times really hard almost pushing the button out of the key. "Son of a bitch!" Eric shouted. "My car key isn't working. He deactivated my key. Fuck!"

A youth among the crowd got his attention, he instantly recognised Eric, he too joined in on the filming on his phone. He chuckled as he filmed Eric. The man in a suit kept on filming him.

Just then a young blonde woman who was passing by approached Eric. "Mr Helix? Is something wrong?" she asked.

"Nothing's wrong! Get lost!" he turned and barked in her faced. Aghast, the lady walked away.

"Hey Eric. Any idea where your father is?" another passer-by asked.

"No!" Eric yelled back.

"Don't you care?" the passer-by asked.

"He can rot in hell for all I care!" Eric yelled back again.

Eric had conjured an invisible force-field around him that pushed the commuters away from him as they tried to walk by him on the pavement. They tried to keep their distance. The crowd formed a semi circle around the red muscle car with Eric standing in the middle of it. The youth and the man in the suit kept filming.

"What's your problem?" another passer-by asked.

"Look!" Eric burst as he spun around to face the asker. "First my bank account doesn't work and now this! God damn it!" He turned to face the car. "Fuck you!" He threw a tantrum as he punched and kicked the car. Suddenly the car came to life by emitting its loud screeching car alarm. "Ahhh! Fuck you! Fuck you!" Eric screamed. He kicked the car again and again. The alarm was so loud it echoed along the streets as it bounced off the tall buildings in the street. Everyone around him was taken aback by such behaviour, the rest walked away in disgust. But then more people started filming on their phones and taking pictures. At that moment, a black cop who saw what he was doing approached.

"Sir," he said. "Calm yourself down. You're causing a disturbance."

"It's not me, you idiot! It's this fucking car!" Eric yelled. "This damn thing doesn't work."

"I won't tell you again, sir. Calm down," said the cop.

"Don't you know who I am?" he shouted at the cop.

"Yes, and you're acting like a felon."

"No, I'm not. I know my rights."

"Then you will obey my authority. Now move along, sir."

"Could somebody turn off that alarm?" A voice called out. A chubby cafe owner in his fifties stepped out. "It's so loud," he complained.

"Shut up and get back to work!" Eric yelled and pointed at him. The youth giggle as he filmed on his phone.

"Hey! Stop filming me you little prick!" Eric lunged forward to grab the phone. The youth jerked away. Eric lunged again and caught the youth, wrestled the phone off him and threw it onto the pavement. It didn't break. It was a Brooks phone. The phone cracked and the screen went black. Every onlooker gasped at such a sight. The man in the suit continued to film on his phone while others joined in. The red muscle car continued to blare its alarm at full blast.

"Mr Eric Helix! You are under arrest for causing a public disturbance. You don't have to say anythi–"

Eric threw a punch at the cop's face and then sprinted into the road. He dropped his jacket behind him as he ran along the road so his hands were free. He then threw his arms up in the air as he stopped in front of an approaching vehicle. The startled driver hit the brakes. The white coupe screeched to a halt. Eric ran to the driver's seat, opened the door, punched the driver in the face, pulled him out and threw him on to the road. Oncoming traffic screeched to a halt beeping their horns. Eric jumped into the car, slammed the door and hit the gas. At the crossroad he went through a red light to make a 180-degree turn. The white car spun around like something out of a rally race. Eric obviously had plenty of practice. While doing so, on-coming cars screeched to halt, and then blasted their horns. He hit the gas again and the car sped up going south.

The black cop reach for his walkie-talkie.

"Reporting a carjacking on 32nd Street, 45th Avenue. The stolen vehicle is a white coupe. He's heading south. The suspect's name is Eric Helix."

At that moment, four police cars burst out screeching out of their alleyway hiding places and spun ninety degrees as they shot into pursuit. Their tyres painted thick black lines on the road, and their sirens echoed across the city. The street was a cacophony of distressed commuters and cars.

"Oh my! Such behaviour," said an elderly woman.

"That was intense dude!" said another youth who jumped up and down all excited.

"Did you get all that?" a passer-by asked another who also filmed the scene.

"I got everything," said the man in the suit. "This is juicy stuff," he said as he stopped the recording. He then opened an app and began to upload the footage. "Blue Eagle TV is gonna love this." He had the look of glee all over his face.

"Could somebody do something about that car alarm please?" The cafe owner complained again.

Eric held the steering wheel tight with both hands. He gritted his teeth as he hunched forward. His breathing was frantic. He noticed the brand of the car engraved onto the steering wheel, CM, which stood for Crow Motors.

"Oh shit!" he let out. "Don't think. Just move!" he said to himself.

He swerved the car from side to side with immense accuracy and dodged every car in his path. He pressed the accelerator harder with his foot, making sure it touched the floor. The car went faster and faster. "Gotta get out of this city!" He hissed. Suddenly he was aghast. To his horror, in the distance he saw a line of police cars that barricaded an entrance to an interchange to prevent him from getting onto the highway. The police cars were packed back to front, bumper to bumper.

"Fuck you!" he growled. He hit the gas again. "I'm getting outta here!" He spotted a minor gap among the wall of police cars and aimed to plough through.

The policemen who stood by began to run and they jumped out of the way. "He's mad!" Everyone! Out of the way!" All the police dived out of the road in time.

The white coupe smashed through a small gap between two police cars at which they scattered as if a spoiled child smacked them with the back of his hand. The airbag burst open and held Eric in place while the car kept moving forward at high speed out of control. The white car spun off the road and fell off the ramp. The car then rolled down the hill on its side, until it hit one of the pillars supporting one of the interchange ramps. For Eric, it was the end of the road.

The white car was completely smashed. The car was upside-down. The wheels were in the air spinning like a distressed tortoise on its back thrashing its limbs around trying to get itself upright. There was smoke coming out of the front of the car. Eric was held in place into his seat by the airbag as it gradually deflated. There were cuts on his face, possibly from the smashed glass. He lay there unconscious. A crowd of people ran over to try and help. But they realised they couldn't get him out of the wreckage without injuring him any further. Eric's body was trapped. "Call the fire department," one of them yelled.

One passer-by took pictures of Eric on his phone.

"He needs help you idiot!" another bystander shouted.

"Unbelievable," another man shook his head at him.

At that moment, another group of police cars arrived and stopped next to the wrecked car. Policemen jumped out as the doors flung open. Their sirens were on full blast.

"Cordon off the ramp!" Ordered one cop.

"Get an ambulance here now," said another cop into his walkie-talkie.

"Everyone, clear the area. Get back."

A couple of men choked on the smoke coming from the car. There was no breeze to blow the smoke away. The sky was as sad as the scene, still grey, still glum. The sound of the busy highway hummed from above. The traffic that was made up of all sorts of vehicles flowed along oblivious to the scene below. More police cars arrived on to the scene emitting their sirens.

Chapter 5

That afternoon, the weather was the same. The canvas of the sky had different shades of grey, light and dark, all smudged into one another. There were no defining white lines either. It was enough to make anyone who looked up feel depressed and uncomfortable. It felt cold too.

Once again, Penelope and her mob of protestors descended upon the statue of Jeffrey Irons. She stood on the pedestal where Jeffery Irons stood and started reading out her speech in a high pitched, vengeful tone. The groups of different coloured banners and clothing returned. The Communists, the Feminists, the Environmentalists, the Vegans, the Gay Pride crowd. But this time they were joined by two other groups:

one being the Anarchists. They were clad in black and red. Many of them wore black balaclavas and hockey pads. They carried banners that read 'Abolish All Governments', 'Kill all Fascism!', 'State funded terrorists!' etc.

The other group were Animal Welfare activists, who (apart from a handful in everyday clothes) dressed up as different animals like mice and cows. They held banners like 'Stop animal testing!', 'Stopping killing animals!' and 'Set them free!'

A white van stopped at a street corner. It had the Blue Eagle TV News logo on it. An attractive reporter and a cameraman emerged. They positioned themselves at the edge of the square. The reporter was red-haired with blue eyes. She was wearing a greyish blue blazer with a white Blue Eagle TV logo on it, and a greyish blue skirt that went down to the knee, black stockings, and a pair of greyish blue flat shoes, complete with a white blouse, red lipstick, and a name tag.

The cameraman placed the camera over his shoulder. The reporter tucked her clipboard under her arm while she quickly finger-combed her hair with one hand and held her microphone in the other. "Are we ready?" she asked.

"Almost," the cameraman replied. The reporter stood tall and held her microphone and clipboard ready. The cameraman signalled 3-2-1- and pointed at her.

"Good Afternoon, this is Adee Lee reporting for the Blue Eagle TV News Corporation. Here I am at the Coast City town square where just yesterday the Jeffery Irons statue was vandalised. It was cleaned up only last night by volunteers who live in the area. And now the protesters are back again. But they are here today for a different reason."

She turned her head to look at them "From what I can see... like before, most of them are university students... Oh, I can see environmentalists, animal welfare activists... and many others. They are chanting 'No Aquarium', 'Leave the fish alone', and 'Stop animal cruelty'."

She turned to face the camera again. "Which makes sense because based on what we know so far, an article was published online and circulated all over social media claiming the Mayor is going to build an aquarium backed by corporations across the city. But neither the Mayor nor any corporate executive have come forward to confirm nor deny the claim."

She took a brief look at her clipboard. "The building itself used to be a theatre in the 1930s when it shut down during the great depression. It had been closed since then only to be demolished a few years ago due to poor maintenance and public safety reasons. So far nobody has expressed any desire to buy the property. However, the sources of this article are highly questionable. It says in two places that 'reliable sources' told the writer of the article, who is a blogger, a university student, that the Mayor planned to build an aquarium there. But it seems the writer herself is nowhere to be found today."

The crowd behind her grew louder as Penelope continued to read her speech louder, it sounded like she was shouting at the top of her voice into her megaphone. Her anger excited the crowd that made lots of them jump and down and shout back "Yeah!" followed by clapping and cheering in agreement. Several members of the crowd blew whistles while others used air horns.

The reporter turned to the crowd and walked towards them while glancing back and forth at the camera. "Now, before we approach the ringleader herself, let's ask some of the attendees." The reporter approached one protestor who held a 'No Aquarium' sign made of cardboard.

"Hello there. Can you tell us why you're here today?"

"I'm here to protest the Aquarium that's going to be built," said a university student, she had pink hair on one side and green on the other.

"Why is that?" asked the reporter.

"Well, basically,... it's not right to take animals out of their natural habitats and imprison them here in the middle of a city for our own amusement."

"Is that all?"

"Well...yeah," replied the student.

"You don't seem very passionate. And plus, if I may say so, you do have quite a bizarre appearance. What's with the pink and green hair?"

"There's nothing BIZARRE about it!" She yelled back defensively. "I am different! I am unique! Pink because I'm a feminist who cares about WOMEN's rights. And green because I care for the environment!" Then the student turned to face the camera and made the peace gesture with two fingers. "The future is green y'all! And it belongs to women! Yeah!" she bellowed and then walked away.

The reporter chewed her lip as she turned back to the camera. Penelope's screeching on the megaphone echoed throughout the city centre. It was overheard in the broadcast.

"Well, that was one protestor," said the reporter, "Let's see who else– oh excuse me." She approached an older woman who resembled a hippy from the 1970s. She had long greying brown hair decorated with a bandanna made of pink, orange, and red flowers made of plastic. She wore a large pink and white shirt with flower patterns on it, on top of that she wore a brown waistcoat with laces that dangled from it. To go with that she wore a dark brown miniskirt accompanied by long orange boots that went up to the knee. She came complete with long necklaces made of different coloured beads and a large silver 'Peace' symbol, and she wore a large pair of glasses. She held a sign that read 'Stop Animal Cruelty'.

"It's all part of the mass extinction agenda," said the hippy.

"And what's that?" asked the reporter.

"These filthy corporations are trying to take over the world by destroying all the forests and all the animals that get in their way for world domination!"

"So what's this aquarium got to do with it? How is all this connected?" asked the reporter.

"They are only building an aquarium so they won't have to feel bad about making the poor little animals extinct in the wild."

"Okay," replied the reporter, "What did you think of the article this morning?"

"What article?" the hippy asked.

"It's called 'Mayor wants Aquarium'. Isn't that why you're here?"

"No, I follow Penelope on social media because... because I agree with everything she says. I follow her every protest. She is a strong independent woman. That's what every woman should be!"

"Does that include checking facts first?"

"Of course, but someone has to stand up to these corporate scumbags. It takes guts to do that! And you ain't one of them!" the old hippy replied with a sour look on her face, she narrowed her eyes and curled her lips. She leaned into the reporter's face as if she wanted a fight. There was an awkward silence.

"Thank you," said the reporter who then moved away.

At that moment, Penelope finished her speech. The echo coming from her megaphone that dominated the atmosphere subsided. The crowd cheered. Each group chanted their slogans louder than before. The whistles and air horns continued.

"It looks like the ring leader has finished her speech," the reporter turned to the camera, "Let's see what she has to say." Penelope came down from the pedestal and the reporter moved toward her. The cameraman followed. "Excuse me, coming through," said the reporter as she approached. And then she reached Penelope. "Over here, Ms Helix!" she called out to her while waving her clipboard in the air. "Blue Eagle TV!"

Penelope stepped forward and stood next to the reporter so they were both in shot. "Thank you, Ms Helix," the reporter began, "So can you tell us what this is really about?"

"Isn't it obvious?" Penelope replied. "We're here to stop the construction of an aquarium. It's what the Mayor plans to do without OUR consent!"

"And why is that such a bad thing?"

"Because aquariums are just another kind of prison for animals. It's like the stocks. Just like a zoo. It's wrong. It's cruel. And it's animal abuse. Like a zoo." The reporter fell silent for a moment.

"But Coast City has its own zoo. It was built about a hundred years ago. One of the pioneers was your great grandfather Martin Helix, wasn't it? How come you haven't protested against that?"

Penelope paused to think for a moment before she stuttered

"Well, I... uuh... I don't know the details about that. But from what I can see is that... errr... back when it was built, people had... errr... different ideas about how animals should be treated. And women too. But we're growing in numbers though. This time we're going to fight to the end," said Penelope.

"But the zoo here is part of our history. What would you say to someone who wants to preserve it?" asked the reporter.

"I would say they are part of the problem of domesticating animals for human pleasure. And they have to know that it's wrong. They need to be educated. And uh... yeah, that's also what we're here for. To educate people."

"Okay Ms Helix, what about the article you circulated this morning?" 'Mayor wants Aquarium' What are your sources? Where's the author? Jane Saunders, isn't it? So why isn't she here today?"

"Uh... Jane isn't here because she's not feeling well. But she's a good friend of mine. I trust her sources," replied Penelope.

"You're a liar!" one passer-by yelled.

"You said you're a vegan!" another passer-by called out. "You were caught drinking a skinny latte at Star-Ducks the other day!"

"That's not true!" she shouted back. "That's got nothing to do with this!"

"It's all over social media you dumb bitch!" another passer-by yelled at her.

"Fuck off you sexist misogynist pig!" she shouted back.

A protestor ran up to one of the passers-by with pepper spray and sprayed it in his face. Other people got caught in her fire.

"Aaaah! My eyes" the passer-by screamed.

"I can't see!" shouted an innocent woman.

The reporter backed away in dismay. Then she gestured for the cameraman to focus on the clash between the protestors and the innocent citizens, from pushing and shoving to hurling verbal abuse at one another. Punches and slaps were thrown. One by one, protestors joined in with the fight only for another member of the public to intervene. One fight broke out after another. The protest escalated into a gang fight. There were screams and calls for help from every direction. Slaps and punches were heard from across streets. The rest of the public filmed the whole scene on their phones while trying to avoid the conflict.

Just then, the reporter spotted an army of the Coast City Police in riot gear. Armed with shields, truncheons, and gas masks, they headed towards the town square like a row of Roman legionaries. They blocked off the entire road as they approached. They marched in a slow pace. Every step they took had the rhythmic sound of a hundred drums, a hundred heavy boots slammed the ground and echoed down along the street.

The reporter looked worried. As soon as she looked the other way she couldn't help but let out an "Uh oh." She spotted another line of police men in anti-riot gear marching towards them in another street. That too was blocked off and had its own sound of a hundred boots hitting the ground with a rhythm of its own. The reporter looked down another street only to spot another line of policemen marching towards them. They were surrounded. The police closed in on the entire square and encircled it. There was no escape for the protestors. Behind each row of riot control police were armoured vehicles and water cannons.

The grey sky darkened. It looked as though it might rain. A storm was brewing. The marching of hundreds of policemen in anti-riot gear that beat the ground with their boots sounded like thunder across the city. Upon seeing such a sight, many of the passers-by began to move away from the square.

The anarchists, clad in black and red, took out a variety of weapons, from sticks to truncheons they had bought online. They began their own chant, one of them shouted "Show me what the Police State looks like!"

The group pointed to police officers and shouted, "THIS is what the Police State looks like."

"Show me what the Police State looks like!" shouted the loner.

"THIS is what the Police State looks like!" shouted the rest of the anarchists. They repeated their chant again and again. The reporter looked on in horror, her face went pale, her eyes widened. And then she turned to the cameraman, "Tom! We gotta get outta here. Things are gonna get ugly." With haste, they made their way toward the edge of the square and stood close to their van. The cameraman made another gesture with his hand at her.

"Oh– okay, now, ladies and gentlemen, as you can see behind me, there's fighting going on between the protestors and the bystanders. What was supposed to be a peaceful protest organised by Penelope Helix over an aquarium has escalated into a riot."

The rowdy crowd emitted a cacophony of screams and insults combined with whistles and air horns. Some protestors took out their spray paint and used the sticks of their banners and flag poles as weapons while others took out their bike chains and crowbars. However, new weapons were added to the protestors' arsenal; fire extinguishers, and fire axes. Students had stolen them from their university and college campuses. All were held ready.

"Disperse!" a loud megaphone roared. "Disperse or you will be arrested!" It was coming from one of the armoured police vehicles.

Penelope was enraged as she punched and kicked any citizen who called her names. Her pepper spray ran out, so she ran over to student with a fire axe and snatched it from his grip and swung it around while she screeched like a mad harpy.

"This is your last chance! Disperse! Now!" The police megaphone roared again. But the fighting continued.

"Fire!" the megaphone commanded.

The riot police locked their shields close to each other like an army of Spartans. They began to shrink the circle as they slowly walked forward. They tightened their grips. Blasts were heard coming from behind them. BOOM! BOOM! BOOM! BOOM! Small metal canisters were launched into the sky, with long and thick white smoke trailing from behind them. They landed in the middle of the town square and burst into white clouds of smoke.

"Oh no!" cried a student.

"Tear gas!" shouted a hippy.

"Run!" shouted another student. But it was too late. Two policemen grabbed him, dragged him out of the circle, and threw him into a police van.

"Fuck you!" Another protestor attempted to punch a policeman, but he struck the visor and hurt his hand. The policeman grabbed him, and then threw him to the side.

"Take him away!" demanded the cop.

"Back off!" shouted another student. She waved her stick like a baseball bat at another cop in riot gear, the fearless masked cop marched closer to her, shield and truncheon in hand. "I said BACK OFF you sexist pig!" She made the first move and struck the shield with her stick. The cop retaliated with a swift truncheon hit to her wrist that made the student drop her stick immediately. Then the cop grabbed the protestor and struck her at the back of the leg; she went down instantly.

"Get in the van!" The cop's voice was a woman's. The protestor looked up at her with shock. "Now!" she commanded. She then dragged the protestor along the ground.

The cans of tear gas grew into a thick greyish-white mist that filled the whole town square. Everything within was invisible. Only screams and shouting could be heard. The rest choked on the fumes. There was panic within the circle of cops dressed in black as they closed in on the protestors. The noose drew tighter. Many of the protestors vomited while the rest gasped for air. "My eyes! I can't see!" became the common cry among all the protestors.

Penelope swung her axe around as she screamed in pathetic bravado.

"Get away from me you fucking rapists!" She swung the axe around at the cops that came close to her. She let out a scream as she lunged forward and attacked the cops with her axe. The blade struck one of the shields. She tried again on another cop close by. He lifted his shield and deflected her attack. Another cop went around her and struck her at the back of the leg, she lost her balance in an instant. She screamed in pain. Five other cops seized her. She punched and kicked them. The cops retaliated with punches and kicks of their own. They silenced her with a beating and a couple of truncheon hits before dragging her out of the circle and then threw her into a police van.

One by one, every protestor was arrested and given a brutal beating by the cops before being thrown into a police van. Once all the protestors were rounded up, the grey mist of tear gas faded to reveal the mess all around the statue of Jeffery Irons. Scattered banners, flags, badges, leaflets, and paper coffee cups were all blown around by the wind.

A white van pulled over and a group of cleaners emerged with brooms and latex gloves. "Okay guys, let's clean up this place." One of the cleaners was the black street cleaner. The observant crowd outside the square stopped watching and went back to minding their own business. The filming on phones was stopped, and then some of them opened their Blue Eagle TV apps and then uploaded their footage. The rest of them walked away. The show was over.

All of this was captured by the Blue Eagle TV cameraman. All the reporter could do was watch. Once the cleaners began their work she turned to face the camera one last time.

"Well," said the reporter, "It's over. Another protest escalated into a riot. Another one of Penelope Helix's shenanigans has come to an end. Whatever this was all for, I'm sure the protestors will have a lot of explaining to do."

There was a moment of silence until the cameraman gestured one last time.

"Oh," she almost forgot after such drama. "This is Adee Lee, Blue Eagle TV News. Back to you, Johnny." The reporter concluded. The cameraman gestured a thumbs up with his free hand and smiled. He turned off the camera, took it off his shoulder and held it with both hands to relax.

"Way to go, Adee," said the cameraman. "You did great."

Just then, there was a flash of white light followed by a crack of thunder. Heavy rain poured down on the city at a rate so sudden.

"Oh no, not now," the reporter moaned. She held the clipboard above her head.

"Ha! Even God has a schedule," said the cameraman. "Quick. Get in the van." They hopped into their van and drove off.

The cleaners hurried as they swept and collected all the rubbish scattered around the square. All except one, the black street cleaner. He took his time as he swept with his broom. He didn't seem to care about the rain. His hat kept his head dry. He was in no mood to whistle either. He walked over to the pedestal and stood in front of the statue. He had a sad look on his face. The black street cleaner looked up at the face of the Jeffery Irons statue. He observed the rainwater come down from the sky and hit every surface with such force as if Heaven was trying to wash away the sins of the city below.

Jeffery Irons' face was stern and stoic, but the rain that ran down his face, his solid cheeks, looked as if he was crying. The grief could be held back no more. The black street cleaner could only watch in sadness.

"I know how you feel," whispered the black street cleaner to the statue, "I know." He bowed his head in sadness and then left the square. The grey clouds above darkened even more. The heavy rain turned into a waterfall. Soon, there was nobody around on the streets of Coast City. Everyone had gone inside.

Chapter 6

Later that day, while the storm raged outside, Toby was in the basement of a rundown building. The dirty dark brown brickwork of the walls were visible, the dark grey mortar that held them together was covered in soggy moss that came in different shades of green. Liquid seeped out of their cracks. Probably from the pipes that were coming out of the walls. At the bottom of every wall there were holes where rats crawled in and out through. Every toilet flush echoed along the copper pipes which made some of them shake. Older pipes were cut from different angles, sticking out like spikes in a death trap. The ceiling was blackened with age, old paint was peeling off and falling onto the dirty concrete floor. The only things that stuck out as brand new were the rows of orangey-yellow compact fluorescent lights that that gave every wet surface an orangey-yellow tint. The whole place was humid. The poorly ventilated air was thick with the odour of marijuana. The green marijuana plants were in black plastic pots. Row after row, the whole place looked like a crudely built indoor farm. The warm humidity in the basement made clothes stick to skin, combined with the thick smell of wet soil.

Toby paced up and down the entire basement hastily. He wore the exact same clothes from the day before. He had his fingers in his mouth biting his nails. Nervous and sweating, he inspected every plant. He wasn't alone. A gang of youths and several adults in torn clothing were installing a new ventilation system. Office fans were useless for such a task. Some of them were drilling holes in the ceiling to attach the supports for the larger fans, while some attached flexible vent hoses to the ventilators to lead to them out to the doorway upstairs.

One person was standing around. A Hispanic youth in his early twenties was smoking a spliff as he leaned against one of the walls. He was wearing large black jeans with silver chains attached. He had a black tank top with partially covered tattoos. He was watching a live recording of himself on his phone; he was in a studio to record music earlier that day. He played the guitar in a careless manner while he yelled his lyrics out of tune. His drummer thrashed about at the drum kit. The bassist stood still, bored, and plucked only one string repeatedly with one finger. The youth was the leader of this grunge band; but the music they produced was so bad, that it would make any grunge artist scowl with disgust.

The youth then edited some of the footage on his phone, and got it ready to upload to the internet. He added the 'El-Taco' logo on the top left-hand corner of the screen. He took the spliff from his mouth with two fingers, breathed out a sigh of relief, and then replaced it before he tapped away on his phone again.

"They're gonna love me, man," the youth said to himself. He smirked. "Just a few more likes and followers." He finished editing the footage. He tapped the 'Upload' button. The 'Uploading' screen appeared and displayed the slow upload progress, 5% at a time. "Damn! This is gonna take ages." He cursed at the slow upload speed. He took the spliff out with two fingers again, spat on floor to the right, kicked some dirt with the heel of his boot, and then put the spliff back in his mouth.

Toby walked over to him.

"Hey El-Taco, is there anything else I can do?" Toby panted. He wiped his sweaty forehead with a chubby paw. "This is all new to me."

"You've done plenty already, man," said El-Taco, "Your investment is going to give us a big boost. Thanks for dem fans and all the tools bro. Once we sell enough of the green stuff, we'll have plenty'a money to hire out some venues for live gigs. And then, in the future, bigger ones."

"So how much will I get per sale?" asked Toby.

"I don't know yet. We're just getting started," El-Taco replied.

"You sell this stuff in little bags, don't you? How much are they worth right now?" asked Toby.

"I told you. I don't know yet. We don't even know how much our competitors are selling them on the street for. As soon as we figure that out, we can sell it cheaper. Ya see, that way we'll have more customers. Once we start selling this stuff, then we can work out the costs, and the share you'll get. Okay?"

"Uhhh...well... do you know how long we have to do this for?" asked Toby.

"For as long as it takes," El-Taco replied, "this is our working capital. I don't wanna do this forever either. But I have to. Until I start making good money from my music career, music sales, concerts and merch, then I'll probably quit. Maybe I keep this as a side job for extra money. Who knows? Whatever you do in the future is up to you."

"I have bad feeling about this," said Toby. He adjusted his tight sweaty t-shirt.

"Look man, you signed up to this gig because you wanted to. It's too late to back out now."

"I just want my fair share that's all."

"You will! Relax already," El-Taco took out took a lighter and another spliff. "Here. Take a sample."

"Uhhh, I don't know," said Toby.

"Go on, try it," said El-Taco.

Toby put the spliff in his mouth and lit it. He took a little puff.

"Well? How is it?" asked El-Taco.

"This feels... kind of... good," Toby replied.

"See. I knew you'd like it," said El-Taco. He smiled.

"Heh, I don't see what all the fuss is about," Toby grinned. He leaned on the wall next to El-Taco, "I mean, one minute I were like errr scared, nervous... and now..."

"And now?" El-Taco parroted with a keen look on his face.

"I feel great. I feel like a million bucks already," Toby laughed. El-Taco joined in with the laugh.

"Pleasure doin' business with ya," said El-Taco.

Suddenly a loud 'Bang!' was heard upstairs.

"What the hell was that?!" Toby jumped.

The sound of a dozen heavy boots descended upon them from upstairs. A voice was heard over a radio somewhere in the building. "Go go go!" It was Police Commissioner Banks.

"CCPD!" A SWAT team burst through the doorway. Armoured men in CCPD uniforms swarmed down the stairs. They were armed with MP5 submachine guns with torches attached to them, each one emitted a bright white spotlight.

"Awww hell no!" moaned El-Taco. He rolled his eyes and let his arms hang.

"Wait! I'm innocent!" Toby cried out loud. He tossed his spliff to one side and threw his arms in the air, while doing so it made his black t-shirt go up more and reveal more of his fat belly. He was already out of breath, his breathing unsteady due to panic.

All the other gang members froze. They were trapped. Every member of the SWAT team beamed the lights of their guns into their faces. Each one shouted a command of their own.

"Hold it!"

"Stop right there!"

"You're under arrest!"

More SWAT team members came down the stairs and

pointed their torches in every direction. They briefly scanned every object as they took quick mental notes of everything in the room. They moved around the lines of all the potted marijuana plants. One by one, the basement became even more crowded. While all the gang members in the room held their hands up, dumbfounded. The SWAT team continued to shout their commands.

"Get down! All of you!"

"Lay on your front! Place your hands at the back of your head!"

"Do it slowly!"

Everyone obeyed. One by one, each gang member was handcuffed and then dragged up the stairs, out into the cold outdoors where police vans awaited. The rain had stopped a few moments ago. A crowd gathered around outside and watched with curiosity. The surrounding police officers stepped up and waved them off.

"Alright everybody, nothing to see here. Mind your own business."

By the time SWAT members approached Toby and El-Taco, the uploading of his video to his social media profile was completed. One of them recognised Toby as he laid on the dirty ground shaking.

"Ahhh, Mr Helix," said the SWAT member, "Toby Helix. Thanks for your help. Couldn't have done it without you."

"The fuck?" El-Taco exclaimed.

"I didn't do anything!" cried Toby.

"We monitored your little online chat with Taco here," said the SWAT member as he handcuffed El-Taco.

"You mean you spied on us?" Toby cried again.

"We don't need to," said the SWAT member. "Thank the Taurus game developers who share their content with us. They have the right to report anything suspicious. After all, you did agree to their 'Terms and Conditions.' Besides, a high-profile guy like you getting involved with criminal activity made our jobs easier."

"You bastards - aack!" El-Taco was pulled up by the hand-cuffs and taken away.

"But I didn't do anything illegal! Honest I didn't!" Toby cried again. Tears filled his eyes.

"Toby Helix, you are under arrest for the illegal dealing of drugs." The SWAT member pulled and dragged him out of the building. As soon as they emerged from the building, the observing crowd came to life with excitement.

"Hey! Is that Toby Helix?"

"Oh my god! It is!"

"What's he doing with El-Taco?"

They took out their phones and started taking pictures and filming Toby and El-Taco as they got dragged into a big black police van. The SWAT team shut the doors behind them and sat the two youths down.

Inside the van was the biggest SWAT member of all, fully clad in black armour. He turned to face them, and took off his mask. He was a gigantic muscular black man in his early fifties. It was Police Commissioner Banks. He looked more like a wrestler than Police Commissioner. Toby and El-Taco gasped. He had a stern look on his face. When he looked at Toby, he narrowed his eyes and frowned.

"Well," Banks began, he sounded almost disappointed. "Look what we have here, boys. A Helix." To that, the SWAT team nodded. "Observe," he said. One of the Commissioner's large hands went straight for Toby's throat and slammed him to the wall. El-Taco shuddered at such a sight. "Didn't think I'd get to do this. Did you? See, boys? I have a Helix in my grasp." The SWAT members smiled, nodded, while some smirked.

"Aack," Toby let out in pain.

"This time, Daddy isn't here to save you," said Commissioner Banks.

"Aaaah," Toby cried again. The Commissioner's squeeze made a tear roll out of his right eye and then roll down his round cheek.

"At least I got somethin' outta ya," said Commissioner Banks. He sniffed and soured his face at Toby. "Did you crap yourself?"

"Mmm-No!" Toby squeaked. To that the other SWAT members laughed.

"Get em outta here," said Commissioner Banks releasing his grip and Toby fell into his seat. The other SWAT members commented in mockery as the Commissioner Banks emerged from the van.

"Sheesh."

"What a wimp."

"Alright guys," said Commissioner Banks. He put on his mask. "Cordon off the place and gather all the evidence."

"Yes sir," a SWAT member replied.

The police vans soon drove off with all arrested suspects. Other police cars followed. Their tyres kicked water in the air as they drove over some puddles. The roads were still wet from the heavy rain earlier. Slowly, the crowd outside the rundown building stopped filming, and once again, some of them opened their Blue Eagle TV, social media apps, and then uploaded their recorded footage. The excitement faded, one by one, members of the crowd dispersed. The sky was still a mixture of different shades of grey, but they were a lot darker than earlier. One thing was certain though, it was evening, and the sun was yet to set.

Chapter 7

That night, it was dark and humid. The clouds continued to constrict the sky above, refusing to let it breathe. The motel was a dirty place that sat at the edge of the city like some unlikable child that didn't want to play with the rest of the kids in the playground. There was a gigantic sign on top of an aging wooden building that read 'Edge Motel' in a Hollywood style font that had red neon lights on the edges. There was a smaller sign underneath, with smaller neon lights that read 'No Vacancies'. The motel itself was a long bungalow. The walls were made of wooden siding, old and rotten. The roof had some tiles missing. During the day, the motel would have looked like a quaint little place, an American antique from the 1960s.

At night however, the place had a completely different look and feel. The motel was so poorly lit, the whole thing looked like a big black block at night except for the dark red curtains that were illuminated with dim lights behind them. The curtains were so thin that the interior lighting would reveal all activity taking place inside like shadow puppets. The porch was also poorly lit with dim orange lights. There was no charm. Only degeneracy.

On the right-hand side of the motel was a diner that served breakfast, lunch, and dinner by old people with disgruntled faces who looked as if they drank something so bitter that it left their faces permanently soured.

On the left-hand side of the motel was a bar that was run by a bad-tempered landlord. In the bar, the walls were decorated with newspaper articles that featured the bar itself including celebrities that visited it in the 1950's, 60's, 70's, 80's, and the 90's, but so far no one famous came to visit since. The publicity wasn't always good. But at least it made people talk about it. Every other night or so, there would be an argument between two drinkers that became a fistfight only to escalate into a bar brawl. All the landlord had to do was take out his shotgun, aka his "Party-Popper", blast the sky with it once and that was it, the party was over. Nothing more to see. "Evr'body go home" the chubby old landlord would say.

However, there was special place for fighting. At the back of the bar was "the cage" where there was a platform surrounded by bars and the whole thing had seats circled around it like an arena. During the day there would be a mechanical bull in the cage. But at night, there would be cage fighting. You name it, it had it, from amateur boxing to wrestling. It was the local entertainment. The car park was full of trucks and SUVs. It had been a rowdy night. Usually nobody would have given this place a second glance. But that night was different.

Jodie moaned in pleasure while a muscular man fucked her from behind. She tightened her grip on the bed. The half-black wrestler held her waist tight while he thrust himself harder and faster. The wrestler smacked her ass hard with his right hand and she moaned again.

"Fucking take that you dumb bitch!" He slapped her again.

"More... more..." She moaned in pleasure in between.

There was a pile of cash on the coffee table. Next to the cash were two bottles of champagne and two glasses. Next to them were a packet of condoms and a pack of cigarettes. As rough as the motel looked from the outside, the interior design was no better. The carpet was dark red, rough and hard, dirty, with cigarette marks and dried chewing gum stuck in several places. Aging wooden walls went down vertically with loose nails. Above the bed was a dim orange light with a dark red lampshade. Hanging from the light was a wooden crucifix. They all shook with their hard fucking. It was an indoor earthquake. The headboard of the bed slammed against the thin wall with a loud beat. In this motel, "Rest and Relaxation" or "Peace and Quiet" was impossible.

The wrestler reached out for his phone on the bedside drawers and started filming himself.

"Yeah, yeah, yeah," he panted as he fucked her. He held on to Jodie with one hand while he filmed with the other.

"Yeah, folks. This is Cactus here. And this bitch here is Jodie Helix."

"What are you doing?" She said as she looked over her shoulder.

"Say hello Jodie," he held the camera to her face as he leaned forward a bit. His thrusts continued.

"You prick!" She just about managed to say in between her moans.

"I AM a prick. I am Cactus. The greatest wrestler in a America!"

Outside, there were two fat old men in their late forties dressed like cowboys. They stood by the front door. They both had Stetson hats and blue jeans. The only difference was that one had a blue shirt on and the other a red. The cowboy in the red shirt banged on the door.

"Hey! It's my turn now!" the cowboy in the red shouted.

"Fuck you, asshole! I got a whole hour extra hour with her!" shouted back the wrestler.

"Awww! Hurry up in there, will ya?" The cowboy in red moaned.

"She's mine! Get the fuck outta here!" The wrestler shouted back again.

Another guy went up to the cowboys.

"Forget it, guys. She's spending the night with him. After all, he's loaded after tonight's fight."

"This is bullshit! It's my turn goddammit!" The cowboy in red stamped his foot. "It should be ME in there!" he whined like a toddler.

"Get lost you," the cowboy in blue shouted at the other guy.

"Awww! I'm outta here!" the cowboy in red whined again. He kicked the ground with his heel and walked off.

"This looks like it's going to be a long night," said the other guy.

The commotion inside the room and the noisy sex could still be heard from outside.

Just then, an SUV pulled off the highway and made its way into the car park. It screeched to a halt. Two youths in their twenties jumped out of the car. Both were wearing black jeans, but one was wearing a yellow top with black zigzags, and the other was wearing red top with horizontal black lines. "They're here somewhere!" said the one with the red top with excitement.

The youth in the yellow top spotted the two punters at a doorway. He approached them.

"Hey Guys, I heard that Cactus's here!" said the youth with excitement.

"Yeah, he's in there," said the punter who pointed at the door with his thumb.

"With Jodie Helix?" said the youth in red.

"Yeah. There's a queue here. Back of the line, kid," said the other guy.

"Hey, how did you know that?" the cowboy in red complained.

"He's broadcasting a live stream fucking her," said the youth in red, he took out his phone showed the live footage. "Look!"

"Wha-?" cried the cowboy. "How?"

"Blue Eagle have launched a livestream service," said the youth in yellow who was also watching on his phone. "Here check this out!"

"When you record things, you can send them to Blue Eagle TV. And if they like your content, they give you points," said the youth in red.

"What for?" asked the cowboy.

"Discounts. You know. Coffee shops and clothes and shit," the youth in red replied.

"Yeah," said the youth in yellow, "Even if Blue Eagle don't want your footage it doesn't matter. If enough people like your content, your profile gets a boost. Like 'Broadcaster of the Day' on social media."

"Yeah," the youth in red added, "and so far, this has got the most viewers. Look how many are watching Cactus's live footage right now. Thousands!"

"But how did you know they were here?" asked the cowboy.

"Don't you get it? He's got his location turned on," the youth in red replied.

"That encourages people in the local area to film things too," the youth in yellow added.

The men looked at the phones and watched Cactus have rough sex with Jodie Helix. Cactus held his phone as he fucked her. With her stunning body, her long blonde hair, and her soft sexy voice moaning in pleasure, made her every man's fantasy.

"Dayum!" said the cowboy.

"She is one hell of a dame," said the other guy.

"Nothing beats live porn. Especially when you're right next to it," said the youth in red.

"You know," said the youth in yellow, "I always wanted some of that hot piece of ass of hers. Tonight is our only chance."

"Got the cash?" asked the youth in red.

"You betcha," said the youth in yellow. He dug his hand into his pocket and pulled out a fist full of notes. "All we gotta do now is wait."

At that moment a group of tall men approached them.

"Okay boys, move along," one member of the group said.

"Hey fuck you man!" said the youth in red.

"Who the hell do you think y-" The cowboy started but was cut short.

The group of big men did something that made all four men freeze in mutual shock. Their faces went pale, their eyes widened, and their jaws dropped. They let out a simultaneous "Oh shit!"

Jodie and Cactus laid on the bed breathless. She panted from exhaustion. Her body was wet with sweat.

"That'll be another thousand bucks," she demanded.

"In a second. I'm busy", said the wrestler, also soaked in his own sweat.

Cactus was on his phone. He sat up and typed into his social media feed: 'I just fucked Jodie. You all know who.' In less than a minute, his post received hundreds of Likes and comments. The hashtag #IfuckedJodie trended all over the internet. It was no surprise to any other internet user, but for Cactus the underdog wrestler, it was big news to his small number of fans. He smiled with joy as the Likes increased and the comments kept flooding in. He then uploaded the video of him and Jodie having sex to the internet.

"Alright, get a load of this. You got another sex video added to your collection," said Cactus.

"You're a prick!" she spat. She folded her arms.

"Don't mention it. How about a selfie? Come here, baby," he put his arm around and tried to pull her towards him.

"Get lost asshole!" She pushed him away, "Now gimme the cash."

"Okay. Fine," said the wrestler. He reached into his denim biker jacket. It was decorated with silver spikes. At the back it had a crude drawing of a cactus in green paint. He pulled out a fist full of cash and then held it out in front of her face. "But I've another hour witcha." He threw the cash at her naked breasts. "And another," he said, he pulled out another fist full of cash and threw that at her as well. She sighed.

"Here we go again," she moaned.

"Wassa-matter? I would have thought you enjoyed getting fucked on a bed full of money," said Cactus.

"Let's get this over with," said Jodie.

Suddenly the front door was kicked in with a BANG!

Four cops burst through the door and pointed their guns at the naked couple on the bed. They held their guns with one hand and a torch in the other. The dimly lit room was illuminated with beams of bright white light. The bed itself was a stage in some theatre. The room had a new set of vocals. The cops shouted commands of their own:

"Freeze!"

"CCPD!"

"Hold it right there!"

"Don't move!"

"Oh shit!" the wrestler exclaimed.

"What the fuck?!" Jodie yelled.

The cops kept their distance as they pointed their guns and torches at the couple. They backed into the walls to give themselves space and then positioned themselves around the bed. One cop stood in front of the bed.

"Alright now," said the cop, "Both of you get out of the bed, lay on the floor facing down, and put your hands behind your head."

"Move slowly!" another cop boomed.

The naked couple obeyed. And then they were handcuffed. The leading cop continued, "Jodie Helix, you are under arrest for the illegal activity of prostitution. You know sex in exchange for money is against the law here in Coast City."

"We didn't do nothin'!" said Cactus.

"Oh yeah? Then what's this?" Another cop kicked over the coffee table that had cash on it.

"Those are my winnings, dumbass," said Cactus

"Get him outta here," said the leading cop. Two cops grabbed Cactus, pulled him up and dragged him outside naked. "And her too."

"At least let me put something on before we get of here!" Jodie complained.

The other cop pulled Jodie up onto her feet by the handcuffs. And then the leading cop picked up the spiked denim jacket, he laughed at the picture of the cactus, and then he put it over her shoulders.

"There!" said the cop with a mocking grin. "Something for you to remember him by. Property of the one and only Cactus after all. Looks like you're HIS property now. Hahahahaha!" The other cops joined in with the laughter. "Now get her out of here." The cop dragged Jodie along with only the jacket over her shoulders. The couple were escorted out of the motel and shoved into a police car.

Outside, there was a whole crowd of people who stood and watched. Several members of the crowd filmed and took pictures with their phones. Some cheered with howls and whistles, while others booed and hissed. The rest jumped up and down with excitement to see.

The youth with the black and yellow top took out his phone and started filming himself next to his friend in the black and red top. He had his own Blue Eagle TV livestream app turned on.

"Hey guys, this is Bumble-Bee Charlie with Ladybug Linus here. We're at the Edge motel, get a loada this. What we are seeing here, is that err... Jodie Helix and Cactus are getting arrested. Apparently, from I overheard anyway, that Jodie was working as a whore."

"Ooooh! Busted!" said Ladybug Linus with excitement and then let out a laugh.

"I know right," said Bumble-Bee Charlie, "but errr... yeah, they got dragged out naked, man. I mean that's totally fucked up."

One of the punters overheard and approached the two youths.

"How the hell the cops know?" he asked.

"I don't know," said Bumble-Bee Charlie.

"I guess somebody must have tipped 'em off," Ladybug Linus replied.

"But it weren't us, man," said Bumble-Bee Charlie, he turned back to his phone. "Anyway, that's all folks." He stopped filming his own broadcast. Then he looked at the Likes, Shares, and comments he got from his broadcast. He received thousands. The number of his discount points jumped up every few seconds. He smiled with satisfaction, and then turned off his Blue Eagle TV app. The punter walked away disappointed. The cowboy with the blue shirt who overheard the conversation looked around. He spotted the cowboy with the red shirt leaning against a wall, close to a payphone. As soon as he made eye contact, he looked the other way.

"You bastard," the cowboy in blue whispered under his breath. He spat on the ground and walked away. One by one, the police cars left the scene, the last two cops waved off the crowd before they made their way to the police car.

"Okay everybody, nothing to see here, get outta here," said one cop.

"Show's over," said the other.

The crowd didn't move except for a few bored individuals. Suddenly there was a blast of a shotgun close by that made everyone jump.

"You heard em'! Get the fuck outta here!" Shouted a big fat man in his forties. He had long grey hair and a big grey beard. He was wearing a dirty white vest that covered his pot belly and a pair of baggy blue jeans with torn holes in them.

"Oh shit! It's Big Billy the landlord!" A voice said.

"With his party popper!" Another voice added.

"Let's split," said the two youths. They ran back to their SUV and then drove off. The rest of the crowd dispersed immediately. They scattered into every direction as they walked off while the rest of them ran back to their cars and raced onto the highway as fast as they could. One of the two cops rolled his eyes at the landlord and sighed.

"You can leave it to us, sir. We can handle this ourselves," he moaned.

The landlord said nothing. He gave them a dirty look. The same sort of look anyone would give to a trespasser. He stood there and chewed as he held his shotgun. His face said it all for him; "Get off my property." The last two cops went into the last police car and drove off. The landlord spat whatever he was chewing to the ground as they left. Only the landlord remained as he stood in the middle of the car park. The motel had gone from a noisy place of drama to a place of peace and quiet, except for the sound of chirping crickets all around, dogs barking from far away, and the occasional car that drove by on the highway. He looked around, turned back to his bar, and slammed the door behind him.

Chapter 8

The next morning was a Saturday, but there was no sign of a blue sky and the sun was concealed by clouds again. The sky was no longer a mixture of different greys mixed on a canvas, this time it was only one shade of grey. A damp grey cloth hung over the city with periodic drips of rain every few minutes. The skyscrapers of Coast City stood tall, but the greyness made them look as sad as the citizens, the sad news of Gerald Helix's absence still raw in their minds. At least there was a gentle breeze that blew in between them. The walking pace of the citizens wasn't as slow as the day before. But at least everyone tried to carry on as normal after the day Coast City had witnessed.

The newsagent sat in his newsstand, surrounded by tall piles of newspapers stacked on top of one another. "Read all about it. Read all about it," he called out. After every purchase of a paper he would read the out the headlines. There was plenty to read out. The Helix siblings dominated the news.

The black street cleaner made his way along the pavement as he swept the gutter with his broom. He wasn't whistling that day either. He pulled along with him his wheeled bin, collected the dirt and then threw it in the bin. He took his hat off, wiped his forehead with the back of his hand, and put his hat back on. He took a deep breath and sighed. He walked over to the newsstand.

"How you doing, Lou?" the black street cleaner greeted the newsagent.

"Morning Kamau, busier than ever. I mean look at all this, I ain't seen nothing like this for a while," said the newsagent. One by one, someone had a paper to buy. The black street cleaner observed the piles of newspapers stacked high. The look on his face said it all. Even he couldn't remember the last time the Helix siblings being talked about in the news at such a scale. He observed one pile at a time.

One stack of newspapers showed pictures of Eric Helix and the wreckage of the white car he was in. The headlines read: "Helix Road Rage", "Petrolhead Crashes", "End of the Road, Eric"

Another pile of newspapers showed pictures of Penelope shouting in her megaphone, the rioters, and the anti-riot police fighting them. The dramatic pictures resembled a battlefield. Some of the other papers had pictures of the Jeffery Irons statue on them. The headlines read: "Jeffery Irons Statue Defiled Again", "Helix Troublemaker Jailed", "Helix Social Justice Warrior Behind Bars".

And then the black street cleaner looked at another pile of newspapers. These ones had pictures of Toby Helix and El-Taco on them as well as the rows of marijuana plants. The headlines read: "Weed Rock", "Toby Helix & El-Taco Exposed", "Helix Drug Ring Smashed", "Helix Rock: Weed Edition", "Weed-Taco".

Finally, the black street cleaner looked at another pile of newspapers. They had pictures of Jodie Helix and Cactus the Wrestler naked with their privates covered with blurred circles. Pictures of the Edge Motel were also featured. The headlines read: "Helix Prostitution", "Underdog Wrestler Goes Under", "Jodie Helix Pricked", "Helix Arena", "Caught in the Act", "Helix Sex Trade Busted".

The black street cleaner shook his head in pity.

"Oh Gerry," he murmured. Then he walked back over to his wheeled bin and pulled it along the pavement to continue his work. The newsagent continued to read out the headlines while one customer after another bought a paper.

***

Miles away from the city centre, Daniel Crawley woke up later than usual, his alarm clock displayed 8:54am in green LED. He yawned and scratched his head. He opened the bedroom window and the cool gentle breeze blew into his face. A smiled appeared at the corner of his mouth. It felt good. He looked down at the suburbs below. It was a relief to be away from the crowded and noisiest part of the city.

A moment later, he was joined by a petite blonde in her night dress. She put her arms around him and rested her head on his right shoulder as she looked outside the window.

"Morning baby," said the blonde.

"Hey," he replied. He put a hand on top of hers. "I'm hungry."

Later, they made their coffee in a nice shiny kitchen made of black onyx marble with elegant thin greyish-white lines that branched around the surface. The sink and the taps were silver. All the wooden surfaces including the cupboards and shelves were glossy white and clean.

Daniel took out a carton of milk from the gigantic silver Helix fridge and poured it into his bowl of cereal. He made himself a coffee and put his mug on the coffee table in the middle of the sitting room. He sat on his dark brown leather couch in front of the Helix HD TV.

The apartment was clean and tidy with modern interior design, with white walls and a white ceiling. The windows let in the daylight. The room was brought to life with plants in glossy white vases on top of oak furniture. The little oak shelves displayed their collection of books. In one corner there was a tall silver lamp, with a wide dome silver base that held two narrow poles up that held an inverted wide silver cone that held a white ball at the top. One of the two silver poles had a little silver knob for a switch.

His girlfriend, Denise, sat next him with a phone in one hand and her own mug of coffee in the other. Daniel picked up the remote and turned on the TV. Just in time for the 9 o'clock news bulletin.

"Good morning, I'm Johnny Perkins and this is Blue Eagle TV News. I'm here today with a special story about the Helix siblings." The news presenter began. He was a slick-looking man in his forties wearing a greyish blue suit. Pale man with grey hair and blue eyes.

"Now, we all know about kids going wild as soon as the parents leave the house, but yesterday, the sons and daughters of Gerald Helix have taken things one step too far. We have a busted drug ring, a riot, prostitution, and a carjacking that almost cost a life. Here's the story:

"Soon after the headlines spread of Gerald Helix going missing yesterday morning, Eric Helix was recorded punching and kicking his own car causing the alarm to go off. Witnesses say that it was because his car key was not working. When a police officer tried to intervene, Eric Helix punched the officer in the face and made a run for it, only to stop a car, assault the driver and steal the car. According to Police Commissioner Eugene Banks, Eric Helix was trying to escape from the city by driving south towards the highway. But Eric Helix, determined of course, crashed through the barricade of police cars which caused the stolen vehicle to roll down the hill and collide with a pillar under the interchange. Eric Helix was found unconscious with minor injuries. He is now in Coast City General Hospital where he is recovering. As soon he does however, he will be jailed to await his trial."

The TV showed footage of Eric punching and kicking his car. And then it showed the footage of him grabbing a youth's phone and throwing it on the pavement to smash it. All the footage that was recorded by bystanders was compiled into one video.

"Later that day," the News Presenter continued, "Brooks Inc released a commercial which compelled thousands of people to exchange their Helix phones for a Brooks phone while many others have placed their Helix phones online for sale."

Daniel Crawley tutted in disapproval, he then took in a deep breath and exhaled.

"Ah Geez. What an idiot," he whispered.

"And now," said news presenter, "As if causing a riot the previous day wasn't enough, Penelope Helix returned to the Coast City Town Square to pull off the same stunt all over again, only this time, it was over an Aquarium the Mayor had supposedly proposed to replace the old Coast City Theatre. It started when an article was published online by an acquaintance of Penelope Helix that turned out to be false. Anti-riot control police were called in, but when the protestors disobeyed orders to disperse, it resulted in a violent clash. Many of the protestors were beaten with truncheons before being taken into police custody. All that over an aquarium? Well that blew out of proportion. Penelope Helix is now in jail awaiting trial. You can watch the live report by Adee Lee by going over to the Blue Eagle TV Extra channel."

The TV displayed footage recorded from phones that were uploaded intertwined with the live report with Adee Lee.

Daniel Crawley threw his head back as he rolled his eyes. His chest raised and declined as he let out deep sigh.

"What an embarrassment," he said.

"She's so annoying," said Denise. She was scrolling through social media apps on her phone. Swiping her finger up and down on her phone, periodically. Her focus went from her phone to the TV and going back to the phone again.

"And if that wasn't enough," the news presenter continued, "famous video game addict Toby Helix was caught growing marijuana in a basement with failed rock-star El-Taco, who was arrested soon after he uploaded his latest video to the internet, which went viral gaining him thousands of views and thousands of more followers. Rumour has it that when his father Gerald Helix cut off access to his bank account, Toby turned to dealing with drugs. He is now in jail awaiting trial."

The TV showed footage of Toby and El-Taco being dragged into the street by the SWAT Team and then thrown into a police van. Some of the footage was uploaded by the bystanders who recorded the arrest with their phones and uploaded it to Blue Eagle TV with their apps. It also showed photos of the dirty basement full of marijuana plants.

"For crying out loud," said Daniel, "What's wrong with these people?" He shook his head.

"Spoilt brats. That's what's wrong with them," said Denise, "When you're born into a rich family like that, why would you want to do anything useful when you already have everything? It's people like that who really piss me off," ranted Denise.

"He's a Video Game Champion," said Daniel. "He has won every single video game tournament in America. You name the trophy, he has it. If I were to play an online game with him right now, he'd beat me in a flash. The trouble is he has too much time on his hands."

"And grease from all the junk food he eats. I mean, look at him. The guy's a fatso. Does that look like a champion to you? More like a champion of masturbation," said Denise.

"Yuck! Oh god." He closed his eyes as he cringed. "Nice going, Dee. That was the last thing I wanted to think about. Now it's in my head," said Daniel.

"Good," she smiled. She leaned over and kissed him on the cheek, and then sat back in her seat. She looked at her phone and then laughed.

"What?" he asked.

"It's that El-Taco video the guy on TV was talking about," she said.

"Huh. At least he's trying to make something of himself, and he wasn't born into a rich family. Not to my knowledge anyway," said Daniel. Denise chuckled.

"His music sucks. I don't know why people even listen to this guy," She said. "Look."

She leaned over and showed Daniel the footage on her phone. He chuckled.

"He's a clown," said Daniel, "At least it's funny. If you can't make good music, why not make a fool of yourself in the process? It will give you publicity but not for the right reasons."

"If this El-Taco thinks his music is any good, then he needs his head examined. I mean, talk about an ego problem," said Denise.

"Wait a minute, let me see your phone... I thought your phone was a Helix. What happened to that?" asked Daniel.

"Ummm... well... alright I exchanged it yesterday. Okay? My friends and I saw the Brooks Phone commercial with Eric Helix in it. And we all decided to exchange our Helix phones for a Brooks phone."

"Yeah but, why?" asked Daniel.

"Look Danny, I dropped this phone twice already and it never smashed. It's second-hand! I dropped my Helix phone only ONCE when it was brand new, it had a crack going down the screen. Don't get me wrong, I love Helix gadgets, they're flashy and easy to use and all that. But you gotta make sure a phone doesn't break when you drop it, let alone smash it on the ground the way Eric tried to."

"Wait, what? Eric tried to...? What do you mean? That was on the news just now. How did Brooks Inc get hold of a footage of Eric Helix trying to break one of their phones?" asked Daniel bewildered.

"I don't know," Denise shrugged as she replied. "Maybe somebody who works at Brooks Inc was present there and filmed it."

"Holy shit," he threw himself back in his seat. "This is bad," he cupped his hands all over his face.

"Maybe Blue Eagle TV and Brooks Inc are working together," Denise added. "I don't know." She shrugged again. "I thought that's how businesses worked. 'Competition' and all that."

"And, last but not least," said the news presenter, interrupting their conversation.

"Oh god no!" Said Daniel.

"Jodie Helix has pulled off yet another sex scandal, but this time it was with failed-boxer-turned-failed-wrestler, The Cactus. She was caught last night at the Edge Motel running her own sex trade with men throughout the day. It was revealed that she too was cut off from her father's bank account so she resorted to prostitution. She is now in jail awaiting trial."

The TV showed footage of the Edge Motel followed by footage of Cactus and Jodie Helix nude with their privates covered with blurred circles being dragged along by cops before being shoved into police cars. Some of the footage was recorded and uploaded by the bystanders who used the Blue Eagle TV app.

"God dammit!" Daniel whispered under his breath.

"Come on. Admit it. You wanna bang her. Don't you?" said Denise.

"Well uh... She's looks nice but uh... nah. Too slutty for me," Daniel replied.

"I know what you mean. I got a name for that; Dick Dilemma. You wanna fuck a girl who's hot, but you know she's been with so many other guys, and that puts you off. So there you go, Dick Dilemma."

Daniel laughed. "Oh god," he replied.

"But that's not all," said the news presenter.

"Uh-oh," Daniel sat up straight as he cringed. Eyes glued to the screen.

"Last night a poll was launched on social media calling for action figures of Cactus to be made to go with their wrestling collection. Many have emailed Osprey Toys calling on them to get Cactus the Wrestler action figures made. But the manufacturer Osprey Toys has openly condemned his actions and refused to make a toy of him saying they 'refuse to glorify a pervert.' In response to this, an independent group of university students came together and launched a crowd-funding campaign this morning with its goal to raise $100,000 to make their first batch of action figures using the latest affordable 3d-printing technology. They call themselves Rebel-Print and so far they have raised $60,000. Their website RebelPrint.com already has a special section dedicated to Cactus merchandise from mugs to t-shirts, posters, pens, and more. Looks like Osprey's loss is Rebel-Print's gain. But sadly for the fans, he is in jail and awaiting his trial. And that concludes today's special story and we'll be back after a short commercial break."

"Phew," Daniel let out a sigh of relief, "Glad that cringe-fest is over."

Just then a familiar person appeared on the TV screen.

"Hey! Stop filming me you little *bleep*." It was recorded footage of Eric Helix lunging at a youth and grabbing him. He took the phone off him and threw it on to the pavement with immense force.

A voice over began; "This is Eric Helix attempting to break a Brooks phone. And this is a video from the phone after he threw it." The advert then showed good quality pictures and videos, and it featured the youth who then looked at the camera and smiled. "With its high definition camera the picture quality is still the same. It remains robust and good as new. The Brooks Phone. Even a Helix can't break it."

"Oh hell no," Daniel buried his head in his hands as he leaned forward in his seat

"Yyyyeeeeah. That was the commercial we saw," said Denise.

"Can this get any worse?" Daniel moaned.

Another commercial appeared on the screen. It showed footage of a man with a bandage around his head. The man's face looked sad. A voiceover began:

"Have you been assaulted by a carjacker lately?"

Then the footage showed the man looking through medical bills, his face looked anxious.

"Did you hesitate to call an ambulance or see a doctor?"

And then a group of well dressed men and women in suits sat next to the injured man and shook his hand.

"Not to worry. We at Crow Car Insurance now cover your medical bills as well as damage to your car. Giving you peace of mind."

Then the advert showed the bandaged man standing next to a white Crow Car identical to the one Eric stole. The bandaged man then stood smiling at the camera with his Crow Car Insurance documents in his hand.

"Crow Car Insurance. Let your driving experience be as the Crow Flies."

"Alright that's it!" Daniel grabbed the remote control, turned off the TV and then put it on the coffee table. "Enough bullshit for one morning."

And then Daniel took out his Helix phone and looked at

all the Blue Eagle TV News reports. He tutted as he shook his head. He read through the comment section of every story about the Helix siblings.

The comment section under Eric's story read like:

"Poor Eric I hope he's ok."

"Somebody could have died!"

"What an asshole."

"He got what he deserved."

"Joy riders should have their licenses stripped from them."

"If Helix inc did a remake of 'The Fast and the Furious' this is what it would look like. Only it's real. HAHA!"

"I always loved the Helix brand but now I'm not so sure."

Then Daniel looked at the comment section under Penelope's story. The comments read:

"Stupid bitch."

"Commie bastard."

"Someone's got daddy issues."

"What a piece of shit."

"I swear every time I hear that high pitch voice of hers I want rusty nails drilled into my ears."

"So this is what students do in their spare time. LOL."

Daniel switched over to the comment section on Toby's story. The comments said the following:

"Fat bastard"

"Go for dope when you're broke. Why not?"

"What a waste of space."

"Hey Toby, when was the last time you saw your feet?"

Daniel took in one more deep breath and looked through the comment section after the news report on Jody. It was flooded with insults and mockery against her and Cactus. Some comments that were hurled at Jodie said the following:

"What an absolute slut!"

"Oh Jodie, can you get any lower than that?"

"She's hot but I wouldn't touch her with barge pole."

"Hey Jodie, get a real job."

"When's she gonna learn?"

"Whore!"

Meanwhile the comments aimed at Cactus said:

"He can't win a championship so he settles for bar fights. LOL"

"He hires hookers. Don't you know that's CHEATING?!"

"Gee Cactus, you really are a PRICK!"

"He didn't bang Jodie. He bought her. What a loser."

"He still banged her though. That lucky bastard."

"He pricks everyone. LOL."

Someone even commented:

"The world is a cactus. No matter what way you turn there's always another prick."

To that someone else replied "Yup, even Cactus himself. Lol."

"Oh man," said Daniel. He sighed. He put his Helix phone onto the coffee table and leaned back in his seat. He placed his hands on his sweaty red face.

"Don't worry, babe," Denise put her phone on the coffee table and leaned onto Daniel. She put her arms around him. "It's not so bad, at least we're not the ones on the screen. Hell, if I was in any of their shoes right now I'd kill myself."

"That's so what I wanna do right now," Daniel replied.

"Don't say that!"

"Now I'm a laughing stock. Every person who knows I work at Helix will want nothing to do with me because of those shitheads. They give the company such a bad name, I don't know how they managed to stay on top of the market."

"Don't worry," said Denise. "This won't last forever. Besides, they're in jail now. They can't do any more damage."

At that moment his phone rang. He picked it up. "Huh? It's work." He said with surprised look on his face before he answered it. "Hello?... Yeah, I heard the news... I know... it was on TV, I saw it... all of it.... what?... Now?! But it's Saturday–" He fell silent. There was a long moment. "Alright, I'll be right there."

"What is it?" asked Denise.

"They need me at work. Right now."

"What? Why?"

"Damage control. Helix Inc. are making losses already and they need me to assist in projects to launch ready for Monday. This is fucking bullshit." He got up and made his way to the bedroom and started to get changed.

She followed him in and stood by the door as he put on his trousers and white shirt with haste.

"Don't worry babe. This is will blow over in time. Besides, you're not alone."

***

Further away from the city was the Edge Motel. In the bar sat Big Billy reading a newspaper. It had pictures of Jodie Helix and the Edge Motel on the front. There was a small TV set broadcasting the Blue Eagle TV news. Even with daylight coming in through the windows, the bar was a poorly lit place with dim orange lights. The walls were built from bricks of different shades of brown. There were plenty of aging antler wall decor to go with the frames photos of the famous people who visited the bar in the past. The table of the bar was a dark coffee coloured marble. In one corner stood an old jukebox that played Elvis records on repeat. It was playing 'Heartbreak Hotel.' Everything else was made of aging wood: tables, chairs, and stools. Big Billy was sitting on a small chair in another corner with his feet up. He was alone until the cowboy with the blue shirt walked in. The small TV caught his eye showing Jodie Helix and the Edge Motel. He smirked as he chewed. He placed his thumbs into his pockets.

"Look Billy, you're on the tube," the cowboy said with excitement.

"Yeah yeah," Billy mumbled with disinterest.

"C'mon, I thought you'd be happy to see yer motel on TV for a change. Yer famous."

"That don't mean jack shit!" Big Billy bellowed. "Now ever' body's gonna think we host orgies here because of that Helix bitch! If we go out of business it will be because of her." Billy let out a bitter rant as he got up. He tore up the newspaper in his hands and threw it in the bin. He then picked up the remote control and turned off the TV. He walked into his small office, slammed the door shut, and began to sulk. The cowboy stood there alone for a moment, he looked around, when he found nobody to talk to, the song on the juke box ended. He chewed again, and then left the bar. He slammed the door behind him.

Chapter 9

Months later, the day of judgement passed, the day of sentencing arrived. Despite the hot and sticky summer, the sky remained a messy canvas of greys, light and dark, all carelessly mixed into one another. The rain came and went like a fickle visitor. But on that day, one group of people stayed in one place.

"Helix siblings found guilty!" the newsagent called out. "Get your copy today. Read all about it. The Helix siblings get their sentence today. Read all about it."

Just then the black street cleaner walked along the pavement with his wheeled bin. He wasn't whistling. He noticed the stack of newspapers in the newsstand. They had all four mug shots of the Helix siblings on the front cover, the headlines read in bold 'Helix Siblings Guilty.'

"Oh Gerry," he whispered in pity. "I wonder what you're feelin' right now." Then he looked up at the sky and sighed. "God knows." He pulled his wheeled bin along and continued along the pavement.

The Coast City Court of Justice was surrounded by cordoned off security that set up railings to keep the crowd away. Only the press was allowed to be close by as they waited outside the building. The public, from every walk of life, gathered around the front. Loyal fans had pictures of individual Helix siblings in their hands while others made placards mocking them by drawing and spraying graffiti onto the Helix faces.

The haters chanted; "Throw away the key!"

While the fans chanted a variety of their own;

"Free Jodie!"

"Let Penelope go!"

"Eric Marry me."

"Toby the Martyr."

The Court itself looked like an ancient Roman temple. The front of it was built to look like the Pantheon of Rome. The roof of the front was held by Roman Doric columns. The light grey bricks were darkened with age throughout the years. The rain added new layers of dark lines on top of another that made the whole place look as if it bled dark grey. The frosted windows were tall with grid panes. It only allowed a small amount of white light to be visible from the outside. The roof had dark grey tiles. The building was complete with a gigantic dome, also clad with dark grey tiles, and on top of the dome stood a gold statue of Lady Justice. She was blind-folded. In her right hand she held a sword, and in her left she held the scales of justice. She wore a toga that covered one of her breasts. It was as if Coast City had a Greek Goddess of its own.

Adee Lee adjusted her outfit with her free hand while she held a microphone with the other.

"You ready?" asked the cameraman.

"Almost," she replied. She adjusted her name tag, took a brief look at a pocket mirror, and then she put it away. "Okay, I'm ready." The cameraman placed the camera onto his right shoulder and held it in place steady. He gestured with his fingers; 3-2-1, and then pointed to her.

"Good Morning, this is Adee Lee reporting for the Blue Eagle TV News Corporation. Here I am outside the Coast City Court of Justice. The Helix siblings have been found guilty.

What the siblings have done are unrelated cases and yet they are about to receive their sentences by the same Judge. This City has never seen anything like this, all four children of successful billionaire Gerald Helix are about to be given their sentences at the same time. These are unusual circumstances. There is a massive crowd here, thousands of people, some have come to support the siblings while others have come to condemn them, the rest, from what I can see, are spectators. While we wait the for the sentence let's talk to some of them."

It was packed inside the courtroom. The crowd jeered at the four siblings who sat next to their lawyers at a rather long Defence table. The judge was an old man in his 70s who leaned on his left hand as he sat in his black leather seat. He looked rather sad. The siblings sat silent with their heads down, depressed. At the back of the courtroom stood Commissioner Banks with his arms crossed and a smirk. The judge watched the courtroom for one moment longer before he reached the gavel and banged it twice with little effort.

"Order in the courtroom," said the Judge. He didn't need to shout.

Behind the Judge was an oil painting of a golden eagle with its wings spread out. On each side of it were two flag poles. On one side it was the American flag, and the one on the other side was a dark blue flag with the Coast City emblem on it. The Coast City emblem was a tricorn hat with two muskets crossed underneath surrounded by two fish, one facing up, the other facing down, all within a circle of stars. Above the golden eagle was a portrait of George Washington. The walls were nothing but plain walnut brown wood. The white ceiling was lit with bright white LED panels that made the room very bright. The frosted windows had crimson red curtains on each side, held up by gold rails.

"Okay now listen here," a lawyer quickly leaned into Eric's ear, "this guy is irascible. Anything can make him increase a sentence. You piss him off, you're screwed. So keep quiet." The Judge watched as the whole courtroom fell silent.

The Judge put the gavel down, took off his glasses, massaged his eyes with his fingers, and then put them back on. He began with a sigh.

"Does anyone have anything to say?"

"I do, your honour," said a lawyer in a suit who sat next to Eric. He got up and stood up straight before the Judge. "Eric Helix was having a bad day, you know. Let us consider for one moment the emotional distress he was dealing with." To that Eric chuckled. He couldn't suppress a smile. The Judge's eyes darted over to Eric. The Judge narrowed his eyes. He was displeased. The lawyer swallowed. "His father went missing only hours prior to the incident in question," the lawyer continued, "He lost access to his bank account. And then his car wasn't working. All in one day. We've got to take his feelings into account."

"Mr Bloom," said the Judge, "We all have bad days. We are all capable of doing nasty things. However that does not justify assaulting a police officer and then a driver, or a carjacking. Would you agree with that statement?"

"I'm afraid that's an unfair question, your honour, I–"

"Would you, or would you NOT agree with that?" asked the Judge. His lips were firm. His eyes burned into the lawyers soul. The lawyer fell silent and bowed his head in submission, the Judge absorbed all the energy he had.

"Yes, your honour." He sat back down.

"Anyone else?" asked the Judge.

"I do, your honour." A lawyer who sat next to Jodie rose from her seat. She wore a black blazer. She marched over and stood in front of the Judge like a teacher's pet. She had a smug look on her face that gave everyone the impression she can soften the judge. The Judge was as stern as ever. "In defence of Jodie Helix here, I can assure you this is all a misunderstanding. When the police came to arrest Jodie, yes she and Cactus the man in question, were naked, but the money that was found just happened to be there. Cactus won a cage tournament that night and all he wanted was to spend his winnings on Jodie. A gift for his girlfriend if you like. Like any lover would." Jodie chuckled, she covered her mouth. She too didn't escape the sharp eyesight of the Judge.

"Ms Ameer," said the Judge in an angry tone, "That does not explain why throughout the day there were men going in and out of that same motel room all day. We saw the surveillance camera footage. And I have right here a statement from Gerald Helix's Bank Manager that says she was cut off access to his bank account the night before. There was live footage of her having sex with the man you mentioned. And we have witness statements to confirm all this."

"But your honour," the lawyer replied, "Those witnesses could be lying."

"Do you have any evidence to prove your claim?"

"Well, not at the moment, your honour, but–"

"Take your seat," The Judge commanded. The lawyer turned around and sat back down like a spoilt little girl who didn't get what she wanted from her father. Her smiling smug face had changed to frustration.

"Anyone else?" asked the Judge.

"Sir–I mean, your honour, I do." A lawyer raised her hand timidly.

"Proceed," said the Judge. She got up and stood before the Judge. She too wore a black blazer.

"Your honour, Penelope is only a youth. Idealistic of course. I'm sure you and everyone can understand that at some point in our lives we wanted to change the world. Penelope stood for something. Equality, diversity, the environment etc. But sometimes we slip up and do it the wrong way. I can assure you, your honour, Penelope here is innocent." Penelope giggled. That definitely didn't escape the Judge's sinister stare. His eyes went back to the lawyer.

"Then how do you explain the attempted assault, if not attempted murder with a fire axe, on a police officer?" asked the Judge.

"Um..." she swallowed, "Sir– I mean, your honour, it must

be stated that the riot control police were very rough-handed. I mean, being in a situation like that must have been terrifying. Especially for a youth like Penelope. All that tear gas and all the beatings, which in itself needs to be put to question. But Penelope was scared. She felt under attack. Being surrounded by armoured policemen with weapons, one could say her only way of defence was to get an axe. So she can feel safe. I don't think she intended to hurt anyone."

"Ms Day," said the Judge, "We have already heard the witnesses and seen recorded footage of Penelope trying to attack the riot control police. Repeatedly. In the situation in question she was the offender. Would you agree with that?"

"But she–"

"I said, would you agree with that?" asked the Judge.

"Yes sir– I mean, your honour," she replied.

"Take your seat," said the Judge.

The lawyer bowed her head and sat back down next to Penelope. The Judge took in a deep breath and sighed.

"Anyone else?" asked the Judge.

"Yes, your honour." Toby's lawyer got up and stood before the Judge. "Toby Helix is innocent. Yes there were messages between him and El-Taco talking about growing cannabis, but that doesn't mean he wanted to be part of the drug trade. After all, we are free to talk about what we want, online and offline." To that Toby smiled and nodded. "But when the SWAT team cracked down on the drug den, Toby was just unfortunate to be present. I can assure you, your honour, that Toby had no intention of dealing drugs or growing marijuana. He was just meeting with a friend who he met over an online video game." To that Toby chuckled as he covered his mouth with this chubby paws. That didn't escape the glare of the Judge either.

"Mr Gonzales," said the Judge, "I have here the messages Toby sent to the youth in question: "That weed thing. I want in. I wanna help. Let's grow this business together. As long as we keep this quiet." The lawyer swallowed.

"Ah, but sir, those words are very subjective. The message 'I wanna help' could mean anything. Help with what exactly? Keep quiet about what, exactly? Or perhaps he considered starting a business together about something else. Like I said, such statement are open for debate."

"Whatever statement you wish to claim he meant, do you have any evidence for them?

"No but—"

"Then, Mr Gonzales, the evidence is clear and already been discussed, now take your seat," said the Judge. The lawyer bowed his head and sat next to Toby.

"All rise," said the Judge. Everyone in the courtroom rose to their feet. "In all my years of working as a judge, in this courtroom, I didn't think this would ever happen. Each and every one of us, regardless of our race, colour, or creed, have a responsibility to uphold the values of this city. And pass them on to our children. Of course, we make mistakes, we go off the rails from time to time." He raised his voice. "But there is a limit!"

"People must learn discipline!" He said that even louder. His voice echoed across the courtroom. The siblings flinched. It was clear he was referring to them.

"Never in my life..." he lowered his voice, "did I ever expect to see the children of Gerald Helix, who comes from a family of successful men, stand right here in front of me. He was a good friend of mine. God knows where he is but at least I'm glad he is not here to see this."

He picked up the few sheets of paper in front of him.

"Eric Helix, you've been found guilty of causing a public disturbance, physical assault, car theft, speeding, and causing damage to public property."

"Jodie Helix, you've been found guilty of the crime of prostitution. Any sex in exchange for money is illegal in Coast City."

"Penelope Helix, you've been found guilty of inciting a riot on false pretences. The article in question about a new aquarium being opened in Coast City was false. In fact, it has been confirmed after further investigation that it was written by your friend Jane Saunders who wanted to cause emotional distress to the public. In short, you organised a protest over nothing. On top of that, you assaulted police officers, and again the statue of Jeffery Irons was vandalised, therefore you are held responsible for damage to public property."

"Toby Helix, you've been found guilty of supplying drugs knowing full well that marijuana is an illegal substance here in Coast City. Manufacturing illegal drugs is a worse criminal offence than that of possession."

He put the papers down and linked his fingers.

"To conclude," he continued, his voice sounded vengeful, "all four of you, sons and daughters of Gerald Helix, are a disgrace to the fabric of our society. This City was founded on decency, and you have none of it! Your father would be ashamed of you."

He paused for a moment to let that sink in. But the siblings were not moved. They had blank stares.

"He is a good man. It is a shame that his own children could not uphold any of his values. So I am going to make an example of you all by giving you six years in prison."

The siblings' jaws dropped. There was a mutual gasp and bewilderment among the crowd as they looked among themselves. Commissioner Banks raised an eyebrow. The Judge unlinked his fingers, reached out for his gavel, and struck.

"Court adjourned."

A group of policemen then walked over to the siblings and held them by the cuffs to lead them out.

"Hey, don't touch the watch!" Eric jerked away, but the cop grabbed his handcuffs and yanked them towards him as he led the siblings out of the courtroom.

Only Commissioner Banks remained after everyone else left the public seating area. He frowned with scepticism. The Judge was getting all his paperwork together and putting them into a folder. The Commissioner walked over to the Judge who heard his approach and didn't take his eyes off his papers.

"Hello Banks," he greeted by only lifting his eyebrows before taking them down again.

"Sir... all of this, you know, four different suspects, for four different crimes, all of them in the same courtroom given the exact same sentence? Seems strange."

The Judge stopped shuffling through his papers. The Judge lifted his head and glared at the big black man. His face was stern. The fire in his eyes were magnified behind the lenses of his glasses. He was elderly, but the spirit within was beastly. He glared at the Commissioner for a while. His secretary, the Court Reporter, and the Court Deputy observed the two. Was there some inaudible conversation going on between them?

"Oh... gotcha," said Commissioner Banks. "Have nice day, sir." He smiled, turned around, and then left the courtroom. The Judge got up, tucked the folder under his arm.

"I need a moment alone," said the Judge.

To that, everyone else in the courtroom left the Judge on his own. He looked around and observed the empty contrast from earlier. The sight of the silent empty courtroom put a slight smile on the corner of his mouth. He took out his phone, made a call, and said "It's done." Then he turned off the phone, put it back in his pocket, and left the courtroom. He shut the door behind him.

The doors at the side of the building burst open, and out poured a group of police men escorting the siblings. The crowd erupted with jeers, curses, and insults. There was also a mixture of boos and hisses. The police led the siblings into police vans. The siblings had their heads bowed down.

"Ladies and Gentlemen," said Adee Lee, "I have just heard that the Helix siblings have been given six years. All four of them. I repeat, all four them have been given the exact same sentence of six years in prison. How bizarre. I can't understand why but here they are being escorted to the police vans as we speak."

"Hey! We've gone out of business thanks to you! You

fuckin' bitch!" Big Billy yelled out from the railings. Jodie got a quick glance at who said it before being led into a police van. She caught sight of Big Billy before the van doors were slammed shut. One by one the Helix siblings were dragged into a police van and then driven away. The police then ordered everyone to disperse.

Adee Lee approached the old bearded man in denim.

"Excuse me sir, Blue Eagle TV, tell us who you are. And what was your business?"

"I used to own Edge Motel. But it's gone now. The whole world thinks we run orgies. We don't. We never did, ya hear! My motel was never intended to be used as a brothel, and now nobody wants to stay at our motel no more. I came all the way here today to give that bitch a piece of my mind. When she gets out of jail, there will always be job waiting for her. Looka-me. I have nothin'! Nothin' I tell ya!"

At that moment, there was a flash of white light followed by a crack of thunder. Heavy rain began to pour down. Every person was wet in an instant. "Ahhh great. JUST GREAT!" Big Billy threw his arms around in fit of rage.

"I'm Adee Lee reporting for Blue Eagle TV News, over and out."

The crowd dispersed as they hurried to get out of the rain. Many ran into the subway while others ran into the nearest coffee shops and cafes for shelter. Their clothes were soaked, the air was hot in the humid despite the dark grey clouds in the sky. The Coast City Court of Justice stood alone in the rain. The streets of Coast City were empty in an instant. The rain came down and washed every surface like a vast shower, the water ran down every surface down to the pavements, flowed along the gutters and down the drains.

The next day, the city was drenched. The hot summer heat made a thick cloud of water vapour in the air which made everyone sweat and their clothing stick to their skin. The sky remained covered by a vast damp grey cloth. The newsagent had new piles of newspapers stacked on top of one another.

He sat in his newsstand with three fans that blew cold air at him. Despite all this, he fanned himself a with a magazine in his hand.

"Read all about it," he called out, out of breath. The humidity of the city made it hard to breathe.

The black street cleaner made his way along the pavement as he swept the wet gutter with his broom. After every few sweeps, he took a breather, pulled his wheeled bin along, and then swept away again. He was in no mood to whistle. In between he took off his hat, wiped his forehead with the back of his hand and put his hat back on.

"Hey Lou," said the cleaner, "How's it goin'?"

"Hot. Too hot," the newsagent complained.

The cleaner looked at the damp pile of newspapers. The Helix siblings dominated the news again. There were pictures of their mug shots and getting escorted to the police vans in hand cuffs. The headlines read:

"Helix Siblings Jailed."
"Two Boys, Two Girls, One Sentence."
"Helix Family Disgraced."
"Father Helix, Where Art Thou?"
"Helix Shame."

The cleaner looked sad as he shook his head.

"What do you think of all this?" asked the cleaner.

"Pfff. I think they got what they deserved, Kamau," said the newsagent. "Those kids are nothing like their father. Useless idiots, I'd say. Oh well, at least they can't cause any more trouble."

"Hmmm," said the cleaner as he nodded, "For now. They'll be out in six years."

"Oh, when that day comes... God help us all," said the newsagent.

The cleaner tipped his hat and then pulled his wheeled bin along with his broom. "See ya later."

Chapter 10

That December, every building had white sheets of snow covering every surface. It was late at night when Denise was lying on the couch in a bath robe for an extra layer of warmth. Her finished microwave meal was in front of her on the coffee table. While she watched TV, she leaned on her right hand and her eyes tried to stay awake.

"Good evening, I'm Johnny Perkins and this is Blue Eagle TV News. And tonight, I bring you a very special story about a new competitor in the market. For the newly emerged superstar company Horus Inc. Christmas has come early. The construction of their needle monument shaped skyscraper is now complete. It towers over the Helix tower with a whopping height of 1,680 feet with 120 floors, while Helix Tower has only 100 floors at 1,400 feet tall. What took Helix Inc. years to build, Horus Inc. has achieved in less than a year. Using the latest technology and construction techniques imported from China, all 120 floors of the Needle Monument tower was built within four months. Making Horus Inc. the first ever company to build something so big so fast in Coast City. Due to height restrictions, Horus Inc. was only able to build 120 floors because of its proximity to the Coast City airport. Had it not been here, who knows how much taller the tower could have been.

"Now, we've all heard of the Chinese's capability of building 3 storeys in a day. If that wasn't enough, there's always 57 storeys that can be built in 19 days. But Horus Inc. achieved their goal within 4 months, making Horus Tower the first and fastest built construction in the history of Coast City. It's as if some ancient Egyptian needle grew out of the ground to fill the void left by Helix Inc. Only this structure is made with glass and steel. Our reporter Adee Lee was invited to the tower where she was given a tour of the lounging area and the mezzanine seating area. Over to you, Adee."

Blue Eagle TV News then switched over to Adee Lee holding her microphone. Next to her stood a tall and beautiful woman, tanned with long black hair. Her face was a combination of North African and Middle Eastern features. She wore a black blazer, a white blouse, black stockings, and black shoes. Her makeup was a combination of blue and green eye shadows that went well with her dark brown eyes, all of that went well with her clear lip gloss. She came complete with gold bracelets, a gold necklace, and a gold pair of earrings. She looked like a modern version of an Ancient Egyptian Queen.

"Thank you, Johnny, here I am in the lounge of Horus Inc, and looking at this place alone takes your breath away. I'm here with the Head of PR, Yazmeen Shaheed, who will be giving me a little guided tour of the lounge and mezzanine. And my goodness," she turned to Yazmeen, "This place is extraordinary."

Yazmeen laughed. "Thank you very much." She had a soft voice.

"So, tell us about Horus Inc. and its origins."

"Firstly, it is our reverence to the Sun, and given that is a great ball of fire, it drives our passion for greatness and progress."

"Wow!" said Adee. "And what's with this lovely setting?"

"We want to make all our visitors feel as welcome and as comfortable as possible. Come, let me show you." She showed Adee the interior design of the place.

The walls, the ceiling, and the floor were all made of a cream coloured marble. And every surface had Egyptian hieroglyphics etched into them with gold ink, and they were decorated with stones: green, blue, turquoise, and red. The rest was all gold. The walls had depictions of Ancient Egyptian Gods painted on them. There were cream coloured marble columns that went up to the ceiling. They were decorated with green floral patterns of the Cyperus Papyrus. Above and below each were green and red geometric patterns. Right in the middle of the seating area was an 8-metre wide square garden that was decorated with all sorts of plants from Egypt including the real Cyperus Paperus and the Egyptian blue lotus flower to name a few. In the centre of the garden was a huge water fountain that held a statue of Ancient Egyptian Pharaoh holding a crook and a flail. They were surrounded by Ancient Egyptian statues, of Egyptian Pharaohs and Queens from the past, as well as solid marble statues of cats in turquoise, and black jackal structures. And right at the back was a modern structure of the sphinx with escalators on each side of it.

In every corner stood a security guard who was tall and built, dressed in black suits and black sunglasses. They looked like members of the FBI.

The seating area had soft leather sofas, also cream coloured, decorated with cushions that were dark red, dark green, and dark blue with gold tassels on them. Some of them were covered with cloth, they also came in dark red, dark green, and dark glue. And they all had gold Ancient Egyptian patterns on them. The seating area had its own coffee machine built into one of the columns, that served beverages in tea cups and saucers. All them products of Horus Inc.

Adee Lee couldn't hold back her amazement at such a sight. "It feels like... like I am no longer in Coast City. More like I have travelled through space and time, only to find myself standing in some modern version of an Ancient Egyptian Palace."

Yazmeen laughed again. "It's so we can make our guests feel special, like royalty," Yazmeen added.

"Well, I feel uplifted just by being here."

"You're welcome Ms Lee," replied Yazmeen.

"So what is the goal of Horus Inc? And why of all places did you choose Coast City?"

"We recognise that Coast City is one of the greatest cities in the world, and we want to contribute to it. Coast City was the ideal place to start so we can grow. It's the perfect place to invest. We offer a wide range of products and services. And we love it here."

"Thank you so much for your time, Ms Shaheed. Oh and Merry Christmas."

"You're welcome, Ms Lee. Merry Christmas to you too," Yazmeen replied.

"This is Adee Lee reporting from the lounge of Horus Inc. Back to you, Johnny." As soon as the words passed her lips, the Blue Eagle TV News switched back over to Johnny Perkins.

"Yes," said Johnny, "And speaking of a wide range products, Horus Inc. has a huge selection ready for purchase in time for Christmas. With its own fashion range, from clothing for men, women and children. Footwear, sportswear, and swimwear, although it's not yet the weather for it. To go with that they have brought out its own range of golden jewellery. Horus Inc. has its own tech division for TVs, PC, laptops, and of course phones. Horus Inc. has launched a new competitor into the smart phone market. There is already a Brooks Phone and Helix Phone, and how there is the Horus Pharaoh phone, available in gold, and black with a gold frame, decorated with the Horus eye at the back of it. And if that wasn't enough, they released their very own video games console; The Horus Pyramid, the first ever game console that is shaped like a pyramid, available in gold, or black with gold patterns. Both come with a red disk on the front with the yellow sun logo on it. Along with other household items like refrigerators, microwaves, washing machines, and dishwashers.

"And speaking of technology, Horus Inc. has released its own range of vehicles: The Horus Falcon range of sports and muscle cars, the Horus Jackal range of transit vehicles, and the Horus Ibis family range of people carriers and station wagons. Of course, we heard earlier they offer services. Horus Inc. have launched its own delivery service, Horus Wing-Deli, that will deliver directly to you wherever you are by your phone, where you work, your local Horus Package depository, and of course, your home. Restaurants have signed to their scheme so they can deliver to you their takeaways. And that's not all. With the approval of the Mayor, Horus Inc. are now designing new subway trains for public transport with built-in heaters for winter and air-conditioning for summer. Giving the public a comfortable commute everywhere in Coast City.

"With the Mayor's approval, and sponsored by other companies, Horus Inc. has been given the green light to construct a new Aquarium where the old Coast City Theatre once stood. The designs have already been decided and the construction will be completed by the end of next year.

"So with Helix Inc. at the bottom, it is no surprise that Horus Inc. is now at the top and leading the market not only for this Christmas, but for what may seem, many more to come. But the one question on everyone's mind is: Who is the CEO of Horus Inc.? And that concludes tonight's special story. We will return after a short commercial break."

A commercial showed an Egyptian Queen surrounded by her servants putting on her make-up. One of the servants brought a tray that had a bottle on it. The Queen picked it up and sprayed it on her neck. Just then, an Egyptian King walked into the room with his bow in his left hand. The King took out a bottle from his belt with his free hand and sprayed his chin. The Queen turned to face him after catching a whiff of his aftershave. The King puts the bow away, and then embraces the Queen. Like an ending to a movie, they kiss. The commercial ended with the following voiceovers.

"Isis - The Horus fragrance for Women," said a woman's voiceover.

"Osiris - The Horus aftershave for Men," said a man's voiceover.

"Bring out your inner divinity," said both voices.

Denise sat there staring at the TV.

"Wow... just wow," she said out loud. "This Horus thing is constant."

Just then, Daniel walked through the door. He came home later than usual. His back was hunched in exhaustion, he looked like he was about to fall over. He had bags under his eyes. He looked at the clock. It was 11:26 pm. "God dammit," he whispered to himself. "I have to get up in less than 8 hours. This is going to be the worst Christmas ever."

"Hey honey," Denise called out to him.

"Hey babe," Daniel replied. "Have you been waiting for me?"

"Yeah," she replied.

"Don't do that, you'll do yourself more harm than good. I'm late as it is."

"How was work?"

"Ah man, we're running low on steam. People are losing interest in Helix products and yet we're expected to make profits. All because of that goddamn Horus company. I've heard nothing but Horus all day every day. I'm sick of it," said Daniel as he took off his suit and tie.

"Me too. I've seen nothing but Horus commercials all day today. I mean, those guys are huge," she said.

"It's like this Horus thing came out of nowhere and has taken over the whole city. Everyone keeps talking about them. It's driving me crazy," he went to the fridge and got himself a can of beer. Then he sat on the couch next to Denise. He drank his can of beer one sip at a time.

The TV was still on and his eye lid twitched every time he heard the word Horus. There was another Horus commercial. It was showing their winter clothing range. A family were playing in the snow, laughing as they played. And then it displayed the Horus Fashion logo in the middle of the screen.

"I have to say," said Denise, "their stuff looks good. You know, I was tempted by one their commercials earlier. They were offering a trade-in service for smart phones with a new contract. It was only slightly cheaper."

"Alright, that's enough of this shit," he grabbed the remote control and turned off the TV. He exhaled in relief. "I just want to unwind and go to bed."

"I don't know about you, but something seems funny about all this," said Denise.

"What do you mean?" asked Daniel.

"I'm not being a conspiracy theorist or any of that, but... doesn't all this seem strange to you? As soon as Gerald Helix goes missing the siblings are jailed. And all of a sudden a brand new corporation comes along and takes over the market. I mean... this is all too convenient. It's as if this whole thing was planned from the start," said Denise.

"That's ridiculous," said Daniel. "Gerald left because he wanted to. He was due to retire anyway. The siblings, well, they have no one to blame but themselves. We knew what they were like. And good-ole Daddy Helix kept them out of jail. And as for this Horus Inc. my only guess is someone, or some organisation, must have planned this whole thing in advance. No way can this be planned overnight. Rome wasn't built in a day. Neither was this. I mean, imagine, how much time and effort this would have cost to plan all this and get it done. And the timing too. With Gerald gone. The timing couldn't be better."

"That's what I'm saying," said Denise, "It's too convenient. Like you said, Gerald was about to retire, and somebody must have known about it. So then maybe this was the right time to act. Like a set-up. Do you think they could have planned to get rid of Gerald Helix and the siblings to make way for them. Maybe even a kidnapping?"

"No. Don't be stupid. Nobody's gonna kidnap a guy like Gerald. I'll bet right now he's probably sitting next to a fire stove in some cottage far away from here, laughing as we speak," said Daniel. "So don't worry about him."

"So, who's in charge now?" asked Denise.

"I don't know, the Senior Management team, I guess. We have to continue. The Captain of the ship may be gone, but the crew has to keep sailing it. And that includes me," said Daniel.

"By the way," said Denise, "Don't get mad at me okay, honey, but I've already done some Christmas shopping with

Horus. They've got a really nice online store and plenty of great deals. I bought a lot of stuff from them, their prices are cheaper and their delivery is swift. I've got more stuff coming. I did all this on my phone with the Horus app. I needed to get my shopping done as quickly as possible. The grocery shopping is done too. It's on it way, it'll arrive tomorrow morning."

Daniel sighed.

"All these things are cheaper with Horus as it is. But I could have had a discount if I had the Horus Pharaoh phone with their own contract. The more products I buy with the Horus, the more discounts I get. But not with the Helix phone. I could have saved more money," said Denise.

"God damn it!" he growled.

"Sorry, babe. But we have to make life easier for ourselves. Just because you work at Helix Inc. doesn't mean I have buy everything from them. Besides, the market decides."

"Thanks," he said. "I'm going to bed."

"Aren't you going to take a shower?"

"No, I haven't got time. I need to sleep."

He went into the bathroom to brush his teeth. "Wha– Oh come on. Horus tooth paste? Horus liquid soap? Seriously?"

She chewed her lip. "Ummm, yeah. Delivered today. Cheap. Fast delivery. Sorry."

In a sudden fit of rage he threw his tightened fists down at his sides, he lifted his head up, opened his mouth wide and screamed. "AAAAAAAHHHH!!!" She closed her eyes tight as she flinched.

There was a sudden moment of silence.

He growled. "Fuck! Fuck fuck fuck! Those fuckers have ruined everything!" He shouted. "Those cocksuckers are gonna haunt me for the rest my life. I never should have taken this job!" he ranted. He marched into the bedroom and slammed the door shut so hard and loud it made her jump.

She took in a deep breath and let it out slowly. She looked at her finished microwave meal, she got up, picked it up and threw it in the bin. She put the plate, knife and fork in the sink. The washing can wait until morning. She went into the bathroom, and brushed her teeth. She entered the bedroom doorway, she paused after she placed her hand on the door knob, she waited a few moments before she slowly opened door and made her way in. She looked in. He didn't even get changed. Daniel lay in bed facing away from her in his shirt and trousers, with the same socks on his feet. His belt rested on the chair, underneath that were his work shoes. She lay next to him, she put her arms around him. She felt his muscles, they were tense all over. The anger within was still boiling. The dragon was trying to sleep.

"Daniel," she said with a soft voice of compassion, she pressed her head on his back. "I love you."

That did it. Her words took the sting out. A short silent pause later, he took in a deep breath and let it out nice and slowly. His muscles relaxed. She too relaxed, and then she whispered, "Goodnight."

Chapter 11

There was a loud buzz. The steel doors ahead opened, and revealed the dim sunlight that came from outside. Once again, the grey clouds concealed the sun from the afternoon sky. The dark grey clouds above hummed as there was thunder in the distance. The cold air blew into the faces of Jodie and Penelope. They both crossed their hands over the chests and rubbed their forearms as they shivered. They wore only their blue jumpsuits and white plimsolls. Jodie had her long blonde hair, but it was far from gold. There was nothing to shine. Penelope allowed her light brown hair to grow and reach her shoulders. Apparently that was "long enough" for her. Their cheek bones were visible since they had lost a bit of weight. They were a lot thinner than before they went in. Their sentence was reduced from six years to three years.

"Come on. Get going," said the security guard. The megaphone was so loud it made both of them jump. The guard sat in the security gatehouse with his feet up on one desk, put the microphone down on another desk beside him, and went back to looking through his phone. Was he reading the news? More likely, checking his social media feed or playing games.

The Coast City Detention Center for Women was nothing but a bunch of long and grey cuboids with thick windows blackened from the outside. The brutalist architecture made it look as though it came out of some totalitarian dystopian movie. All the grey surfaces were slabs of concrete stuck together with an even darker grey mortar. Every time it rained, new lines of dark grey would bleed out of the mortar, that painted a new coat of grey water-colour paint onto the grey slabs that made them look older. On the darker surfaces, there was green moss growing on them. Such ugliness for a building, with an immense hatred of the outside world, it was no surprise it stood isolated outside the city. Like a bitter unwanted relative with a disdain for all humanity. No one in their right mind would want to go near it, let alone be in it. From above it looked as if some toddler threw her grey bricks onto the floor with disgust at the dull grey colours. The layout of the place was random, nothing was consistent, the Detention Center was a poorly arranged group of grey blocks that looked in different directions to one another as if even they couldn't stand the sight of each other. All of them joined together with electric fences and barbed wire. At last, after three years, Jodie and Penelope were free. And yet they had their heads down as they slowly walked out into the cold.

"Smile, honey, you're free now," said the security guard with mocking tone. That woke Penelope up. She turned to look at him and give him a dirty look as she held her fists at her side, tight.

"What did you call me?!" Penelope screeched.

The guard looked at her angry face and laughed.

"Whyyyyyyyou! I am NOT your 'HONEY' you lil–" she

attempted to march over to the gatehouse to bang on the windows with her fists.

Jodie jumped in front of her and grabbed her forearms and squeezed her grip on them.

"Don't! You're gonna get us in trouble again! Now move!" She shoved her in the opposite direction.

"That fuckin' pervert," Penelope said through gritted teeth. Her eyes went red with rage.

"Shut up!" said Jodie. "Don't look at him. It's what he wants. Just grow up and walk away."

The guard sat back in his chair and laughed as he filmed her on his phone. They walked on and then the large steel doors slammed shut behind them.

Right in front of them was the main road. And in the distance was Coast City. Miles away. Probably the furthest from the city they had ever been. They breathed out a sigh of relief.

"Oh man," moaned Penelope, "Where did all that time go?"

"I don't know," said Jodie. "And I don't care. I'm glad it's all over. No more plastic meals, no more uncomfortable hard beds, no more freezing room temperatures, and no more inmates screaming at night. All I want right now is a shower."

At that moment there was a clap of thunder and the rain began to pour.

"Eeeeeeek!" Penelope jumped as she squeaked in her high pitched voice. She crossed her arms over her chest tightly and rubbed her forearms with her hands as she jumped up and down.

"Uh no!" Jodie growled. "Well this is just perfect! Just fuckin' PERFECT!" Jodie shouted. She stamped her right foot. They noticed the security guard having a hearty laugh in his gatehouse. They looked at one another and then they turned their backs to him. They looked around. But there was nobody to pick them up. They stood there in the rain and looking lost.

"Now what do we do?" said Penelope.

"Get a cab, I guess," Jodie replied.

"Forget a cab. Nobody would even want to come here," said Penelope.

"Oh I don't know, I–" Jodie stopped. She saw something in the distance. A pair of bright white headlights in the distance were coming towards them. It was a people carrier, all black with blackened windows. Her jaw dropped.

"Oh thank god!" she stuck out her arm and waved around her thumb.

"What're you doing?" said Penelope.

"Fuck the cab. I'm hitchhiking," said Jodie.

"Are you crazy? You don't know who's in there. Put your hand down, you idiot."

"No. You can stay here and–" Jodie's response was interrupted by tyres screeching to a halt right next to them. The black vehicle was a large Helix MPV. Both of the front doors opened in an instant. Two big men in black suits emerged. They both wore black sunglasses. They were both muscular. One of them was a black man with a small finely trimmed afro. And the other was a pale man with long blonde hair tied into ponytail. They both had square jaws and broad cheeks. They would have been suitable as wrestlers. But in the suits, they looked like ideal bodyguards.

"Are you Jodie, and Penelope Helix?" asked the black bodyguard.

"Yeah," they both nodded.

"Helix Security," the blonde bodyguard presented his idea card. The black bodyguard also showed his ID card. "Get in the car," he commanded.

"Oh thank god," said Jodie

"No way," said Penelope. She crossed her arms even tighter and shook her head. "I am not going anywhere."

The two bodyguards looked at each other, and made their move. The black bodyguard went over to Penelope, he picked up her up like a doll, she thrashed and kicked about as she screamed while the blonde bodyguard slid open the side door and shoved Jodie to get in.

"Heeey! Get off me!" Penelope screamed, "This is kidnapping! Aaaaah– huh?"

"What the hell?" said Jodie.

"Toby?!" Penelope screeched.

"Eric?" Jodie exclaimed.

"Yeah yeah," said Eric in a disinterested tone as he leaned his head against the window. Eric was in the grey suit he wore on the day of the accident, partially torn and dirty.

"Well duh," Toby replied. Toby had the same small black t-shirt with the blue hedgehog on it, partially faded and torn, along with his extra large jeans from the day he was arrested. Both men had stubbles with messy hair, and carried with them a foul smell of body odour.

"Get in there," said the black bodyguard. He threw Penelope onto a seat and then slid the side door shut. Both men hurried back to their seats at the front to get away from the rain. The driver hit the gas, made a u-turn, and then sped off in the opposite direction.

"You misogynist pig!" Penelope said to the black bodyguard.

"There she goes again," Jodie sighed.

"You touched me without my consent. That's sexual harassment! I'm gonna get you fired from your job!" Penelope complained.

"My job is to protect you ma'am," the black bodyguard turned to face her, he lifted his sunglasses, there was a slight smile on his lips, "I'll do whatever it takes to keep you safe. Got that?" He rested his sunglasses back onto his nose and then turned around to face the front. Penelope growled. She folded her arms and looked out the window to sulk.

"Where were you guys?" asked Jodie.

"The fortress," said Eric.

"The what?" Jodie asked.

"The Coast City Fortress, damn it," Eric replied.

"Ha! Fit for animals like you," said Penelope.

"No, I'm not," said Toby.

"Yes you are!" said Penelope.

Eric and Jodie looked at each other, and then they rolled their eyes as they let out a huge sigh.

"Give it a rest, will ya?" said Eric.

"You two are giving me a fuckin' headache. Enough already," said Jodie.

"You shut up!" Penelope screeched.

"Hey!" The black bodyguard turned around to face them. "Shut up back there."

"Fuck you," said Eric.

In a flash, the black bodyguard pulled out his taser gun and pointed it at Eric's face.

"Holy shit!" said Eric. There were light blue sparks on the end of the electrodes that stuck out of the nozzle.

"I wouldn't hesitate to use this on you right now," said the black bodyguard.

"He will do it, buddy," the blonde bodyguard chimed in casually as he looked into the rear-view mirror. "Do as you're told, and you won't get hurt. Simple as that."

The siblings sat up straight in their seats. Silent.

"Good," said the black bodyguard. He put away his taser gun and then turned around to face the front.

The rain continued to pour so heavily it sounded more like thousands of small metal balls hitting the roof of their people carrier. The wipers squeaked as they swayed from side to side trying to keep the windscreen clear. Already they reached the suburbs of Coast City. The roads were not as busy since it was in the middle of the day in the middle of the week. Nobody gave their vehicle a second glance.

Jodie waited a few moments before she asked:

"So where are you taking us?"

"Helix HQ," the black bodyguard answered.

"You said you are Helix Security. How come I've never heard of you guys?"

"We're new," he replied. "Helix Inc. started a security company with a bodyguard service."

"Started?... You mean Dad's back?" Jodie asked with hope.

"No. Still missing," said the black bodyguard.

"Did it not cross your mind to call the cops?" asked Penelope.

"He left by his own free will," said the black bodyguard, "There is nothing the police can do."

"How do you know that?" asked Jodie.

"The Police Commissioner told us not to worry. He said he doesn't want to be found."

"But–" Jodie began.

"You'll find out everything else when you get there. Now shut up," commanded the blonde bodyguard.

The rain continued to pour. When they reached the city centre, they took a slight detour as they entered the basement of the Helix Tower through the freight entrance. And then the bodyguards pulled the siblings out of the black Helix MPV, and then they led them into the freight elevator. They touched their cardkeys onto the small panels on the walls to open the elevator doors. The doors opened straight away. The bodyguards touched their cardkeys again to enable them to go straight to the top floor. The elevator doors shut. While the elevator hummed as it made its way up, the siblings looked at each other with puzzled looks on their faces. It would have been an awkward silence otherwise. The elevator pinged and then the doors opened.

"Come on," said the blonde bodyguard to hurry the siblings. Right ahead of them were the double doors to the CEO's office. The bodyguards marched over to the double doors at the end of the corridor, they stood where the panels were to touch their cardkeys. They opened the double doors. And signalled them in. The siblings were slow at their pace. As soon as they reached the doors, the bodyguards pushed the siblings into the office and then slammed the doors shut behind them that locked automatically. Then the bodyguards stood still and silent as they folded their arms. There was no escape.

"Hey! What's your problem?" said Toby as he turned to the bodyguards.

"You rapists!" Penelope shouted at the bodyguards. "I'm gonna get you jailed for this!"

"Huh?!" Eric spotted someone sitting in the black leather chair behind the main desk. "Hey you! Get out of that chair!" Eric barked loudly. He stormed over towards the desk. "That chair belongs to my Dad you little piece of shit!" He suddenly stopped in his tracks aghast when the chair spun around to reveal who it was. The siblings gasped.

"Welcome back," said Gosia. She was in a sharp black blazer with a white blouse where she still had her little crucifix necklace hidden, and a black skirt that went down to the knee. But this time, her long brown hair went down her back. The cute bun with the pen was gone. Her black blazer had a silver badge with the Helix Inc. logo on it. She looked like a stunning businesswoman, the sort you would see on the front cover of a business magazine or on a successful women's poster.

"I've been expecting you."

"What?!" Jodie exclaimed.

"You can't sit in that chair!" Penelope screeched.

"Where's Dad?" asked Toby.

"Take a seat," said Gosia. There were four empty chairs in front of the desk.

"You ain't telling ME what to do!" Eric barked. "I'm outta here." As soon as he spun around, the black bodyguard unfolded his arms and cracked his knuckles in a slow calculated manner. Eric couldn't see his eyes through the sunglasses, but he knew he meant business. It was obvious Eric was no match for him, the black bodyguard could easily break him in two like snapping a matchstick. Eric gulped. "Ah fuck you asshole!" he growled at the bodyguard. And then he turned his back on him. To that, Penelope burst out laughing. She sounded like the most irritating hyena with the highest pitched voice possible. The laugh was so hysterical she had tears in her eyes and held her arms around her stomach.

"What's so funny?" asked Jodie. Annoyed at such a sound.

"What's the matter little white guy?" Penelope taunted Eric. "Scared of a big black man?"

"Ooooooooooh!" Toby giggled.

"Hey, shut the fuck up! I'm not ready for a fight yet anyway! I didn't come here to get my ass kicked!" said Eric.

"Sure you didn't," Jodie mocked.

"Doesn't change the fact that you are a racist pig!" said Penelope.

"I am NOT racist!" Eric protested.

"Yes, you are!" Penelope screeched. "You punched a cop 'cause he was black."

"No I didn't. I acted in self-defence. I would have done the same if he were white or hispanic," Eric protested again.

"Yeah right," Toby chimed in.

"Fuck off!" He threw his palms into Toby's shoulders and made Toby fall onto the floor and land on his ass.

"Ow!" Toby cried.

"Stay there, fatso. Before you break the floor," Eric shouted. He pointed at him the way an owner would shout at his dog.

"Oh Jesus Christ, Eric!" Jodie shouted. "Have you not learned anything after being in prison for three years?"

"Fuck you, bitch!" he laughed sarcastically. "You're in no position to take the moral high ground with me. You're a hooker!"

"Fuck you!" she growled through gritted teeth.

"The only thing YOU'RE good at is what's between your legs!" He spread his arms out as he ranted.

"Why you–" Jodie growled, she stuck out what was left of her nails ready to claw him.

"Now you're being a misogynist pig! You men are ALL the SAME!" Penelope screeched.

"No, I'm not!" Toby moaned as he got up. "I'm better than the likes of him."

Gosia stared at the siblings with anger, followed by disappointment. She took in a deep breath and sighed. While the siblings squabbled, Gosia pressed the red button under the desk. The panels behind the siblings opened up to reveal the red curtains. The red curtains opened up like a theatre to reveal the painting of their mother. The beautiful Katherine Helix. The cacophony became instant silence. They gasped as they froze.

"Ma!" said Eric.

"Mom!" said Jodie.

"Mommy!" said Penelope.

"Mama!" said Toby.

The moment of silence grew longer. It was then interrupted when flashes of lighting brightened the whole office for a few seconds before thunder cracked again. The clouds outside were darker. The rain hit the floor-to-ceiling windows so hard that it looked like the glass was held under a waterfall. Gosia folder her arms. She was the third person in the room to look at the siblings with disapproval along with the bodyguards.

At that moment, the CEO office of Helix Inc. was a cathedral. Gosia and the bodyguards stood still like the statues of saints looking down at the guilty sinners with intense scrutiny. The siblings stood frozen, caught in the midst of their bad deeds. They looked at the painting of their mother, guilt-stricken, the same way a sinner would look at the icon of Mary before begging for forgiveness. Even at the top floor of one of the tallest buildings in the city, at this rate, this was as close to Heaven as they could get. As if that wasn't enough, the wrath of God himself could be heard and felt all around, with his thunder and lightning outside. The siblings felt weak. Defeated. They could not hold back their tears.

"Oh my god," Penelope cried as she covered her mouth with a hand.

"My god. She... she's beautiful," said Jodie. "I'll never be like her." Tears rolled out of her eyes and down her cheeks.

She covered her face with her hands and began to cry.

"Why didn't Dad tell us about this?" moaned Toby. He wiped his tears with his chubby paws, and then he sniffed.

"She's exactly how I remember her," said Eric. "She was always..." his jaw trembled, "...lovely." He slouched.

"Is this how you want your mother to remember you?" Gosia said sternly. The siblings looked down at the floor. Each one slowly shook their heads. "It's not too late," said Gosia. "You still have one last chance. If you won't do it for yourselves, your father, or for everything he built, do it for her."

"But what can we do?" asked Penelope.

"We're broke," said Eric.

"Dad deactivated our cards," said Jodie.

"He blocked access to his bank account," said Toby.

Gosia took out a remote control and pressed a button. And then, as before, at the back of the office, in the north-west corner of the room, the large steel cabinet opened up. The doors hissed again as they opened. The metal panels opened up to reveal the four shiny black leather briefcases with the gold handles. The tags on the each handle were still there. Green, blue, yellow, and red.

Gosia put away the remote control. And then she gave each sibling her first command.

"Eric, the one with the red tag is yours. Helix Motors."

"Jodie, the one with the yellow tag is yours. Helix Gen."

"Penelope, the one with the green tag is yours. Helix Press."

"Toby, the one with the blue tag is yours. Helix Tech."

"Now, take them and go, quickly. Read through all the documents. We don't have much time," said Gosia. "You have everything you need. If I can be of any assistance, you know where to find me."

"Wait a minute," said Eric. "You're the secretary, aren't you? How did you get involved in all this? Who are you anyway?"

"My name is Gosia Kowalski. Your father appointed me as the Vice-President until he gets back," Gosia replied. "You own the subdivisions of Helix Inc. he set up. The rest is up to the four of you to get this company back on track. We are running out of time. We have fallen behind, and we are losing a lot of money."

"But where do we start?" Jodie asked.

"What do we do?" Toby hesitated.

"Yeah, where do we go from here?" asked Penelope.

"But we don't have our keys," said Eric. "We can't go back to our apartments."

"I put copies of your keys in your briefcases," Gosia replied.

"Oh thank god," said Jodie.

"Yeah, and then what?" asked Eric.

"You have board meetings tomorrow morning. They are expecting you. You all have new phones in your cases. I have emailed you the details."

The siblings looked amazed at her efficiency.

"And yes, your father set up new accounts with some cash for each of you. Don't piss it all away. Use it wisely."

Their jaws dropped.

"Now go!" She urged.

In that instant, the four siblings looked at one another. They sprinted towards the metal cabinet. They seized their designated briefcases. And then they ran straight for the double doors. The bodyguards opened the doors and stepped aside.

"Out of my way! Eric shouted.

"I'm first!" Jodie barked.

"No! I AM!" Penelope screeched.

"Wait for me!" Toby whined.

The four siblings rushed to the elevator at the end of the corridor. The doors pinged open as they approached. With such haste, they crashed into the back wall of the elevator. Their hands reached out to the press the ground floor button, they piled on top of each other like a game of Snap. The elevator doors shut. The bodyguards closed the doors and then crossed their hands in front of them. Gosia sat back into the leather chair.

The elevator hummed as it descended. The siblings leaned back on the walls to take a breather. They looked at each other, not knowing what to say, then they looked down at the floor. Toby held his briefcase with both hands to admire the clean shiny black leather. He looked at the tag. He opened his briefcase like a laptop. His face brightened with joy.

"Hey! There's a handful of cash in here," Toby said with excitement. "A new Helix phone, new Helix tablet with login details, a Helix cardkey, a Dove Bank card, a copy of my home key, and errr... folders of papers. Wow. Dad err– Gosia has taken care of everything."

The other siblings followed suit, they opened their briefcases and looked. Yup. All there. Then they all closed their briefcases and let them hang by their sides as they waited.

"You know," Toby said, "things are not so bad after all."

"What do you mean? We're still in the shit here. Look at us," said Eric.

"Don't you get it?" said Toby, "As soon we come out of prison we are given a job. Just like that. I mean... this is too easy." He smiled with excitement.

"That's because Dad owns the business," said Penelope. "If we were anybody else we would definitely be in real shit."

"Exactly, nobody wants to hire a felon. Which means I can't work anywhere else if I wanted to," said Eric.

"Oh please." Toby soured his face at Eric. "If you had any intention of doing anything useful you wouldn't be in this mess."

"Fuck you," said Eric, "I'll work when I feel like it. I wanted to do all the things I wanted to do first and THEN get a job. I didn't want to end up like this."

"So what did you want to do?" asked Toby.

"How the fuck should I know? Nobody has their whole life planned ahead of them."

"Well at least now you've got something to work on," said Toby.

"Oh yeah? What are you gonnna do, fatso? Go back to gaming? You're not a champ anymore. Your game is over, man. Heh! More likely go back to eating." Eric taunted Toby with a mocking laugh followed by a smirk.

"Yeah!" said Toby. He nodded as he walked right into Eric's face with glaring eyes. He tightened his fists and held his chin high. "All of that." he replied, "And this." He showed his briefcase. "So I've got a plan. What have YOU got?"

"That's none of your business. Get out of my face," said Eric.

"Translation: NONE!" said Toby.

"Fuck you," said Eric.

"Will you two shut up!" Penelope screeched. "Enough already," she lowered her voice. And then she let out a growl. "Men!"

"Whatever," said Eric. There was a brief silent pause.

"What's the matter with you?" Penelope turned to Jodie. "Why do you look so sad?"

"I feel like shit," Jodie replied.

"Huh?" Penelope looked puzzled.

Jodie held her briefcase with both hands in front of her and looked at it.

"I look at this and I'm thinking... this whole thing could have been avoided. Why didn't I take the chance Dad gave me all those years ago? Three years." She paused to let that sink in. "My god. Where did all that time go? You know, come to think of it, back then I thought I was smart, but now... uch... I feel so stupid. I just want to get out of here and move on." The elevator pinged. The doors opened. The siblings emerged with less haste than before. They headed for the exit ahead of them. Once they passed through the doors, they noticed the rain eased off the shower a little. The clouds had softened their grip on the sky, but it was still grey.

"Thank God for the rain," said Jodie, "there's nobody around to see us."

"Or recognise us." Penelope added as she gestured to their blue jumpsuits.

"I'm getting a cab," said Jodie.

"Me too," said Penelope.

"Can I come with you?" asked Toby.

"Fuck that. I ain't takin' a cab," said Eric.

"What you gonna do? Walk in the rain?" Jodie asked with a mocking tone to her voice.

"My place is only a twenty minute walk from here," Eric replied. "I'll get there in about 10 minutes if I run. I'll see ya later." He placed the briefcase on top of his head and ran down the street.

"See ya," said Jodie called out.

"Taxi!" Penelope called out so loud it made Jodie and Toby flinch. She waved with her free hand while she held her briefcase on top of her head with the other. In that moment, a yellow cab pulled up in front of them. The three remaining siblings jumped in, and the taxi took off.

The rain subsided.

Chapter 12

Eric Helix was out of breath when he stopped running, he changed his gears to fast walking. He panted as he made his way along the pavement. To give his swag a little boost he swung his arms out a little further while he held his briefcase in his right hand. He felt his diaphragm muscle go up and down, pushing out the air like a steam engine. It felt so good to walk freely down the street.

When he turned the corner, he was only a few paces away from the entrance of his penthouse when something made him suddenly stop in his tracks. He looked on in horror, his face went pale and his mouth gaped open.

"What the-?!" he exclaimed.

The parking space ahead of him was occupied by a white transit van. His red Helix muscle car was gone.

"Oooh no! No!" He panicked. He resumed his running speed and rushed over to the front door. He opened his briefcase, and then took out his new cardkey, and tapped it onto the panel by the door. A little green light flashed and unlocked the door.

"Yes! It works!" He said to himself. He pushed the door open and made his way into the elevator. He pressed the 'Up' button multiple times with his left thumb.

"Come on. Come on. Come on." His breathing became frantic.

He tapped his heel on the floor in a fast rhythm. The elevator arrived, pinged, and then opened.

He rushed in and ploughed into a fat man.

"Hey! Watch it!" said the fat man.

"Move dammit!" said Eric as he made his way around the fat man and reached for the buttons.

"You damn fool. Have you no manners?"

"Shut up!" Eric shouted.

"Wait a minute, don't I know you? You sure look familiar."

"Get lost, fat ass!" He pushed the fat man away from him and pressed his finger on the 'Close Doors' button. The elevator doors shut. He couldn't stand still. He paced around in a circle, frantic in his breathing, and checked his watch every few seconds. As soon as the elevator pinged, the doors opened, Eric raced over to his front door. He took out his key and opened the door.

"Oh thank god." He breathed a sigh of relief. He put his briefcase onto a shiny white coffee table and pulled out his new Helix phone. Registered his details and then dialled. And then he paced around his penthouse.

"Hello? Helix Motors? Yeah it's me. Eric Helix... Yes, of course the same Eric Helix. I own you now!... No I ain't calming down until I find out what's happened to my car! Where is it?... You what? You sold it?! Why?!..." There was a silent pause.

"So what if my car was in the same spot for more than a hundred days?... I'm a resident here. I have every right to park my–" There was a longer pause.

"Wait. Let me get this straight, just because my car was in the same parking spot for more than hundred days, it was declared abandoned by the Police?... Oh no... But I was in prison God dammit! I just got out today. Couldn't you have collected it and kept it safe for me?... What do you mean you can't do that? Don't you know who I am? I am Eric Helix. You know? The son of Gerald Helix. I'm telling you right now, I OWN Helix Motors, so you better do as I say otherwise you're fired!... I already told you what you have to do. Find my car and get it back!... What do you mean it's no longer mine?" There was another silent pause and then all of a sudden Eric took the phone away from his face, and threw the phone across the room. He tilted his head up while holding his out fists as he screamed in rage. "AAAAAAHHHHHH!" He kicked the nearest wall with bang.

He went over to the coffee table, sat down on a white leather couch, and then buried his head in his hands. It was during that time he heard a faint "bleep bleep" from his phone. The call was over. Then he leaned back in his seat to take a breather. His chest went up and down in exhaustion. He got up, tore off his suit jacket and threw it in the trash. He looked for his phone, found it. It had a crack on the screen already. "Fuck!" He said to himself. He dialled again and paced around his penthouse.

"Hello? This is Eric Helix. Listen up," he said. "I want a brand new Helix Muscle Car outside my penthouse as soon as possible... What do you mean there are none left? You stopped making them? Why?... The losses you made over the last few years are not my concern. I was in prison." There was a pause. "So what have you got? A recent trade-in? Are you

KIDDING me?! I am not driving around a car that belonged to someone else. Don't you get it? It's been fucking USED! God knows what the previous owner did to it. I want a brand new one!...." He sighed. "Oh man!" He sounded like he was about to cry. He put his hand on his forehead and then slid it down his face and pressed his fingers into his closed eye sockets. "Uh-huh... fine. By the way, what colour is it?... Dark Blue? Oh phew, that's not so bad." He exhaled with relief. "Okay fine. Just make sure it's outside my place by tomorrow morning, okay?... What?! Two business days? Why?... It's in New York?... Wait a second, I have to PAY for the delivery service?... Dammit!... Okay. Tell the New York branch to reserve that car for me and I'll arrange the delivery myself. Got it?... Good." He took the phone away from face and got off the line. At that moment he let out a long sigh.

He went back to his white leather couch and collapsed onto it. As he regained his breath, he looked around his penthouse. At least there was solace in seeing everything else he owned exactly where they were when he last left it.

His penthouse was a modern white palace. Almost every surface was white and shiny. The dinner table was a long slab of white marble surrounded by ten white leather chairs, all held up by silver legs. The floor itself was a white marble. The surrounding floor-to-ceiling windows gave him a panoramic view of the city. The rest of the furniture were some miniaturised versions of the Crystal Palace, silver poles and panels that held thick glass. One of them was his drinks cabinet that stored all the wine and whiskey bottles, along with rows of stylish glasses. Another cabinet, long and wide, was right by the windows and it held a gigantic Helix 120-inch HDTV. This glass and silver cabinet stored all his video games, DVD and Blu-ray collection. Next to that was another glass and silver cabinet that held his black Helix hi-fi system. This one stored all his music CDs. In front of the TV was a group of huge white leather couches that formed a crescent around it. And right in the middle was the white shiny coffee table that held his new briefcase. The rest of Eric's penthouse was decorated with ornaments related to cars. All the other glass and metal cabinets had small models of cars from different eras: vintage cars from the 1950s, 60s, and 70s, as well as sports cars from the 80s and 90s. The rest were all models of modern concept cars. You name the brand, it was there: Lamborghini, Ferrari, Maserati, and Aston Martin to name a few. On the walls were pictures of the luxury cars in thin black metal frames. What stood out of his living room penthouse was his small kitchen in the corner. The tiles were black and white like the checkered flag. The table in there was a black marble slab surrounded by black leather stools with silver legs. The cupboards were black and shiny, within every panel was a sort of red brake-light pattern that glittered against the light.

He let out a sigh of relief. It was good to be home after three years in prison. He got up to undo the buttons on his shirt. He noticed his gold Helix watch. He gently took it off to look at it for a moment. It stopped working years prior due to lack of activity to get the kinetic mechanism to function. He shook his head at the watch, and then he tossed it onto the coffee table, as if it was a piece of junk. He undid the rest of the buttons on his shirt as he walked towards the bathroom to take a shower. Along the way, something caught his attention that stopped him in his tracks. There, in the distance was the Horus Tower. With its imposing structure, it stood out of the cityscape. "Son of a bitch," he growled under his breath. He went into the bathroom and slammed the door.

***

Penelope Helix opened the door to her small apartment. She leaned on it after she closed it. She took in a huge deep breath as she relaxed her shoulders. She allowed a big smile on her face, and then it suddenly disappeared. She gasped. She dropped the briefcase on the floor.

"Oh no! My babies!" She rushed over to her window sill. Rows of flower pots had dead plants in dry soil. The crunchy leaves broke apart as she tried to feel them.

"Oh my god. I'm so sorry," she said to the plants. She shook her head in dismay. She looked around the rest of her apartment, all the shiny white clay pots had dead plants in them. They would have breathed life into the place.

"Oh," she said to herself. She rushed over to her fridge and opened it.

"Oh my god. Ewww. Uuugh," she yelped. She slammed the fridge door shut. She flapped her arms around to fan away the ghastly smell of rotten food she had accidentally released. "Oh man," she moaned. Then she went over to the cupboard under the kitchen sink and took out a roll of trash bags. She opened all the windows to let in some fresh air and allow some ventilation. In her head she counted 1-2-3, and then opened the fridge door. She seized everything in the fridge and put them into a trash bag, one at a time. Once the fridge was emptied, she went over to her dead plants. She sniffed as she emptied all the contents of the clay flower pots into the trash bags. "I'll get some new ones soon," she said to herself. She let out a sigh of relief as she threw one bag of trash down the garbage chute at a time. And finally, she took off the blue jumpsuit from the detention centre, and the white plimsolls, and threw them down the garbage chute. She wrapped her arms around herself as she looked around her apartment whilst naked. The only thing she wore was her black glasses with large lenses and thick frames. All her piercings were gone. She felt relieved to be home.

Her apartment was small. Quaint, by modern standards. It was minimalist with little furniture. Her sitting room had a shelf full of books on plants, nature, politics, the environment, and women's literature, along with magazines that covered such topics. In the corner there was a beige couch with a Helix HDTV in front of it, 38-inches in size was big enough for her. The couch itself had dark brown cushions that matched the dark brown rug on the floor. It even came with a soft dark brown shawl to decorate it with. Next to that was a lanky white lamp that stood next to the shelf. On the dark brown rug was a little light brown coffee table. The large windows allowed plenty of daylight into the apartment, even on cloudy grey days like this one, especially when the white blinds were up. The place would have looked more lively had there been plants around. All the walls were white and so was the ceiling. Except for the few surfaces that went a slight yellowish colour over time. The floors were all of oak coloured laminated flooring. There was a rug in each room, each one a dark shade of earth colours, from dark brown to dark green. The cupboards and all the other surfaces in her kitchen were all a light-cedar-tone coloured wood that matched the laminated wooden floor. Light brown shelves on the walls had vegetarian and vegan cookbooks that rested next to each other. The fridge, the oven, the hob, and the microwave were the only things that were black and silver, all of them Helix products. The kitchen table was a square piece of thick wood, three feet long, and three feet wide, held up with black metal poles, that matched the two chairs next to it, also made of wood and held together with black metal.

She remembered the briefcase she dropped by the door. She picked it up and placed it on the kitchen counter. She opened it, took out her new Helix phone, registered her details, and then ordered and paid for a vegan pizza with her new Dove bank card. Then she put them aside to take a shower.

When she came out of the shower, she was fresh and clean, wearing nothing but a white bath robe and a white towel wrapped around her head. She buzzed the delivery man in. She went into the bedroom to get her Helix laptop. There it was, on her desk. Closed. She picked it up, and blew off the layer of dust on it. She brought it to the kitchen and wiped it with a kitchen towel. Placed it on the coffee table in the sitting room, plugged it into the mains, and turned it on.

There was a knock at the door. When she answered, she found a big man in a biker's outfit and a balaclava, he had her pizza in one hand, his tablet in the other.

"A vegan pizza?" he asked.

She nodded.

"Here's your pizza ma'am," said the delivery man.

She took the pizza box and slammed the door in his face. She put the pizza box on the kitchen counter, opened it and dug into her first piece. She couldn't suppress a smile. With her oily hands she went over to one of her cupboards and took out a wine glass and bottle of red wine. She devoured the rest of her pizza while she gulped one glass of red wine at a time. Once she finished her meal, she went over to her couch in front of the coffee table where her laptop was ready. She went online and logged into her social media accounts. Her number of followers had over the years declined. But at least she still had her few loyal fans who were always ready to 'Like' and share anything she posted online. She posted her first comment in three years.

"Guess who's back, guys?"

There was little response apart from a handful of messages that welcomed her, while others mocked her return.

"Whoooooo!"

"Hey Penelope. Are you okay?"

"Great to see you."

"Yay!"

"She's back!"

"Who are you?"

"Where have you been?"

"Oh god, what's she up to now?"

"Huh!" she responded. She cracked her knuckles, stretched out her arms, tilted her head left and then right to stretch her neck muscles. She opened up the word processor to write a new article.

Upon writing the title "Three Years: How Prison is Systematic Misogyny" her inner keyboard-warrior went off on a rampage, in a frantic speed as she typed a lengthy rant about her experience in the Coast City Women's Detention Center. She typed away into the evening, ready to upload her article to the web.

***

Toby Helix panted as he ran over to the front door of his apartment. As soon as he opened the door, he jerked his head away.

"Woah," he said. "Oh god." He covered his nose with his free hand while he carried his briefcase with the other. He walked into the pitch black apartment. The black horizontal blinds were down. When he turned on the lights, all was revealed.

His studio apartment was a junkyard. All the leftover foods were in the places he last left them. Dirty clothes hung on every surface, the trash can in the kitchen overflowed with card and plastic packaging for microwave meals, unwashed pots on the hob and in the sink, and every other gap in the mess was filled with empty potato chip bags. Crushed cans of soda and beer were scattered all over the floor. Under the couch was an opened pizza box with a half-eaten pizza in it. Under the closet bed was a box of half-eaten nachos. The closet bed was undone with sheets unchanged for who knows how long. The bed also had some unwashed clothes on it.

After three years of seasons come and gone, the stench of all the rotten food, the garbage, and all the dirty clothes, blended together into a thick cocktail of one foul stench that could make anyone want to vomit. It was like walking into a giant trash can. Even for Toby, the place was nauseating.

The only thing that looked spotless was his big black leather gaming chair with large soft black leather cushions on it. It curved gently like a flattened crescent. When one sat on it, it rocked like a rocking chair. The only thing that made it dirty were the oily finger marks that shined on the black leather surface. And right in front of the chair was a big black Helix HDTV, 120-inches big, but it wasn't big enough for him. The TV rested on a wide black wooden cabinet that displayed his collection of video game consoles, it had light blue LED lights around the edges to give it a futuristic science-fiction feel to it. And right in front of that cabinet were his video game consoles, the Helix Discus, the Brooks Box and a pile of video games next to it. The Helix Discus was a wide black cylinder with a blue Helix symbol on the top. The Brooks Box was a white metal box with the letter 'B' engraved all over it to form a pattern on its surface. There was another game console with its own pile of games next to it, the Taurus Bull, it was shaped like a black drum, on top of it was a white, silver, and a purple design of a bull's head. All were linked to the back of the TV, ready to play.

The walls were nothing but black wooden shelves that held all the merchandise and video game paraphernalia that he had collected over the years. From action figures to plush toys of popular video game characters, along with accessories he brought from Anime and video game conventions; Mugs, key rings, sunglasses, Rubik's cubes, figurines, plastic toys, custom chess sets, trading cards, special editions and so on. All these things surrounded the cups he had won over the years, Gold, Silver, and Bronze for his video game champion-ships. All of them gathered dust, but his three year absence only added another layer on them.

"Oh man," he moaned.

He brushed everything out of the way with his feet as he made his way to his gaming chair. He put his briefcase on it. The next thing he did was open the blinds by pulling the strings down. Something about the cloudy sky made him smile for moment, he opened the windows to let some air in before he pulled himself away. He looked at the mess all around him, and looked almost lost in his own home. He bit his nails and scratched his head as he thought for a while. He shrugged his shoulders.

"Oh well," he said to himself. He ploughed though the mess, he picked up the first handful of trash next to his feet, waded though the mess over to the garbage chute and threw everything down there. Handful after handful, he grabbed whatever was mixed in with the mess; all the clothes he hadn't washed, all the rotten foods, all the cans and all the packaging, even the unwashed pots and pans. He picked up the trash can and turned it over as he poured all the rubbish that remained out of it. He tore off the sheets from his bed and threw them down the garbage chute too. While dumping all the rubbish in his studio flat, he uncovered a black coffee table.

"Oh, there you are," he said with surprise. "I was wondering where you'd gone." Soon he had thrown away everything he could get his hands on. "There." he said to himself. The place looked almost bare in comparison with before he came in.

There was a grumble in his belly. "Oooh, I'm hungry." He went over to his big silver Helix fridge, when he opened it, it let out a stink in the air. It also had unfinished food in there. "Oh man." He moaned again. He grabbed everything in the fridge and threw them down the garbage chute. He looked around the kitchen, the only thing he could find was a cereal box, that expired years ago. He opened his mouth wide and poured it down his mouth. He didn't care that some of its contents spilled on to his face, chest and onto the floor. He chewed all the sugary flakes before he poured another mouthful down into his mouth. He put the box down onto the kitchen counter.

He dragged his black coffee table next to his black leather chair. He opened the briefcase and took out his new phone and laptop. He registered his details on both devices and logged into them. On his Helix phone he ordered two pizzas, a box of fried chicken, a big plastic bottle of soda, a king-sized bucket of strawberry flavoured ice cream, a bucket of popcorn, 2 hot dogs and some candy bars. He salivated like a dog.

"Oh boy," he said to himself with excitement. And then he surfed the internet on his laptop, he ordered the latest video game consoles; The Brooks Box II, The Taurus SpaceBull, The Horus Pyramid, the gold version, and he ordered all the top ten video games for each console. And he paid extra to get them all delivered within 48 hours.

He logged onto all his social media accounts and onto his favourite gaming forum.

"Hey guys, I'm back!" Toby posted.

The internet erupted with joy.

"OMG, I don't believe it."

"Hey!"

"Heeeeere's TOBY!"

"It's the martyr."

"Heeeee-lix. Heeeee-lix. Heeeee-lix."

"How ya doing buddy?"

"The champ is back."

"You got a lot of catching up to do."

"I know I know," said Toby in his next post. "I just got out of prison. I'm feeling a little rusty. I got myself all the latest consoles, I'm so excited to get back in the game. For sure ya'll."

"So what you gonna do now?" one commenter asked in response.

"I have to wait till tomorrow or Friday to get them delivered here. Besides, my Brooks Box is exactly where I left it. There are still some trophies I need to get. Perfect time to practice," Toby replied.

Later, there was a buzz by the door. He picked up the phone, and buzzed the delivery man in. "Oh boy!" said Toby with excitement. "Everything's back to normal." Soon he was dancing around his apartment with joy with a big smile on his face. The floors creaked as he skipped around like a school boy. He turned on his TV and his Brooks Box, he placed the top game in there, and loaded it. The game was called 'All-Out-Assault IX: Space Warfare', a sci-fi shooting game.

While the game was loading there was a knock at the door. He opened the door, and the delivery man was huge, dressed in a biker's outfit with a balaclava. Next to him were two big square bags.

"I got a delivery here for Toby Helix," said the delivery man.

"That's meeeee," Toby sang.

"Okay, here you go, sir," said the delivery man as he gave him the two big square bags.

"Thank you, man," said Toby.

"Thank you, sir. Have a good night." Toby shut the door and put the bags down. He opened the first one, took out the two pizza boxes and placed them onto his black coffee table. He opened the box on top, and breathed in the smell of a freshly cooked meat-feast pizza. He grabbed a piece and watched as the cheese stretched from the surface to form long strings of greasy yellow fat. He devoured the pizza, one piece at a time. The hot cheese burnt the inside of his mouth, but he didn't care. The taste was too good. As soon as he finished the first pizza, he tossed the box over his shoulder. He reached into the bag and pulled out a big plastic bottle of sugary soda, he opened it, and then drank it. Then he opened the other pizza box, and he breathed in the smell of a freshly cooked Mexican Barbeque pizza. He devoured that pizza too. He wiped his mouth with his hands. Crumbs went everywhere. All over his face, his tight t-shirt, his jeans, and on the dark grey carpet floor. He picked up his control pad with his oily fingers, put on his headset, and sat back in his black leather gaming chair.

"Alright. Let's do this," said Toby.

**

Later that evening, Jodie Helix took her time as she made her way down the hallway after coming out of the elevator. She opened the front door to her penthouse and walked in with relief as she closed it behind her. She put her briefcase on a couch. She walked straight to her bedroom, took off her white plimsolls, and lay on her bed. After a few minutes rest she got up to observe her bedroom. Every wall in her penthouse was coloured French Vanilla, with various floral designs of lighter colours. All her furniture was a sort of cream colour. The white ceiling had an organised grid of warm coloured LED spotlights. The cream carpet matched the cream coloured drawers, cupboards, and the large makeup table. The makeup table had a huge square mirror with small warm coloured spotlights on the edges. All the handles and hinges were gold.

She got up from her bed and walked over to a wall of mirrors, she slid them to one side and turned on the lights inside. This was her walk-in wardrobe, there were rows of clothes and dresses on hangers. This room was also French Vanilla coloured with warm spotlights on the ceiling. Everything was exactly where she left them. Her handbags and shoes were in their cream cabinets. It was as big as her bedroom.

"There you are, my darlings," she said under her breath. She felt the textures of all her dresses and outfits with her fingertips. She allowed her hands to brush along while she walked beside the dresses that hung. Her hands chose a dress and pulled one off the wardrobe rack.

It was a long dark purple dress that reached the ground, and it had a v-cut. She held it in front of her as she turned around and looked at herself in the mirror inside the walk-in wardrobe. She smiled with delight at first, but then, after a longer look in the mirror, her smile faded. Her long blonde hair didn't shine. But there was something else. She put the dress back where she found it. And then walked over to the mirror to take a closer look at herself. She touched her face. It was at that moment she began to think.

The three years she spent in the detention center had transformed her look. Her weight loss made her cheek bones stick out more than before. Three years with many sleepless nights gave her bags under her eyes.

Despite being in her nice and quiet penthouse, she could still hear the screams her inmates emitted in the middle of the night. Her face said it all. Exhaustion. Her face without makeup looked like she had aged another ten years. She looked at her face one last time, as if she noticed something.

"Mum," she whispered. "I wish I was more like you." She turned away, turned off the wardrobe lights and closed the wall of mirrors. She took off the blue jumpsuit she wore, picked up the white plimsolls, and threw them in the trash.

She went into her bathroom and took a long hot shower. She crossed her arms over and embraced herself as she leaned against the wall. She took her time to feel the hot water land on her head and roll down her face, and then down the rest of her body. She kept her breathing steady. Pressing her back against the shower wall, she gently slid down and then sat down. She allowed her eyes to close. She placed her arms on her knees, rested her head onto her arms, and then she began to cry. The hot water vapour and the hot water that came down from the showerhead massaged her skin. Her tears were washed away by the hot water that came down from above, like a compassionate angel caressing her head in sympathy. She let it all out until she stopped crying.

Later, she came out of her bedroom with a cream coloured bathrobe. She massaged her blonde hair with a large cream coloured towel. And then put it on her shoulders. She walked into the sitting room where the briefcase rested on the couch. The couch itself was a soft cream coloured leather. The couches formed a large L-shape next to a gigantic Helix HDTV. They were decorated with coffee coloured cushions, one dark accompanied by a light coloured one. The coffee table was a solid block of wood, also coloured cream, that held a large dark coffee bowl for a decoration. In the bowl was a mixture of seashells that were gold, silver, and bronze, flower-scented, but it had long gone. Right in the middle of the room was a large dark coffee coloured rug. She too had floor-to-ceiling windows, they too gave her a panoramic view of the city.

There were cream coloured curtains that hung down from the ceiling. The floors of her sitting room were light brown tiles. The ceiling was cream with warm LED spotlights. In every corner were gold vases that held green plastic plants.

She opened the briefcase and took out her new Helix phone and Helix laptop. She placed them on her coffee table, turned them on, and then registered her details. She looked online to see what was going on in the world. She noticed already there were articles going around spreading rumours about the Helix siblings on the internet. Penelope and Toby had already brought attention to themselves with their on-line activity. Penelope posted her article online and people were arguing about it on social media, meanwhile the gaming community cheered on the arrival of Toby getting back into his gaming routine. Each fan commented on what he was up to on his Brooks Box console, and already working on getting a new trophy.

She cringed with embarrassment at first, she took a deep breath and held it in as she bit a finger, shook her head, and then she exhaled. Relieved that at least she wasn't under the spotlight for once. Nobody had mentioned her or Eric yet. She turned off her laptop and her phone. She took out the folder that Gosia prepared for her to look through the documents. She held it in her arms as she got up and went back to her bedroom to read. But as soon she lay down on the bed, her eyelids felt heavy. She couldn't keep her head up or concentrate. She lay back on her bed, closed her eyes and fell asleep. For her, it had been a long day.

***

That night, Denise was in the middle of changing her baby when her husband Daniel came back from work.

"Hi honey," she said. "Look who's here, Nadia, Daddy's back." She pretended to give the baby the look of a pleasant surprise.

"Hey babe," he replied. He put down his briefcase by the door, took off his shoes and then loosened his tie. He breathed a sigh of relief to be home.

"How's she been?" he asked.

"Not as demanding as yesterday. Say Hello to Daddy," she smiled at the baby again.

"She's gorgeous," he leaned over and kissed his daughter's head. And then he kissed Denise on the lips. He put his suit jacket and his tie on the living room chair and undid the buttons on his shirt.

"What's for dinner, honey?" He asked.

"Nothing, yet. I've been busy," she replied.

"Don't worry, babe, I'll put a frozen pizza in the oven for us. Has she eaten?" asked Daniel.

"Yes, I'm putting her to bed soon. How was work honey?" asked Denise.

"Tiring. It's been a long day. We're still trying to keep the company afloat. It looks like there may have to be some more 'restructuring'. That can mean anything. Either I get demoted, moved to another sector, or..." he took in deep breath, "I lose my job." He said as he exhaled.

"Don't say that," said Denise.

"You have to think about these things, Dee. You can never know what happens. So you have to prepare for the worst."

"But we mustn't let it come to that," said Denise.

"Don't worry, honey, I'm just tired," said Daniel.

"Well you must be," she replied. She held the baby in her arms.

"What do you mean?" he asked.

"Haven't you heard? They're back."

"Who's back?" He asked.

"The Helix siblings," She replied.

"Oh god no. I totally forgot about those guys. Holy shit, they were jailed like what... three years ago?! And now they're out?"

"Looks that way," she said.

He took out his phone and scrolled down his news feed. The news had spread that the siblings were out of prison. Even an online magazine had a picture of Eric at the top of the article. He was spotted running in his messy suit with his briefcase by a bystander who had recognised him. It was posted on social media earlier that day, many comments confirmed it was definitely him. The title read "Where's he going in such a hurry?" Articles showed pictures of the Helix siblings.

As Daniel read through some of the articles, he came across Penelope's article and of Toby's announcement of his return to gaming.

"Oh no," said Daniel.

"Come on, it's not so bad," said Denise.

"This IS bad," he replied.

"How?" she asked.

"Toby can do harm, but god damn it, Penelope is at it already. On the DAY she comes out of prison. Of all the days. Her activism is embarrassing."

"At least she's giving Helix Inc. publicity."

"But that's not the kind we need. I swear, if we go down and out, it will all be their fault. So far, Eric hasn't been arrested or crashed a car yet. And as for Jodie, she hasn't been caught in another sex scandal yet either. But I'm dreading the times they do. Like I said. You've got to prepare for the worst."

At that moment his phone rang.

"Huh? It's work." He said, and then he answered it. "Hello?... Yeah, I'm good. I just got home... Yeah I know, I heard... what? Tomorrow morning? With Eric Helix?... And who?... oh...oh..." He had the look of horror on his face. He swallowed. His voice began to croak. "Uuuuhh, yeah, okay. I'll be there. Bye." He slowly took the phone away from his head and put his hand on his face. He swallowed. He looked dizzy. He slowly sat down on to the couch.

"What a nightmare," he whispered to himself.

"What's wrong?" asked Denise.

"I'm meeting them tomorrow," Daniel replied.

"Who?" she asked.

"The siblings."

"Oh really?" she asked with excitement. "Which one?"

"All of them."

Chapter 13

The next morning, Eric was at a meeting with a group of men in suits in the Helix Motors subdivision of Helix Tower. The boardroom had large windows with long and thin white curtains that decorated them, like the veil of a wedding dress, they went from the rack on the ceiling down to the floor. The blinds were up to allow the daylight in. It wasn't too bright outside. The huge LED screens on the walls displayed the presentation with graphs and sales charts. The weather was partly cloudy, the sky was bright blue, but the sun was hidden behind the clouds, which gave their edges a white glow. The floor was covered with milliken carpet with various shades of dark blue lines going across it. The walls were white and so was the ceiling that came complete with white LED spotlights. The blackish-blue table in the middle was a wooden surface so shiny that it reflected like a mirror. With the daylight outside and the white spotlights from above, the whole boardroom with the dark blue surfaces gave the whole place a tint of blue.

The long table had black leather seats, enough for twenty people. All the men were in suits who sat up straight. Their eyes focused on the main screen while they ignored the ones on the walls around them. Most of them were middle aged-men, with various hairstyles. Each of them wore jewellery of the Helix brand, be it a Helix watch, Helix cuff links, some preferred gold while others wore silver. Their suits were also various shades of dark blue, grey, and black. All of them had the iconic dark blue handkerchief with the Helix symbol on it. To them, it was a mandatory uniform, an expression of loyalty to the company they worked for. Some of them went as far as to wear a tie that also had the Helix logo on it, while others had a plain tie with a pin that came in gold or silver, bearing the Helix logo engraved on to it.

Daniel Crawley, the Project Manager, stood by the biggest screen on one end of the boardroom, he held a remote control in his hand that came with a built-in laser pointer. He was in the middle of giving a presentation.

Eric, the youngest of them all, sat at the other end of the boardroom table, relaxed as he had his head tilted up to stare at the ceiling. He was in his dark greyish-blue suit with a white shirt, top two buttons undone. No tie, no handkerchief. His only accessories were his gold cufflinks and his gold watch. He rolled his eyes and then looked out the window. He irritated the board members who sat closest to him with his constant clickety-click-click with his pen. They narrowed their eyes at him. One of them couldn't take it anymore, he was the oldest of the annoyed. Eric didn't stop clicking his pen until the older board member growled under his breath.

"Will you quit it?"

Eric stopped and looked at the angry board member who scowled at him. He noticed that among his gritted teeth one of them was gold. And then, like a child, Eric rolled his eyes, slammed his pen down on the table which made other board members turn their heads before turning back to the presentation. He rested his head on his right fist as he stared at the windows. He exhaled from sheer boredom.

"And so, gentlemen, that's how it is," said Daniel Crawley, "In order to increase our sales, we need to invest in our marketing campaign."

"I agree," said James Knight, the Chairman who sat at the front end. He had dark brown hair brushed back and grey sideburns. His suit was dark grey and he had blue eyes. "We can invest some of the profits to fund the research for further improvements to our current models."

Eric got up and walked over to the window and looked down at the city. All the board members turned to look at him.

"Eric Helix? Do you not want to participate?" asked the Chairman.

There was a long moment of silence.

"Yeah," Eric replied. "Yeah, I have an idea." He spun around to look at his team. "Gold!" he said with excitement.

"Gold?" asked another board member with raised eyebrow.

The other boardroom members had puzzled looks on their faces.

"Look at all the cars down there," Eric pointed. "They all look the same. The only thing to distinguish from the similar shapes and sizes are the colours. Red, white, blue, black, and silver. Whatever." He counted the colours with his fingers. "We need gold cars, man!"

"Gold cars?" asked the Chairman.

"Yes! Let's bring out a new model with a nice shiny golden coat of paint. People love bling, man!" Eric said with excitement. The board members looked at each other with confusion.

"Nonsense," one board member said.

"Where did you get that idea from?" asked another member, to which the old member with the gold tooth covered his mouth with his hand and turned away from the table.

"Well," said Daniel, "We could do that. Since we are working on a new model that is yet to be released, we could bring out a gold version of it. Like a concept car perhaps?"

"Really? When is it coming? Is it a sports car?" Eric asked with excitement. He placed his hands on the table and leaned forward. He had the look immense optimism on his face.

"It's a station wagon," the Chairman replied.

"Oh man!" Eric moaned. He pulled himself away from the table. "Oh well. At least we can make that one gold."

"A gold station wagon?" said a board member, "Don't be ridiculous."

"Yes. And there is the customer's budget to consider. This model is aimed at families who live in the suburbs," said the Finance Manager.

"Cars are not toys, Mr Helix," the old board member with the gold tooth. He couldn't help but smirk as he joined in with the group who expressed their discontent at Eric.

"Speaking of which," said Daniel. "It's still in the design stage. It won't be in the showroom for the next six months."

"Oh come on! We don't have time!" Eric shouted.

"Calm down, son," said the Chairman.

Like an irritated teenager, Eric rolled his eyes and puffed out loud. He went back to his seat, sat down, crossed his legs and went back to clicking his pen again. The oldest board member's face went red as he tightened his lips shut firmly. Eric thought for a moment.

"Mr Crawley, you were saying?" the Chairman urged.

"Yes. So I think it's best we advertise the new model well in advance, right about now. And we can give a free test drive of an early prototype for those who place a deposit, like a few months before the release. Think of it as an early bird deal."

"Sounds like a good idea," said a board member.

"My main concern," said the Chairman, "is safety. Will the prototypes be as fully functional for the test drives?"

"I think it's best you speak to the engineers about that," Daniel replied.

"What else do you think we can do?" asked a board member

At that moment, Eric clicked his fingers, put down his pen and then stood up.

"I got it! I've got a better idea. We're going to release a gold version of EVERY model we have!"

One board member smacked a palm on his forehead. "People can exchange their current models for a gold one," said Eric with excitement. The other board members rolled the eyes and sighed.

"Mr Helix," said a board member, "We don't only make cars. We manufacture trucks, and vans, and other vehicles for farming, and construction. Do you want to make them gold too?"

"Ha ha ha. Really?" Eric laughed. "A gold Helix tractor? Now there's a thought. But errr... nah man. I'm talking about cars here. Whatever model we have now, let's bring out a gold one. With gold hubcaps and some gold accessories, like a gold car key."

"With all due respect, Mr Helix, do you have any idea how much this will cost? We need to be careful where we channel our profits," said the Finance Manager.

"What? Spray paint? That's cheap. People like buying gold, man. Even when they don't need it. It's a nice thing to have. It's all about status, man. I mean, come on. Don't tell me you never owned anything to make yourself look better than your underlings. So gentlemen, let's come clean and admit it. Yes?"

The boardroom fell silent.

"Exactly," Eric went on. "So that's what we are going to do. And that will boost our profile. We will be the only company with gold cars in its inventory," said Eric.

"And if people don't want it?" asked the Chairman.

"It doesn't matter," said Eric, "It's about presence. We are Helix Inc. People have to know that we exist and do whatever it takes to burn our brand into their brains. Ha! We'll spray it on in gold. We can slap on a price tag for like uhh... $200,000 for a new car. Or they can exchange their current cars for a gold one for a few extra dollars."

All the other board members sighed.

"Fine," said one board member.

"If it means that much to him, go ahead," whispered another member.

"Very well," said the Chairman. Then he turned to Daniel. "How soon can we get this project started?"

"I'll have to get back to you on that one. But in the mean time we'll see what we can do," said Daniel.

"Yeah! That's the spirit," said Eric. He went over to the window to look at the cityscape. "We're gonna rule this city! Ha ha."

The meeting concluded. All the board members put all their papers together, put them into folders, and then put them in their briefcases. They got up, one by one, they left the boardroom. Eric was the last to leave and shut the door behind him.

"Phew. Man, that was hard work," Eric said out loud. The other men ahead of him raised their eyebrows while others compressed their lips as they looked at one another.

Chapter 14

The next meeting was meant to start, but Toby was nowhere to be seen. All the seated men in the boardroom took their turns to check their watches followed by a sigh of dissatisfaction, be it a puff through the nose, a head shake, or a frown. Daniel Crawley sat at the end of the table with his laser pointer.

"He's not coming," said one of the board members.

"We are forty minutes late already. Time is money, god damn it," said Alex Thomson, the Chairman.

"We might as well start now," said Daniel. He got up and stood by the large projector screens. "Okay gentlemen, I present to you–"

The two doors burst opened with a bang.

"I'm coming! I'm here!" Toby barged in with heavy panting. Some of the paperwork had spilled out of his briefcase. He panted as if he ran a marathon, his face was wet with sweat. He wore a poorly buttoned up shirt and a tie that wasn't done up properly. What stood out were his light blue pyjama trousers with little white spots, and his pair of large white trainers.

"Did you just wake up?" asked the Chairman.

"Yes– I mean no! I errr… so uh what did I miss?" As soon as he spotted an empty seat, he parked his fat backside on it. Three men closest to Toby covered their noses and moved away from him.

"Christ almighty," said a board member.

"This guy fuckin' stinks," another whispered.

"We were just getting started, Mr Helix," said Daniel. He opened his presentation. "Okay gentlemen, at the moment, since we have to cut costs from our Research and Development team, we're going to have to look elsewhere. Right now there is an increasing number of small chipset developers, I suggest we pick a few and purchase them."

"Wait a minute!" Toby called out. He raised his hand like a school boy. "Why are we buying someone else's chipset when we can make our own? We are Helix Tech! The best in the world!"

"Now now, Toby," said the Chairman, and then he spoke a little slower in a gentle father-like tone, "First you have to take into account it costs a lot of money for us to design and develop our own chipset. It's a long expensive process. We don't have the budget for it. However, when we purchase a few smaller chipsets from other companies we get to keep production costs down. Do you understand?"

"Okay," Toby replied. "So when is the next console coming out?" asked Toby.

"Console?" asked the Chairman.

"He means the Helix Discus video game console," said another board member.

"Forget it, kid," said the Chairman, "We're out of that competition. We no longer make consoles."

"Naaoooooo! That can't be! No!" Toby cried. "Wait! So who's leading the console market now?"

"The Brooks Box X, and the Horus Pyramid," one board member answered.

"Recently," another board member joined in, "The Taurus game development company announced the release date for their new console, The Taurus Bull II. Taurus has been growing for years."

"Thanks to you," said an older board member who glared at Toby.

"Me? I had nothing to do with it!" Toby moaned.

"If it weren't for you and your shenanigans with the drugs and that Taco fellow, they would never have gained such popularity!" the older board member growled.

"But...uh... we can fix that," said Toby.

"No, we can't!" said the old member, his face was turning red. "We have lost a valuable product, we had to make a sacrifice. A lot of people lost their jobs so we can stay in the tech competition. So you better get video games out of your head right now."

Toby's jaw trembled.

"You mean... Helix will never make video games again?"

"For the time being, yes," said the Chairman. "But we still have the Helix software. This is where we make the operating systems and develop the software for our tech, like phones, laptops, and PCs."

"You mean... we can still make games?" There was spark of hope in Toby's eyes.

"Yes we can, but–"

"Let's do it!" Toby boomed with joy as he got up from his seat, knocking back his chair down to the floor, and threw his arms in the air like he had won the lottery.

"What do you have in mind?" asked a board member.

"Okay, well, let's see what video games are the most popular, and then we'll make our own version. I mean, like, you know, turn a popular sci-fi game into a fantasy game. Or uh, we can get first person shooter, use the same story but in a different setting, like a World War 2 instead of modern warfare," said Toby.

"And what will be the purpose of this? How will that make us money?" asked the Finance Manager.

"Micro transactions," said Toby. "You know. To progress

in a game you have to purchase a weapon, or level up, or to purchase an accessory. Or like instead of losing the game, you can continue from where you left off by paying a small fee. You know. These little things will all add up. Think about it. At least we can start with these. I mean, we gotta remind these people we still exist. Like, you know, 'hey guys, we at Helix Inc. still make games.' Get it? We've got to try."

"And then what?" asked another board member.

"If we still make popular games like we did before, we can put ourselves back on the console market. Then we can use the sales of the games to make more games and buy more chipsets," said Toby.

"Hmmm," a board member began, "I suppose we could use this as a marketing strategy."

"Toby," said the Finance Manager, "Developing games costs a fortune. We don't have the budget."

"Not exactly," said Toby. "We're startin' small, right? I know a lot of guys who make games on small budgets. Look!" He took out his phone and opened up a web browser. "See? When we go to HireMeNow.com, there are people you can hire to program games, design websites and design logos for you. So instead of spending millions developing one game, we can spend thousands to make a dozen. At least we have variety."

There was a long silent pause in the boardroom. The Chairman sighed.

"Think about it, guys," said Toby. "Instead of buying chipsets that can lead to nowhere, right now we can get these games made right here right now on tiny little budgets. Once we release them, then we can start making money again."

"So be it," said the Chairman. "We might as well try this out and see how people respond to our marketing. We can advertise our products with them."

"Yes, like a new Helix laptop or phone could come with say five games built in or free trials," said a board member.

"Well that doesn't sound so bad," said a board member.

"So, are we going along with my idea?" asked Toby.

"Yes," said the Chairman.

"Yipeeeeeee!" Toby cheered with glee so loud it made the other board members flinch.

Daniel Crawley stood there with his presentation. "And the chipsets?" he asked to remind everyone in the room.

"We're going to have to put purchasing new hardware on hold for the time being," said the Chairman. "Right now the best thing we can do is see how much money we can make. Maybe after that, we may consider purchasing better chipsets for our hardware. For now let's focus on getting some budget games made and see how much revenue we generate though that."

"Very well," said Daniel. He nodded his head.

"Okay, gentlemen, meeting adjourned," said the Chairman. All the men gathered their paperwork and put them in their briefcases, packed up and left the boardroom, one by one. None of them wanted to look at Toby. But the Chairman took his time.

Toby was about to leave.

"Toby," the Chairman called him.

"Yeah?" Toby replied.

"Now don't take this the wrong way, son. But I think it has to be said and some things have no... how shall I put it, politer way of saying it."

"I don't get it," said Toby.

"At Helix Inc. we do our best keep at least two things constant. Punctuality and hygiene."

"Oh, uh, I'm sorry I was late. I didn't mean to, you know. I was up last night-well... till this morning. Heh. I was on a mission to kill as many aliens in a map in the shortest time possible. I lost count of the number of times I tried. It took longer than expected. But... I won! I got another trophy. I'm back in the game," Toby smiled.

"We don't have time to play video games," said the Chairman. "Our main concern, Toby, is to keep the business your father built afloat. He was dedicated to Helix Inc. It is that dedication in him that we honour, and respect. We apply that to our lives too. That is how Helix became a giant in the market. A video game can be completed. Our work here is never done."

"Well, neither is mine," said Toby. "See ya later." He walked away and left the boardroom. As soon as the door closed, the Chairman hurried over to a window and opened. The cool air breathed life into him. He stood there to take a breather.

Chapter 15

Jodie was a few minutes late when she walked in to the boardroom. All heads turned to look at her, disgruntled by her interruption. All except the Chairwoman who smiled at her. Daniel Crawley was the only man who stood by the biggest screen at the end of the boardroom.

The boardroom had a different interior design, the colours were mostly wooden with a warm atmosphere. The windows were separated by square columns made with an oak wood texture to go with the mahogany walls. The lights had round orange lamp shades. The carpet on the floor had lines going in one direction with various shades of dark brown that resembled ebony wood. The table in the centre was shaped like an elongated oval, also oak coloured. It was surrounded by twenty-four leather seats that were cream coloured with ebony arm rests. The walls had gigantic Helix HDTVs to display the presentation for those who couldn't see the main screen. Jodie was in her iconic black dress with a long v-cut that showed her cleavage, and the diagonally cut lower half that revealed an entire leg.

"Hey guys," said Jodie.

"Ah, Jodie Helix," the Chairwoman stood up, approached Jodie and shook her hand. She was a woman in her 60s with short silver hair in a Tousled Pixie style. She was in a dark blue Helix blazer along with all the other women in the boardroom. She was the oldest and senior. "I'm Stephanie Lawrence. Glad you can join us. Here, take a seat." She gestured. The leather chair next to hers was vacant. Obviously reserved for Jodie. They sat down. Jodie relaxed, sat back, crossed her legs and flicked her golden blonde hair like a model.

"So what did I miss?" asked Jodie.

"We're going for a new range of clothing for formal wear, like for parties, and balls, and wedding parties, christenings, bar mitzvahs etc."

Jodie sat quietly for moment to roll her eyes.

"Okay let's cut the crap. This is all boring. Helix has been making the same shit for years. We need something new. Now!" said Jodie.

All the board members gasped as they sat frozen in place. Their jaws dropped. All except for Stephanie who only raised an eyebrow.

"What do you have in mind, Jodie?" asked the Chairwoman.

"Lingerie!" Jodie said as loud as she could to make sure everyone in the room heard. "This is a market Helix has never touched. Well I say it's time it did. People love lingerie," Jodie announced with immense pride.

The ladies in the boardroom looked at one another. And then they took turns to shake their heads at Jodie.

"Errrrr."

"Not us."

"I don't think so."

"Maybe not."

"Now now, ladies," said the Chairwoman. "Jodie is new here. So let's be patient." She cleared her throat. "You see, Jodie, we at Helix Inc. are, how shall I say, a little conservative." The she paused to look at Jodie with stern eyes to let that sink in. "We don't resort to sexual provocation in order to sell. Even Hollywood celebrities buy Helix clothing."

"But wait," said one board member. "Has everyone forgotten the sexual liberation movement in the 1960s? We had some designs that were highly controversial back then. We were chastised by the press. We kept with the times. Helix Inc. stayed on people's minds ever since."

"Yes, but we didn't make lingerie. We didn't go that far," said another member.

"Neither should we do it now," and another board member.

"Outrage sells," said another.

"Well I still think we should do it," said Jodie. "With Valentine's day coming, the timing couldn't be better."

"Oh Jodie, you just don't get it," said a board member.

"We'll lose our existing customers," said another board member.

"They'll hate us for this," said another.

"Now now, ladies," said the Chairwoman. The boardroom fell silent. "We all know companies take risks from time to time. But Jodie..." she paused to look at her again. "As interesting as your idea may be, why should we do it?"

Jodie smiled, she laughed. And then she got up to walk around the table. She addressed the board members as she slowly made her way towards Daniel Crawley.

"Isn't it obvious? If we do the same thing, over and over again, people will get bored of us, and our products. Sooner or later, someone else will come and take over the market with a niche that we were too scared to try."

She got closer to Daniel Crawley who stood up straight, in his black Helix suit. He had a raised eyebrow. And then she stood next to him.

"Like I said," Jodie continued, "People love lingerie. I see it in movies, and TV shows. It looks hot. And it makes men drool like dogs. Our target audience is not just women, you know. It's men too. They can't resist sex."

She grabbed Daniel's tie and gently pulled him towards her. His face went red with embarrassment. He looked at the

Chairwoman with the look that cried 'Oh God. Help. Get her off me.' The Chairwoman frowned with disapproval, while the rest of the women in the boardroom gasped. Some of them covered their mouths with their hands.

She leaned in close to him and smelled. "Mmmm. Helix Aftershave for Men. I am impressed by your loyalty, Mister..."

Her seductive blue eyes looked into his brown eyes, the smell of her Helix perfume was the same one he gave his wife. This gave him a rapid heartbeat. He kept a straight face, but his forehead was sweating, and his knees were shaking. He gulped.

"Crawley. Daniel Crawley." He answered as coldly as he could. He almost croaked like a frog.

"Thank you for volunteering," said Jodie. She let go of his tie and turned back to the board members. "You see. As you all saw just now, sex turns men on. Of course they'll buy it for their girlfriends and their wives. There's a lot of potential here."

Daniel adjusted his tie. He grabbed one his folders to fan his face. He took a deep breath. Jodie went back to sit next to the Chairwoman.

"So what do you think?" she asked.

"Very well," said the Chairwoman with a sigh. "Since Helix Inc. has never done it before, at least now we can give it a try." Some of the board members shook their heads. Jodie smiled. "Aaand..." she looked at Jodie in a way a concerned grandmother would advise her mischievous granddaughter, "In a NON-pornographic kind of way. If it succeeds we continue. If it fails, we won't make lingerie ever again. One lesson is enough for us."

"Good!" said Jodie with excitement. "And I'm going to model them. The Jodie Helix line. There! It has a name already."

The jaws of the board members dropped. One of them placed her head in her hands. The Chairwoman sighed.

"What are we waiting for? Let's get them designed

already," said Jodie. "Oh, and Mr Crawley, make sure you get the best designers on this."

"Yes, ma'am," he said.

"Alright. Meeting adjourned," said the Chairwoman.

Everyone in the boardroom packed their papers into their folders and briefcases.

"Jodie," the Chairwoman leaned in to her. "May I talk to you for a second, in private please?" Jodie nodded.

Daniel hurried as he made his way out. He kept his eyes away from Jodie's direction. One by one, the board members left until it was only Jodie and Stephanie in the boardroom.

"Jodie, I have to say that I am not impressed by your behaviour. What you did back there was unacceptable," said the Chairwoman.

"I didn't do anything," said Jodie.

"You knew exactly what you were doing. And I won't tolerate it," the Chairwoman said. To that, Jodie frowned like an angry teenage girl. The Chairwoman sighed. "Jodie, listen, Helix Inc. is a professional place of business. We treat people with dignity, respect, and we don't invade other people's personal boundaries. This is not a place to flirt with married men. He has a baby girl too."

"Okay, I didn't know he was married. So what? Besides, if I didn't do what I did back there, none of you would have listened to me. I have my ways." She twirled her hair with her finger.

"It was inappropriate," said the Chairwoman in a stern tone.

"I wasn't going fuck him, you know." Jodie soured her face.

"Jodie, you have to understand, this is a place of work. Word gets around here very quickly. Misunderstandings are hard to undo. This is not the way we conduct ourselves here. Do you have any idea how you look? Don't you care how other people perceive you?" said the Chairwoman.

"No," said Jodie in a defiant tone.

"Well, it's about time you did because you are making us look bad. People will distance themselves from us. It will affect sales too."

"But that's got nothing to do with me," Jodie protested.

"My dear, this company has everything to do with you; first of all this is your father's business, and you are his daughter. So therefore anything you say or do has consequences. You have one of the greatest names in the history of Coast City. So don't defile everything your ancestors built. Whether you like it or not, Jodie, people associate you with the company. But since you have no respect for yourself, then at least show some respect for other people." She looked at Jodie with stern eyes. "You may not care right now, but maybe when you have a family of your own you'll understand. But in the mean time, control yourself. That's all I have to say," said the Chairwoman.

"Thanks," said Jodie. She stopped playing with her hair, spun around and left the boardroom.

The Chairwoman then slowly took in a deep breath and slowly exhaled. She packed her things and then left the boardroom.

Chapter 16

Penelope walked through a pair of double doors without knocking. The board members lifted their heads up from the paper work and magazines laid out on the big table. They looked annoyed by the rude interruption at first, but when they realised it was Penelope, they all smiled. Among them was Daniel Crawley.

"Oh, Penelope Helix, hello," said the chairman.

"I'm glad you can join us," said another.

"Yeah yeah," said Penelope, "Let's get this over with." She sat down on the first empty chair she could find, opened her briefcase and took out her files. The board members looked at one another. The Chairman approached Penelope.

"I'm Jonathan Cropp, Chairman of the board," he reached out to shake hands as he smiled. She looked at his hand, then her eyes met his. She sighed, annoyed, and then took his hand, shook it briefly, and then let go. The Chairman went back among the group who huddled around the table.

Penelope kept her light brown hair short that went down to her shoulder. But she still had her big glasses with thick black frames. She wore black jeans, and black high heel shoes to give her some height.

"Penelope, you look different," said a gentleman who gave her a warm smile.

"What does THAT mean?" She glared at the gentleman with a confrontational tone.

"I mean you look nice," he said startled.

"Are you trying to flirt with me?" Penelope frowned.

"No," the gentleman replied.

"You better not, or I'll get HR on you for sexual harassment! Better yet, I can get you fired, you sexist pervert!" she screeched.

"Good lord," said one board member.

"Oh my— I didn't mean anything else," said the gentleman who backed away.

"He was only being friendly, Ms Helix," said a board member.

"Relax," said another.

"Ms Helix, control yourself. This is not the way to behave in a boardroom," said the Chairman.

"Oh yeah? What is the right way then? Misogyny?" Penelope replied.

"No," said the Chairman, "Politeness. There's no need to take things out of context and jump to conclusions. This isn't something to fire someone over. We talk like grown-ups."

"We'll see about that. As long as you all co-operate with me everything will be fine," said Penelope. There was moment of an awkward silence. "So what's on the agenda?" asked Penelope. She took out some files from her briefcase. Everyone else in the boardroom sighed and then resumed. Daniel Crawley cleared his throat.

"We are looking at raising awareness about the difficulties of living in the city," said Daniel, "How it impacts mental health. And the differences between an urban life and suburban life. We have facts here provided by researchers."

"We are looking at pollution around the world too," said the Chairman, "Human rights. The environment."

"And," another member of the board said. "We are also looking into how a growing population increases the demand for more resources, like food and–"

"I still think we should protest the aquarium," Penelope cut in.

"Ms Helix," said the Chairman, "there is nothing we can do about the aquarium. It's been open for business and growing in popularity. Now will you please get over it?"

Penelope huffed in irritation. She sat back in her chair and sulked for a moment. And then she got up. "Wait. You mentioned food and resources, right?" said Penelope. "That means there are shortages, right? Well, I have the answer. The Vegan Diet! We need to change the way people consume. For those who are still eating meat and all animal products, we need to shame them for doing so. Make them feel guilty! Yeah!" she announced. "And then the meat industry will go out of business. And we at Helix Press will have delivered the final blow. And then, we're gonna take pictures of people who eat meat, contact their employers and get them fired! Fear is the ultimate weapon. Yeah!"

There was mutual head-shaking across the boardroom. Except for Daniel Crawley who stood frozen with his lips compressed.

"No," said the Chairman. "Penelope, listen. We are not an activist group. We are the press. Our job is to inform people. Educate the public."

"It's not our job to tell people what to do," said the oldest member of the board. "If we insult them they will not read our literature. On and offline. It's certainly not our job to contact anyone's employer to get them fired from their jobs." He began to fume and frowned at Penelope. "Do you have any idea how immoral that is? It's costing someone else's livelihood. It affects their families, husbands, wives, and children. There are people who depend on them. You have no right to take that away from them. You have to show some respect." He raised his voice.

"You solve problems with dialogue, not by shutting them out," said the gentleman.

"Call yourself a liberal, eh?" the oldest board member continued. "Well, I'll tell you one thing, it's about tolerance. And that includes working with people who don't agree with you. Get the picture?" He pointed to a large framed photograph of the Statue of Liberty in New York. "Freedom of speech is a value we hold here. It's one of the things that makes America great."

"Yes, said another board member, "Whether you like it or not you have to show some respect."

"Fine!" said Penelope. She sat back down and crossed her arms. There was a long moment of silence. Everyone else in the boardroom exhaled from exhaustion.

"What do you suggest we do then?" said Penelope.

"Well," Daniel Crawley cleared his throat, "We can start by raising awareness on climate change around the world and how it affects us."

"Oh that sucks!" said Penelope. "We've been going on about it for years. Nobody's listening. There's gotta be something that will get people's attention. To make them think... But what? Hmm... I know! Animals! People love animals. So if we take pictures of them and show the world what we are doing to them and their habitats, then they will think twice."

Suddenly the whole boardroom was full of smiles with some mutual nods.

"Yes," said the Chairman.

"Of course, the destruction of habitats," said another member with a nod.

"I like it," said another board member.

Daniel Crawley smiled and relaxed his shoulders.

"Yes. But what is your message?" asked the oldest board member.

"The Vegan diet!" said Penelope.

Suddenly all the smiles were wiped off everyone's faces. One board member put a hand on his face.

"Ms Helix–" the Chairman began.

"Call me Penelope!" Penelope commanded.

"Alright, Penelope. Listen. Habitats are being destroyed because of our constant expansion. Our increasing consumption of more resources means more litter that ends up in the oceans. Trees are cut down. Animals lose their homes because we–"

"Just listen to my idea. Okay. You won't know unless you try. I am a vegan, right. Because I love animals. Right? Right. So I will be a model with animals. You take pictures of me with animals. That way people will get the picture."

"Oh god," said one board member. The rest of them sighed except Daniel Crawley who chewed his lower lip.

"But you have tattoos all over your body that have nothing to do with your message." One board member pointed to the side of his neck to signal to Penelope the sickle-hammer tattoo on her neck.

"Why is this all about you?" said the oldest board member. "Why should we do this?"

"Because I am Penelope Helix," she began. "I am the voice of Helix Press. So therefore it makes perfect sense to have me in it. I understand you have all suffered and made losses over the last three years. Well I wasn't around to stop it. So here I am. I am going to fix things up. Once everyone knows about me, they'll know about Helix Press, and, most important of all, what we stand for. In a nutshell, when people see ME, they will who know what Helix Press represents."

The board members looked at one another.

"We have to start somewhere. If we don't start now, we'll never get anywhere," said Penelope.

"Very well, let's try that," said the Chairman.

"Sweet, I'll call a modelling agency and I'll get the graphic design team on to it. Don't worry, guys. Leave it to me. Meeting adjourned."

She packed up her files and folders put them in her briefcase.

"Phew," said Penelope, "incredible. One woman solved a problem a whole group of men could not. See ya later." She walked out of them room.

The whole boardroom sighed. There was an awkward silence among them. Some of them shrugged their shoulders. One by one each board member took their time to pack their files and folders into their briefcases and left the boardroom.

Chapter 17

One late Friday night, Daniel Crawley was at home in the living room. His wife and daughter were already in bed. He was looking through all the advertising campaigns that Eric, Jodie, Penelope and Toby had launched. They all failed. He read through the sales figures and found that all the Helix subdivisions made losses.

"Oh god," he whispered to himself. He bit his fingernails as he looked at the adverts and the marketing campaigns for Helix. And then he read the comment sections on his social media feeds. Each one made him cringe and wipe the sweat from his forehead.

First he looked at the adverts for Helix Motors. There were posters and billboards with pictures of Eric Helix, in his suit and expensive golden jewellery, posing next to every Helix vehicle that was painted gold. Even a Helix Bulldozer. And then there was the promo for the upcoming Helix Station

Wagon, a prototype was painted gold, and the advert had Eric Helix leaning on it as he grinned. Next to him was a model who had her arms around him. The slogan at the bottom read; The new Helix Station Wagon. Book your test drive now." As a result, a small number of people arranged for a test drive but nobody made a pre-order for the soon to be released Helix Station Wagon.

Daniel Crawley had the look of dismay and embarrassment through the comment sections on social media sites. The comments posted were the following:

"I'll buy one when I win the lottery."

"Gold cars? Sure, why would you NOT want to attract thieves into your neighbourhood?"

"200k for a gold car? No thanks."

"I can get gold spray paint in my local hardware store for 8 dollars a can. So yeah, it's a lot cheaper to do it myself. You Jackass!"

"Picking up gold-diggers won't get easier than this."

"Is that solid gold? Or gold paint? If it's the former instead of the latter then real gold will make it heavy and consumer even more gas. Think about the environment you idiots!"

"I just spray painted my son's bike gold. But it didn't go any faster."

"Now we know who painted the girl in Goldfinger. It was Eric Helix. You bastard!"

Daniel covered his face with his hands and then pulled them back over his head to stretch his face upwards. "Eric, you dumbass." He whispered. Daniel then leaned back in his chair to take a deep breath and look away from the screen for a few moments. He sighed as he shook his head.

And then he looked at Jodie's campaign. Helix Gen had launched the new Jodie Helix line of lingerie. To promote her new line there was a video uploaded to the internet that featured Jodie herself.

The video began when a man in a suit comes home from

work tired, and then Jodie approached him in a red satin robe. She grabbed his tie and led him into the bedroom. She then pushed him onto the bed with white satin sheets only to hand cuff him in place. She then climbed onto the bed, stood above the man, and suddenly threw off her robe to reveal herself in her red bra, thong, and suspenders.

Daniel quickly jerked his head up from his laptop, paused the video and looked around to see if his wife was around. He breathed a sigh of relief. He was still alone in the sitting room. He turned the volume down to its lowest setting and continue to watch the advert.

Jodie gave the man an erotic dance before sitting on top of him to ride him like a horse as she laughed, swinging around long blonde hair in joy. The advert ended with a voiceover by Jodie Helix herself, "The new lingerie line by Jodie Helix." Daniel curled his toes and tried to dig them through the floor. He tightened his fists as he cringed.

And then Daniel looked at the other adverts, all of them had Jodie Helix in different lingerie styles and different colours, red, black and dark blue.

"Stupid bitch," he growled as he shook his head.

When he looked though the comment section in the social media feeds, he rested his head on his left hand. He prepared himself for a moment of depression. The comments posted were the following:

"Great. Her Daddy must be very proud."

"Slut!"

"Dayum she's hot."

"I never thought Helix would sink to this level of low. I'm taking my custom elsewhere."

"Once a slut, always a slut."

"WHORE."

"Isn't that the girl who got pricked by the Cactus? LOL"

"Helix Porn."

"Nice going Jodie. You sell yourself very well."

"Too pornographic for me."

"Hey Jodie, please message me your number. Please, I wanna meet you. Please. Pleeeeeease."

"Where's daddy to spank that ass? Hell, I'll do it for him. lol."

"No pink? I'm offended."

"Hey Jodie, will you be my valentine?" The profile picture of the person who posted the comment was an elderly hillbilly with a grin full of wonky yellow teeth.

Next, he looked at Penelope's campaign. There were pictures of Penelope semi-nude surrounded by various taxidermy animals; lions, tigers, polar bears, and penguins with a jungle in the background. Penelope was skinny and pale, and had all sort of tattoos on her body. The slogans read "Stop Killing Animals. Go Vegan."

"What the hell?" he whispered as he put a hand on his forehead. "Put some clothes on. For Heaven's sake."

In another photo Penelope was topless, and smiling while holding a cat in her arms to cover her small breasts. The slogan read: "Fur is murder. Love all animals."

In another photo, she was riding a taxidermy bull in a black bikini and a cowboy hat. In her hand she had a burger and it looked as though she was about to take a bite out of it. The slogan read: "Who needs beef when you can have a Veggie Burger?"

The images made Daniel shudder. He cringed again.

"Ewww. Oh god, why did they let her do this?"

Another photo had a picture of Penelope completely naked, laying on her front as she kissed the mouth of a taxidermy crocodile. The slogan read: "Say NO to Croc skin." She protested overfishing in another photo where she was also completely naked, but partially covered with some fishes. She was in a pool full of fish, with a large one in her arms while giving the camera an erotic look. And in another photo she is kissing the big fish on the mouth.

The slogan read: "Save the fish. Don't eat them. Love them."

"I think I'm gonna throw up," said Daniel. He closed the tab on the web browser and then he braced himself as he took a look at the comment section in the social media feeds. The comments posted were such as the following:

"Why would Helix do this?"

"None of this makes any sense. What are they trying to do?"

"I like my beef burger thank you."

"If fur is murder, then why is she holding a house cat? Is somebody out there making coats out of them? What the hell?!"

"This is disgusting."

"OMG she is repulsive!"

"That poor fish."

"I wish that crocodile would eat that dirty bitch."

"You idiots! There are children out there who are going to find these. Where are the censors?"

"LOL. Penelope, you look ridiculous."

"Ugh!"

"PP the Jodie wannabe"

"At first glance I thought this was some breed of insect."

"You do know that penguins don't live in the jungle? Right?"

"You are not your sister, Penelope. Jodie is hot. You're not."

"If this was meant to promote veganism then what's with the tiger? Who's eating all the tigers out there? I want to know!"

"Penelope, I read that article you wrote about your experience in prison, and you compared it to a concentration camp. What you went through was NOTHING compared to what my grandparents suffered during the holocaust. To say that your article is offensive is an understatement. I swear I am never buying Helix products again!"

"Yuck!"

"A spider web tattoo on your shoulder? A hammer-sickle

on your neck? A butterfly above your ass? Hmmm. I'm guessing you were once a pretty little thing, and then you turned into a commie that likes to get caught."

"Filth!"

"You degenerate bitch."

"My goodness, Penelope. You are too skinny. You ought to eat more deer." And then the comment was followed by a reply, "I think you meant 'Eat more, dear.' Lol."

"Penelope, what have you done?" said Daniel. Then he found an article written by Penelope herself. The title read "How Meat eaters are no different to Murderers." He couldn't bring himself to read that nor to read the comment section below it. Instead he closed the browser, got up from his seat, and opened the window to take a breather. He felt the late night breeze hit his face that gave him instant relief. He looked out of the window to observe the black cityscape with white lights, behind that was a dark navy curtain for a sky. "Christ almighty," he whispered to himself, "Those pictures have scarred me for life. I think I need I little therapy."

He went to the kitchen, and then got himself a can of beer from the fridge. After a few sips, he sat back down.

Finally, he had a look at Toby's line of a dozen video games he released. They were only available on phones to be downloaded, installed and then played. Toby hired freelancers and independent video game developers to make the games on the cheap and released them quickly. Daniel took out his phone and tried to play one of the games released by Helix Tech. The game was called 'Viking Raider: Forest Quest.' It took a while to load. He rolled his eyes.

The bright colour palette looked child-centred but it was rated '18' due to the bad language and the dark red blood that oozed out of the orcs and octopuses when they got killed. The user played the role of a Viking by killing monsters as he went around a forest. It was a 2D platform game about a Viking who went into a forest to avenge the death of a his tribe who was slaughtered by a giant demon hiding in the forest.

It had the appearance of a video game from the 1980s, with the characters and environment all made of large coloured blocks.

The experience was repetitive and boring. To get to the next level, the player either had to kill thousands of orcs and octopuses until he gained enough experience points, which would have taken weeks, or the player could pay $20 through the Helix app for a key to open a door to enable the player to progress. The game had only one weapon, the standard axe, but better weapons were only available through the Helix app, such as $5 for the Bronze axe, $10 for the Silver Axe, $20 for the Golden Axe, and $50 for the Thunder Axe. The standard axe never broke, but all the other axes that were meant to be better broke after few kills which meant the player had to buy a special axe all over again. The game did not allow the progress to be saved either, which meant after hours of playing the game, the player had to start all over again unless they purchased a Timer through the Helix app.

The animation didn't flow. It had poor sound mixing, the soundtrack was so short it was on constant loop and it had no variety. It didn't match the theme of the game either. There was no consistency in this game.

Daniel chuckled as he tried to play a little bit of the game. He shook his head in dissatisfaction.

"Oh man," he whispered to himself, "This game is bad." He turned it off and put it away. He then looked through the downloads and sales records on his laptop where he had access to his work documents.

Thousands of people downloaded the games, but they received negative reviews. The average score each game received by critics and the audience was either 2 out of 5, or 3 out of 10. This made Daniel shake his head again as he tutted.

He looked at the discussions on social media where Toby and his games received immense backlash. He felt the rage and anger among the gaming community as if Toby had betrayed his fan base. He couldn't help but chuckle as the games and Toby received nothing but ridicule. He read the comment section, and the comments were posted as followed:

"I was really excited when Helix was back on the gaming market. But these games suck."

"Get a real job Toby."

"Fat ass."

"Your games are dogshit."

"Is this the best Helix could do?"

"Here I was, wondering why Helix would bring out such crap, and then I saw Toby's face. The rest made sense."

"Toby, you are a fat ugly fuck."

"He's still high on that weed."

"I can't believe Helix hasn't been sued for plagiarism yet. Helix's 'Space Pod-Racer' is an exact copy of 'Galactic Racer' on the Brooks Box and the Horus Pyramid. At least that one has better graphics and it's actually enjoyable to play. Have you not heard of ORIGINALITY?!"

"Get a real job Toby you fat bastard."

"The in-game adverts are annoying. Get rid of them. Please."

"$50 for a laser scope on 'Space Shooter Pro'? Not a weapon. But an accessory FOR a weapon that I already paid for? Seriously?!"

"My god. Why is the music on constant loop? Could you not find a better musician?"

"These games gave me brain cancer!"

"THESE GAMES HAVE VIRUSES! DO NOT INSTALL!"

"Too late for me. My Helix phone doesn't work anymore, which is why I am posting this review with my new Horus Phone. Fuck you Helix!"

"My little brother is only 12 years old and he knows how to program games on his tablet. Let that sink in. A 12 year old boy is doing a better job at making games than a multi-billion dollar corporation!"

"The graphics are shit. They look awful. Who did you hire for these games? An amateur?"

"Don't buy anything on these games. The Helix app is full of glitches. It charged me 6 times for a purchase I made only once. I want my money back!"

"Yup. He's still fat."

"These days I buy Helix Tech for the TECH. Not for the games. Give us something new."

"Looks like Helix needs Tech support. lol."

Upon reading all the comments and negative reviews, all Daniel could do was laugh. To him this was all a tragic comedy. He kept his laugh quiet so that he didn't wake up his wife and daughter.

"Oh, Jesus," said Daniel. He sighed. He tilted his head back to gulp down some more beer. Some of it leaked through the sides of his mouth which he then wiped with the back of his other hand. He turned off his laptop and let out a sigh of relief for a moment to see the screen go black in front of him. It was no longer emitting the bright light. The room became dark. He sighed with relief again. He picked up his can as he went over to the window again. Among the cityscape in the distance, he saw the needle tower which was Horus Inc. He couldn't suppress a chuckle.

"I bet you're all laughing over there," said Daniel. "Well, you're not alone. I hope you enjoyed the show." He held up his beer can against the window. "Cheers." He drank the remaining beer and put it in the trash can. He closed the window. Brushed his teeth. And then he went to bed.

Chapter 18

One morning, back in the CEO office of Helix Inc. Gosia slapped a handful of magazines onto the main desk. Then she spread them out with her hands. She picked all the ones that had one of the siblings on the front covers along with their featured products.

One magazine had Jodie and her erotic pictures with her

new lingerie. The title read, 'She's at it again! Obsessed with sex!'

Another magazine cover had a semi nude picture of Penelope kissing the large crocodile on the mouth. The title read, 'Helix Bestiality?'

Another magazine had a picture of Eric Helix standing next to a Helix Sports car that was painted gold. But Eric himself was edited to look gold in a mocking way. It looked as though he was made of solid gold to go with the car next to him. The title was in bold 'Goldfingered!' followed by a small subtitle that said 'Butter-fingered was so yesterday.'

And another magazine had a picture of Toby's face on the front cover. It was an old screenshot of him from one of the webcams he filmed himself years earlier. It showed him eating popcorn while he watched a video game cut scene. Surrounding his bloated face were pictures and screenshots of all the bad games he released. The text was big and bold '3 out of 10 is the best THIS GUY can do!'

Gosia stood with her hands on her hips. She took in a deep breath. "What the hell do you call this?" said Gosia sternly. She frowned. The four siblings sat on the chairs in front of her. They had sheepish expressions on their faces like kids getting told off by the school principal.

"Gold, man. It's the real deal," said Eric.

"It was an experiment for Valentine's day," said Jodie.

"Real activism," said Penelope.

"Nah. That's not right. The media demonised me. It's not fair. These are my first games," said Toby.

"Stop right there!" Gosia commanded. She sighed and then massaged her eyes with her fingers. She took in a deep breath and slowly exhaled. She placed her hands on her hips. "Look," said Gosia. "You don't make money by putting out products and expect people to buy them. That's not how it works. You have to find out what people NEED. Your fellow board members have contacted me and they are not happy with you. Especially with your behaviour.

NONE of them had anything positive to say about ANY of you."

She paused to let that sink in.

"I understand you are all new to this business, but there are people here who have worked at Helix Inc. for years. They have knowledge and experience in these fields. You have to listen to them. It also doesn't help that we have competitors who are way more ahead of the game than you. You are in no position to dictate to the market how it should be. We have limited budgets. We have to use them wisely."

The siblings bowed their heads in shame for a moment.

"You cannot do this alone," she continued, "you have to work together. You are brothers and sisters. By working as a team, you succeed. But first you need to repair the damage and then get back to competing in the market. You have to adapt."

Eric shrugged. "So what can I possibly do?" he asked. Gosia paused for a moment to think.

"First of all, you can go to that cop you punched and make a public apology," said Gosia.

"Oh hell no!" Eric exclaimed.

"Yes you will! That's a start. Even if you really don't care about other people, you can at least have the decency to re-build your company's public image. Find him. Apologise to him. Shake his hand. Make it public. Maybe give him a free car as a gesture of kindness or something. I'll leave that bit to you."

"What else?" asked Eric.

"Your carjacking stunt gave Crow Car Insurance quite a boost. When Horus Inc. emerged and brought out its own range of Horus cars, it formed an alliance with Crow Car Insurance. So if you can create a Helix Car Insurance company, it will go with those who own a Helix car. Give your existing customers discounts for owning a Helix car. That way our customers don't need to go anywhere else. And you can try giving them discount points for staying loyal to you so that they could use those points for other Helix products. This will demonstrate that you have thought about your customers. They will like that," said Gosia.

"Yeah. That's it! I'll do it," said Eric with excitement. He got up and rushed out of the CEO office.

"What about ME!?" Penelope cried out loud.

"You can start by promoting healthy products," said Gosia. "You don't promote the vegan diet by demonising everyone else who doesn't conform to your standards. Nor by posing with animals naked! Try vegetarianism first. Be a little subtle. And since you care so much about animals, why don't you try saving some animal lives for a change. Try cleaning up the ocean or something. Our charities help not only animals and the environment, but we also help young people. Helix Inc. offers apprenticeships to help them get into work. We give them opportunities to volunteer too. One thing your father could not stand to see was idleness," Gosia continued. "He loves young people. He believed they all had something to offer this world. So that's why he founded the Helix Foundation. Your father didn't like seeing youth unemployment. So he gave them something to do. Charity is about helping those less fortunate than you. You can try talking to Daniel Crawley about some projects you can do. See what he has to say."

"Who? I don't know who you are talking about," said Penelope.

"You will do when you speak to him properly," Gosia replied. "He's a Project Manager. You need to listen to him." Gosia paused for brief moment. "But before you put anything out there, you have to think carefully about your message. What you published was a mess. First you need to plan WHAT you are going to do, then HOW you are going to do it, and then, most important of all, WHY you are going to do it. The 'why' is the key. Because if you don't know, then all your campaigns will fail. Do you understand?"

"Umm, kind of," Penelope replied. "So what you're saying is I have to do some research?" To that Gosia sighed.

"Well that's a start," said Gosia, "but my point is, Penelope, actions speak louder than words. You will only inspire people when they see you in action. You have to get out there and prove it. So commit yourself to a cause you care about and do something about it."

"Right," said Penelope. "Is that it?"

"There is another important matter," Gosia replied. Penelope rolled her eyes and sighed.

"What?" she asked.

"Your father and the Mayor are good friends. So I think it's time you set things straight with him by apologising. Try working with him instead."

"What?!" Penelope squeaked. "No way!"

"You upset a lot of people with your protests and your riots that got you nowhere. Taxpayers cleaned up after your every mess. And for what?"

Penelope fell silent not knowing what to say.

"You don't achieve anything by protesting or virtue signalling. Nobody wants to hear your complaints. So, going forward instead of criticising, condemning, or complaining, try complimenting, use words of praise. Words of kindness. Show support. That way you will win people over. That is how we grow our business. You win by making friends, not by making enemies. Do you understand?" Said Gosia.

Penelope bit her nails. She hesitated for a moment before she shrugged her shoulders.

"Errr, I guess so. I'll try."

"There is no trying. Only doing. Start today," Gosia commanded.

"Okay I will." Penelope got up and left dragging her feet.

And then there was only Jodie and Toby left sitting in front of Gosia. Gosia took in a deep breath while the two siblings that remained waited anxiously to see who she will pick on next. They both avoided eye contact. Jodie looked up at the ceiling while she twirled her blonde hair with her fingers. Toby crossed his legs and stared at the floor while he bit his nails.

"Jodie, I think you have a lot of amends to make," said Gosia. Jodie rolled her eyes.

"Like what?" Jodie asked.

"You can start by going over to Barry Brooks of Brooks Inc. and apologise to him," said Gosia.

"No way!" Jodie protested.

"It's not going to be easy. But you have to learn to be strong. You have to learn to deal with people in difficult situations."

"I'll just call him," said Jodie.

"No. You are going to go and meet him, and apologise to him face to face. Make it public too, so that people can see. You will win people over by demonstrating your sincerity," said Gosia.

"Oh man! Does that mean I have to apologise to that girl's family as well?" The one who committed suicide?" asked Jodie.

"You won't have to worry about them. They left the country. But you still have to build bridges with Brooks," Gosia replied.

"Damn! But that won't make money," said Jodie.

"It will improve your public image. Bad publicity is bad for business."

"What else can I do?" asked Jodie.

Gosia thought for a moment.

"Here's an idea or two. That motel you spent the night in went bankrupt after you went to jail. You can get in touch with the previous owner and negotiate a deal with him. You can build it into a brand new hotel. Or maybe it can be a shared ownership. See what you can do."

"Hmmm, okay," said Jodie, "That doesn't sound so bad. So what's the second idea?"

"Get back in touch with Cactus the wrestler," said Gosia.

"What?! No way! I am not going anywhere near that guy!"

"You are connected to him whether you like it or not. He was an underdog until you increased his popularity. While you were gone I heard about his ups and downs with alcohol, bar fights, gained and lost weight. He could do with someone like you to help him," said Gosia.

"Why would I want to help HIM?"

"Helix Gen can make fitness products. You can build gyms and promote healthy eating. He will be your ultimate model. You can promote energy drinks and snacks. Healthy eating, and things like that. Speaking of healthy food, this is a good opportunity to build bridges with your sister, Penelope," said Gosia.

"Eww," said Jodie. She cringed.

"Swallow your pride and do it. Now go. Don't forget to get in touch with Barry Brooks."

"Alright," said Jodie. "Fine." She got up to leave.

"And one more thing," said Gosia. "Wear something decent. You are a business woman." Jodie nodded, and then she left.

Toby sat in his chair shaking. He wiped the sweat off his forehead with his chubby paws.

"And as for you, Toby," Gosia began. Toby jumped as soon as he heard his name. "You need to forget about video games for the time being. You need to work on other things."

"Like what?" asked Toby.

"For example, Helix phones are not as durable as the Brooks phone nor the Horus Pharaoh. Eric's stunt promoted the Brooks phone only to pave the way for Horus Inc. See if you can make ours better."

"That's it?" asked Toby.

"No, you'll have to talk to your brother. Build bridges between you two."

"Oh no!" said Toby. "He won't see me. He wants nothing to do with me as it is," Toby moaned.

"Quit whining!" Gosia commanded. "Learn to be a man! You are family. Family is the most sacred thing anyone can have. What would your mother think? Seeing her own children like this?"

He leaned forward and shook his head. His jaw began to tremble as if he was about to cry.

"But... he scares me," said Toby.

"Was he always abusive towards you?" asked Gosia.

"No," Toby replied.

"Then you have to learn to be brave enough to confront people like him. Even if he doesn't like you, he has to work with you. Think about your father. Toughen up!"

"Well...okay," said Toby. He sighed.

"And while you're at it," said Gosia, "You can make amends with your sisters too. Starting with Jodie."

"Oh no. Not her. But why?"

"You could get into shape using her fitness products and facilities. You don't want to die alone and obese, do you?"

"No."

"Then do it," said Gosia, "For your own sake."

"Okay," said Toby, "Is that all?"

"Hmmm." Gosia paused to think for a moment. "Jodie's last publicity stunt gave Blue Eagle TV quite a boost. We can have our own streaming service or something. A new app perhaps. Ideal for phones, computers, and TV. It's an idea. You're going to have to figure out the rest yourself."

"Yeah, I'll do it." He slowly got up from his seat and made his way to the double doors.

"And one more thing!" said Gosia. It made him freeze on the spot. He turned to look at her like a lost child. "Take a shower. Daily. And have a shave too. When you meet with Jodie you may want to try out some of her products. You two can make shower gels for men or something. You two have amends to make as it is."

Toby leaned towards his left armpit, took a smell and jerked his head away. "Okay." He said. And then he left.

When Gosia was alone she picked up the magazines on the desk and threw them into a small bin.

Chapter 19

One night, it was a few minutes after 10pm, Penelope sipped on a glass of red wine after she finished eating her vegan lasagne microwave meal. She sat by her desk in her bedroom, in her light purple pyjamas.

"Phew," she let out. "That was good," she said to herself. She typed away on her Helix laptop as she typed up another article. She took out her phone and made a call.

"Hello?" a woman's voice said.

"Hello... Marcy? Hi, it's me, Penelope."

"Oh my god!" Marcy exclaimed. "Where have you been?"

"In prison. Don't ask," Penelope replied.

"Oh yeah. It's been so long. Are you alright?" she asked.

"Yeah, sure. I'm fine. Listen. I've got to get back in the game. I'm organising a protest," said Penelope.

"For what?" asked Marcy

"The aquarium!" Said Penelope.

"Huh? What for?" asked Marcy.

"I'm going to launch a campaign to get it shut down once and for all. I put out two online polls this morning. One for the aquarium and one for the zoo. Most people still want to keep them open. We need to educate these people. We've got to get them to learn that aquariums are bad. And also, that previous protest got me thinking, while we are at it, we can campaign to shut down the Coast City Zoo too," said Penelope.

"Ummmm–"

"So I am organising a big protest this Saturday afternoon," Penelope continued, "Trust me. It'll be just like the good old days. Think about it! You and me. The strong independent women who set the animals free from Coast City's patriarchy. I swear. People will be talking about us for years."

"Errr... I don't think so, Penelope," said Marcy.

"What?! What do you mean you 'don't think so'?" Penelope asked.

"It's just that I have other commitments," said Marcy.

"Like what?"

"I have baby."

"WHAT?!" Penelope shrieked. "But you said you didn't want to have kids. What about overpopulation? The environment? Consuming resources and–"

"I'm sorry, Penelope, but those days are over. I have a family now," said Marcy.

"Family, eh? Well that doesn't stop you from changing the world for the better," said Penelope.

"Penelope, I can't. I passed all that. Besides, my family is all that matters to me. I have a baby girl, she is one now. I've never been happier. Oh, and I got married last year."

There was a silent pause. Penelope's face went red. She clenched her free hand into a fist and tightened the grip of her phone with the other.

"Well?" said Marcy. "Aren't you going to congratulate me?"

"C - cuh - congratulate you? Are you kidding me? I feel betrayed right now! You were supposed to be my friend. You stab me in the back and you expect me to be happy for you? FINE! Congratulations!" Penelope took the phone away from her face, in her blind rage she tapped the screen several times and missed the red 'Hang up' button. After a few more attempts, she hung up the phone and then slammed it on her desk. She slammed both fists onto her desk and gritted her teeth. She let out a long "GRRRRRRRR!"

She went back to work on her laptop. Her fingers typed away at a frantic speed. She looked at the results of the online polls she setup. One poll asked 'Should the Coast City Aquarium be closed?' The results showed 14% for 'Yes' and 86% for 'No'. The poll displayed the following comments below it:

"The fish are amazing."

"Went there on a school trip recently. I enjoyed it."

"What I like is that I don't have to go scuba diving to see such amazing animals."

"I love this place."

"It makes a nice addition to the zoo, which is only a walking distance away."

Penelope frowned and gritted her teeth again. She got up and went to the kitchen, grabbed another bottle of red wine and popped it open. She brought it into her bedroom and poured herself another glass. She then looked at another online poll she created to see the results. It asked 'Isn't it time to close the Coast City Zoo?' and the results showed 2% for 'Yes' and 98% for 'No.' She breathed through her nose. Then Penelope grabbed her phone and dialled another number.

"Hello?" A woman's voice answered.

"Sue? Is that you?" asked Penelope.

"Yeah. Who is this?"

"It's me, Penelope."

"Oh my god. This is a pleasant surprise. Hey Penelope, how have you been?"

"In prison," Penelope replied, "Okay now let's cut the crap. I'm organising another protest this Saturday. There's a war going on. We've got to get out there." There was a desperate urge in Penelope's voice.

"Huh?"

"Remember that aquarium campaign? It's still on. It's not over. And this time we are going to target the zoo. Think about it. You and me, and all the right-thinking women are going to free all the animals back into the wild. We're going to make history! We are going to be the women who saved the world!"

There was a brief moment of silence.

"Uhhh... look, Penelope," said Sue. She sighed. "That was a long time ago. It's water under the bridge now. There's nothing anyone can do."

"Yes there is!" said Penelope. "Listen to this. Animals are held captive against their will by an evil patriarchy so it can profit from captivity, right? Right. And we women will overthrow the patriarchy by setting the animals free. We will be heroes. We will be remembered forever."

"Yeah well I'm not interested in that anymore. I've actually visited the aquarium. It's a really nice place, you should go there and see it for yourself," said Sue.

"WHAT?! You... VISITED... that aquarium?" said Penelope.

"Yeah. And not only that but– get this– that was where I met my husband," Sue said with excitement.

"HUSBAND?! Why? Whatcha do that for?" Penelope bellowed.

"What do you mean? I love him," Sue replied.

"But Sue... I thought you were a feminist! Like me! Strong independent women! We don't need men! Remember? What about all the battles we fought?" said Penelope.

"Yeah well I've changed my mind. I'm over all that. I got sick of all the drama. Besides, I'm a lot happier now. I'm married to the man I love, and I'm going to have a baby in a few months," said Sue.

There was along moment of silence.

"Wwwwwwwhat?!" Penelope screeched.

"I said I am pregnant. Five months in. I'm going to have a little boy. I can't wait," Sue replied with joy.

There was another long and silent pause.

"Hello? Penelope? You there?" said Sue.

"Yeah. All this time I thought you were my friend. And I learn you went and stabbed me in the back. Fuck you!" Penelope hit the 'Hang up' button on her phone and threw it across the room.

"AAAAAAAAAAH! I HATE YOU! I HATE YOU ALL!" she screamed.

In a fit of rage she went back to her laptop and created another online poll and then turned it off. She slammed the lid of the laptop shut. She marched into the kitchen, opened the freezer and took out a jumbo-sized tub of chocolate and vanilla flavoured ice cream. Like a warrior seizing a weapon, she dug her hand into the kitchen drawers and took out a large spoon. She slammed the drawer and freezer shut with immense rage. She huffed and puffed as she went over to the sitting room, threw herself onto the couch, put the spoon and ice cream tub on the coffee table, grabbed the remote and then turned on the TV. The TV displayed a commercial that showed a product from Horus Inc. It was an aftershave for men.

"Fuck you!" said Penelope. She changed the channel.

The TV then showed a program where a woman was drowning in the sea, an athletic lifeguard comes to the rescue. He brings her to the beach and resuscitates her with a mouth-to-mouth.

"You fucking rapist!" Penelope yelled at the screen. As the show progressed, the woman coughed at first, and then when she saw the lifeguard, she smiled and thanked him with a kiss on his cheek.

"You bastards!" Penelope growled. "Fuck your male propaganda!" She bellowed.

She changed the channel. The next channel showed an elegant music video. It played Spanish music and it showed a beautiful couple smiling as they danced to salsa music.

"AAARRRRR! Fucking men!" Penelope screamed. "Damn them! Damn them to Hell!" In a fit of rage she turned off the TV with the remote, and then she threw it across the room. She picked up the tub of ice cream and the spoon, and then made her way back to her bedroom. She put the tub and spoon on her desk for moment.

"Where are you?!" She said in anger as she looked for her phone. She found her Helix phone and then picked it up. It had a crack on the screen. She logged in to her social media profile one last time and posted her comment: #KILLALLMEN. She turned it off, and then slammed the phone onto her desk.

"Fuck you! Fuck you all!" she whispered. She picked up the bottle of red wine, and put it on the small bedside table. She grabbed the ice cream tub and spoon, then threw herself on to her bed. She tore off the lid of the tub and threw it to one side. She plunged the spoon into the ice cream like wanting to stab someone with a knife, and gobbled every spoonful. One by one, she devoured a heaped spoon full of sugary ice cream as she stared at the wall ahead. Her breathing had slowed down. In between a few spoonfuls, she grabbed the bottle of red wine and drank it. No longer bothering with the glass. Her breathing had slowed down. She took in a deep breath and exhaled slowly. She ate and ate until the ice cream tub was empty. She drank and drank until wine bottle was empty. Her face was sadder than ever before. She put the spoon and the tub on the floor next to her bed. She then pulled over the covers, put her face in the pillow and pressed it onto herself with her hands as she tightened her eyes shut. And then she cried herself to sleep.

Chapter 20

Later that night, it was around 2am and the party was still going wild. Eric Helix walked out of the party drunk while a young brunette held onto his arm.

"Man... what a night," said Eric. He laughed.

"I know right," said the brunette. She mirrored his laugh.

"Yeah. It takes me back," said Eric.

"You haven't done this for a while, have you?" asked the brunette.

"No. Can't party in a prison. Come on. Let's go." He stumbled as he led her along. Her hands latched onto Eric's forearm. He was in his dark grey suit, and she was in a dark red dress.

After a little walk around the block, they approached the dark blue Helix muscle car. Eric took out his key and pressed the button. *Beep Beep.* The hazard lights flashed for a second. He poked it awake. Then he stopped in his tracks. And began to stare at the car. The brunette jerked back at the sudden halt almost losing her balance. She looked up at Eric. His laugh ceased. All joy was wiped from his face. The front of the car had a stern face, with its glaring headlights, it looked at Eric with disapproval.

"What?" asked the brunette.

He stared at the car for a moment. Then he looked at the key.

"What is it?" She pressed him.

"Uh... this isn't a good idea," said Eric.

"What? Us?" Asked the brunette.

"No. I can't drive. I'm drunk," said Eric.

"So what are you going to do?" she asked.

He paused to think for a moment. Then sighed.

"I'm getting a cab," said Eric.

"What?! But you said we were going for a ride!" The brunette complained.

"I know. I didn't think."

She flung his arm away from her.

"Why?" said the brunette. "Backing out in the last minute 'cause you're too chicken?!" she shouted.

"No. It's not that," said Eric. He closed his eyes tightly as he bowed his head and pressed his fingers into his eyelids.

"Then what?!" She shouted even louder.

"Ah. Keep your voice down, will ya?" said Eric.

The brunette folded her arms and tapped her foot. She stood there like an angry mother waiting for an explanation from her naughty teenage son. She narrowed her eyes and tilted her head to the right.

"I'm waiting." She lowered her voice. She breathed through her nose while her mouth was firmly shut.

Eric took his hand away from his face and gave her the same stern look his car gave him. He breathed in deep.

"Look," he said, "what do you think I went to prison for? Huh?"

"Carjacking," she replied swiftly with a patronising tone.

"No– well– yes and no. That is–" Eric shook his head.

"You weren't drunk at the time." Came another swift

response from her. "It was in broad daylight. I know it. It was all over the internet. And the papers. By that time you sobered up. So what's your excuse now?"

"I put other people's lives in danger. I almost killed a lot of people. Including me. I was stupid. Okay? I'm not doing that anymore."

She shook her head as she smirked. "Eric Helix," she began. "From petrol-head to pussy," she said even louder. "I've seen guys come out of prison a lot tougher than before they went in." The volume of her voice increased. "But you! You're a faggot!"

At that moment, a small number people in the area opened their windows to listen in while there were other people and a few couples who walked past. Eric looked around and noticed the watchers.

"You're making a scene," said Eric.

"And?!" She shouted even louder. Her arms still folded.

"There are people looking at us."

"Well I don't wanna be seen with you!" she shouted.

"Fine. Get outta here," said Eric.

"Yeah. And I'll get my own cab. Maybe the driver will have more balls than YOU!"

She spun around and walked in the opposite direction. Her high-heeled shoes echoed along the street as she stormed off.

"Good riddance," he whispered to himself.

Then he looked at the windows of the surrounding buildings. One by one, each onlooker turned out their lights, and went back to bed. The show was over. He stood there alone, in the empty street, next to his car. He pointed the key at the car and pressed the button. *Beep Beep.* The hazard lights flashed again. The Helix muscle car went back to sleep. The face at the front of the car eased off its sternness as if it spoke to him, "You did the right thing, Eric." He relaxed, bowed his head, and exhaled. He put the key into his suit pocket, and then walked on with his hands in his pockets. He felt a cool and gentle breeze on his face that helped put his mind at ease. At that moment, a car emerged from around the corner. It was a taxi. As if the Heavens rewarded him for the choice he made. Eric raised his arm. The taxi stopped by the curb, and then Eric hopped on board. The driver was a plump man in his 50s. He didn't turn to look at his passenger.

"Where to sir?" He mumbled after a yawn. His seat was positioned so far back he didn't bother to sit up straight.

"Fort Street, 36th Avenue," said Eric.

"Okay," the driver replied.

He drove slowly. Eric rolled down the window next to him. He looked up at all the buildings with fascination like they were giant toy blocks. The architecture of each one grabbed his attention. The gentle breeze that cooled his face helped him relax more. He looked and felt like a kid being driven around by his parents, enjoying the view. He smiled slightly. He was enjoying the view so much that he forgot about the brunette and the argument already. The driver noticed him when he looked at his rear-view mirror.

"You new in town, kid?" Asked the driver.

"No," Eric replied.

"You're acting like some kid in a theme park. As if you've never seen a city before."

"Not like this," said Eric. "Not for a long time."

"Where have you been?" asked the driver. To that Eric chuckled.

"In the driver's seat," said Eric. "As soon as I got my license, I took the car everywhere I went."

"Hmmm. So where's your car now?"

"Back where we started," said Eric. "I'm drunk, okay."

"Attaboy," said the driver gently. "You did the right thing."

That made Eric relax even more. He let out a big sigh of relief as he leaned back in his seat.

"Because you know we don't like drunk drivers around here in this city." The driver continued.

"Yeah. You're right. I used to be one of them," said Eric.

"Oh yeah? What happened?" asked the driver. To that Eric chuckled.

"I went to prison. I've learned my lesson. Okay."

"I see," said the driver.

A moment later, they arrived outside Eric's penthouse.

"Here we are, kid," said the driver. "That'll be uh..." the driver was about to look at the counter.

"Forget that," said Eric. "Take this." He held out a hundred dollar bill. The driver looked surprised.

"That's a lot of money," said the driver.

"Take it. I insist. Think of it as extra tip. I mean it, thank you for the ride."

"Well... okay," said the driver. As he took the bill from Eric's hand he took a longer look at Eric's face. He frowned.

"Say kid, you look just like Eric Helix," said the driver. To that Eric chuckled with a little embarrassment.

"I am Eric Helix," he replied.

"Get outta here. Eric takes no cab," said the driver.

Eric took out his business card and showed it to the driver. As soon as the driver saw the Helix Inc. logo, his eyes widened.

"Told you I learned my lesson," said Eric.

The driver gasped. He sat up straight and rubbed his eyes.

"Oh my god! I'm sorry– I didn't mean to be rude. I..." said the driver with haste.

"It's okay," said Eric. "I enjoyed the ride."

"Oh man," the driver said, "The boys are never gonna believe this."

"Oh yes they will," said Eric. He took out his Helix pen and signed his business card. "You now have my autograph." A big smile lit up the driver's face as he took the card and marvelled at the signature in dark blue ink.

"What's your name?" asked Eric.

"Uh... Ha-Harold Jones," the driver answered.

"Pleasure to meet you, Harold," said Eric as he took out his hand for a handshake. The driver took it shook it with excitement. "Cool name," Eric commented. "It sounds like Gerald, my Dad's name."

"Oh yeah," said Harold, "Your father's a great man. Say errr, I don't mean to be a pain in the ass but... can we have a selfie? Please?"

"Good idea," said Eric.

Harold took out his phone, Eric put a hand on Harold's shoulder. They smiled. Flash. "Now let me see... Wow! Perfect! Thanks again, Eric– I mean, Mr Helix," said Harold.

"Call me Eric, good night, Harold."

Eric got out of the car. And then he made his way to the front door. He took out his phone and went to the Coast City Cabs website and gave them a five-star review while it was fresh in his mind. He mentioned Harold the driver and openly thanked him online. He let out another sigh of relief as a big smile appeared on his face that was followed by a silent laugh. He stumbled towards the door. And went in.

Chapter 21

That same night, Jodie and a young man were kissing in a white sports car. He held her waist with both hands while she dug her fingers into his hair as she kissed him. They paused to look each other in the eyes. They smiled.

"Great party tonight. Huh?" said the young man. He was in a white suit, with a black tie and black shoes. His hairstyle was a dark brown uppercut. Jodie was in a pearl dress.

"Yeah," said Jodie. She giggled a little.

"Get a load of this," said the young man. "Me! Marc Ginnis the best actor in Coast City with the one and only Queen of Coast City herself, Jodie Helix." Jodie giggled again.

"I guess," said Jodie. Marc took out his phone and leaned in.

"Here, let's get a selfie." He took a picture of himself and Jodie. He then uploaded the picture to his social media feed.

"Now," said Marc, "It's not over yet." He panted with excitement as he placed his hand on her naked leg. "Let's go over to my place."

Jodie smiled at first, blinked, and then the smile vanished. She looked away from him.

"What?" said Marc.

Jodie looked ahead. She placed her hand on top of his and gently took it off her leg and placed it on the steering wheel. That wiped the smile off his face.

"I'm sorry, Marc. I can't," said Jodie.

"What? What do you mean you can't?" He moaned.

Jodie turned her body away from him to face the front. She sighed.

"Look," she began, "I've been here before. Many times... and.. and–"

"And now what?" He interrupted. He raised his voice as he lifted his shoulders and displayed his palms.

"It's not exciting anymore," said Jodie.

"You mean I'm not exciting?" said Marc.

"No. It's not you. It's me. I can't do this anymore."

"Oh! So now that it's my turn to have you, you pick NOW to become a nun?!" said Marc in a ranting tone. She folded her arms and turned to face him.

"Yes!" said Jodie.

"Well, can't it wait until tomorrow?" said Marc.

"No," Jodie replied.

"Riiiiiight," said Marc. He lowered his voice as he nodded slowly. "In that case, I know exactly where to take you!" He turned the key in the ignition, the engine roared, the headlights turned on. The car jerked forward and sped off as soon as he hit the gas. The car raced off. Jodie grabbed her seatbelt and buckled up as quickly as she could. She sat tight as she held on to her seat.

"Marc? Calm down," said Jodie.

Marc frowned as he held the steering wheel tightly with both hands while he gritted his teeth. He was a monster at the wheel. At such a speed, he took a sharp turn that threw Jodie away from him and hit her head against the passenger window.

"Agh! Watch it you idiot!" She placed a hand on her head.

The white sports car raced down the road and took another turn, and then stopped.

"There!" He pointed. Jodie looked. They were outside the St Luke's Cathedral. "Now that you're a fucking nun, THAT'S where you should be!" he bellowed.

Jodie grinned. "With pleasure, thanks," said Jodie. She unbuckled her seatbelt, picked up her little handbag, and opened the door. She stopped and leaned in as she got out. "Oh, and by the way, Marc. Your ex Linda told me everything about you. You suck in bed." She slammed the door and walked away. His face went red. In a fit of rage he hit the gas again and raced off at an immense speed. The engine was so loud it echoed around the city. And then it was followed by police sirens that chased after it. He got busted. Jodie laughed out loud.

"Stupid bastard," she said. And then she took a moment to breathe and recover. Her heart rate began to slow down. She let out a sigh of relief, turned to face the cathedral, and walked up to the front steps. She sat down on the cold stone steps and took a moment to relax. The gentle night breeze massaged her skin, she closed her eyes and then smiled. The city was quiet. No cars. No people. She took in a deep breath and opened her eyes. She got up and went for a stroll around the cathedral. She admired the Gothic architecture, with its flying buttresses, narrow arches, and tall towers with spires, it looked like something out of a fairytale. She marvelled at the stained glass windows, illuminated by the light coming from inside, all the glass was held together with floral tracery around the arches. And then she stopped and looked at one stained glass window that caught her eye. It was a portrait of Saint Luke the physician, he held a scroll with one hand, and in the other he held his staff with two snakes intertwined at the top, he had brown hair and a big brown beard. She stood there and admired it like a grand painting. Then she looked at another stained glass window, this one had a portrait of Mary holding baby Jesus. She tilted her head as she looked in admiration.

At that moment, a car emerged from around the corner. She turned around and saw that it was a taxi cab. It was as if the Heavens had sent it to her. She raised her hand as she hurried towards it. The cab pulled over at the curb. There was delight on the driver's face when he saw Jodie. As soon as she sat in the back seat, the driver turned to face her.

"Excuse me, Ma'am, but are you Jodie Helix?" he asked.

"I am."

"Oh my, tonight is my lucky night!" He let out with joy.

"I guess," she smiled.

"Oh yeah," said the driver, "it sure is. I just gave your brother Eric a ride home a few minutes ago," said the driver with excitement. Jodie looked puzzled for a moment.

"No offence, but I think you mistook him for someone else, sir. He never takes the cab."

"He did! Tonight! Look!" He took out his phone and showed her the photo with him and Eric in it. And then he took out Eric's business card with his signature on it. "He gave me his autograph too."

Her eyes were fixed onto the phone, her jaw dropped. She didn't notice the card he tried to show her.

"No way!" she whispered. She took the phone with both hands and took a longer look at the photo with Eric and Harold the driver in it. "Eric?... What the hell?" she whispered.

"He gave me a five-star review on our website too," said Harold.

"What possessed him to take the cab?" asked Jodie.

"He was drunk. He didn't want to get into trouble. He told me he learned his lesson and I told him he made the right choice. Yeah. Good man," said Harold.

Her face remained astonished. "I still can't believe it,"

said Jodie. She handed the phone back to Harold.

"Come on, let's get you home," said Harold. "Where to, Ms Helix?"

"Moat Street, 38th Avenue," Jodie replied. "And please, call me Jodie."

"Sure."

"What's your name?"

"Harold Jones."

"Mr Jones, can you please drive slowly?" said Jodie.

"Yes Ma'am," Harold replied.

As Harold drove, Jodie rolled down the window to let in the cool breeze. She smiled at the sensation as she looked out of the window. Harold noticed that when he looked in the rear-view mirror.

"Your brother did the exact same thing," said Harold, "Rolling down the window and enjoying the breeze." To that Jodie laughed.

"I never thought we were alike," said Jodie.

"Siblings usually are in some way. My kids are similar," said Harold.

She leaned towards the window and looked up at the buildings with fascination. There was a long and silent pause.

"Say Jodie, what were you doing at the cathedral anyhow?" Asked Harold.

"Oh, I needed some time alone. That's all," said Jodie.

"With God?" he asked.

"Maybe."

"Your parents got married there, you know," said Harold.

"I almost forgot about that. Mum told me about her wedding when I was a kid. Haven't thought about it since."

"It was a lovely wedding ceremony. I remember it was on TV and all the papers. Are you considering getting married there one day?" asked Harold.

She laughed. "No. I'm not cut out for that," said Jodie. She shook her head.

"I thought the same thing when I was young. My wife and

I have been married twenty-three years. We had no idea how things were going to turn out and look where we are," said Harold.

Jodie smiled. "That's really sweet," said Jodie.

"The point is you've got to work at it. Besides, a fine lady like you deserves a fine husband. You'll meet him some day. Heck. You may have already met him," said Harold.

"Maybe," said Jodie. Despite her best efforts, she couldn't keep the scepticism from her voice.

"Here we are," Harold parked the car outside Jodie's penthouse. "Now let me see..."

"Mr Jones, please forget what's on the counter and take this." She held out a one hundred dollar bill. Harold's eyes widened.

"Uh, but that's too much," said Harold.

"This was the most enjoyable ride I ever had. Think of it as a 'Thank you' gift. From me," said Jodie.

"Thank you," said Harold. "Umm, I don't mean to be bother ya but... can I have your autograph?"

"Sure," said Jodie. A big smile flashed on her face. She took out her business card and her Helix pen, signed it, and then gave it to him. "I got an idea. How about a little video? Who do you work for?"

"Coast City Cabs," said Harold.

"Perfect," said Jodie. He gave her his phone, she put her arm around him and started recording a video together with both of them in it.

"Hey everybody, Jodie Helix here, and I just want to say a big thank you to Coast City Cabs for their wonderful service. Harold here has given me a pleasant ride home. Byeeee." She blew a kiss at the camera before turning it off. Harold's smile was engraved onto his face. "Here." She gave the phone back to Harold. "Feel free to put it online. Thanks, Harold." She exited the cab.

"You take care now. Good night," said Harold. She blew

him a kiss and waved goodbye. Harold then drove off. While it was fresh on her mind, Jodie took out her phone, looked up Coast City Cabs on her phone and gave them a 5-star review. She noticed Eric's review too. A big smile appeared on her face. Then she walked over to her front door with a spring in her step. She let out a sigh of relief to be home, safe and sound. She opened the door and walked in.

Chapter 22

That same night, it was a few minutes past 5am when Toby was focused on the screen. With a control pad in his greasy hands, he sat back in his black leather gaming chair as he rocked back and forth with excitement. He was in his same black t-shirt with the blue hedgehog on it, his extra large jeans with holes in them. To his right was an extra-large bucket of popcorn, to his left was an extra-large bottle of soda. He had a headset on that was attached to his brand new Brooks Box II console. He was in the flow of the video game he was playing online when he yelled "Go! Go! Go!" He and his friends were playing a modern warfare game. His avatar and five others followed as they charged forward in a virtual war environment. "We got'em!" Toby yelled.

"Damn right mudafucka," a voice called out over the headset.

"For sure," another voice called out.

"Boonch-boonch-boonch-boonch," another voice chimed in with a rhythm.

"R269, will you cut that out?! You're not a fuckin' drum machine!"

"Geez, lower your voices will you guys!" yelled Toby.

"Speak for yourself, fat ass," a voice replied.

"Why you! I'm warning you, you little dipshit! I'm the fuckin' leader here. Gimme one good reason not to fire you right now!" Toby shouted back.

"Don't do it, Toby. We've come this far. Don't screw this up."

Throughout the whole video game, there were ongoing sounds of gunshots, rifles, and explosions, like a war zone. They were in some kind of war zone surrounded by crumpled buildings in a deserted city.

The avatars shot and killed more enemy avatars as they defended a building they were in.

"Okay guys," said Toby. "Sniper, you stay on the roof, XtraLargeD, BaboonBoom, you two follow me. The rest of you stay here. We're going right. Hold the fort.... Okay, you guys ready?"

"Yup."

"Yeah."

"Okay, follow me," commanded Toby. The three soldiers exited the building they were defending. One of them spotted activity in a distant building to the right.

"I see'em!"

"Take'em out!"

Toby's avatar threw a smoke grenade into the building where it exploded and emitted a massive cloud of smoke. They turned on their heat vision goggles, spotted the enemy combatants in red, and then they unleashed a storm of bullets into them. Toby's avatar and his teammates went up the stairs. There were three soldiers left. Toby's team gunned them down.

"That's it! We did it!" Get the objective!" Toby commanded.

One of the teammates grabbed the metal carry case that was the objective. A message appeared on the screen: 'Objective 6/8 Captured'

"Got it!" shouted BaboonBoom.

"Let's get back to the base," said Toby. "This one will tell us where the next objective is." Toby leaned to his right to grab a handful of popcorn and stuffed them in his mouth. He was too busy to notice that some of them clung to his beard. And then he leaned to his left to grab the bottle of soda to drink. Some of it leaked out of the corners of his mouth and onto his dirty t-shirt. He belched. Then he wiped his mouth with the back of his left hand.

As Toby's avatar and his friends went downstairs, an enemy soldier emerged from beneath and started shooting at them. They all took heavy damage.

"Oh no!" Toby screamed.

"Shit!" exclaimed BaboonBoom.

"Fuck!" shouted XtraLargeD.

"Y'all supposed to clear the fuckin' area!" Toby bellowed.

"Fuck you! He weren't there before!" BaboonBoom shouted back.

"Watch out!" shouted XtraLargeD.

They took even more gunfire, BaboonBoom died. He dropped the objective and was out of the game. And then XtraLargeD died, and he too was out of the game.

"Noooo!" Toby screamed. He was running low on health, he rushed over, picked up the metal carry case objective, but there was nowhere to run. More enemy soldiers were running into the building.

"Toby! They know you are there! You've got to get out!" another voice among his team shouted over the headset.

"Someone help me! I'm surrounded! I'm going back upstairs," said Toby.

"We can't leave our posts, Toby. We have to guard the tower," a voice said.

"They're all coming after us!" another voice shouted over.

"R269, come and help me!" yelled Toby.

"Boonch-boonch! Boom-chika-boom-chika- boom-chika-" went R269 with his mouth drumming.

"Shut up! You prick! I told you to stop doing that! I can't hear myself think!" Another voice bellowed.

"Baoooka-baoooka-baooka," R269 continued.

"Guys! What's taking so long? I need help!" shouted Toby. Just then, R269 emerged, one by one he killed the all the soldiers who trapped him.

"About time. Let's go. Quick," said Toby.

Toby and his teammate R269 ran back to their base and placed the objective into their radio tower. The location of the next objective was revealed on their maps. It was a lot further away than all the previous objectives. Almost as if on the other side of the map where there was a high number of enemy combatants. The mission was getting harder, and the war was getting longer. A message flashed onto the screen, 'OBJECTIVE 7/8 LOCATED.'

"We're almost done!" a voice said over the headset.

"Two more to go," said another.

"Yeah!" another cheered.

"Badoom-Tshh," went R269.

Toby panted. He took a moment to put the control pad down, he lifted his glasses from his face to rub his eyes with his chubby paws. He noticed his apartment was brighter than before. He looked at the window, it was dawn. He looked at the clock, it was 5:47am. He had the look of disbelief and gasped.

"Oh no!" said Toby. "I've got to be at work in a few hours. Where did all that time go?!" he said to himself. He yawned. He had bags under his eyes. His eyelids felt heavy and he struggled to keep his head up. He was sweating all over.

"Hey Toby! Are you still there?" a voice called out from over the headset.

"What now, Toby?" another voice asked.

Toby hesitated as he picked up the control pad. He remained silent. All he could do was stare at the screen.

"Awaiting orders!" a voice shouted.

"Come on!" shouted another.

The loud voices made Toby jump. He snapped out of his daze and looked around and then focused back on the screen.

"I... I... Listen guys," said Toby, "I can't do this. I have to go to work soon. I need some rest."

"No! You can't!" A voiced shouted back.

"Don't even think about it!" another voice shouted over.

"We have come THIS far! You can't bail out now!" another voice shouted.

"Guys...listen to me...please. I got a headache. I feel really tired. And... and... I don't think I can do this as much as I used to. I can't do this anymore," said Toby.

"There are only two objectives left," one voice replied.

"Toby, don't forget that we've been trying to complete this mission since– like what? 8pm. We have come this far. If you bail out now, our whole mission will be aborted. And all that time will be gone for nothing," said another voice.

"Can't I just make someone else the team leader?" Toby said. His voice was began to break.

"You know the game doesn't work that way!" a voice bellowed back.

"Come on, man! You can do it! We've come this far. Let's get this over with," said another voice.

"Holy shit! They're coming after us. There's more of them!" a voice shouted.

"What now, Toby?" a voice asked.

There was a long pause as Toby sat there with a blank stare at the screen. His eyes began to fill with tears, his jaw began to tremble.

"Toby, I swear if you leave us now we'll never play with you again. D'ya hear me? No one is gonna wanna play with you if you bail out!" another voice shouted over the headset.

Toby croaked. Tears rolled down his chubby cheeks. He gulped. He wheezed as he panted. His jaw continued to tremble. His chest contracted and expanded at a rapid speed.

"TOBEEEEYYYY!!!" the players screamed.

"No!" Toby jumped to his feet. He threw the controller on the floor. He pounced onto the Brooks Box II console and yanked all the cables out in one go. He growled through his teeth when he picked himself up, picked up the console, and threw it to the ground with all his might. The console dented. He stamped on it. The console smashed at every stomp of his foot. He broke down and cried with his mouth wide open like a big baby. He struggled to breathe as he cried even louder. Then he went over to his 120-inch HDTV, latched both paws onto the right of it, and flung the whole thing to the left, and broke the screen with cracks that resembled a spiderweb on it. He cried harder and louder as he threw himself onto the floor, seized the control pad and whacked the shattered console with it again and again until the control pad broke. And then he threw it across the room where it hit a wall and smashed. On his knees, he buried his face into his chubby paws and cried uncontrollably as more tears rolled down his cheeks. He croaked a few more times until he got his breath back. He crawled over to his bed, put his face in the pillow, and held it tight as he cried himself to sleep.

Chapter 23

In the morning that soon followed, it was around 6am when Penelope woke up with a groan. She placed her hands on her stomach and curled up into the foetal position on her bed.

"Awww," she moaned in pain. "What the hell?" When she opened her eyes she saw the empty tub with some melted ice cream at the bottom.

"Oh man, what was I thinking?" she said to herself.

She pulled herself out of the bed and stumbled into the kitchen. Her hair was a mess. She took some pain killers, drank a glass of water, and then drank another. But it did little to soothe the pain in her abdomen. She still felt bloated. The whole bottle of red wine gave her a headache. She rubbed her eyes as she went back to her bedroom. She reached for her phone and then turned it on. It came to life. Bzzz Bzzz Bzzz Bzzz.

"What the hell?" she whispered to herself. When the phone overcame its excitement, it displayed notifications for two messages. One by Sue, the other by Marcy. She opened the messages. Sue's message read: "You've got a problem."

And then she read the text by Marcy that said: "Well since you're such a 'strong independent woman' go ahead enjoy living the rest your life alone."

Penelope covered her mouth with her hand.

"Oh geez," she said to herself.

And then she opened the social media app on her phone. She gasped at what she saw. Hey eyes widened. Her comment '#KILLALLMEN' received thousands of dislikes as well as hundreds of comments:

"Nice going Penelope."

"She's gone genocide mode. lol."

"Oh ok thanks"

"What did I ever do you?"

"Someone definitely has daddy issues."

"You fucking bitch."

"Excuse me, I have a father, a husband, and a 2 year old son. If you want to kill them you have to get through ME!"

"What's your problem?"

"No wonder she doesn't have a boyfriend."

"She doesn't mean that, really. She's just angry."

"Well thanks for letting me know how Helix Inc. really feels about their male customers. I won't be buying their products again. #BoycottHelix"

"Um, don't you have like two brothers? You want them dead too? What about your Dad? I seem to remember him going missing a few years ago."

"Good luck with that lol."

"You need help."

She had lost a lot of followers.

Penelope dropped her phone. She lowered herself, on her knees she sat on the floor. Weak. She buried her face into her hands. Her body shrank as she crossed her legs tightly and locked her ankles in embarrassment. She sat like that for a while until she croaked. "Oh no." And then she picked up her phone, and then deleted her comment along with all the replies. She pulled herself up and sat on the chair by her desk. And then, with a shaky hand, she opened her laptop and turned it on. Her whole body shook, her breathing was unsteady. She opened the internet browser that displayed her latest poll. The overnight results were in. She looked at it with dread; the question she posted was: 'Men are evil. True or False?' The results showed 8% for 'True' and 92% for 'False'. The poll also had hundreds of comments below which displayed as such:

"Wow. Thanks a lot."

"Well, I'm not. The last time I checked."

"Sure, a lot of men do bad things but I wouldn't go as far as calling them all evil. Sheesh."

"Jesus Christ."

"Having a bad day, honey?"

"Well there was Hitler and there was Ghandi. So yeah, whatever."

"Does that include your Dad too?"

"I'd like to report this for misandry please."

"You got problems. Keep my dad and my boyfriend out of them. Okay."

"Oh well, at least she is honest about her man-hating."

"Seriously. What have you got against men, Penelope?"

"I swear to God, as long as Helix Inc. has this Penelope pest in its midst I am not buying any of their products. #BoycottHelix"

She had lost a lot of subscribers to her articles too.

Penelope shook her head in disgust with herself. She swallowed.

"Shit. What was I thinking? God damn it." In a moment of haste she deleted the online poll along with all the comments. She growled. She slapped herself round the face several times with her hand in rage again and again. "Stupid! Stupid! Stupid! Stupid! Stupid!" Each slap was followed by a rapid "Stupid!" until the whole side of her face was red and too sore to continue. Her eyes swelled with tears. Her breathing became unsteady again.

And then she opened up her inbox to read through her emails. As much as she hesitated, she couldn't resist, her curiosity got the best of her. Something possessed her to look through her newsfeed. She gasped at what she saw as she placed her hands on her forehead. Her jaw almost hit the desk when it dropped. Her poll and her comment were on the news, they had spread like wildfire all over the internet. The screenshots were the eye-catching images of the day along with pictures of her in her protests from years ago. It was too late. Whatever was posted could not be unposted, nor be removed from the public eye. The headlines read:

"Feminist shows her true colours"

"Helix Brat calls for Male Genocide"

"FemiNazi"

"Today's Broadcast: Daddy Issues, featuring Penelope Helix."

"Bitterness Personified"

"Little Miss Bad: Human Form"

Her popularity had dropped even further.

Penelope rushed over to the toilet, threw herself down on to her knees and vomited.

"Bleuuurgh!" All the evil spirits that possessed her inside came pouring through her wide open mouth. She choked and gagged in desperation as she forced everything out of her once and for all. All the sugar, and lactose, and fat from the ice cream, and all the alcohol from the wine formed a gungy cocktail in the toilet. She vomited some more until it was all emptied from her stomach. She raised her weak arm to flush the toilet. She began to cry and hyperventilate. She picked herself up and then made her way to the sink to wash her hands and her face. She splashed cold water on her face and massaged her eyes. Soon she stopped crying and her steady breathing resumed. When she saw her face in the mirror, she could not hold back her disgust. She washed her face one more time and dried herself with a towel. A thought occurred to her in her mind. There was sudden rush of alert. She went back to her bedroom and sat in front of her laptop. She took in a deep breath and exhaled. She turned on the webcam and pressed 'Record.'

"Hello everyone," she began, there was brief pause. "Uhhh... I...I am guessing you have all seen that nasty comment and that poll I posted last night. Yeah, I know. I know. It was horrible." Her voice was already beginning to croak as her jaw began to tremble. "It was a horrible thing to say. I shouldn't have done that. I don't know what came over me. All I want to say is I...I...I..." Penelope was beginning to cry again as tears filled her eyes and rolled down her cheeks. "I'm sorry!" She burst out. "I'm sorry. Okay. I–" she sniffed, "I just want to apologise and tell you all I'm sorry. That's all. I won't waste anymore of your time. I promise. Again, I'm sorry." She stopped the recording, uploaded the video to her social media feed, and then she shared it among the small number of followers and subscribers she had left. She turned off her laptop and then looked at the time. It had passed 6:30am. Work won't start until 9am. She picked up her phone and set the alarm. And then she went back to bed to take a power nap.

Chapter 24

That morning, grey clouds covered the sky. There was a knock on the double doors of the Helix Inc. CEO office.

"Come in," said Gosia. Eric walked in, he had a new clean suit on. He scratched the back of his head.

"Hi Gosia, I uh, I want to ask you something," said Eric.

"Sure. What is it?"

"Can I see the painting of Mum again?"

"Of course," said Gosia. She pressed the button under the desk. The panels gently split open, and then the red curtains opened to reveal the painting of Katherine Helix. He took his time to look at the painting. It put a smile on Eric's face at first and then he bowed his head and looked sad.

"What's on your mind?" asked Gosia.

"I just want to hear what she would say to me," said Eric as he slouched.

"First of all, I think she would say, toughen up. You can't go around looking like this. Keep your head up. You are Eric Helix, the son of Gerald Helix, CEO of the most successful corporation in all of Coast City. You must remember that, repeat it to yourself."

"Hmmm," Eric nodded.

"By the way, you should be pleased with yourself. Especially after last night," said Gosia.

"Really? Why?"

"I heard you took the cab last night," said Gosia. "Apparently you were drunk and you decided not to drink and drive. Good on you. It's what every responsible citizen would do. Not only that, you swallowed your pride, and showed some humility. By taking the cab, now you're just like everybody else in Coast City. Even your father took the cab from time to time."

"It's nothing." Eric shrugged his shoulders.

"The whole city is talking about you right now. You, Eric Helix the petrolhead of the city, took the cab instead of going back to your old habit of drink-driving, and speeding. You changed the image of yourself and this will affect Helix Inc. in a good way. So keep it up."

"I guess," said Eric. A smile appeared on his face.

"It seems prison has taught you well," said Gosia.

"It was horrible. I am not going back there again. That's what changed my mind," said Eric. "But now that I am out. I thought to myself, what am I doing? Sure I can go out partying and drive cool cars. But..." He sighed. "I have a business to run. If I don't it'll go bankrupt. And I'll have nothing."

"Exactly," said Gosia. She nodded. "You are now learning to be a responsible adult."

"Yeah. Helix Motors is mine. I've got to run it. I'm doing this for me. And for Mum and Dad."

"Don't forget you need to talk to your brother and sisters," said Gosia.

"Oh man." He rolled his eyes. "I can't stand them."

"They're not so bad. Not really. When did you last spend some time together?"

"Not since were kids," Eric replied.

"Then you better start now. Part of running a business is dealing with people you don't like. But this is your family we're talking about. And the company your father built." She pointed out of the floor-to-ceiling window. "Look out there." Out in the distance, the Horus Tower stuck out from the cityscape, "That is what you are up against," said Gosia. Eric closed his mouth firmly. He clenched his fists as he looked at the needle tower.

"You are the oldest, Eric. Your siblings will look up to you. You've got to lead them. You have to be good role model. You must learn to be a man. What you did last night was a start. The rest is up to you."

"Ah man," he sighed again.

"You'll have to face them sooner or later. You need each other. You are family. Don't forget, your mother is dead, your father is missing. Right now you need each other. More than ever. From where I'm standing," she crossed her arms, "they are all the family you've got," said Gosia. Eric nodded.

"Yeah," said Eric. "Thanks Gosia, I'll see you later."

He marched out with his head held up. She waited for him to leave and then she pressed the button under the desk again. The red curtains closed, and then the wall panels closed.

***

Later that morning, there was another knock at the double doors.

"Come in," said Gosia.

Jodie walked in, she was dressed in a black blazer and high-heeled shoes.

"What is it?" asked Gosia.

"Gosia, I need to talk to you," said Jodie.

"Yes?"

"Last night, I was outside Saint Luke's Cathedral, there was something about that place that got me thinking. I can't help but feel there is a connection to that place. I just can't put my finger on it."

"Yes there is," Said Gosia. "Your parents got married there."

"Is that it?" Jodie asked.

"During the Civil War, it used to be a small chapel where all the sick and injured were cared for. It was built by Jeffery Irons and John Helix. I think he was your great grandfather, was he?"

"I don't know," Jodie replied.

"Anyhow. After the war ended, everyone in Coast City, including Jeffery Irons, John Helix and many others came together and commissioned a cathedral to be built. They hired architects from Europe, like France, England, and Germany, using all the local material, they built the cathedral which stands to this day."

"Hmmm." Jodie smiled. She looked outside the window to look at the spires of cathedral that stood out form the city-scape. She tilted her head.

"Of all the other Saints, why Saint Luke?" Asked Jodie. "Do you know? "

"Saint Luke was a physician. A doctor. During the Civil war, injured soldiers from both sides of the war were cared for. Of course, they took care of the sick too. The chapel was dedicated to him because he was what brought everyone together. They put their differences aside and built a new place to live. A fresh start for themselves and their families. Soon after that, the hospital was built, which became the Coast City General Hospital. These are all the things your father committed himself to. When your mother got cancer, your father did everything he could to find a cure. No matter how many hours he worked, or how much money he invested in research, there wasn't a cure at the time. But since then, he donated money to causes he cared about. Like the Coast City university, and Coast City General Hospital so no one will suffer the same fate he did."

"I did not know any of this. Oh Dad," said Jodie. There was long and silent pause. "Can I ask a favour?"

"Yes."

"Can I see that painting of Mum again?"

"Of course," said Gosia. She pressed the button under the desk, the wall panels opened up to reveal the red curtains, the curtains opened up to reveal the painting of Katherine Helix.

Jodie and Gosia stood in front of the painting. Jodie couldn't help but marvel at the painting.

"She is so beautiful," said Jodie. "There needs to be a painting of her in that cathedral too. She looks like a saint."

"In a way I think she was," said Gosia. She was a nurse at the General Hospital. That was where your father met her. They got married in the Saint Luke Cathedral and then she committed herself to motherhood. Her family was all she cared about."

Jodie sighed.

"I wish I could do that," said Jodie.

"What? Marriage? Of course you can. When you have a family of your own, you can be just like her. It's not too late. You're still a young and attractive woman. There are plenty of good men in Coast City."

"I guess."

"By the way, I have to say. Well done."

"For what?"

"For not going back to your old promiscuous ways. I don't know what you were doing at the cathedral, but I have a feeling God spoke to you."

"Oh, huh. I didn't want to take it further with Marc Ginnis. He was a jerk anyway. He left me there to be nun. Haha." She laughed. Gosia also laughed.

"You did the right thing," said Gosia. "Remember, you are the daughter of Gerald Helix, you are representing this company. You must get it back on its feet."

"Yeah. I'm tired of all the drama. I don't want it anymore. I want to do something worthwhile. And this is it," said Jodie. She turned to look at the panting of Katherine Helix one more time.

"Then go for it," said Gosia. "Helix Gen is yours. But remember, you have to talk to your brothers and your sister. You are not alone. Okay?"

"Sure. I will. Thanks Gosia."

"Good luck," said Gosia.

As soon as Jodie left the office, Gosia pressed the button again to close the panels to shut away the painting. As the panels closed, she made her way to the wall where she stood in front of the paintings of Mary and Saint Luke. She closed her eyes, recited a prayer. And then she crossed herself with her finger tips.

***

Later that day, there was another knock on the double doors.

"Come in," said Gosia.

Penelope walked in. She was dressed in a black blazer and high-heeled shoes. She was a little shy. She slouched as she walked in timidly.

"Yes, Penelope. What is it?" asked Gosia.

"I'm guessing you saw everything. You know, the post, and the poll. Umm. Yeah. I feel rotten about it. I thought I'd come and apologise to you personally. To let you know that I am sorry."

"Yes, I saw them," said Gosia. "I'm not amused. But it's not me you should be apologising to."

"Well... then... what do I do?" asked Penelope.

"Learn from it and move on," Gosia replied.

"That's it?" Penelope paused. "Look... I... I was drunk.

What I said was stupid… I made a mess of things."

"Penelope, we are all capable of saying things we only end up regretting. But you must remember you are part of Helix Inc. It's attached to you whether you like it or not. There are consequences for everything you do," said Gosia.

"I was drunk too," said Penelope.

"That does not excuse bad behaviour. When I saw your apology video I kind of had that impression anyway. But right now I think it's best you stay off social media for a while."

"You're not mad at me?" asked Penelope.

"No," said Gosia, "You have shown the world you have acknowledged your mistake. You have demonstrated that you are aware that you have hurt a lot of people's feelings. Therefore you took responsibility for it and acted accordingly. It takes a lot of courage to do that."

"I still feel bad about it," said Penelope.

"You don't have to," said Gosia. "It's water under the bridge now. What you need to do now is start making friends. Come let me show you."

Gosia led Penelope to the wall where all the framed monochrome photos hung.

"Look," said Gosia, "Your father was a well known respectable man because he contributed to the society he lived in. He worked hard. And people respected him for it. Not because he was descended from a wealthy family, but because of everything he gave to Coast City. He wanted to make the world a better place." Penelope observed each photograph, one with the photo of Gerald Helix having a whiskey with the President, another with him accompanied by the graduates of Coast City University, then the one with the charity ball, and then the ribbon cutting ceremony for the clinic next to Coast City General Hospital.

"One key to running a successful business is maintaining good relationships. We don't live alone. The world we live in gives us so much that we must give something back," said Gosia. "It's about showing gratitude. You still need to speak to the Mayor."

"Oh god, the thought of that makes me nervous," said Penelope.

"He won't bite," said Gosia. "He's a good man."

"I guess so," said Penelope.

"But most important of all, you must talk to your brothers and to your sister. They are all you've got left."

"Oh god." She shuddered.

"Like I said, we don't live alone. You have to learn to work with them," said Gosia. "You too can have successful relationships like your father did. But it must start with your family."

"Well, I guess I have to face them sooner or later. Hey, thanks."

"No worries," said Gosia. "If you need someone to talk to, I am here."

"Sure."

Penelope left the office.

***

Later that day, there was another knock on the double doors.

"Come in," said Gosia.

Toby walked in. He was wearing an extra large suit. But he still had his large white trainers on. His tie was poorly done up and his face wasn't properly shaven, parts of his beard were still on his face. He had sweat on his forehead, he slouched as he approached.

"Now that's more like it. Without a suit, a Helix is incomplete," said Gosia.

"Oh. Really? Uh... thanks."

"When did you last use a razor?" asked Gosia. She gave him a concerned look as she put her hands on her hips.

"Um... a long time ago. I can't remember."

"What you need is some practice. There is still some facial hair on your face and on your neck."

"Oh? Well, I rushed it. I didn't really check before leaving home this morning. I'm guessing you heard I was late again..."

and... errr... I'm sorry," said Toby. "But uh, I need to talk to you."

"Go on."

"Last night– I mean, this morning, I made a decision. It was really hard for me. I realised I can't keep playing video games. It's draining me of all my time. Every time a new game comes out, I feel I have to complete it, and master it. And now I can't."

Gosia folded her arms.

"Isn't that a good thing?"

"I can't live the way I used to and run a business at the same time. If I commit to playing video games, then Helix Tech will go bankrupt. But if I focus on Helix Tech and leave video games forever, I will lose my Champion Gamer status," said Toby. He put both hands on his head as he shook his head. He closed his eyes. "I'm so confused."

"What I want to know is this," said Gosia, "Why was playing video games so important to you in the first place?"

Toby put his hands down and took his time to think. There was a long and silent pause.

"Errr... it's hard to explain. You see ever since I was a kid, I was never good at anything. I was always a fat kid. Getting bullied and all that. People made fun of me all the time. No one ever liked me. I was a loser and hated it. But video games gave me a reason to live. It was the only thing I can beat. I was a winner. I was good at it. I had a purpose. It's the only thing where I win. The only place I feel like... like I really achieved something. To really be somebody. And people respected me for it. Every time I went to a video game convention, people were happy to see me. They cheered me on."

There was a smile on Toby's face, and then it faded.

"And now it's gone. All gone." He bowed his head and let his arms hang down on his sides. "I feel like I'm a loser again."

"Don't talk like that!" snapped Gosia angrily. Toby jumped. And then she lowered her tone. "Look. That is not the right attitude. You are part of a huge corporation that your father built. People respect your father for what he has done, his commitment to his work. That he was running a business that contributed to society. He gave people what they needed. He worked hard for it. It wasn't easy for him. And it won't be easy for you either. You have an important role to play. Helix Tech is yours. This is your chance to make something of it."

"When you put it like that, it makes it sound important. Like, it only confirms my decision," said Toby.

"It looks to me like you have finally acknowledged you need to take responsibility for yourself and for the company you run. You said so yourself that every time a video game comes out you feel you have to complete it in order to get a sense of accomplishment. Right? There will always be another video game, Toby. But there is only one Helix Tech. This your last and only chance. You can't afford to lose it."

"I know, but what do I do? I've never done this before. I don't know how to run a business," Toby moaned.

"I can't run your business for you," said Gosia. "You need to figure that out for yourself. See what's on the market. Find out what people need. You can start by listening to your board members, and see what they have to say. Remember, you have a limited budget. You can't afford to waste it on pet projects."

"Is that all?"

"No. You need to talk to your brother and your sisters."

"Yikes."

"You don't have a choice in this matter, Toby. They are your family. You've got to work with them. Don't forget that you have competition out there." She pointed to the Horus Inc. needle tower that stuck out from the cityscape. Toby looked at the needle tower and then frowned.

"Yeah, we gotta beat those guys." He clenched his fists.

"That's the spirit, Toby. Now go."

As Toby turned to leave he was interrupted.

"Hold it!" said Gosia. She walked over to Toby to adjust his tie, she braced herself for a smell of bad body odour as she approached him.

"And one more thing," said Gosia. "You might want to eat less and move more. You need to start thinking about your health too. You can start by eating healthier foods and–" she sniffed. "I have to say, you don't smell as bad as you usually do. Did you take a shower?"

"Uhh... Yeah, this morning," said Toby.

"Good for you. You are learning. Now all you need is a little bit of aftershave. Try the Helix brand. You know? You can talk to Jodie about that." She winked as she nodded.

"Yeah. Got it," said Toby. He walked on and then he left the office. After Toby closed the door behind him, Gosia let out a long sigh of relief.

Chapter 25

The next day, Eric was in his suit as he sat in his large office looking through some paperwork. He worked on his Helix laptop periodically. The office was a smaller version of the boardroom he was in. All the thin white curtains were pushed to one side, but there was little sunlight because of the cloudy grey sky. The white walls were accompanied by a white ceiling with white LED spotlights. His desk was blackish-blue with shiny surfaces. The milliken carpet had various shades of dark blue going across it. There was a large Helix HDTV on the wall, in one corner there was coffee machine, in the other there was a small pool table.

Eric looked at the paperwork with fury. "Those Crow Car Insurance bastards," he whispered.

The phone on his desk rang. He picked it up.

"What?!" He barked.

"Sir, Toby Helix wants to see you," said his secretary.

"Huh? Uhhh, let him in."

Toby was slow in his pace as he stepped through the door. He too was wearing a suit. All was done up properly. All except his large white trainers.

"Ha! You shaved!" Eric laughed. He threw his head back with his mouth wide open to laugh out loud.

"Yeah," said Toby. He put a hand on his left cheek.

"You now look like a baby! Ha haaa!" Eric laughed again.

"Stop that!" Said Toby.

"Sure thing, chubby. Whadya want?"

"Well, uh, I want to talk to you," said Toby, timidly.

"Shoot," Eric replied.

"You know that thing you did?" Toby began.

"What thing?" Eric asked.

"You know. That Brooks phone you threw and it didn't break. And that carjacking."

"Oh for God sake! I'm sick of hearing about it!" said Eric.

"Wait! Just hear me out for one second. It got me thinking. How about I make a Helix phone that doesn't break? And a car that doesn't get stolen?" said Toby.

"Yeah? So?"

"And the car key that didn't work?" Toby continued.

"Get to the point already!" Eric barked.

"I can fix all that with Helix Tech. But I need someone to promote them for me. Who better to do it than you?"

"No thanks," said Eric.

"But Eric, we have to work together. Horus Inc. has beaten us already," Toby urged.

"I'm busy as it is. I have to beat Crow Car Insurance. Later this afternoon, I'm going to speak to the guy I stole the car from. For that, I'm gonna have to bite the goddamn bullet," said Eric.

"That's it. That's a great idea. We can get them to promote our products," Toby said with excitement.

"You don't need to get involved. I wanna get this off my back as soon as possible," said Eric.

"I got another idea," said Toby, Eric gave off an irritated sighed. "You like gold, right? Like gold watches. We can put a car key into gold watches too," said Toby.

"You've got problems of your own, chubby. Shaving that

neck beard isn't going to make a difference," said Eric.

"Why won't you work with me?" said Toby. He was beginning to look sad.

"I don't need to," Eric replied. To that Toby, frowned.

"Don't think for one second you can beat Horus Inc. on your own 'cause you won't."

"I can."

"Oh yeah? How did that gold car project go? Huh?" Toby stepped up towards Eric.

"It was a little experiment. Okay? I have other tricks up my sleeve. What have you got, pork chop?"

"I already told you! That's why I'm here. To talk to you. To work with you," Toby urged again.

"Why should I work with YOU?" Eric raised his voice.

"Because we're FAMILY! Is THAT not enough?" Toby also raised his voice.

The room fell silent. They looked at one another with determination. They both breathed through their noses and breathed through their mouths. Then Eric walked up to the window and looked out.

"Family, huh?" said Eric.

"Yeah," Toby replied.

"What do you think family is?" asked Eric.

"The people in your life who stand by you no matter what," said Toby. And then there was a long silence. "Well? What do you think family is?" Toby asked.

"I don't know," said Eric. He put his head down. "I never really thought about it until now." And then he turned to face Toby. "To me..." Eric paused to think. "It's like what you see in the movies. A mum, a dad, and some kids. Maybe even a pet." He chuckled. "They do things together. Like uhhh... birthdays, Christmas, vacations, family outings, that kind of stuff. When Mum died everything came to an end. We saw less of Dad because he was working all the time. We had several nannies taking care of us. I guess my idea of a family was never going to happen."

"That makes sense," Toby said. "I'm no expert in this, but I don't think a kid can bond with strangers the same way it can bond with a mum."

"What makes you say that?" Eric asked.

"I'm not sure, but I saw more of those nannies than I saw mum. You should know, you're the oldest."

"Looking back, the nannies that looked after us didn't really care. We didn't know who was going to take care of us next," said Eric.

"What happened after that?" asked Toby.

"Since Mum was gone, I wanted to be with Dad. But he wasn't around. He was always working. I hardly ever saw him as a kid. And as for me, I was only concerned about myself. I guess we all drifted apart after that."

Toby nodded slowly to allow a little silent pause.

"Did you ever talk about this with Dad?" asked Toby.

"No. You don't talk about things like that. Not with your Dad anyway. The last thing you want to do is look weak in front of him. He'll laugh."

"Do you think he's laughing now? Look at us. We only have each other," said Toby.

"Yeah," Eric sighed.

"But Eric, you said that a family is when there is a Mum and a Dad with kids. Well, don't you want that?" asked Toby. Eric chuckled.

"An Eric Junior? Now there's a thought," said Eric.

"Well? Since family is so important, then why don't you have a family of your own?"

"What about you?" asked Eric.

"You know. I was never sure," said Toby. "I always wanted to have meaning in my life. I didn't think I ever had a purpose until now."

"Neither did I," said Eric.

"You can be a good Dad. If you wanted to," said Toby.

"Maybe," said Eric. "What about you?"

"Uuuuh, well, I can be a good Dad I guess," Toby replied.

Eric smiled. "I think you got potential," said Eric. "But you need to shed some pounds first."

Toby looked at his reflection in the window.

"Yeah, maybe I should," Toby replied.

"Don't be a chicken. You gotta look tough. Put yourself forward with confidence. So lay off the fries, fatso," he laughed.

"Hey, shut up," said Toby. But then he couldn't suppress his laughter.

"So anyway, what did you come here for?" asked Eric.

"Uuuuh, Oh yeah!" Phones. Cars. And, errr...watches."

"What about them?"

"Well I wanted to share some ideas with you. I'll make a Helix phone that doesn't break. Oh yeah, we need better batteries that last longer as well. Finger print recognition on car handles that won't open to carjackers."

"Don't start that again!" said Eric. He rolled his eyes. Toby laughed.

"I mean cars that recognise your watch like a key," Toby continued.

"Sounds like we have potential here," said Eric.

"You mean you'll work with me?" Toby said with excitement.

"Sure. Why the hell not?" Eric replied. "We're family after all."

At that moment, the clouds split open like drawing curtains in the morning. They slowly parted as they widened the gap to let the sun shine through the windows. It made the office feel warm and gave every surface a joyful shine. The two men smiled at each other. Then they looked outside to see a bright view of the city.

When Toby turned to look at the sun, he took out his Helix phone and looked at it.

"That's it," he whispered. "Solar Power."

Chapter 26

Later that day, the clouds moved even further apart. Penelope was in her office. She was wearing a black blazer and a white blouse to go with the black skirt that went down to the knee. She wore flat black shoes. But she still had her large black thick framed glasses. Her light brown hair went down to her shoulders. She was looking through her paperwork, when the phone on her desk rang. She picked it up.

"Yeah?"

"Ms Helix," said her secretary, "Jodie Helix would like to see you."

"What?!" She squeaked. "Are you sure?"

"Positive."

"Okay then, let her in." She put the phone down. There was knock at the door.

"Come in," Penelope called.

The door opened and Jodie walked in. She too had a black blazer on, with a white blouse, all buttons done up, a black skirt that went down to the knee, and a pair of black high-heeled shoes. She walked in slowly and gave an affectionate smile. Penelope raised an eyebrow.

"Okay now. What's up?" Penelope asked with a cynical tone.

"I had a meeting down at Helix Fashion this morning," said Jodie. "We were talking about alternative materials. You know, the kinds that don't require animals. And then you came to mind."

"Huh! So I am only a source of income to you. Is that it?" Penelope barked.

"No. It's like what Gosia said. I've come to make amends."

Penelope jaw dropped. Her eyes widened almost as large as the large frames of her glasses. She paused.

"That...is so NOT you," said Penelope.

"I guess not," Jodie laughed. She blushed as she played with her long blonde hair.

"No, it isn't," Penelope hissed. She narrowed her eyes. "You can fool anyone. But you can't fool me."

"What are you talking about? What's your problem?" asked Jodie.

"Come on, Jodie, don't play the innocent with me. What's your game?" Penelope asked. "Did you come here to prove you have influence over men and rub it in my face?"

"I didn't influence anybody. Just because men don't find you attractive it doesn't make me a bad person," Jodie replied.

"But you ARE," Penelope screeched louder. "You fuck married men!"

"Not anymore. Okay. I quit that," said Jodie.

Unsatisfied, she huffed and puffed, Penelope got up from her seat and walked up to Jodie in confrontational manner.

"What the hell has happened to you? asked Penelope. "It's as if you're a completely different person."

"I don't know. What do you want me to say?"

"I want you to be HONEST!" Penelope screeched.

"I am being honest. That's why I'm here," said Jodie.

"Oh yeah? Then PROVE it!"

"How?" Jodie asked.

There was a brief moment of silence.

"To start," Penelope lowered her voice, "What made you change your mind?"

"About what?"

"What made you quit?" asked Penelope.

"Sleeping with married men?"

"Well, it's simple. I realised I was wrong," said Jodie.

"That's it?" asked Penelope.

Jodie turned to face the windows, she saw her reflection, and took her time to have a look at herself. She walked over to the window and looked out at the city below. The spires of the Cathedral caught her sight.

She crossed her arms, closed her eyes to recollect some thoughts; the rage in the eyes of Marc Ginnis, the roaring engine of his speeding car, the thought of a possible death, the stained glassed window depicting Saint Luke, the Portrait of Saint Luke in the CEO Office, and then the portrait of Katherine Helix with her loving affectionate eyes. And then the words of Gosia returned to her mind, "When you have a family of your own, you can be just like her."

"When I was in that car with Marc Ginnis, the way he hit the gas, he was going so fast I thought I was going to die. Something hit me in the gut," said Jodie. She allowed a gentle pause. "When I stood outside the cathedral, I was relieved. As if... as if I was given another chance. And then I remembered how I've been. And then I thought of Mum. How I wanted to be like her."

Penelope remained silent. Still sceptical, she scratched her teeth with her nails. She raised an eyebrow to accompany her unsatisfied look.

"But... what made you want to do it in the first place?" asked Penelope.

"Do what?" asked Jodie.

"Having affairs," Penelope said. "A girl like you can have any man you want. Yet you went from one guy after another. Why?"

There was a long silence. Jodie took in a deep breath and exhaled slowly.

"You know, I never really thought about that until now. I guess it's because deep down I was jealous," said Jodie.

"Jealous?!" Penelope looked shocked. "Of whom?" Penelope frowned.

"Women who have what I wanted the whole time. A husband who will love me and take care of me," said Jodie.

"No way!" said Penelope.

"I thought I could get the best by taking him away. Get him to leave his wife for me." She turned to face Penelope. "But when a man betrayed his wife for me, I hated him even more. Because he had no loyalty. That's when I learned that he didn't love his wife. He only wanted my body."

Jodie paused, and then continued.

"So after I fuck them I ditch them. There was something about it that was thrilling. People would gasp. I liked the look of shock on people's faces. It made me look cool in front of the other girls. All eyes would be on me. I had all the attention. It felt good. Everyone would talk about me. But still, I learned later that they don't care about me." She paused. "I guess, maybe all this time, all I wanted was to be loved," said Jodie.

"Attention? Care? Love?" Penelope whispered to herself. She covered her mouth with her hand as she looked down at the floor.

"Yeah," said Jodie.

There was silence again.

"Ever since Mum died," Jodie said, "we never saw Dad. He was always busy with work that maybe... maybe I thought that he forgot all about me."

"I felt the same way too," said Penelope. She removed her hand from her mouth and looked at Jodie. "Have you noticed whenever we wanted something, like toys or nice clothes, we were given them straight away? How nobody told us 'No'?"

"Yeah," Jodie replied.

"But what I really wanted was a hug," said Penelope, her voice began to break. "Compassion. Those nannies were not Mum. They didn't care." Her eyes began to swell. "I wanted Mum and Dad back. To hold me. Kiss me. And tell me everything's going to be okay." Penelope was fighting back tears, trying her best not to cry.

"You know," Jodie said. "I was always a naughty girl. I was never punished for my actions until I went to jail. That was the first time in my life I learned about consequences."

"So did I," said Penelope. She dried her tears. She sniffed.

"I thought I could live my life by giving Dad the finger, telling everyone in this world to fuck off and not give a damn," said Jodie.

"Me too," said Penelope, "but you know what... I wanted

respect. I thought I could get it by demanding it. But all people did was gather around me and mock me. I felt alone. I wanted to do something good for mankind and be loved for it." Her eyes swelled with tears again.

Jodie couldn't help herself anymore, she walked over to Penelope. "Come here," she said. She opened her arms out and embraced her little sister close. Penelope embraced and Jodie began to cry as she closed her eyes tightly. Tears rolled down their cheeks. All tension was released. They breathed heavily as they felt their stomachs relax.

They held each other for the longest time ever. They both took in deep breaths and let them out slowly. When Penelope stopped crying, they slowly let go and held each other's hands. Then Penelope dried her eyes with her fingers. And then they sniffed. When they looked into each other's eyes, they let out little laugh. They smiled.

"There," said Jodie. "Feel better?"

"Yeah. So, uh, back to business I guess," Penelope laughed.

"Yeah," Jodie let out an emotional laugh.

"Where were we?" asked Penelope.

"Uh... clothes. Fashion. Yeah."

"Oh yeah. What about them?"

"I'm going to need an expert in alternative materials. So, it looks like Helix Gen and Helix Press are about to collaborate," Jodie smiled.

"Yeah, sure. I'll see what I can do," said Penelope.

"You know," said Jodie. "Now that we've made up. We need to get together with the boys."

"Yep. We can't do without them," Penelope replied.

"If you want to you can find yourself a nice boyfriend," said Jodie.

"I guess so," said Penelope.

"It's not too late, Helix Cosmetics can help you." Jodie smiled. "Your hair looks better like this. Brown, down to the shoulder. Smaller framed glasses will look better on you too. No more piercings, except little earrings. Diamond studs will look good on you. And we can get rid of all those tattoos. To give you a nice clean body again. Courtesy of Helix Cosmetics." She winked.

"Yeah, okay. I can live with that," said Penelope.

"But we're going to have to do something about that voice of yours," said Jodie.

"How?" asked Penelope.

"I'll think of something," said Jodie.

Chapter 27

Later that day, Jodie was looking through some designs for new dresses. She stood over her ebony wood desk as she looked at drawings from designers that were laid out in front of her along with some samples of animal-free materials. The sun shined through the windows that made her office feel warm. The walls in her large office were white, but the laminated floor had various shades of dark brown wooden textures. The leather chairs were cream coloured with dark brown wooden arm rests.

The phone on her desk rang.

"Yeah?" Jodie answered.

"Ms Helix, Toby is here to see you," said the secretary.

"Sure! Let him in," she said with glee.

Toby walked through the door.

"Toby!" said Jodie impressed by his new look. "Look at you, you shaved."

Toby blushed as he smiled.

"Oh," the smile was wiped from her face when she noticed his large white trainers. "They don't go with your outfit."

"Uh, yeah, shoes. Um, they're too small for me. They hurt me feet. But I want to lose weight though."

"Don't worry," said Jodie, her smile returned. "We'll see what we can do about that. Besides, I'm glad you're here."

"Really?" asked Toby. His face lit up with optimism.

"Yeah. I've been wanting to talk to you," said Jodie.

"You have? Well I, uh, me too, to you I mean."

"You go first," said Jodie.

"Uh... when I saw that painting of Mum, and the way you looked at it. Something about that moment hit me hard. I don't know how to explain it. She died when I was a baby. I do have a confession to make, Jodie. I was kind of, I don't know if it's the right word, jealous. Of you and Eric. Because, like, you were born way before me and you two had plenty of time to spend with Mum. Do you think she loved me as much as she loved you?"

"Of course she did," said Jodie. "Don't be silly. You were her baby. Aaaand, you are my little baby brother," she grinned.

"Stop it!" said Toby. He couldn't suppress his laughter.

"Come here," said Jodie. She went up to Toby and gave him a hug. To him, it felt good, he embraced her too. "Listen," said Jodie, "Just because you didn't spend time with her as I did, it doesn't mean she loved you less. Okay. So get that out of your head."

"Do you mean it?"

"Yes. You're like a little teddy bear."

"Stop that," said Toby.

She laughed.

"Hey listen," said Toby. "I've got an idea I want to share with you. Maybe I could combine fashion with tech."

"Like?"

"I just bought some chipsets that we will research and develop further. Penelope is into all that animal-free stuff, right? Well, I was thinking, I could make a dress out of small OLED screens that display different images and footage. I think the best model for that is you," said Toby.

"That's very sweet of you," Jodie replied.

"I've got something else too. I found El-Taco," said Toby.

"Really? Wait, how did you get hold of him?" asked Jodie.

"He reached out to me over social media. He heard about my return and got in touch. We exchanged numbers and got talking," said Toby.

"So what happened to him after you... you know?" asked Jodie.

"He spent two years in jail," said Toby.

"After that?"

"He's been a hobo ever since. Nobody employs a felon."

"So how does he get by?" asked Jodie.

"He has a ViewTube channel where he films himself singing along to rock songs on his phone. He's got a few thousand followers that give him monthly donations. It ain't much though. It's the only thing that keeps him going."

"Damn," said Jodie, "that's fucked up." She shook her head in pity.

"I wanna help him," said Toby.

"How you gonna do that?" asked Jodie.

"I got an idea. Helix Tech makes equipment for music production. I can give him whatever he needs. But errr... the problem is," Toby scratched his head and then he sighed. "His voice is terrible. He can't sing." He soured his face at the thought.

"Hmmm. I know someone else who could do with a voice coach," said Jodie. "Let's see if we can find one."

"Sure, keep me in the loop."

The phone rang Jodie answered.

"Hello?... Oh Hey Penelope!" A big smile flashed on her face. "Lunch together? Sure. A little girl's day out. Yeah."

To that Toby winked, nodded, and then he mouthed "I'll leave you two alone." He tip-toed out of the office as he slowly opened the door and gently closed it.

"Hey Chubby?" A voice called out.

"Gyaaah!" Toby jumped. He turned around and saw Eric approaching. "Hey! Don't do that again!"

"Ha! Can't promise," laughed Eric. "What were you doing in there?"

"Oh uh, I asked Jodie to see if she will work on some projects together," said Toby. "She said yes." Toby let out with excitement.

"Sounds good. But why were you trying to sneak out?" asked Eric.

"She's on the phone to Penelope. I didn't want to be heard."

"Oh, yeah, I need to talk to her at some point," said Eric.

"Me too," said Toby. "Say, are you free this lunch time?"

"No I can't," said Eric. I'm meeting that cop, remember? And the other guy."

"Oh," said Toby.

"But, I do have an idea though. Why don't we all come over to my place for a snack. A movie or something. Tonight," said Eric.

"Yeah! That's a great idea. You know, I could bring one of my video game consoles. I could do with a player number two."

"It's okay, I've got all of them already. Only I don't play them."

"Huh? Then why do you have them if you don't play them?" asked Toby.

"For show," said Eric. "They go well my with big Helix screen."

"Oh."

"I only have a few driving games for each console," said Eric, "I could do with a few beat-em-ups and shoot-em-ups."

"Ha! You leave that to me. I know just the sort you'll like. Anyway, I'll catch ya later," said Toby.

"Laters," said Eric. And then he turned to Jodie's secretary and asked, "Is she free?"

The secretary in her late twenties looked at her phone, saw the vacant line. "Looks that way," she replied. "Here, let me call her." She picked up the phone and called. "Ms Helix, Eric is here to see you.... Okay." She put the phone down. "She's ready to see you Mr Helix."

Eric walked through the door.

"Eric! What a pleasant surprise," said Jodie with glee.

"Hey Jodie. Yeah. I errr... Can we talk?"

"Sure," said Jodie. "Shall I get you anything. Like a coffee?"

"No thanks," said Eric. He walked up to her. "Toby came to see me earlier today and uhh, something about what he said got me thinking."

"What did he say?" asked Jodie.

"We're family after all," said Eric.

"That's it?" asked Jodie.

"Toby and I are working on new projects together. But that's not what I'm here for." He paused for a moment. "I've come to say sorry. For the things I've said."

Jodie smiled. "That's alright. I'm sorry too," said Jodie.

"What do you remember about Mom?" asked Eric.

"She was always kind and beautiful. She was always in a good mood and she never let her misery show. She didn't want us to see her like that. We went everywhere together. I was like her best friend. And she was mine too," said Jodie. "What about you? What do you remember about Mom?"

"She always made me feel good. Like whenever I was down, I remember she used to make me a toasted cheese sandwich. She always made me feel kind of special. She used to call me handsome. The way she always used to hold me. But... now that she's gone, that's never going to happen again."

Jodie walked up to Eric and gave him a big hug. To him it felt strange and good at the same time.

"She may not be around to hold you anymore. But I am," said Jodie.

"Thanks," said Eric. They embraced again. There was something about Jodie's golden hair that felt similar to his mother's. The softness. He couldn't suppress a tear when it rolled down his cheek. Jodie closed her eyes, she also had tears in her eyes. For once she felt the much needed affection from a man. They both took in deep breaths and exhaled. Then they dried their tears as they both allowed smiles on their faces.

"Listen," said Eric, "I was thinking, why don't we all crash at my place tonight?"

"Good idea," said Jodie.

"Sweet. I better go," said Eric. "I'll keep you in the loop."

"Sure," said Jodie. "See ya later."

After Eric left the office, Jodie went back to her desk to look at the designs and materials that were laid out on it.

Chapter 28

The headquarters of Dove Bank was one of the tallest towers of Coast City, although it wasn't as grand as the Helix Tower or as the Horus Needle. With its white dome, and shiny mirror-like surfaces on the outside, it looked like one of the Financial centres in New York City. Except that in the centre of the tower was its small iconic motif, the white bird shaped like a shield. It stood in the central area of the city.

Eric stood outside on the pavement as he looked up. His breathing was unsteady. His neck was stiff. The noisy city around him didn't ease his mood. He was dressed in his iconic dark blue Helix suit, he had a white shirt on, his dark blue tie matched the colour of his suit. It was decorated with a gold pin that had the Helix Inc. symbol on it. His hair was freshly cut by the local barber. He tightened his fists, took in deep breath and walked towards the doors. He walked right up to the reception desk. The receptionist in her mid-thirties instantly recognised him and smiled. "Good Afternoon, Mr Helix. How can I help you today?"

"Good afternoon," said Eric. "I have an appointment with someone who works here."

Roy Henson was a balding man in his fifties. He looked half-Irish, half Italian. He was an Operations Manager. He had a white shirt on with a black tie and black trousers. He was typing away on his computer when there was a knock at the door.

"Come in," said Roy.

Eric walked in. "Mr Henson, hi." Eric smiled as he walked

in with his head up. But Roy didn't smile.

"Good afternoon, Mr Helix. Please, take a seat." He gestured.

Eric sat on one of the chairs in front of Roy Henson's desk. Eric looked around the office, it was neat and tidy, just like all the offices at Helix Tower. He was impressed by Roy's cleanliness. He took in deep breath and exhaled.

"So Mr Helix, since it was me you specifically wanted to talk to, what can I do for you?" said Roy.

"Yeah. Look, I've come to say sorry. I know I served my time in jail, but, I don't think it was enough for us to make up. So Mr Henson, I have come to make amends," said Eric. Roy didn't smile, nor was he impressed.

"A phone call would have sufficed, Mr Helix," said Roy.

"I'd rather come and talk to you face-to-face to show you that I am sincere in my apology," said Eric.

"Is that all?" asked Roy.

"No," said Eric. "I've come to give you this." He took out a Helix business card and offered it to him. When Roy looked at the card he frowned when he noticed another telephone number was written on it in dark blue ink with a biro.

"What for?" said Roy.

"It's got my personal number on it."

"Why?"

"Well, I recently started new businesses, Helix Car Insurance and Helix Car Repairs. If you need any of these services, just mention my name and I can give you custom service. Specially for you, sir," said Eric. Roy eased off on his frown but he still wasn't pleased.

"I thank you Mr Helix, but, I already have car insurance and I know someone who can repair my car for me."

"There's something else too." said Eric. "I heard you have a son, he will be sixteen soon, is that right?

"Right." Roy replied, he gave Eric a cynical look.

"I am also about to open a Helix driving school. Helix customers get reductions, and discounts on other services."

"I can see you are trying, Mr Helix, but you cannot buy me out like this," Roy said in a cold tone.

"I can assure you Mr Henson, that is not what I'm here for. Like I said, I'm here to make amends. Saying sorry is not enough for what I did to you. You see, my father was committed to serving the community he lived in, he cared about this city and all its citizens. One of his commitments was helping young people. And I want to follow in his footsteps. If your son ever needs a job, all you have to do is give me call, and I promise I will see what I can do for him." He paused for brief moment. "Look, I know the CEO of Dove Bank and my father are friends. But this is different, this is an invitation from me to you, for you and your family to become part of the Helix family too. My father would have wanted this. And so do I."

Eric offered his business card again and leaned forward as he did so.

Roy didn't move, first he looked at the card, then into Eric's eyes, and then he looked at the card again. He leaned forward and took the card.

"Thank you, Mr Helix," said Roy. Eric smiled.

"Friends, Mr Henson?" Eric stood up and put out his hand.

"Certainly." Roy got up, took Eric's hand and shook it. He allowed a slight smile in the corner of his mouth. They nodded.

"Thank you for your time, Mr Henson. I shall see myself out," said Eric.

"Come back any time, Mr Helix," said Roy. He put the card in his shirt pocket.

When Eric left the building, he let out a big sigh of relief. The cool air breathed life into him. He walked over to his car at a fast pace. He sat in it. He took in one deep breath and let it out.

"Glad that's over with," he said to himself. "One down. Two to go." He buckled his seatbelt, started the engine, checked his surroundings, and gently blended into the slow moving traffic.

*****

Later that afternoon, Eric stood outside a Coast City Police Station. A solid grey building that had no variety of colour. The windows were frosted with black frames. There were green lanterns on both sides of the front door. Out in the front was a row of CCPD police cars, some of them were Helix models, all were on standby in case of emergency. Eric stood outside. More nervous than before. He swallowed, breathed through his nose and made his way to the entrance.

The policeman behind the reception desk had a cold unpleasant look on his face. He recognised Eric Helix but he looked at him with indifference as he approached.

"Name?" He asked of course, he already knew but it was his job to do so.

"Eric Helix."

"What can we do for you?"

"I've come to see officer Bradley. James Bradley. I called to meet him earlier."

"Hold on a second." The receptionist picked up the phone, exchanged a few words, and put the phone down. "Okay, Mr Helix, take a seat over there." He pointed to a row of chairs by the doorway.

A little while later, Officer Bradley emerged. He was a chubby black police officer in his late forties.

"Good afternoon, Mr Helix, so you wanted to see me. What's it about?"

"Officer Bradley, it's good to see you." They shook hands. "I won't take too much of your time. I thought I'd come over personally to say that I'm sorry for what I did to you all those years ago."

"Water under the bridge, Mr Helix. You did your time and that's enough," said Officer Bradley.

"Not for me. I want to make amends. For us to be friends."

"Friends, huh?"

"Yes. You see, I understand that my father and the Commissioner are good friends. He has a good relationship with the police force. But I've had none until now. So I want us to start with a clean slate," said Eric.

"That seems fair enough."

"As a gesture of my friendship," Eric took out a Helix business card with his personal number on it. "Here's my card."

"What for?" asked Officer Bradley.

"VIP service with Helix Motors, Officer." Eric smiled. "Helix Car Insurance, Car Repairs, even discounts for a new Helix car."

"That's okay, Mr Helix, I won't be needing any of those."

"There's more," said Eric. " I heard you have two daughters, your eldest had her sixteenth birthday yesterday. Am I right?"

"Right."

"I'll be opening a new Helix Driving School soon, and they can have a whole driving course on me. And if they ever need a job, all you have to do is give me a call. Helix Inc. offers career opportunities for everyone, from every background, especially young people. My father cared for the youths of this city. And so do I." Eric offered the card again. "I mean it."

Officer Bradley looked into Eric's eyes. Something about Eric made him nod.

"Sure," said Officer Bradley, he took the card and then smiled. "Have good day, Mr Helix."

"You too, Officer."

They shook hands again. And then Eric left.

Eric let out big sigh of relief as he walked along the pavement. As if the whole weight of the world was lifted off his shoulders. As he walked, he dug his hand into his suit pocket and took out one more of his business cards with his personal number on it. He looked at it. "One more to go," he whispered to himself.

He was lost in a world of his own until he bumped into someone.

"Oof!" A stranger a let out. The person stopped his whistling too.

"Watch it! I mean– I uh... I'm sorry. Are you okay, sir?" asked Eric.

"Eric Helix?" It was the black street cleaner, Kamau.

"Yes. That's me," said Eric.

"As I live and breathe!" exclaimed the cleaner, his eyes widened. He had the look of joy on his face.

"Pardon me, I didn't look where I was going, and I was preoccupied with other things and..."

"It's alright, Mr Helix." He tipped his hat. "It's good to meet you."

"I have to say," said Eric. "These days I've been doing a lot of walking and I never realised how clean the streets were until now. It's all thanks to you and your hard work."

"Why, thank you, Mr Helix." The cleaner had a big smile on his face.

Eric put his hand into his pocket and took out a five dollar bill, it had a picture of Abraham Lincoln on it.

"Here," said Eric.

"What for?" asked the cleaner.

"Think of it is as a tip. Take it."

"Bless you, sir."

"What's your name?" asked Eric.

"Kamau Johnson, sir."

"Nice meeting you Kamau," said Eric. They shook hands. "And call me Eric. I'll see you around."

"Have a good day, Eric," said the cleaner. He went back to sweeping the pavement with his broom while others walked by. His whistling resumed, the tune was Summer by Vivaldi.

Unbeknownst to Eric and the cleaner, the whole encounter was filmed by a passer-by. He opened his Blue Eagle app and then uploaded the footage to the internet. And then he walked away in the opposite direction.

Chapter 29

Eric was in his dark blue Helix tracksuits with white stripes that went diagonally across them. He relaxed on a couch in his penthouse. There were rows of empty plates on the kitchen table. He was watching TV to unwind after the day he had. He flipped through the channels as soon as he saw a commercial for Horus products or services. He huffed and puffed with irritation.

"God damn it," he ranted. "They are everywhere. It's a fucking disease."

Almost every channel he flipped over to had a commercial for Horus Inc. products. He shook his head and then he thought, "That's it, I've had enough. I'm not having you spoiling the night." He turned off the TV and put the remote control to the side. He relaxed for moment to enjoy some peace and quiet.

There was a knock at the door, Eric jumped from his seat and opened it, the delivery man gave him plastic containers of food. Eric opened them and he laid them all out on to the plates that waited for them. He had ordered a Spanish Tapas party buffet; Cheese, ham, and chorizo appetizers, grilled octopus, pickled vegetable skewers, stuffed peppers, clams in green sauce, garlic shrimp, fish cakes, some paella. The end result was a wide variety of colours. When he stood by the table to look at them, he smiled. He looked at his watch. 7:28pm.

At that moment there was a buzz at the door.

Eric picked up the phone by the door.

"Hello?"

"Eric, it's me, Penelope."

"Come on up."

When Penelope entered, she was smartly dressed. She was wearing a dark brown party dress with black floral patterns on it, to go with that she wore a light brown bead necklace, and pair of dark brown shoes. She had a little bunch of flowers in her arms.

"Hey Penelope, you look lovely," said Eric. Stunned by her new look.

"Oh, ha, thanks. I've never seen your place before so I thought I... you know. Be little presentable." She smiled.

"You shouldn't have. Take a look at me. I look like a hobo compared to you," said Eric. He laughed and Penelope giggled.

"Here, for your place." She held out the flowers.

"Thank you." He took them. "Uhhh."

"What?" asked Penelope. "Don't you like them?"

"I don't have a vase. Does a tall glass count?"

"Yeah, as long as you put them in water," said Penelope.

"Sure," Eric took out a tall glass and filled it with water from the tap and put the flowers in.

"Where is everybody?" asked Penelope.

"They'll be coming a little later. I gave you the earlier time on purpose," said Eric.

"Why?" asked Penelope

"I've been wanting to talk to you," said Eric. He walked up to her and sighed. "Listen. I called you a lot of names. I treated you like a piece of crap. All these years I viewed you as an annoying pest. And that's no way to treat a little sister. So I want to say I'm sorry."

"I'm not exactly a saint myself," said Penelope. "Because I always resented you and I didn't know why. I said a lot of mean things to you too. Especially in my articles. I feel bad about them now, and I was beginning to think you never wanted to talk to me because of them. I've deleted them all. But... you know, the damage is done. But I... I'm not sure if you've read them, but... what I'm trying to say is... I'm sorry too, Eric."

"Come here," said Eric. He held his arms out and pulled her towards him to give her a hug. She put her arms around him. She hadn't felt such an embrace by an affectionate man for a long time. "I'm here for you. Okay."

"Me too," said Penelope. She wiped a tear from her eye.

"Anyway, I need a little favour," said Eric.

"What?" asked Penelope.

"You're good at social media, right?"

"Yeah. Kind of."

"You're good at finding people, right?"

"Yeah."

He took out his phone and showed her a video. "You see this Brooks phone commercial. It was from years ago." It showed the one with Eric getting mad at the people around him before attempting to break the Brooks phone.

"Oh god. What about it?" asked Penelope

The commercial showed an attractive blonde woman expressing her concern for Eric as she approached him.

"Mr Helix? Is something wrong?" she asked.

"Nothing's wrong!" shouted Eric. "Get lost!" he turned and barked in her faced. Aghast, the lady walked away. Eric paused the footage.

"Gee, you were rude," said Penelope.

"Yeah. I know. It's embarrassing. But you see that blonde woman there?" said Eric.

"Yeah."

"Can you find out who she is?"

"Sure. But why?" asked Penelope.

"Another person I need to apologise to." Eric replied.

"Yeah, I can find her. You know what they say 'A jealous woman does better research than the FBI.'" She winked. "Send me the link."

"Okay. Research, huh? Be sure to keep that in mind before you start another riot."

"Shut up!" she laughed, she smacked him in the shoulder. "I ain't doin' that no more."

"Old habits die hard," said Eric. "Here let me get the wine."

A few moments later, the buzzer rang. Eric picked up the phone by the door.

"Hello?"

"Hey Eric. Let me in," said Toby.

"Come on up."

A little later, there was a knock at the door. Eric opened it and let Toby in. He had a huge rucksack with snacks, packets of popcorn and potato chips, as well as beer cans and soda cans. All of them ready to go with the Blu-ray movies and video games he brought.

"Holy crap," Eric said with amazement. "You got more than enough to last a whole night."

"It's for a special occasion." Toby was also in his Helix track suits, only his ones were light grey with dark blue lines that went diagonally across.

"Hi Toby," said Penelope. She had a glass of red wine in her hand.

"Oh, hey Penelope," said Toby. "Can I talk to you for a second?"

"Sure."

"Uh, I know I hurt your feelings in the past. A lot. And err... I know it's late but I just want to say sorry," said Toby.

"That's alright, Toby. I've said some mean things to you too. Come here." She put her arms around him. In turn, he embraced her. Eric came over and put his arms around both of them.

"Come here, you two." Eric pulled them both towards him and gave them a playful squeeze.

"Stop it. You're crushing me," said Penelope.

"At least he's not on top of you," said Eric as he pointed to Toby. Eric and Penelope giggled.

"Hey! Stop that," said Toby.

The buzzer went off. Eric went over to the phone by the door. He answered it.

"Hello?"

"Hi Eric," said Jodie.

"Come on up." Soon Jodie made her way to the door. Eric opened it. Jodie was also smartly dressed, she wore a dark purple dress with gold swirly patterns on it. She wore dark purple high-heeled shoes to go with them.

"Hey Jodie. We're all here now."

"Thanks, here, I got some champagne."

"Thanks, Jodie." Eric took the bottle, went over to the kitchen to open it.

"Hey Toby. Hey Penelope." Jodie walked over and embraced Penelope and then Toby.

Eric popped open the bottle of champagne and poured it into four glasses. "Come and get'em guys."

"Cheers." They all clinked their drinks.

"Hey Eric, those tracksuits look way cool," said Jodie. "Where did you– oh." She noticed the Helix symbol. "Oh my god. Sports gear never crossed my mind until now. I totally forgot Helix Fashion made those too. I was more concerned with what I would wear." She laughed at herself.

"They only come in Black, white, grey, and blue," said Penelope. "Why don't you add some pink and purple for the ladies?"

"Hmmm. I have green in mind. Like... a lime green," said Jodie

"Sounds better," said Penelope. "Environmental."

"Green! Now there's a thought," said Eric. "We never see green cars on the road. We can paint them green. That will add variety to our auto range."

"Green cars that pollute?" asked Penelope. "You may want to rethink that."

"People drive hybrid cars these days," said Eric. "Don't they? Hey Toby, doesn't Helix Tech make... like rechargeable batteries?"

"Yeah we do, but not for cars," Toby replied.

"That's it then," said Eric. "We need better batteries for cars. And we can make them green."

"Good thinking," said Penelope, "I can drink to that."

They clinked their glasses.

"Make sure the batteries last long enough," said Jodie, "You don't want to get your customers stranded. The Helix phonef battery runs out too fast. Speaking of which, I need to charge my phone. You got a spare cable?"

"Sure, it's in the drawers. So yeah, green cars, battery powered, high capacity and... ah geez this all sounds like a lot of work," said Eric. "It's going to make my head explode."

"You can worry about that when you get to work. Right now, we need to eat," said Toby.

"Yeah, come on guys let's eat," said Eric.

"Oh wait, let me get the drinks out." Toby opened his large rucksack and pulled out all the drinks he had. He put the beer bottles and cans of soda in the fridge.

"Come on, let's have a little selfie together," Jodie suggested.

"Sure," said Eric. The siblings came close together and smiled at Jodie's Helix phone. She took the photo. It was the first time they had a picture of them taken in years.

After the four siblings finished their little feast, they grabbed a drink from the fridge, they had a beer bottle each. And then they threw themselves onto the couches that formed a crescent in front Eric's big Helix HDTV. They sat back and relaxed.

"Man," said Eric. "We haven't had a meal together like this in years."

"I know right," said Jodie.

"Sounds crazy," said Penelope.

"When was the last time we did something like this?" asked Toby.

"Since I finished high school," said Eric. "As soon as I was old enough I was out with my friends every night."

"That's true," said Jodie. "I did the same thing as soon as I was allowed to go out. I guess we drifted apart after that."

"I don't think we spoke to each other, or did anything together since," said Penelope with a note of surprise. "Do you know why?"

"Easy," said Eric. "With no Mum or Dad around, we were left to do our own thing. I guess we had no glue to hold us together back then."

"Do we have a glue now?" asked Toby.

"Yeah, we do," said Jodie. "It's us. The way things have turned out recently has made us want to come back together again. After all, we are family."

"I wouldn't want to change it for anything," said Penelope.

"Neither would I," said Toby.

They all leaned forward, clinked their beer bottles and drank.

"Something dawned on me lately. I've been doing a lot of drifting until now," said Eric. "I mean. Suppose we didn't take the cases Dad gave us all those years ago. Or go to prison. Where do you think we'd be right now? What do you think would have happened to us instead?" He paused to think for a moment. "Knowing me, apart from travelling around, racing cars and dating women, I don't know. I have got to admit I didn't have a care in the world. No responsibility for anything. Now I have a company at hand. It's Dad's legacy. I guess what I'm trying to say is... I finally have a purpose."

"Me too," said Toby. "As for me, I would have pissed my life away playing video games. I would have surrendered to the conveyor belt of the gaming industry. New consoles, new games. That will never end, but my life will."

"I don't know what I would have done," Penelope replied.

"Neither do I," said Jodie. "I guess we needed some kind of calling in life. I think we found it."

"Hmmm. Yeah. A calling," said Eric nodding. "I'd drink to that."

The siblings raised their glasses and took another sip.

They all let out a relaxed sigh. Toby, Jodie, and Penelope took their time as they looked around at Eric's apartment.

"Where do you think Dad is right now?" asked Eric.

"Oh man," said Toby.

"Beats me," said Jodie.

"Do you think he's still mad at us?" Penelope asked.

"It wouldn't be the first time," said Eric. Then he chuckled. "But that wouldn't explain why he would desert his own company. He committed his whole life to it."

"He left us in charge," said Jodie. "Sort of."

"At least before he gets back maybe we can get Helix back on track. Make it lead the market again," Toby said with optimism.

"Yeah," said Penelope, "maybe that will make him want to come back."

"First we have to put our heads together and work on some projects together," said Eric.

"Green cars, again?" Jodie laughed.

"That's one of them. I've done all I can to rebuild some relationships, to improve my image as well as the company's. Toby and I have some projects we need to work on."

"That reminds me," said Toby, "Look." He took out his phone, opened his Blue Eagle app and showed the video that was uploaded earlier that day. "It's you. Talking to some black street cleaner. You were trending all afternoon."

The video was called "Eric bumps into Cleaner and then Tips him."

Below the video the comments displayed the following:

"That is not the Eric Helix I know."

"My god. Prison has done him wonders."

"Is that him smiling?"

"How do you like that? He's now kind."

Toby then showed it to Jodie and Penelope who smiled at the video.

"Way to go, Eric," said Jodie, impressed.

"Good move," said Penelope.

"Oh yeah, how did your meetings go?" asked Toby.

"They went okay, I guess," said Eric.

"Anyone we know?" asked Jodie.

"The cop and the driver I assaulted," Said Eric.

"And one more," Penelope winked.

"Who?" asked Jodie.

"Some blonde he shouted at," said Penelope.

"Oooooooh. A crush?" asked Jodie.

"Nah," said Eric. "I just want to say sorry to her that's all. Whoever she is, she may be a potential client, or a customer."

"What will you do?" asked Jodie.

"Take her out for a coffee, I think," said Eric.

"I knew it. It's gonna be a date," said Jodie.

"Hey, we've got to do our part to make amends with people outside the family," said Eric. "It's our only chance. If we get people to like us, they will like our company."

"Yeah, you're right," said Jodie. "Oh god. I've still got to meet Barry Brooks at some point."

"I still need to meet the Mayor," said Penelope.

"By the way, Penelope, I've got a laser tattoo removal booked for you tomorrow afternoon. You can't go talk to the Mayor with that," said Jodie as she pointed to the side of her neck. And then Penelope placed a hand over the hammer-sickle tattoo on her neck.

"Yeah, you're right. I'm scared," said Penelope.

"Of what?" Said Eric. "Him or the laser?"

"Both!" Said Penelope.

"Why of him?" asked Eric. "The guy's an old fart."

"He's a friend of our Dad's. Remember? And I wrote A LOT of articles badmouthing him. I may have deleted them all but I have no doubt he has read them."

"I'm sure he'll be fine once you talk to him," said Eric. "You're going with good intentions after all."

"What do we do after that?" asked Toby.

"We're going to need to put our heads together and find ways to make the company grow again. We can worry about the rest later," said Eric.

"Yeah," said Toby. "Come on. Let's watch a movie. I bought some Blue ray disks." Toby got up and rummaged through his rucksack. "I've got 'Just Business', 'School Shooter', 'Trevor', 'The Forest'..."

"I want action," said Eric.

"I want romance," said Jodie.

"I want horror," said Penelope.

"I've got just the thing with all of that. And fantasy too, 'The Kingdom of Konendara' it is." He presented the box.

As they all gathered around the big Helix TV and relaxed on the couches, Toby dug out all the snacks from his bags and laid them out on the coffee table close by. There was plenty of room for them to lie on each couch. They watched a movie together for the first time in many years.

Chapter 30

One morning, on the top floor of Brooks Tower, Barry Brooks was in his CEO office. He stood by the windows to look outside while he held onto his cane. He was a skinny man in his seventies with white hair. He was in a beige suit with a white shirt, his dark tan coloured tie went with his shiny dark brown shoes. His tie was decorated with a gold pin that had the Brooks Inc. emblem engraved into it. He watched the city. His entire office matched his clothing. His favourite colour palette no doubt. Everything was either beige, cream, tan, or gold. The carpet was a cream colour that had dark brown floral designs on it. The walls were a light beige colour that had dark tan coloured wooden square columns. In between some the columns, he had dark tan cabinets that displayed his trophies, golf and bowling were his favourite sports. The white ceiling was dotted with warm LED spot lights. On every wall was a painting of horses running bareback and free around the landscapes of America.

The cream and gold coloured phone on his desk rang. The elderly man walked up to his desk and picked it up.

"Yes?" said Barry.

"Sir, Jodie Helix is here to see you," his secretary replied.

There was a moment of silence. He gritted his teeth. There was a silent growl under his breath.

"Sir?" The secretary's voice snapped him back into focus.

"Let her in," he answered. He put the phone down. He

leaned on his walking stick to hold himself up as tall as he could. But his old back wouldn't allow him to stand as tall as he used to be.

The doors in front of him opened and the stunning blonde entered. Jodie was in a black dress that went down to the knee, and showed no cleavage this time. It was decorated with dark blue Hellenic patterns on it that shined when light hit it. She wore black high-heeled shoes. She held in her hands a long black box with some gold text printed on it. The doors closed behind her.

"Good morning, Mr Brooks," said Jodie with an optimistic tone in her voice. She stopped in her tracks to give a well-rehearsed little curtsey – the ladies at Helix Gen had taught her well. Barry Brooks stood unimpressed. He didn't move. Defiant. He only glared. His old red eyes burned through her soul. She was already intimidated by his wrath. She swallowed.

"I, I brought you some whiskey," she said as she stepped closer, she held out the box to him. "It's your, um, the kind you like. You and my Dad enjoy whiskey so I thought you might like this." She attempted a smile.

He stood unmoved. His frown was etched into his face. It wiped the smile off her face. To look away from him she put the box on the table nearest to her. She felt embarrassed. She brushed her soft golden blonde hair to the side with her fingers and swallowed again. And then her beautiful blue eyes met his fiery glare.

"Mr Brooks. I'm sorry about what happened. I, I didn't mean to ruin your son's wedding. And when I heard about his fiancée I... I feel bad now. Really, I still do."

He stared for a moment. His firmly closed lips finally moved to reveal the gritted teeth within. The angry face began to talk.

"It was a good thing you were in prison," he growled through his teeth. "That way you could not have ruined his new relationship. Even if you didn't 'mean' to."

Jodie stood there and took it; she placed her hands behind

her back like a naughty schoolgirl, and then bowed her head in shame. His fiery eyes and his angry voice burnt through her soul. Guilt finally kicked in. Barry's hand on his walking stick shook a little.

"He is happily married to someone else now. And I finally have a grandchild. That means the world to me. They have another child on the way. Until you have children of your own, you will never understand." He paused to let that sink in. "What else did you come here for?"

She swallowed again. She didn't want to say the wrong thing.

"Sir," she said, "I want to make amends. You're my father's friend. And uhh, that makes you a friend of Helix Inc. And I want us to be friends too. I feel... I feel that the best way to start is for me to invite you to a grand opening. A ribbon cutting ceremony to a new place I bought."

"And what is that?" he asked, and raised an eyebrow.

"I am going to make Edge Motel into a nice and cosy hotel on the edge of Coast City." She said as she smiled with pride. "I reached out to the previous owner recently. After all, I took away his livelihood, so I thought I'd give it back. In its place there will be a brand new hotel as part of Helix Hotels. And I will be assigning him as the Branch Manager. He accepted my offer, and he's happy with this decision. We're going ahead with it." She said with excitement. "So when we open, I'd be delighted for you to come and cut the ribbon with me."

His mouth remained shut. But then his eyes opened wide, he had the look of such surprise that his white eyebrows almost reached the top of his head. She cleared her throat.

"Mr Brooks, of Brooks Inc. I, Jodie Helix of Helix Inc. call for an alliance." She reached out her hand for a handshake.

He frowned again. "Hmmmmm." There was a sceptical growl in his throat at first. He looked at her hand. Looked at the way she dressed. And then her eyes. To him she was still a child, but he knew a genuine apology in one's eyes when he saw one. He reached out his hand and took hers. They shook hands. While he looked stoic, she couldn't help but smile with joy. It was as if she made up with someone who could have been her father. Her spirits were uplifted.

Chapter 31

One morning, the Mayor was sitting in his office when the phone rang. He picked it up.

"Yes?"

"Sir, Penelope Helix is here to see you," said the personal assistant.

"Send her in." He put the phone down. He did not look happy. The Mayor was a man in his seventies, close to Gerald's age. He was dressed in a black suit. He had a pin badge that had the Coast City emblem on it. The office was well furbished, with walls that were made of shiny brown wood. The windows were decorated with dark blue curtains. The carpet was a cream colour. The desk was a well polished mahogany that proudly held his name plaque in gold, and next to that was a black telephone. In front of the desk were two brown wooden chairs with dark blue upholstery. Behind the desk was the big black leather chair where he sat. Behind him were two flags, one of the American flag, and the other of Coast City. On the wall behind him was a gigantic oil on canvas painting of a bald eagle flying, with its wings spread.

Penelope knocked on the door. He kept a stern face.

"Come in," said the Mayor.

Penelope walked in. She had a black blazer on, a black skirt that went down to the knee, black tights, a white blouse, and a dark blue silk square neck scarf that partially covered the bandage around her neck. The hammer-and-sickle tattoo was still yet to be removed completely. She had flat black shoes. She came complete with a new pair of glasses that had smaller frames. In her hands she held had an expensive bottle of French red wine. She scratched the itch at the back of her leg with other shoe. She forced a smile on her face. As she looked around his office, she noticed a small monochrome photo of the Mayor and Gerald Helix enjoying a glass of red wine together as they laughed. She cleared her throat.

"Good morning, Mr Mayor." Penelope greeted him as formally as she could. She did her best to keep her voice low and calm. The Mayor got up from his seat and walked up to her.

"Good morning to you too," said the Mayor.

"I have something for you," said Penelope. "You and my father drank one of these in a charity ball years ago." She presented the bottle of wine to him.

"Ahh, yes. That takes me back." He took it and then put it on his desk. His stern face had a smile in the corner of his mouth. But he still wasn't impressed.

"So, Ms Helix, what is it you'd like to see me about?" the Mayor asked.

"Please, Mr Mayor, call me Penelope."

"Very well, Penelope, what is it?" Already he was getting impatient. She swallowed and took a deep breath.

"I've come to say I'm sorry. For all the damage that I've done." Good, she let it out, went straight to the point. "You are friends with my father, so that makes you a friend of Helix Inc. So I have come to make amends."

"Is that so?" asked the Mayor. He raised an eye brow.

"Yes, sir," said Penelope. She began to get nervous.

"You are quite a harsh critic of my policies. But I don't think you are fully informed enough to know what you protest about," the Mayor chastised her. She fiddled with her fingers while she stood before him. She looked down in shame. Her voice was beginning to break, better say something before it falls apart.

"I must admit," said Penelope, "I'm not as informed as I should be." She looked up at him as she answered.

"Very well then. Allow me to enlighten you. One of your protests about my policies was the lack of regulations regarding overfishing, wasn't it?"

"Yes sir." She crossed her legs while she stood and placed her hands behind her back. The bandage under the silk scarf gave her an itch, she scratched it quickly.

"You accused me of being a greedy fish eater," said the Mayor. To that Penelope cringed. "Hence your vegan propaganda demonises people who purchase animal products. You even had me down as a monster." She cringed again, closed her eyes tightly in embarrassment, and then looked at him.

"I'm sorry," she whispered.

"I know why you did it," said the Mayor. "You love animals and you care about wildlife, and the environment they inhabit. Overfishing has been a complaint here in Coast City for years. You see, Penelope, as the population increases, so does the demand for fish across the country. Of course, we all need to take responsibility for our actions, and consider the impact our decisions make on the environment. However, you must know that it is not for me to tell fishmongers what to do. It is not for me to regulate the market, or tell businesses how I think they should be run, or tell them how many fish they are allowed to catch. That's not my job!"

She bowed her head in shame before she looked up at him.

"Oh god," she thought, "Am I going to get a lecture now? Whatever you do, you're here to rebuild bridges." Her inner voice went on. "Don't argue back, just listen to what he has to say, then leave."

He walked over to the window with his hands behind his back. He looked at the blue seascape beyond Coast City. He continued: "All I can do is monitor the outcome. So, when the sea becomes underpopulated with fish, that's when I have to step in. Should there be any species or animals facing extinction, we can only place a temporary ban on fishing for a short period of time. This is so that the fish population can regrow, and it gives us an opportunity to find alternatives." He then turned to face her. "Now do you understand?"

"Yes sir," said Penelope with a croak. She nodded. She was beginning to feel sick.

"Now," said the Mayor, "Another one of your protests was about immigration. You accused me of being 'racist'."

She cringed again.

"Sorry," said Penelope.

"I understand why you did it. You want everyone to have the same opportunities as you. You want everyone to be safe and secure with the freedoms we have. You want everything to be 'equal'. But you must know, Penelope, the world doesn't work that way. Life is not fair, and we have to accept it."

He paused for moment.

"Can you imagine what would happen if we let everyone in the world into the United States? Our cities would be over-crowded. Public services would be overstretched. We would have to raise taxes. People don't like high taxes. People don't want to see the cost of their living expenses go up. A reduction of migrants can only stabilise this city. We permit workers based on skills. Not simply because they want to be here. I understand. There are disadvantaged people in this world who would give anything to live here in the United States. But we cannot open our borders to the world."

He went over the window again and looked at the city-scape outside. Her eyes followed him. To her it felt like getting told off by the school principal. What has been only a few minutes felt like an hour.

"Oh my god," she thought "When is this going to end?" But then her inner voice intervened. "Just stay quiet, keep calm, and listen. It'll be over soon." The bandage around her neck gave her an itch again, she quickly scratched it hoping he didn't see or hear it.

"It would cause instability," he continued. "We need to make sure the right amount of people settle here. People cannot become citizens as soon as they arrive, legally or not. There are processes involved. For example, I would love to live in France. But that doesn't mean I have a right to be there. Like everyone else, I have to get a passport, speak French, sign an integration contract, obtain a VISA, and so on. We can only let in sustainable amounts of people here." He then turned to face her.

"We live in a world that is full of borders," he continued. "Borders are everywhere. The roof of a house keeps the rain out. The walls of a house divide the rooms accordingly, and they keep intruders out. Your mind is a border, it's where you keep your private thoughts. Your bank account has borders, that's why you have a pin number to access it. Do you understand?"

"Yes," said Penelope. She began to sweat.

"Or perhaps something a little closer to home for you," he stepped up to her with a stern look that made her shudder. "What makes America great is its diversity of ideas as well as its people. And that includes conservative and liberal values. We are conservative here in Coast City. If people cannot respect our customs. They can leave."

He paused for a moment to let that sink in.

"As you can see, Penelope, these things are a little more complicated than you can imagine. Politics, economics, social changes, it is my job to keep these things under control in Coast City."

Penelope nodded in agreement.

"So going forward," he concluded, "before you lash out to the public, I suggest you check your facts, or have a word with me first. Is that clear?"

"Yes, Mr Mayor, thank you," said Penelope. "Again, I'm sorry for all the things I've said about you."

"Very well. Is there anything else I can help you with?" asked the Mayor. He kept his hands behind his back and he was still stern.

"I do have a question," said Penelope. "Actually two. Whose idea was it to convert the theatre into an aquarium? And why an aquarium?"

"Very good questions," said the Mayor. "Let me deal with the why first. The decision for the aquarium came as a result of your last protest against overfishing. Before that, there had been no plans for it. Coast City used to be a small fishing village on the coast, right here. It used to be called Coast Town, but as the population grew, so did the demand for fish. More harbours were built. As a result, more aquatic life was facing extinction. We were all worried. Crabs, lobsters, and so on. Coast City used to be abundant with sea life, but due to the danger they faced, we decided to preserve them in an aquarium. Of course, scuba diving is expensive, not everyone can afford to go on a course or go out to see them. So, Horus Inc., Brooks Inc., Dove Bank, Osprey Toys, Crow Cars, Blue Eagle TV, along with other companies approached me and proposed a plan. That's the answer to the 'who' question. They presented the research and the benefits. Facts and figures. We all agreed. We had all the money we needed for a swift construction. We have a wide range of sea life in there now. Such as the mantis shrimp, sea horses, the cuttlefish, octopuses, squids, all sorts. They even brought in a blue ringed octopus from Australia. I was amazed when I saw them for the first time. They will give others the same thrilling experience they gave me. And I have Horus Inc. to thank for that. People don't have to pay much nor travel far to see these magnificent creatures. You should go and visit it. It educates the public. And it makes me and the companies money too. It's a successful project."

"I will," said Penelope. "However, I do have one more question. Who is the CEO of Horus Inc.?"

"That information is classified," he said in a cold tone and frowned. "Is that all?"

"Yes," said Penelope.

"There's a Mayoral election coming up next year," said the Mayor. "And I intend to win it." To that Penelope smiled.

"Mr Mayor, I want to help you win it. I promise I will do everything I can to get the public to vote for you," said Penelope. The Mayor raised an eyebrow. Did she just say something nice? "I run Helix Press," Penelope continued, "I seek a friendship between us. I mean Helix Inc. Would you be interested?" She walked up to him and held out her hand. "Friends?"

"That's good to know," said the Mayor. He looked at her hand, and then into her eyes. He took her hand and shook it. Penelope couldn't help but smile. In her eyes, there was hope. The Mayor eased off his frown and back into a stern look, but he allowed a smirk to appear on his face.

"Thank you so much for your time, Mr Mayor. Have a good day." She bowed her head.

"Have a good day too, Penelope." The Mayor replied.

She left the Mayor's office. She let out a big sigh of relief. Her knees felt weak. "Oh thank god it's over at last," she thought. She wiped her forehead with the back of a hand, and then she left the building. The bandage gave her another itch, this time she gave it a harder and a more thorough scratch. She looked around and then hailed a cab. It pulled over by the pavement. She got in. "Helix Tower, please." She sat back and relaxed in the backseat of the cab and then took off the dark blue silk square scarf. "Phew. Glad that's over and done with," she whispered to herself. She felt her energy had drained. But nonetheless she felt relieved.

The Mayor watched as the yellow taxi cab blended in with the rest of the traffic. He sat back in his leather chair for a moment thinking it all over. And then he went back to work.

Chapter 32

Later that day, lunchtime to be exact, Eric sat in a Star-Ducks coffee shop. He was in his suit. He leaned on his hand while he waited. He stirred the coffee in front of him slowly as he watched the foamy bubbles on the surface turn. He took his time as he looked around the coffee shop. It was a quaint little place. The interior had an Art Deco style from the 1930s. The counter was a large black table that curved into the wall. At the back was a large black and brown shelf that displayed various brands of coffee from around the world as well as Star-Ducks merchandise, like mugs, coffee coasters, and little plush toy ducks. Each one had pictures of ducks decorated with stars. At the top of the shelves were blackboards that had the menu written in white chalk. The windows were tall and narrow as they reached the ceiling. The walls and panels in between were all a brown colour with wooden textures. The laminated floors were oak that also had wooden textures. The lights were white balls that hung from the ceiling, about a foot and half in diameter, they illuminated the place with a gentle whitish-orange light that gave the whole place a warm feel. All the leather seats were a dark orange colour with dark brown wooden legs. Every surface had faint white patterns on them that were shaped like ducks and stars to go with the Star-Ducks logo. There were small shelves in corners where people could share and donate books. This was the ideal place to read and have a coffee. To Eric, it felt like a large living room. He observed the people sitting around him, university students and their laptops, chatting away about online gossip and laughing about funny things that were shared on social media, elderly couples chatting among themselves next to a few mothers who held their babies in their arms as they spoke to each other. Some tables sat a few men and women in suits having business meetings. Something about this atmosphere made him smile.

And there she was. The blonde passer-by from years ago who he shouted at, entered through the doors. Marie Baker. She had long blonde hair, straight at the top and then curled at the ends. Just like his mother's. She had a gentle tan, brown eyes, almost as tall as him with brown high heeled boots. She was wearing a light-greyish wool sweater under a long coffee-coloured leather coat that went down to her thighs, and dark brown jeans. Her makeup was minimal, with a little bit of mascara and lip gloss, it was all that was needed. She walked in and recognised Eric instantly. She had a constant smile as it was, but she was delighted when she saw him. He got up and walked over to her. They shook hands.

"Hello Ms Baker, it's good to see you," said Eric.

"It's a pleasure to meet you, Mr Helix," said Marie.

"Call me Eric. What can I get you?"

"Oh nothing, please."

"Come on, I insist. I'm getting a cappuccino. You can have one on me."

"Okay." She blushed.

They sat together.

"So I heard you work at the Ducklings Day Care Centre," said Eric.

"Yeah, I look after children," said Marie.

"Do you like it there?"

"Of course I do." Marie gave an affectionate smile. "Someone's got to look after the children when their parents are out working. Besides, I love children."

That put a smile on Eric's face.

"Marie, I invited you here because I wanted to say sorry."

"For what?" asked Marie.

"Remember when I yelled at you? Yeah, that was the day we met."

"Oh... well, that was a long time ago."

"Yeah I know. But I didn't mean to be nasty. So I thought I should make amends."

"Thank you, Eric. But you didn't need to go through all this trouble."

"You see, back then I was a shape shifter. I morphed into a monster that bites people's heads off whenever I'm in a bad mood." He smirked.

"You skipped breakfast, did you?" She asked.

"Yeah. How did you know that?"

"Because I'm the same." She cracked a cheeky smile.

They both laughed.

"We've all seen that commercial 'Have you had your Weet-Brownies?' right. But that's not it. Back then, I... I was someone else. I want you to see that I'm a different man. Prison gives you a lot of time to think things through. I've changed a lot since then."

"Oh?"

"Yeah. Listen, are you free for the rest of today? We'll go for a walk."

"I can't, Eric. I have to get back to work.

"Okay, next time."

"Do you do this with every person you have misunderstandings with?" She asked.

"No," said Eric. "I was thinking we could spend some time getting to know each other. Properly."

"Why would you want to date me when you are out and about with other women every day?"

Bzzz Bzzz. His phone vibrated. She noticed.

"Is that another one of your girlfriends?" She asked.

"No, it's not, whatever it is can wait," said Eric.

"Even so. It's all over the internet. It's one woman after another with you," said Marie. "What I look for in a man is commitment. No offence, Eric, but I do not want to be another one of your trophies. I have to get back to work. Thanks for the cappuccino." She got up and left the cafe.

"But..." he didn't get up. He stayed in his place as he watched her leave. He clenched his fists as he closed his eyes tight. Then he looked at his phone and picked it up. The message read.

"Hey Eric, we still on for tonight?"

"Dammnit," he growled.

He replied back with his hasty fingers tapping on his phone. "No."

He put his phone down on the table, sat back in his chair and exhaled.

"I'm such an idiot." He whispered to himself. He sat there to look at the surface of his cappuccino. He slowly leaned on his hand again as he stared at it, with his other hand, he stirred it with a spoon. He watched the foamy bubbles spin on the surface that formed different shapes and patterns.

Every turn formed a new spiral shape. Perhaps it was an unconscious expression of the state of his mind. He took in a deep breath and exhaled. He looked around the coffee shop again. He noticed how everyone was with someone. He was the only one who sat alone.

He picked up his phone and sent Penelope a text.

"How did it go?" he asked.

A few minutes later she replied.

"Not too bad. How did your date go?" she asked.

"Like shit. Thanks for finding her anyway."

"No worries."

"I'm at Star-Ducks across the road. Wanna join me?" he asked.

"Sure," she replied.

A short while later, Penelope arrived at Star-Ducks, in the same outfit she met the Mayor with. She greeted him with a smile.

"Hey. What happened to you?" she asked.

"Nothing," said Eric. He adjusted his tie.

"That bad, huh?"

"Could have been worse." He shrugged.

"I'm getting you a drink."

As Penelope turned to make her order, someone behind the counter had a familiar face.

"Jane?"

"Penelope?"

"Oh my god, what are you doing here?" Penelope let out with delight.

"Ummm, Oh god," her eyes darted around as she tried to avoid eye contact. Jane was a youth, the same age as Penelope except she was slightly taller, she was skinny, pale, and had long black hair that was tied into a ponytail. She had blue eyes, and was also covered with tattoos that ranged from heavy metal bands, quotes and slogans to symbols of witchcraft. All over her body, except her face.

"Hey. What's wrong?" asked Penelope.

"Look, I know you're pissed at me because of that article I wrote years ago. It's my fault you got jailed. Just don't kill me, okay?!"

"Don't be silly. I'm over that."

"Really?" She looked puzzled.

"Yeah. Oh god. It's been so long," said Penelope.

"I thought I was over that until you came along. I feel bad now," said Jane.

"Listen, you have nothing to feel bad about. Okay?"

"Okay. Uh... what can I get you?"

"Latte, coconut milk please. With a little honey. And whatever my brother had."

"Coming up."

"Oh, and make them large too."

"Sure."

"Look, I'll be sitting over there with Eric. Come and join us for a bit. Please?" Penelope gestured to the table Eric sat.

"Uh, okay, sure," said Jane. She went over to her manager and asked if she could have a small break, the manager saw Penelope and Eric and then nodded.

Penelope brought the hot beverages over to Eric's table, pulled an extra chair, and sat down.

"Who was that?" asked Eric.

"Jane Saunders. And old friend from uni. She's the girl who wrote that false article about the aquarium. That was the last thing I protested about."

"And?"

"She's okay. I don't think she'll do it again."

"You forgive too quickly," said Eric looking a little stunned.

"I'm trying not to hold grudges," said Penelope. "Life is too short to be angry all the time."

Eric looked at his cappuccino while he stirred it with his spoon.

"Let me guess," said Penelope. "She left. Didn't she? Rather than sit here on your own, you asked me to accompany you. Right?"

"Is it that obvious?" asked Eric.

"You look sad," Penelope replied. Eric remained silent. "Well? You said sorry, didn't you?"

"Yeah."

"That's it then. That's all that matters. So move on. She doesn't have to like you."

"I guess," said Eric.

Jane came over and joined them, she sat on the extra chair.

"Hey," she said timidly.

"Eric, this Jane Saunders," introduced Penelope.

"Nice to meet you," said Eric. They shook hands.

"So Jane, listen. I met the Mayor earlier today," said Penelope.

"Oh my god!" Jane exclaimed. "Really? What did he say?"

"Let's just say that I promised him I am never going to cause trouble again."

"He must have read all those articles we wrote about him," said Jane.

"He sure did. Anyway, I took them all down," said Penelope.

"I need to do that too," said Jane. She began to bite her nails.

"So how long have you been working here?" asked Penelope.

"Since I finished uni."

"That's it?" asked Penelope.

"Well...yeah. Ever since I got my multimedia degree I haven't been able to get a job anywhere. Employers say they want people with three to five years work experience. So I am stuck here," said Jane.

"What do you want to do?" asked Eric.

"Lots of things," said Jane. "Graphic design. Web design. Interactive media. Marketing. Online Media Analyst. Pfffff... pretty much anything related to what I've spent all those years studying for." She leaned on her hand. That made Eric and Penelope smile simultaneously. They looked at each other for

a moment. They had the exact same thought at the same time
"Are you thinking what I'm thinking?" asked Penelope.

"What?" asked Jane.

"Dad always cared about young people and helping them
get into work. It's time we did the same," said Eric.

"Did what?" asked Jane.

"You know, Jane," said Penelope, "we could do with an
extra pair hands in the marketing department at Helix Inc."
She winked at Eric.

"And we're going to need some marketing analysis too."
Said Eric.

At that moment, Jane's eyes glittered with hope.

"Um, are you.. errr... offering me... a job?" Jane asked.
She swallowed.

"Let's just say I'm giving you another chance," said
Penelope.

"Really?!" she exclaimed with excitement.

"Yeah, sure. Why not?" said Eric.

"Oh thank you, thank you." Jane gave Penelope a hug.
Then she faced Eric. "Thank you." She reached to shake his
hand, he took his hand out and she shook it with both hands.

"Okay now," Penelope said, "Your first assignment is to
get to the Coast City Library. Going forward I want something
concrete in the research."

"Oh yes. I won't let you down," said Jane.

"We need to come up with a plan," said Eric. "Right now
Horus Inc. is leading the market. We need to find a way to
beat them. But how?" He placed a hand on his chin.

"I say we study them," said Jane. "Analyse them to the
finest detail. And then we can hit'em where it hurts."

"Hmmm...This will sound crazy to you guys but I say let's
go visit the aquarium," said Eric.

"I was planning on going too. But what got you interested
in it?" said Penelope.

"I want to see what all the fuss is about. After all, it was
pioneered by Horus Inc. And... and..." He looked around the

coffee shop. "We don't have a coffee shop either. Maybe we can look into making our own coffee franchise."

"Good thinking, Eric," said Penelope. "Now that you mentioned the aquarium, that has got me the thinking... during my last protest some reporter asked me about the Coast City Zoo and it was some kind of Helix project."

"If that's true then we need to look into that," said Jane. Eric smiled.

"What you got planned today, Penelope?" asked Eric.

"Oh, Jodie and I are working on some new designs for an animal-free fashion show we're planning."

"Why don't you come with me to the Aquarium? Right now."

"Now? Are you crazy? No wait, on second thought, yeah. That'll be good publicity. Which reminds me, the Mayor did recommend I go and visit the place."

"Alright, let's do it," said Eric.

"But what about Jodie?" asked Penelope.

"Call her, she can come along too. I'll call Toby. Hey Jane, what time do you finish here?"

"Uhh, in a couple of hours," said Jane as she checked her watch.

"Good. You can join us too." I'm taking you ladies to the Coast City Aquarium," said Eric. He winked.

They got up from their seats. Jane went back to work. Penelope took out her phone and called Jodie. Eric took out his phone and called Toby. He led Penelope out of the coffee shop and then he raised his hand to call for a taxi. They jumped in and set off for the Coast City Aquarium.

Chapter 33

That evening, after another boxing defeat, Cactus sat on a bench in the locker room. He leaned forward to hang his head in shame as he looked down at the floor. He slowly closed his eyes. The announcer and the crowd could be heard from the boxing ring. The sound echoed along the corridors. Many people clapped and cheered, but the rest made mocking remarks against Cactus. "Once a prick, always a prick!" They shouted. The chants were too much for him to bear. It forced him to open his eyes. He was alone. The locker room was a dirty place. There was a stench of male body odour, urine from dirty urinals, shit from the toilets, and bleach on every other surface. The lockers were a grid of metal boxes, each one had patches of red rust, scratches, dents, some with all of the above. The built man undid his boxing gloves and pulled them off. Each one emitted a whiff of sweat from within to reveal his hands wrapped with boxing straps, wet with sweat. Though topless, he wore his boxing shorts which came with red, white and blue stripes. They matched his boxing boots that had the same colours. He sighed. He got up and turned the dial to his locker. He opened it, but not before punching a few of the closed lockers next to his in rage, adding more dents to them. He gritted his teeth as he threw more punches until his bare knuckles hurt. He leaned against a wall and took in one deep breath after another to collect himself. Sweat dripped from the top of his bald head down to his face. He opened his duffle bag to take out a black towel.

Just then he heard footsteps coming from the other side of the locker room. The cracked tiles on the floor were wet due to the leaking showers close by. It was more than enough to alert him to the presences of three men. The man leading them was the fat venue manager, a middle-aged half Italian, with a bald patch, he had a dirty vest that yellowed with time and dirty black jeans. Behind him were two men who looked like FBI agents. They were both tall muscular men in black suits with black sunglasses. One was a black man with an afro, the other was a pale man with a long blonde ponytail.

"Hey Cactus, your new bodyguards have come to take ya?" said the manager and then he walked away.

"Bodyguards?" asked Cactus.

"Are you Malcolm Henriks?" asked the black bodyguard.

"Yeah, what do you want?"

The two tall men presented their ID cards.

"Helix Security," said the black bodyguard. "Our employer wants to speak with you."

They set off in a black Helix MPV. The rain was drizzling. Cactus looked out of the windows as they made their way to the city centre. The blonde body guard drove the vehicle down into an underground car park. And then the two bodyguards escorted him through a fire exit and up the freight elevator, down a corridor with a rows of doors and a fine carpet on the floor. They led him further until they reached a set of double doors. The black security guard took out a card key, touched the panel on the wall with it to open the doors.

"This way," he gestured.

Cactus walked in. And then the black bodyguard shut the door behind him with speed, and then locked it. The two guards stood outside with their arms crossed.

"Hey! What gives?!" said Cactus. He grabbed the door knobs, pushed and pulled but the doors didn't budge. And then he looked around the room he was in.

Cactus walked into the centre of the large hotel room. It was well-lit with the luxury of a 5-star hotel. He noticed the dark cityscape through the windows. The sun had set. Judging by the height he figured he was somewhere on the 10th floor. Everything in the Helix Hotel room had various shades of cream and white. The furniture was light grey, almost white. But what stood out were the iconic dark navy-blue satin sheets with dark blue satin pillows. The ceiling was white and the carpet he stood on was a darker cream colour. The curtains were also a dark navy-blue colour. The sofas were made of light grey cloth. The sweaty boxer looked out of place.

"We need to talk." He heard a familiar voice.

He turned to look around. Jodie was seated in a corner on a comfortable sofa. Next to her was a small table. There was a champagne bottle in an ice bucket. Standing next to them were two empty champagne glasses.

"Feel free to take a shower here," said Jodie. "There are some new tracksuits in there too. It's on me. Courtesy of Helix Fashion."

"Look, I've already been in jail because of you." Cactus started. "I ain't–"

"Relax. Nobody knows we're here," said Jodie.

"So whatcha want?"

"I want to help you," said Jodie.

"I don't need your help," said Cactus.

"Really? I've read all about you, Malcolm Henriks."

"That's Cactus to you, bitch. You don't know nothing about me."

"Amateur boxing to keep up with the rent? It's not easy," said Jodie.

"It's the only thing I know and I'm going to stick with it," Cactus replied.

"You have a load of medical bills to pay. In their thousands. If you don't pay them back soon, you're going back to jail anyway," said Jodie.

"Shut up. I can handle this."

"It doesn't have to be this way."

"You don't know what it's like to have a shitty life. I do!" Cactus barked. "When I was a kid, after my parents separated, I had to take care of myself. I had to live with my Ma. But she dead now. The landlord kicked me out when I lost my job. I did everything myself, you hear? So the only thing that kept me going was boxing. Amateur boxing wasn't enough. So I got into wrestling to make a name for myself. Make enough money to retire on." He paused for a brief moment. "But you. You were born with a silver spoon in your mouth. You never tasted desperation. You don't know what it's like out there. On the streets. You don't know jackshit."

"Don't condescend," said Jodie, "You don't know anything about me."

"I know enough," Cactus replied.

"Oh yeah. What's that?" asked Jodie.

"You're a spoilt rich kid... and a good fuck," said Cactus.

"Fuck you, you little prick!" Jodie hit back.

"Yeah, I am a prick," Cactus shrugged.

"I had dicks bigger than yours, asshole."

"Yeah. Well I had you. You're the one who resorted to being a hooker when you could have had any man you wanted."

She fell silent.

"What happened after you got arrested?" asked Jodie.

"You gave my popularity a boost for a while. People bought my merch. For once I had some extra cash. But then Wrestle Arena kicked me out and hung me out to dry like I was nothing. I had nothing left. So I went back to amateur boxing. Sure, it wasn't an easy ride. Bar fights, cage fights and shit. But hey, I have to keep the machine working."

"Listen, Malcolm, I have a proposition for you. I run a company called Helix Gen. I have got fashion and beauty products."

"Not interested."

"Just a minute. Instead of working for Wrestle Arena or getting your ass kicked in bars, you can work for me instead."

"I don't work for nobody," he said, "I work for me."

"Listen!" she insisted. "I'm launching new products that are down your street. Sports gear, protein shakes, gyms. Helix Fitness. I'm going to need someone to promote all this. And you're the right guy to do it."

"So that's it? Use me as a billboard, then bye-bye is it?" Cactus replied.

"No. You can work as a fitness coach in my gyms. A Boxing Trainer in your own ring. You name it. You can do anything you want. The decision is yours."

The hotel room went silent. Cactus turned away from her to think. He saw the black and lime green towel on the bed, it had the Helix fitness logo on it. Next to that it had the black and green shower gel and Helix Fitness fruit protein bars.

Above the headboard of the bed, he saw hanging on the wall was a gigantic monochrome photo of Mohammed Ali looking down at his defeated opponent.

He turned to face her. "Deal."

"Great." Jodie smiled. She uncrossed her legs and got up. "Let's celebrate." She poured the champagne into the two glasses and then brought them to him. "This looks like the beginning of something new," she said as she gave him a glass.

"It sure is." He replied with a warm smile.

They clinked their glasses and drank. He held her close to him.

"Take a shower first," said Jodie.

"You're coming in with me," said Cactus. He took her by the hand and led her into the bathroom.

He pulled her close to him and they kissed. They slowly undressed each other and then made love in the shower. They embraced and gently caressed each other as the hot water ran down their naked bodies, lost in a world of their own as the hot water vapour wrapped around them. After they dried themselves with towels, they went from the steamy room into the bedroom where they turned out the lights and continued to make love on the bed, and then they slept in each other's arms.

Chapter 34

The next morning, Toby and Eric were in a Helix Motors showroom. This branch was closed for the day. Similar to Helix Tower, it had the interior of a white marble with Roman Doric columns that held up the ceiling. With rows of Helix cars, black and dark blue made it look like a modern version of a Roman Army. All the white blinds were down to stop people from looking in. The whole place was well lit with bright white studio lights. In the middle of the showroom was the brand new Helix station wagon. It was the first prototype. Also dark blue. The lighting gave it a beautiful shine.

Toby and Eric were in their suits. But they weren't alone. They were accompanied by three groups of people. One was a group of engineers who stood on one side of the showroom with clipboards and tablets. The other group were scattered photographers and cameramen who made sure everything looked good. The last group were a group of men in suits who were the board members of Helix Motors and Helix Tech. Among them were the Chairmen, James Knight of Helix Motors, and Alex Thomson of Helix Tech.

"Lock," Toby said into his gold watch. The station wagon flashed its hazard lights and beeped twice. The sound of the doors locking was heard. "Okay, now try it," said Toby.

Eric stepped up to the car to open it. It wouldn't budge.

"Yup. It's locked," said Eric.

"Great! The gold watch's voice recognition works!" Toby shouted out with excitement. The engineers smiled. They ticked the right boxes.

"Not bad," said Eric, impressed. "Now test the fingerprint scanner on the door handles."

Toby walked up to the car, placed his fingers under the door handle, the white light underneath lit up which signalled the activation of the unlocking mechanism, and then Toby opened the door.

"Success!" Toby shouted with joy. The engineers smiled again.

"This is awesome," said Eric. Amazed.

"But wait!" said Toby with excitement. "There's more!" He closed the door. He then took out his new Helix phone and brought it close to his mouth. "Lock," he commanded. The car flashed its lights again, "Beep Beep." The lock mechanism was heard. "Now try it."

Eric tried to open it. "It's locked," said Eric.

"Perfect!" Toby shouted with joy. "The four-way locking system works!"

"Four?" asked Eric.

"Yeah. The key of course," Toby took the key out of his pocket. Locked and unlocked with it. "See? The watch, phone, fingerprint scanner, and the key. All in one!" said Toby. He had the biggest smile in ages.

All the engineers looked at one another as they nodded. They ticked all the right boxes on their tablets and clipboards.

"Wow," said Eric, looking pleased. "I can't believe it. This is our design. It's way better than I expected."

"Of course it is, son." The Helix Motor Chairman walked up to Eric and pat him on the back. "You see? When you give customers what they want, business can only succeed."

"Indeed," said the Helix Tech Chairman walked up to Toby and put a hand on his shoulder. "This only goes to show when we work together, we can achieve great things."

"Yeah, I guess so," said Toby. "I wish Dad was here to see this."

"Me too," said Eric.

"Someone else is here instead," said a board member, "Commissioner Banks is here to see you."

In walked the gigantic black man in a Police uniform, looking as stern as ever.

"Mr Helix, I'd like a word if you don't mind." He looked at Eric.

"Uh, sure," said Eric. "I'm free to talk."

"In private please," said the Commissioner.

"Oh. Hey guys, can you all excuse us?" said Eric. Everyone left the showroom. Toby was about to leave too.

"I wanna talk to you too, Toby Helix," said Commissioner. Toby jumped.

"Uh oh. Ummm. What did I do?"

"Just a minute." The Commissioner waited for everyone else to disappear from the showroom. The doors closed. The three men were alone. "Now," said Commissioner Banks, "Eric Helix, I don't know what you were trying to do the other day, but I don't care. Don't think for one second that can buy out my cops." He frowned.

"Oh, that? I was trying to make an amends. I was only–"

"I'm warning you. You screw up once, I'm comin' for you. Ya hear?" To that, Toby gulped. And then the Commissioner turned to face Toby and then pointed at him. "And the same goes for you!"

"Sir," said Eric, "I've learned my lesson, okay. I spent my time in jail and I'm doing my best to never break the law again. I'm only trying to make it up you and everyone else." Eric showed the palms of his hands, the Commissioner noticed.

"Me too," said Toby.

"Listen. What this city needs is role models," said Commissioner Banks. "Our forefathers were decent men who built this city and made the society the way it is. It is the law abiding citizens who uphold such values. Because of Helix Inc.'s success, the spotlight is always on you and your family. You wanna make amends? You owe it to your ancestors."

"Okay. How do I do that?" asked Eric.

"You can start by acting like model citizens. Become someone people want to aspire to. Understand?"

"Yes sir," said and Eric and Toby.

"Good. Have a good day gentlemen," said Commissioner Banks. And then he left the building.

Both Eric and Toby let out a big sigh of relief.

"Phew. Oh man," said Toby, "I thought he was going to arrest us. Or accuse us of something."

"Me too," said Eric.

"He scared the crap out of me," said Toby as he leaned on the car.

"So he wants us to be role models, huh?"

"Yeah. Well I'm guessing that's what he meant," said Toby.

"Maybe he wants us to be more like Dad," said Eric.

"What? Rich and successful?" asked Toby.

"No, you idiot. Something else," Eric replied.

"Whatever the Commissioner meant, the city has a lot

more respect for Dad than they do for us. Compared to him we're clowns."

"You think I don't know that?"

"So how do we get people in this city to like us?"

"I don't know," said Eric. "We're meeting Jodie and Penelope later today anyway. Maybe we can ask them."

"That reminds me," said Toby, "I'm expecting a delivery today. Jodie's new fitness equipment will be arriving."

There was a knock at a distant door.

"Excuse me, is everything alright?" asked an engineer.

"Yeah sure," said Eric. "Everybody can come back in. We have a photo shoot to finish."

The photographers, the engineers, and the board members returned to the showroom.

"Photo shoot?" said Toby. He looked at all the cameras the photographers had. "Hey! I got an idea. Eric, throw it on the floor."

"The what?" asked Eric.

"The Helix phone. It's durable. Throw it on the floor."

"Are you crazy?" said Eric.

"Remember that Brooks phone commercial? Where you tried to break one of theirs? Now we can test ours. Roll them cameras!" At Toby's command, the photographers and the cameramen pointed their cameras at Eric.

"Okay. Here goes nothing," said Eric. He threw his Helix phone on the floor.

It didn't break. Not a scratch. And then Toby walked over to one of the cameras and said:

"The new Helix Phone. Even a Helix can't break it." To which everyone in the showroom laughed.

"That takes me back," said Eric. "Great idea. This can go on TV."

"Excellent," said the Chairmen.

The teams ran a few more tests on the new station wagon and then left the showroom.

Chapter 35

That afternoon, Daniel Crawley sat in the boardroom of Helix Tech. He looked around at the interior design and smiled at it. What got his attention were the white curtains that gently billowed against the gentle breeze that came in through the open windows. Then his eyes went back to the documents in front of him. One by one, he took out more documents and folders out from his briefcase and laid them out on the table. He checked each one to make sure they were in the right order that aligned with the points in his memo. In between the notes he read, he took a sip of his freshly made coffee. As soon as he laid all the documents ready for the meeting, he got up and stood by the window to look outside. He felt the cool gentle breeze from the window. He took in a deep breath and exhaled. He looked at his watch, the time was 1:46pm. The meeting was due to start at 2pm. He looked out of the window to enjoy the view of the city. And then the door opened. Jodie walked in with her briefcase.

"Oh. Mr Crawley? Hello. I didn't expect you to be here," said Jodie. She was in a black blazer, black trousers, black shoes, and a white blouse. All buttons done up.

"I wanted to make sure I had everything prepared," Daniel replied. He stood up straight. She looked at the documents laid out in on the desk in front of the chairs.

"Looks good. You're more organised than me," said Jodie. She smiled.

"Hmm." Daniel kept his mouth shut.

"Actually, Daniel, I'm glad we're alone," said Jodie. "There's something I want to tell you."

"Uh oh," he whispered to himself. He clenched his fists as he cringed. Jodie walked over to him.

"I want to say I'm sorry for embarrassing you at our previous meeting. I didn't mean to make you feel uncomfortable like that."

"Oh," said Daniel. "It's nothing. I thought nothing of it at all." He forced a fake smile.

"I didn't want there to be a misunderstanding. I was trying to prove a point and I messed it up. Big time," said Jodie.

Daniel relaxed his shoulders. "Regardless, we have much to cover."

"Great. And please, call me Jodie. I hate formalities."

Just then, Penelope walked through the door with Jane behind her. They too had black blazers, black trousers and shoes, and white blouses. All buttons done up.

"Hi there," said Penelope with excitement. "I thought we were early."

"Me too," said Jane. She had a big black box file in her arm and a laptop in the other. She put it on the big table.

"Now we need to wait for the boys," said Jodie.

"Yeah, for once we beat them to it," said Penelope.

"Excuse me, I have not seen you before," Daniel said to Jane.

"Oh, I'm new here," said Jane. "I uh, am a marketing analyst. Also a researcher."

To that, Daniel smiled. "Very good, that's exactly what we need for what we are about to discuss. I'm Daniel Crawley. Project Manager." He reached out his hand for a hand shake.

She took his hand and shook it. "Please understand, I'm a little nervous."

"Everything will turn out fine as long as we work together," said Daniel.

Then the doors opened and in walked Eric and Toby in their suits.

"You two look like you've seen a ghost," said Jodie.

"Worst than that," said Eric. "Commissioner Banks came to the showroom earlier today."

"I thought he was going to arrest us," said Toby.

"What did you do?" asked Penelope.

"Nothing," said Eric. "I apologised to the black cop I

punched years ago to make amends. And then Commissioner came in to accuse me of trying to bribe the guy." He gave a sigh of relief. "At least that's all over. Come on, let's start this meeting."

Everyone sat on the chairs and looked at the documents that were laid out in front of them. The boardroom was quiet for a few moments. Daniel Crawley took another sip of his coffee.

"Now," said Daniel, "Our first order of business is to see what we have ready to release. Eric, let's start with you, Helix Motors. What have we got?"

"Toby and I were at the showroom today. We tested the security system on the new Helix Station Wagon. It all works great," said Eric with excitement. "This thing is ready!"

"Wonderful," Daniel replied as he smiled. "Do you have the engineers' report?"

"Uhhh, no, I didn't think I'd need it. So I didn't bring it."

"It's okay. I'll ask them to send me a copy. So the next thing we need to do is to see if we can get some test drives available and see how many deposits we can get. It's looking good so far. We have a car," said Daniel with delight. Everyone in the boardroom looked at each other with smiles.

***

"Now, next up. Helix Tech. Toby, what have you got for us?" asked Daniel.

"I got the new Helix Phone right here." Toby took out a prototype of the latest Helix Phone and showed it to everyone in the boardroom. "It's been on test drive for the last few days. It works like a charm." He had a big grin on his face.

"Let me see it," said Daniel. Toby handed over his phone. Daniel held the phone in his hands and looked at it in different angles, and then he frowned.

"Hmmm. Why is this thicker than the previous one? And

why does it have the headphone jack? The Horus phone is thinner, it doesn't have a headphone jack, and it's lighter as a result. Same with the Brooks phone," said Daniel.

"I figured there are lots of reasons to keep the headphone jack. So why get rid of it?" Toby replied.

"Such as?"

"First of all, you can just plug in your headphones. It works straight away. But with bluetooth headphones you have to sync your devices. That by the way is another device you have to recharge. At least with a headphone jack, you can listen to music while you recharge your phone at the same time."

"I see," said Daniel. "But Horus Inc. is leading the market in this field. Along with Brooks."

"Just because some other company is doing something doesn't mean we have to follow. Besides, it's the customers' needs that are more important to us. I thought that was the whole point of Helix Inc.!"

"Relax Toby, there's no need to get defensive," said Eric.

"Um, pardon me guys," said Jane. "I did some research on this very topic. And according to my market analysis, there's a link between a bigger battery and a longer battery life. Having a thinner phone by removing the headphone jack actually forces the battery to be smaller in size, hence the shorter battery life."

"Point taken," said Daniel. To that Jane and Penelope looked at each other, and they fist bumped with big grins.

"Then, how about this?" Daniel continued. "Why not make two versions of the Helix phone? Thinner phones without a headphone jack but low battery capacity. Thicker phones with headphones jacks, but longer battery life. At least that gives customers options. And it gives you the upper hand in the market."

"Let's do it," said Toby. "Speaking of batteries, we are applying the same technology to Helix Motors too. Along with the rest of the toys and gadgets made by Helix. I'm also developing new drones with cameras attached. That'll be an exciting new addition to our gadget range."

"Very good," said Daniel. He made few notes.

***

"Next thing on the agenda is Helix Gen. Jodie, what have you got for us?" asked Daniel.

She opened her briefcase and took out some products that were black and lime green. One was a tank top, one was a shower gel, a protein candy bar, a protein shake, and a pair of gym gloves. Then she took out a small portfolio continuing new designs for Helix Fashion. They were followed by another folder. "Check this out. I have created a new brand. Helix Fitness. All black and green. I'm opening up new gyms around the city. Starting right here in Helix Tower, we're going to have our very own on-site gym too. So our employees don't have to go anywhere else. With the help of Helix Tech, thanks to Toby here, I'll be getting new gym equipment. We can sell those too. To promote all this, I have invited Cactus the Wrestler. He will model all this for us."

"That's all well and good, but why Cactus?" asked Daniel with raised eyebrow.

"He has a track record of boxing and wrestling. So he's no stranger to sports. Besides, he deserves a chance in the spotlight. After all, Helix Inc. is about giving people the chance to contribute. He has signed up to become a fitness coach too," said Jodie.

"Hey, I've got an idea. Let me model with them too," said Toby.

"Not so fast, chubby," said Eric as he giggled.

"Cut it out!" said Toby.

"Hmm, maybe," said Jodie. "We could do a 'Before and After' promotion with you as an example. But you have to commit to it. You got that? You let yourself down, you let the rest of us down."

"Yeah sure," said Toby. "I've been wanting to lose weight for a while anyway."

"Okay then, what else?" asked Daniel.

Jodie opened her Helix Fashion folder and showed all the designs for new dresses, shoes, and jewellery.

"With special thanks to Penelope here," they smiled at one another, "we have designed clothing from cotton, linen, seaweed, wood, hemp, and beech tree fibre. Handbags, shoes, and jackets will be made with alternatives to leather, such as paper, waxed cotton, apple fibre, tree bark and cork, pineapple and teak leaves."

Daniel looked through the designs for women. They were modernised version of dresses and other kinds of clothing that resembled the 1940s. "They look good," said Daniel. "So what's with the alternative materials?"

"It's to show we care about animals," Jodie replied. "From now on, we at Helix Inc. use animal-free products. With all this in place we're going to have a big Helix Fashion show lined up. All we need is a date and a venue."

"I see," said Daniel. "But... what if I told you Helix Inc. have been testing products on animals for decades?"

"What?!" Penelope screeched.

"Oh shit!" exclaimed Jodie.

"Uh oh," muttered Jane.

Eric and Toby's jaws dropped. For a brief moment the boardroom fell silent.

"Okay, now that you know," said Daniel, "how can we tell the world that we at Helix care about the well-being of animals while experimenting on them? That gives out the wrong message. No?"

"Then we must scrap it," commanded Penelope. She slammed a fist on the table.

"I agree," said Jodie.

"Me too," said Jane.

"You do realise that alternatives are more expensive," said Daniel.

"Fine," said Jodie.

"We'll do it. I don't care how expensive it is," said Penelope. "Since actions speak louder than words, then God damn it we're gonna scrap animal testing here. And everybody's going to know about it."

"I think this is a risk we're going to have to take," said Eric. "Jane, do the guys at Horus test products on animals? What about other companies?"

"I don't know, but I can find out," Jane replied.

"Get onto it," said Eric, "if we scrap animal testing, this will prove to everybody what we stand for. That way our customers will feel good knowing that no animal was harmed in the making of our products. We can invest in alternatives. Better yet, we win the customers from our competitors. Those in favour?" He raised his hand. Everyone in the boardroom except Daniel raised their hand and let out a mutual "Aye."

"I see you're all very passionate about this. I'm going to have to speak to the finance department about this one. I think we can do this. With new customers, we can invest in more testing alternatives. And for that, we're going to need some research." He turned to face Jane, she blushed. "Anything else, Jodie?"

"I've got more." She took out another folder from her briefcase. "Last but not least. The Edge Motel is now a hotel. Shared ownership with Helix Inc. I had it rebuilt. The former owner is now the manager. And, get this, Barry Brooks himself has agreed to join me in the cutting of the red ribbon on its opening day."

"Barry Brooks? Himself?" said Penelope with excitement.

"No way," said Toby with joy.

"That is brilliant!" said Eric.

"How did you do that?" asked Daniel.

"All I wanted was to improve the relationship between Brooks and Helix. With Dad gone, someone had to do it. Besides, I ruined his life a few years ago. So I thought I'd better rebuild bridges with him. And the manager of The Edge Motel too," said Jodie.

"I have to say I am impressed with this. This will definitely improve the image of Helix Inc.," said Daniel. He made a note of it. "It will be good for the press too. So Jodie, we have a new brand, Helix Fitness, a new range of clothes, animal free, and an opening of a new hotel with Barry Brooks. Great stuff."

***

"And finally, we have Helix Press. So, what does Penelope have for us?" asked Daniel. Penelope grinned.

"We're going to make some documentaries. To inform the public. Take it away, Jane." Jane got up, walked over to a projector, attached her laptop to it, dimmed the lights and turned on the projector.

"Our first documentary is going to be about the history of Coast City. How it came to be, and about Jeffery Irons himself."

"A long time ago, Coast City used to be a village of the indigenous peoples. The original name is not known, some historians say it was originally called 'Agola Amayi' in a Cherokee dialect which translates to 'Fish River'. But it's not certain though. The village was burnt down and massacred by conquistadors who later converted it into a town with a fortress. They named it 'Pueblo de Costa' which means 'Coast Town' in Spanish. In time, as more Europeans settled on the east coast, the town was eventually came to be known as Coast Town."

"When the American Civil War broke out, Captain Jeffery Irons, who was a devout Christian brought his injured men here to recover after a defeat in a battle against the Confederate Army. At this point, Coast Town was almost a ghost town had it not been for the small number of people who stayed here. The fortress was abandoned and partially demolished. He used this place as a chapel and as an infirmary. He dedicated it to Saint Luke, the Physician. His wife Mary-Jane joined him, his sisters and many other women from the North came to the St Luke Chapel to aid the sick and injured.

"When the war ended, everyone who sought refuge here, along with the freed slaves, came together to build a whole new city. Jeffery Irons ordered the demolition of the fortress and commissioned the construction of St Luke's Cathedral in its place. Down the road, a hospital was built, it later became the Coast City General Hospital. Also dedicated to St Luke. Jeffery Irons had other places built like the Town Hall, the Coast City Library, the Coast City Court of Justice, among other things. Everyone contributed, it was the community spirit inspired by Jeffery Irons that brought people together to build this city. And since then, Coast City grew and became the city we know today. So that concludes the first documentary." Jane stopped speaking and the room had a heartbeat of silence.

"Way to go, girl!" Penelope cheered.

"Good move," said Eric.

"That's pretty good," said Jodie.

"Sweet." Toby gave a thumbs up.

"It all looks good and all but, what does that have to do with Helix Inc.?" asked Daniel. "How is this going to help you?"

"To answer that question, comes the second documentary. The History of the Helix Family. I looked through some old family records in the Coast City Library and this is what I found." Jane started a new presentation. "Okay, this is a picture of Kenneth Helix. Long story short, he came to the United States as a Pilgrim from England with his family. They bought more land as they grew. Kenneth invested in real estate which is how he became so wealthy."

She paused for moment. She gulped.

"Now... err. This is the part you guys are not going to like. It's what I found in the library. So please don't kill me. Okay?" said Jane.

"Huh?" Penelope raised an eyebrow.

"Oh come on," said Jodie.

"It can't be that bad," said Eric.

"Spit it out already," said Toby.

"Let's hear it," said Daniel.

Jane took in a deep breath. Her next slide revealed a portrait of wealthy plantation owner.

"Okay now. This is Richard Helix. My research has found that..." The next slide of the presentation revealed a picture of Richard Helix sitting on a rocking chair while watching over slaves get whipped as they worked on a cotton field.

"Richard Helix was a slave owner," said Jane. She cringed in fear as she gritted her teeth. Everyone else in the boardroom looked on in horror.

"What?" said Eric.

"Oh shit!" Jodie exclaimed.

"Uh Oh." Toby cringed.

Daniel sat there in silence with his eyes wide open.

Penelope's jaw fell to the ground so hard it stayed there. She squeaked as she gasped.

"Aaaaoooooooh....myyyyy......GOD!" Penelope screeched.

Jane closed her eyes tightly as she nodded. And then opened them.

"Slaves? Racists? In the family?" Penelope began to hyperventilate. "I don't believe it! I am so ashamed right now. We're doomed!" Penelope slammed her hands on both sides of her head and squeezed it like a vice with her palms.

"Calm down, Penelope," said Eric. "It's not the end of the world."

"No but it will be the end of Helix Inc. if Horus gets hold of this, they will fuck us up for sure," said Jodie.

"What do we do?" said Toby. He began to bite his nails.

"Best keep this quiet perhaps?" Daniel suggested quietly.

"Wait, please, there's more. It gets better," said Jane.

"In what way?" asked Eric.

"I need a glass of water," said Penelope. She rushed over

to the water cooler and seized a glass. Her hands shook as she filled it up and drank it. She sat back down to take a breather.

"That's the worst of it. Okay? But from there it all goes up. Trust me," said Jane as she held her arms up as if she was held at gunpoint.

"Jane," said Jodie in a cold and stern voice. The board-room was dim, but the fire in her eyes were visible, "You don't realise how serious this is. If the whole city finds out that we descended from slave owners, they will think we are RAC-ISTS and no one will ever want to have anything to do with us again."

"Please, let her continue," said Daniel. He pulled at the collar of his shirt.

"Okay," said Jane. On the next slide of her presentation, she revealed a photograph of Richard Helix in a military uniform among the Confederate Battalion.

"Oh my god!" Penelope's voice broke as if she was about to cry. "He fought for the South? Jesus! Just end my life already. Pleeeeeeease." She grabbed one of the folders on the desk to fan herself with it.

"Shut up Penelope will ya?" said Eric.

"Stop that," said Toby.

"Do calm down PP," Jodie joined in.

"Continue," Daniel urged Jane.

"This is the battalion that he was part of during the Civil War," said Jane. "When they retreated from a battle they lost, they came to Coast Town where they encountered Jeffery Irons and his men while they were resting. According to a diary entry of one of the soldiers who rested at the chapel, there was a stand-off. All the men pointed their rifles at each other. But Jeffery Irons offered to give Richard Helix and his men medical aid on the condition they surrendered to them. They accepted. Another diary entry mentions that Jeffery Irons read passages of the Bible to the injured men while they recovered. He gave them tranquillity with the teachings of Jesus Christ. Jeffery Irons saw all men as equals which is why he was against slavery. He saw every person as God's child. To him, this war was nothing but a clash of misunderstandings and ideals, a test from God."

"Now," Jane smiled with excitement. "This is where it gets really good. "Influenced by Jeffery Irons and his goodwill, Richard Helix ran back to his plantation and set all his slaves free. He let them all go!" Everyone in the boardroom smiled and sighed with relief and joy. The boardroom became a theatre. "After that," Jane continued, "he came back to Coast Town and announced to Jeffrey Irons in the St Luke's Chapel that he had released his slaves. He switched sides. Seeing Jeffrey Irons and Richard Helix work together, the rest of the Confederates at St Luke's followed suit, and they joined Richard Helix and switched sides. To fight for the right cause."

"Wow!" Toby let out like a child in a theatre. "He switched sides! Cool!"

"Shh," Jodie hushed him.

"And then, shortly after that, another Confederate battalion heard about Richard Helix and the liberation of his slaves. They tracked him down to Coast Town and they attempted to attack. They knew the chapel was full of injured soldiers and yet they planned a massacre. The St Luke's Chapel was used as fortress again. Jeffery Irons, Richard Helix and their men fought side by side to fight off the last Confederate battalion. They won!"

"Whoohoo!" Toby cheered.

"Alright!" Eric threw a fist in the air.

"Cool," said Jodie.

"Go Richard Helix," said Penelope with excitement. Tears filled her eyes.

"Wow," said Daniel.

"And then, when the war was over. All the slaves Richard Helix liberated came to Coast Town and thanked him for setting them free. The freed slaves were given the right to vote. Jeffrey Irons, Richard Helix, the soldiers, the nurses, and the freed slaves, all came together to rebuild Coast Town and make it into a city."

"Here are some black and white photos with them together. You see the black man on the right? Next to Richard Helix? That is Sherwin Banks."

"Banks? You mean...?" said Eric.

"That's right, he is an ancestor of Commissioner Banks," said Jane. "And, do you see that man with the rifle? That's Roland Stewart. The great grandfather of the Mayor."

"Holy shit," said Penelope.

"And, do you see this man here? That's David Brooks. Ancestor of Barry Brooks."

"Ha. No way," said Jodie with excitement.

"It gets better," Jane winked. "Here's another Helix. This is Martin Helix." She showed a wealthy man in a suit with a huge moustache. "He was the man who pioneered the Coast City Zoo. Why? Because he cared about animals. With Coast City growing so rapidly, it impacted the environment around it. There was a lot of deforestation and overfishing to keep up with the growing population. This caused animals in these areas to become almost extinct. Inspired by the *On the Origin of Species* by Charles Darwin, Martin Helix loved animals and he wanted to preserve them. So in the year 1912, he used his wealth to collect as many of the last surviving wild animals he could find and put them in the zoo to preserve them. Thanks to him, we have the Eastern Black Bear, the Brown River Bear, Deer, the White Wading bird, and many other endangered species right here in Coast City. Safe and Sound."

"Cool," said Penelope.

"But wait, there's more," said Jane. And then she showed black and white photographs of soldiers during World War II. "Now, during the Second World War, a lot of men in Coast City were drafted to fight the Nazis. To bring an end to fascism." The photographs showed the American soldiers at Omaha Beach after the Normandy Invasion. "Look at these soldiers." She took out a laser pointer and showed who was who. "Private Helix, Paul Helix to be precise. He was your grandfather's brother. Next to him are Private Banks, Private Brooks, Private Stuart. Once again, relatives of the Commissioner, the Mayor, and Barry Brooks. Meanwhile your grandfather Jeffery Helix took care of the family business. So as you can see, the Helix family has come a long way. And that concludes my draft of our second documentary for Helix Press."

To that the whole boardroom clapped and cheered.

"What an amazing story," said Eric.

"Oh my god. I didn't know ANY of this," said Jodie.

"Whoohoo," cheered Toby.

"And, finally," said Jane, "this is a quick one, I promise. The last documentary is about the animals Martin Helix rescued. This documentary goes into depth about each and every animal that lived here as well as the environment, such as the forests around the city. This will come in handy to show the world that Helix Inc. really does care about the well-being of animals as we discussed earlier. We are so going to win. Thank you very much." She gave a bow.

The boardroom clapped and cheered. Penelope got up and gave Jane a big hug. They jumped up with excitement before they sat back down. They fist bumped again with big grins.

***

"That was quite a performance, Jane, very uplifting. Thank you," said Daniel. He took in a deep breath and slowly exhaled. "Now, I hate to spoil the fun, but I have to ask... Who is going to make these documentaries? How much will all this cost?"

"We've decided to hire volunteers from Coast City University," said Penelope. "Dad believed in giving young people opportunities. So we decided to give students and graduates a chance to contribute to Helix Inc. That way the whole world gets to see their skills and talent. It's going to be a big team effort. This will boost their profiles."

"Very well then. But what is the point of all these documentaries?"

The boardroom fell silent for moment.

"Don't you get it?" asked Penelope. "The first one is the history of Coast City. There hasn't been a documentary about it until now. If you ask anyone in Coast City today, most people won't even know about its original inhabitants."

"Or the impact of colonization," Jane added.

"Yeah, and Helix Press is the first company to do it best. After all, it's education, a history lesson for everybody who lives here," said Penelope. "Who better to make this documentary than us?"

"Fair enough," said Daniel. "And the second one? The history of the Helix family. What use is that one?"

"Isn't it obvious?" retorted Penelope. "This shows how the Helix family is closely tied into the history of Coast City. It's about who we are. It's our identity. Helix Inc. and Coast City are inseparable."

"Exactly," said Jane, "You see, Helix Inc. has a whole history behind it. A story. Horus Inc. is nothing in comparison. It came out of nowhere and it has taken over the market. This city ain't big enough for both of us. Get it?"

"Alright then," said Daniel, "Last but not least, the animal documentary. What will you do with that one?"

"Oh come on, that's a no-brainer," said Penelope. "We talked about animals earlier. With this animal-free fashion show that Jodie and I are going to host, the scrapping of animal testing, this will demonstrate our love for animals. Our customers will love us for it."

"So that's it then? Animal welfare. Is that all that Helix Inc. is about?" asked Daniel.

"What are you getting at here?" asked Eric.

"I am trying to get you to remind yourselves what Helix Inc. stands for. Apart from the environment, animal welfare, what do you care about? What are your values?" asked Daniel.

"The environment? Oh crap I forgot," said Eric.

"What?" asked Daniel.

"Green! We need to release a green model for Helix Motors. We only have black, red, white, and blue. How can we sell an environmentally friendly car when we don't have a green car? Battery powered cars too. Don't worry, I'll take care of it."

"Is that all?" asked Daniel. The boardroom fell silent.

"You see," said Daniel. "People don't just buy products. They buy ideas. Things that are compatible with their own identity. If you don't know what you stand for, then people don't have a reason to buy anything from you. Now let me ask you again; What are the values of Helix Inc.?"

The four siblings looked at one another in silence.

"Wait, I know!" said Toby. "Hey Eric. Didn't the Commissioner tell us earlier today that the city wants good role models? Well, that's us. We've got to be better role models for the city. Give people something to aspire to."

"I guess so," said Eric.

"I remember a conversation I had with my chairwoman a while ago," said Jodie. "She told me that we at Helix Inc. are conservative. When I saw the Cathedral of Saint Luke on the projector just now, it brought it all back to me. We need to be moral. And humble. I think."

"Conservative," said Penelope. "That's it! The Mayor told me same thing. He also told me about diversity of ideas, diversity of people too."

"Yeah, and maybe that's what Jeffery Irons must have told Richard Helix to get him to change his mind during the Civil War," said Jane.

"So there you have it," said Daniel, "Moral values, and diversity, as well as showing concern for animals and the environment. Now you must show it. Demonstrate it."

"But how?" asked Penelope.

"One way to prove it is..." Jane began, "well maybe... I took an ancestry DNA test a couple of years ago and I have ancestry going back all over Europe, and I have some Asian in me. If I remember correctly I am 3% Native American."

"That's it. I am so doing that!" said Penelope. "If we show the world we are diverse, and everyone in Helix Inc. are diverse too, then this will convince everyone we are what we say we are."

"Is that all?" asked Daniel.

"Hmmm." Jodie put a hand to her chin. "The clothes and dresses I designed are based on designs from the 1940s. We can use that photo of the soldiers during World War 2 to show our diversity. Look at the soldiers from Coast City. They were diverse then. And we are diverse now. We can show it like this. While the men were out fighting the war, we can show the world the sort of clothes that women were wearing. The women of Coast City have all kinds of ethnic backgrounds. And they were conservative back then too. This will be perfect for the fashion show," said Jodie.

"So, looking at what we have so far," said Daniel, he looked at all his notes, "All we have to do now is work out some release dates and make some marketing plans. Best not to release all Helix projects at the same time. Let's bring Helix back into the spotlight one project at a time. First we get those documentaries made and put them online. Remind everyone what Helix stands for. Next we bring out the new Helix phone, followed by the new Helix car. After that, we can bring out the Helix Fitness range with your new products and gyms. And then we can have the Helix Fashion show. Agreed?"

Everyone else in the boardroom nodded in agreement.

***

"Wait a minute. I got another idea," said Jane. "Hey Jodie, that Cactus guy. Helix gives people from different backgrounds opportunities, right? Well, how about I make a video interviewing him? Then we put it online. That way we promote Helix Fitness as well as Helix Inc."

"Good idea," said Jodie, "After all, people are interested

in the lives of other people. Let me talk to Cactus and see what he thinks."

"Hey Jane," said Toby, "I have a suggestion for someone you can also interview. A friend of mine named El-Taco. He's had it rough. He could do with some good publicity. He wants to be a singer. A rock star... I think. Anyway, he's meeting his vocal coach this afternoon." He winked at Jodie. Jodie smiled.

"Sure, I'll interview him," said Jane.

"That reminds me," said Jodie. "Hey Penelope, you need to work on your voice remember? You've got your speech coach booked for this afternoon too."

"Is it the same guy?" asked Penelope.

"No," said Jodie. "One's going to teach El-Taco to sing and the other is going to teach you public speaking. You're just going to be in the same recording studio."

Daniel let out a big smile as he took few more notes.

"What is it?" asked Jane.

"Oh nothing," Daniel replied. "You know. It's just that... it fills me with great pride to work with such a great team. All four members of the Helix family."

"Yeah, I wish Dad was here to see this," said Penelope.

"Family?" Eric whispered to himself. He froze for a moment. He took out his phone and looked at the profile picture of Marie Baker. "Mr Crawley, random question, do you have children?"

"Yes, I have a daughter. Why?"

"I just had an idea for Helix Inc. A built-in day care centre for children. I mean, uh, the children of the employees who work here."

"That is a possibility, Mr Helix. But how do you plan to implement that?" asked Daniel.

"I'm not sure. Like... how many Helix employees have children? Who takes care of them? How much does it cost? What I'm getting at here is... why hire a day care centre and go to work when you can have both in the same place? If not, close by? Know what I mean?"

"I like the sound of that," said Daniel.

"I can research that," said Jane. She raised her hand in a playful way and expressed a big grin.

"Okay, you go ahead, let me know what you find," said Eric.

Jane took down some notes of her own.

***

"Great. I guess that's everything," said Daniel. "Is there anything else anyone wants to raise? Any more ideas?"

"Nope," said Eric. "All is good with me."

"I think we got everything covered," said Jodie.

"Then I guess it's meeting adjourned," said Daniel.

"See ya guys later." Eric got up and walked out of the boardroom.

"Later folks." Toby followed suit.

Jane unplugged her laptop from the projector and then packed all her research material back into her box file. Jodie collected all her samples and put them into her briefcase. Daniel put all his notes and files into his folder, and then he put it into his briefcase. One by one, everyone left the boardroom except Daniel who took his time as he packed his things and closed his briefcase. He picked up his coffee cup and drank the remains. It was cold but he didn't care. He dunked the last few drops and threw the paper cup in the trash bin. He stood by the window to look outside. He took in a deep breath and exhaled as he felt the cool gentle breeze that came through the window and caressed his face. He observed the cityscape and then watched the clouds slowly disperse to reveal the blue sky. He smiled And then he left the boardroom.

Chapter 36

That evening, Penelope and El-Taco sat at a table in the Pelican Pizza Shack restaurant. They shared a Vegetarian pizza, with olives, and spinach. The restaurant was packed. All the bigger tables were full with friends and families. Every group feasted on every piece of pizza as they ate, drank, and laughed. Penelope and El-Taco sat on the stools and ate at the small table by the front windows so they could see the traffic outside; people walked past as they made their way home from work. The air was chilly, so they hurried.

The walls had a reddish-orange and terracotta coloured brick wall texture. The chairs were all grey leather with different black feather patterns painted on to them. Little plastic pelicans hung from the ceiling as decoration. All the red napkins on tables were folded into bird shaped origamis that resembled pelicans.

"Man, that was one hell of a session," said El-Taco. "At this rate my voice is gonna break."

"Tell me about it," said Penelope. "I've been reading the same speech over and over again. I think I'm gonna get a sore throat for life."

"At least you don't have to hold a note for long."

"Ha! I don't have to. But you do."

"Yeah. I guess." He nodded.

"What's your real name anyway?" she asked.

"José Gonzales."

"So how did you come to know Toby?"

"We met online while playing video games. He was my online gaming buddy in our multiplayer campaigns."

"Is that when you two decided— you know, that thing?"

"Yeah. It was my idea to get him involved since he was loaded. But then he told me he had a fight with his Dad and cut off all financial aid, he got desperate. That true?"

"Yeah," Penelope replied. "I was there when it happened, I had a fight with my Dad too and I got the same treatment."

"Dayum. What did you do?" He asked.

"Let's just say that I was a naughty girl. I was embarrassing myself as well as everybody else. And then I went to jail," said Penelope.

"Yeah, I went jail too. That was years ago. I ain't doin' that again. So let's not go there okay, babe?"

Penelope squeaked as she giggled.

"What?" he asked.

"Okay, sure babe, honey, whichever you prefer," said Penelope.

"You can call me Honey, it sounds sweet."

"Hee hee, sure, Honey." She giggled again. "It feels kinda naughty."

"Why is that?" asked El-Taco.

"You know, for years I've been campaigning for language control and one of them was to ban pet names. Like, oh my god it's so embarrassing."

"Come on. It can't be that bad," said El-Taco.

"Would you believe that I've been trying get men jailed for using words like babe, honey, and sugar on women? I used to believe it was degrading women."

"Why?" El-Taco asked.

"Well, it's because now... come to think of it. I guess I was jealous. Jealous that nobody ever called me that. That no other guy ever liked me enough to call me babe." She turned away in shame. "I never had a boyfriend either."

"Things change, babe," said El-Taco.

She squeaked again as she let out a big smile as she faced him again. He smiled back.

"I like it when you squeak like that." He leaned in and kissed her on her lips. She jerked back and gasped.

"What?" he asked.

"Oh God. I'm sorry. I– I." Her eyes darted around. She looked as though she didn't know what to do.

"Wassup?" he asked.

"I feel stupid. It's just that I– I've never been kissed by a guy like this before. And I... errr. I better go." She reached for her bag.

"Wait," he said as he grabbed her hand.

"At least let me say goodbye before you go." He leaned in and kissed her on the cheek. And then on her neck. She smiled and relaxed. She looked into his eyes. Their mouths met and they kissed again. This time she put her arms around him and they embraced. He held her close to him as they kissed again. Their kisses were longer and more passionate.

Just then two youths walked along the pavement. One was wearing a yellow top with a black zig-zag pattern going across, and the other was wearing a red top with horizontal black stripes. They stopped frozen in their tracks to stare at what got their attention.

"Hold up!" said the youth in the yellow and black top. "Is that–? Is that who I think it is?!"

"Penelope Helix? El-Taco? They're an ITEM?!" The youth in the red and black top exclaimed.

"No way!"

"Get your phone out!"

They pulled their phones out of their pockets, opened their Blue Eagle TV apps and began recording a Livestream. The youth in the black and red top filmed the couple as they kissed. Meanwhile the youth in the yellow and black top began filming himself standing in front of the restaurant.

"Hey guys, this is Bumble-Bee Charlie with Ladybug Linus here. We're outside the– uh–" He looked up at the sign, 'Pelican Pizza Shack'. Get a loada this. What you are seeing here is Penelope Helix kissing a guy. That's right. The man-hating social justice warrior is kissing a guy. But not just ANY old guy. It's El-Taco himself! The hobo singer. You heard that right, folks. Look!" He held the phone right by the window.

"I don't believe it," said Linus. "I thought she hated men."

"Not anymore. She's found her man. Of all the guys out

there, she's with El-Taco. HA! Who would have thought. Eh? Love conquers all."

"Amen, brother. Amen."

"Keep filming, we're getting a shitload of likes here."

Another gang of youths were walking past the Pelican Pizza Shack and saw the couple kissing through the window.

"Wait a minute is that El-Taco?"

"He's kissing Penelope Helix?"

"Shit! Get your phone out."

That evening, pictures and footage of Penelope and El-Taco were circulated all over the internet. It got Helix Inc. back on social media feeds where many people commented and expressed their surprise, along with the following hashtags:

#Helix

#Love

#CoastCityRomance

#PenelopeHelix

#ElTaco

#PizzaLoveShack

The next morning Penelope received a text from Jodie.

"Way to go, sis. You gave us a boost already."

"Hey Penelope, you just gave me another idea." Toby texted her. "Helix Live! The Helix version of the Blue Eagle TV app. Where people can broadcast what they record on their phones. I'm going to have this app built into every Helix phone so they don't have to install any other app. Thanks."

"Way to go, Penelope," Eric texted her.

"Thanks guys," Penelope replied. "I love you so much xxx."

After that she sent El-Taco a text: "Hey, thanks again for taking me out. I had a great time."

"Don't mention it babe."

"Laters honey X."

Penelope smiled as she lay in her bed while she looked at the social media feed on her Helix phone. The sun shined through the windows and Penelope smiled. As she read the comments, she didn't reply to any of them despite feeling the temptation. She put her phone down on the bedside drawers, skipped over to the bathroom, and sang as she had a shower.

Chapter 37

It was on a late Saturday morning, months later, when Daniel Crawley leaned at the kitchen window to look outside. It was a quiet morning, people went about their day at a steadier pace than usual. The blue sky was patchy with clouds. He looked at the cityscape and listened to the noise outside, the sounds of cars and vehicles hummed along the roads and people who walked along the pavement.

His wife Denise was also up. She sat at the table while she fed her baby girl Nadia as she sat in a high chair, pulling faces and making her laugh as she spoon fed her with Helix baby food. Then Daniel sat at the table and watched his wife feed her daughter who laughed at her mum's every funny noise and face she pulled as he fed her. It made him smile.

He opened the laptop on the table. The city outside was a little sluggish, but the internet was on fire with immense activity. Thousands of comments were being posted and shared across every social media platform.

Penelope had Helix Press release all three documentaries onto the internet: 'The History of Coast City,' 'The Story of Helix Inc', and 'The Animals Coast City Zoo Rescued'. Thousands of people watched them.

"Holy cow," he said

"What?" asked Denise.

"I wasn't expecting this."

"Bad news?"

"No," he said. He let out a chuckle. "This is good." He nodded. The smile on his face widened as he read through his social media feed. "This is very good. It looks like people like the documentaries we made."

He read through the comments section and people posted the following:

"I had no idea the Helix family was involved in the civil war. That is badass."

"My great grandfather was there when it happened. He fought alongside Jeffery Irons and Richard Helix during the civil war. I'm so happy the rest of the city knows this."

"I didn't know half of this stuff in these documentaries. Now I am more proud to be citizen of Coast City than ever."

"I've been buying Helix products for years, but then I switched over to Horus when Helix dropped the ball. Now I am switching back to Helix."

"I always bought Helix gadgets, feels good to come back to it."

"They kept the headphone jack on their phones. Nice to know Helix listened to their customers."

"I was upset when Helix went downhill after Gerald Helix left. The siblings have come a long way. I have gone back to buying Helix products again."

"I've been buying Helix products for years. Now that I've watched these documentaries, I feel complete."

"My parents got married in St Luke's Cathedral. My God, I didn't know it was a fortress at first. Nice to know."

"When I looked it up, I discovered my great grandfather was one of the German architects of St Luke's Cathedral. Now it fills me with pride every time I walk past it. Thank you Helix."

"I'm Native American. My family were among those who survived the massacres. I am so happy Helix Inc. told the origin of Coast City with its history documentary. Thank you."

"Thank you Helix for shedding light on the history of Coast City. My grandfather was in the D-Day campaign too. As a kid I remember him telling me how he fought the Nazis alongside the Helixes. When I told my friends about this nobody believed me. Now they will!"

Daniel then went over to the website and he saw the videos and photo galleries of the Helix Animal-Free Fashion show that Jodie and Penelope hosted. Celebrities from across America attended, from actresses to fashion models and entrepreneurs. They watched each model walk onto the catwalk in their new modernised version of 1940's style dresses and clothes. All of them made from animal-free materials. He read some of the comments on the social media feed:

"Thank GOD they scrapped animal testing. I was shocked when I found out that Helix have been testing on animals the whole time. I'm so glad they came forward and admitted it. Now that they scrapped it I will be buying Helix products."

"The time for all companies to scrap animal testing is long overdue. Well done Helix!"

"I am going to visit the zoo now, I didn't know we had endangered species living right here in Coast City. I'm so glad Martin Helix built the zoo. They wouldn't be here otherwise."

"Hey guys, I looked it up. Horus Inc. are still testing on animals! I am switching over to Helix now. Fuck you Horus!"

"For once it's nice to see a company act on what they say. They made animal welfare and the environment a priority. I can only applaud them."

After that, Daniel went over to the video site ViewTube and saw the advert for the new Helix phone. It was a parody of the Brooks Phone advert from years ago that showed Eric Helix trying to smash a phone to the ground. This time it was Eric himself throwing down the new Helix phone. Toby Helix revealed himself to the camera and said "The new Helix Phone, even a Helix can't break it." Toby had already lost a little bit of weight since he had started buying Jodie's protein shakes and using some of the gym equipment. The next advert showed Helix Fitness, with Cactus running on a treadmill and lifting weights at a Helix Fitness Gym. And then it showed him drinking a new protein shake and he was wearing the new black and green Helix Fitness sports gear. The comments section displayed the following:

"Hey guys, guess what. I am commenting here on my new Helix phone. Hell yeeeah."

"I tried throwing the phone on the ground too. It's solid as a rock."

"I've got the new Helix phone too. I can't tell you the number of times I've dropped my phone already."

"Is that Cactus? No way!"

"I can see Toby is slimmer than before. He's finally acknowledged he's fat. At least he's working on it."

"Great to see Cactus again."

"I'm glad to see Cactus turn his life around. But I still think he's a prick."

"Is he still banging Jodie Helix? Lol"

Daniel chuckled as he read some of the comments.

"What are you watching?" asked Denise.

"Commercials."

"Huh?" She inquired.

"Ours. It looks like they're doing well."

"Really?"

"Yup, the whole world is talking about Helix Inc. This time we have some good publicity. With better products to hit Horus with. I can see things are getting better already." He said with excitement.

"That's great, hon," replied Denise.

"Yeah, and maybe one day Nadia will be working at Helix Inc.," said Daniel as he looked at Nadia with a grin. "Won't you?" He pulled a funny face at her. The baby giggled.

"Okay, now you're thinking too far ahead," said Denise.

"Maybe. Here's something that's not too far in the future, have you thought about going back to work?"

"No I haven't. Why?" Denise replied.

"Eric Helix has opened on-site day care centres for employees. All I'm saying is we don't have to pay for child care while we work. It's all covered for us. Even if you don't work at Helix, I'll take her there."

"Sounds good– wait a minute. This was Eric's idea? That's not like him," said Denise.

"What do you mean?"

"He's been single for a while now," said Denise. "When he's not racing cars he's dating multiple women. I'm betting he's found someone to settle down with already. Why else would the city's playboy act like a family man all of a sudden?"

"Hmmm. That never occurred to me," said Daniel. "After all, people do change."

"Yeah, and speaking of change, I need to change the baby," said Denise.

"Let me do it," said Daniel. He turned off his laptop and closed the lid. He got up, lifted his baby girl from the high chair, and hold her in his arms. Before he left the room he kissed his wife.

**

That afternoon, a crowd gathered outside the newly-built Edge Hotel. The building itself was like a modernised version of an American Art Deco hotel with four floors. The building was white with blue window frames and ivory coloured wall columns. There was a big sign above the doorway in an Art Deco style font that said 'Edge Hotel'. The car park at the front was decorated with a row of palm trees.

A giant red ribbon tied the front doors shut. Jodie was in her dark blue Helix blazer with the silver Helix Inc. logo pin. Barry Brooks stood in his beige suit as he held on to his cane. And next to them stood Big Billy in a brand new black suit. He had trimmed his beard slightly, and he had a big smile on his face and looked as though he won the jackpot. Next to him stood his wife, dressed in a new black blazer. She too sported a big smile.

Penelope stood with a dark blue cushion in her hands, on the cushion were three pairs of silver scissors. Next to her Jane Saunders stood with her note pad reporting the whole thing.

Jodie, Barry, and Big Billy took the scissors and took

turns to cut the red ribbon. The crowd applauded and then they made their way into the hotel for a little tour and enjoy the buffet.

Adee Lee and her cameraman were present to broadcast the scene for Blue Eagle TV.

Outside, Toby tested his new remote control drones with built-in cameras. He had launched Helix Live a few days earlier. He controlled the device with his Helix phone as it hovered above the crowd and filmed the event. Next to him stood three assistants, one made notes on a clipboard, the other had a spare drone in case the other one didn't work, and the other held a tablet and watched the live stream footage on the internet of what Toby recorded.

"Any progress?" asked Toby.

"Yes sir," said the assistant who held the tablet, "Thousands are watching this right now. We're getting a lot of Likes. I am still getting notifications of pre-orders for the drones. They are flooding in as we speak."

"Excellent," said Toby.

"Excuse me," Adee Lee approached Toby. "That's an interesting device. Can you tell me what that is?"

"Thank you," said Toby. "It's a Helix Camera Drone, I'm controlling it with a Helix Phone and I can see what I am recording. It is linked with Helix Live so I can broadcast what I am filming at the same time."

"Helix? May I ask who you are?" asked Adee.

"I'm Toby Helix," he grinned at her.

"Oh Mr Helix, I must say, you look very ... different," she said in surprise.

"Oh yeah? In what way?" he chuckled.

"You seem to have lost quite a bit of – oh uh – sorry I didn't mean to sound so rude." She blushed.

He smiled. "It's okay. I'll take it as a compliment," said Toby. "Here. Would you like to give it try?"

"Oh, I don't know how to use it."

"How about I teach you? Maybe Blue Eagle TV can benefit from our camera drones."

"I'd be delighted, Mr Helix."

"Call me Toby. What's your name?"

"I'm Adee Lee, Blue Eagle TV." She reached out her hand. They shook hands.

"I've seen you on TV many times, Adee. You're a good presenter," said Toby.

"Oh. Why, thank you." She blushed again.

***

A few weeks later, in the CEO office of Helix Inc. the siblings took their turn to hang a monochrome photographs of their successful projects. Gosia watched with folded arms as she stood by. One by one, each sibling hung a black and white photograph next to the one of their father.

Eric hung a photograph of himself standing next to the latest Helix Station Wagon in a Helix Showroom. Jodie hung a photograph of herself in front of the hotel with Barry Brooks and Big Billy standing next to her. Penelope hung a picture of herself and Jodie standing surrounded by their fashion models and celebrities at their fashion show. Toby hung a picture of himself holding the latest Helix smart phone.

And then they all stood back to marvel at their photographs. They couldn't hold back their smiles of joy. They gave each other a hug and a pat on the back.

"We did it guys," said Eric.

"I can't wait for Dad to see this when he gets back," said Jodie.

"I wish he was here right now," said Penelope.

"He's going to love this," said Toby.

Gosia then unfolded her arms, approached the siblings and gave them a pat on the back each.

"Well done," Gosia said. "Well done to you all." She gave them a congratulating smile.

"Does this mean we beat Horus?" asked Toby.

"No." Gosia shook her head. "Horus are still leading the market. We have a long way to go. But don't worry. We'll get there."

Chapter 38

The next morning, the buzzer at the reception of the Duckling Day Care Centre went off.

"Good morning, who is it?" the secretary said as she looked at the camera footage on another screen and noticed a man in a suit.

"Hi, it's Eric Helix."

"Come in, Mr Helix." The buzzer went off again and he walked through the door and approached the reception desk.

"I've come to see Marie Baker."

"She's in a class right now, is she expecting you?"

"No. It's a surprise."

"Okay, I'll tell her." She picked up a phone and dialled a number. She gestured Eric to take a seat.

Eric looked around the reception area and smiled at all the finger paintings that were hanging on the walls that depicted nursery rhymes and their families. All the houses were drawn with squares and triangles in different sizes while the family members were drawn in different round shapes with added wriggly lines for hairs and limbs. The paint came in seven different colours of the rainbow. Eric was reminiscing over similar things he did as kid, and then Marie came over.

"Oh. Eric." She smiled, delighted. "What are you doing here?" She was wearing a light grey turtle-neck jumper, dark blue jeans, and light brown boots. Her long blonde hair curled at the ends.

"I've come to see you."

"What for?"

"To show you that I am serious." There was determination

in his voice. "I thought about what you said, and you are right. So I have opened a day care centre for all Helix staff. I want what's best for all the families who work at my company. Staff can bring their children to work with them, and while they work their children are taken care of in the same building. All expenses covered."

"That is wonderful news," she said impressed.

"There's more," said Eric. "I want to start a family. Since we last spoke, I have not been with anyone else. This relationship is only open to you."

"Oh Eric, I don't know what to say," she said amazed. She blushed.

"Are you interested?"

"Yes."

"Great. Let's go," said Eric.

"Go where?"

"I'm going to take you out shopping, and then we go somewhere nice for dinner."

"But Eric, I can't go anywhere right now. I'm working."

"Tell your boss it's ME who's taking you out. I AM Eric Helix after all." He said in a smug tone that made Marie frown and place her hands on her hips in disapproval.

"Listen, Eric. You can't turn up unannounced and expect everyone to drop everything just for you. We have work to do."

To that Eric frowned back at first, he didn't like being challenged like that, but then he couldn't think of a comeback. He relaxed his face and sighed.

"Yeah. You're right."

Marie relaxed her face as well. "But I am free this weekend though." She removed her hands from her hips.

"Sweet. Let's exchange numbers," said Eric. "Is this Saturday good?"

"Sure." They put their numbers into their phones.

"Great. I'll see you then." He pulled her towards him and kissed her on the cheek. "Bye."

"Bye." She smiled and blushed again. As she walked back to work there was a skip in her step.

After Eric left the building, the receptionist watched on the surveillance camera screen as Eric threw a fist in the air going "YESSSS!" and then she smiled for them.

***

Later that day around lunch time, El-Taco sat at a table in the Star-Ducks coffee house with his caramel sundae. He was dressed in scruffy track suits and he had a black and green bandana. He looked through his phone as he waited, and watched footage of himself as he recorded some singing rehearsals for a new album he was working on. The cafe was packed. The piano jazz music in the background drowned out by people chatting. Glad he came in on time, otherwise there would have been nowhere for him and Penelope to sit. Just then Penelope arrived, as soon as she saw him through the window and waved at him with a big smile. She walked in, got herself a drink and walked over to El-Taco and joined him. She kissed him on the lips before she sat down.

"How's it going, babe?"

"I met up with Marcy and Sue to build bridges with them. We've made up," she said with relief.

"Who are they?"

"They're old friends of mine from uni. I said some nasty things to them a while back. Now they are happily married and have children. They are so cute." She showed him photos of them on her phone. "I thought I'd pay them a visit and give them some flowers."

"That sounds nice."

"Yeah, and they congratulated me on my documentaries. They saw them all. They enjoyed them. It's the exact feedback I wanted."

"That's my girl," said El-Taco, "Dedicated, hard working,

and popular." To that Penelope squeaked as she giggled. "Hey, your tattoos are gone." He pointed to his neck.

"Yep, they are all removed now. There are now no marks on my body."

"Nice. I ought to check you out myself," said El-Taco. She giggled again. "Speaking of checking things out, have your ancestry DNA results arrived yet?"

"Oh yeah. They came." Penelope looked though the emails on her phone, and opened her DNA results. "Look." She read through the list of ethnicities of her results that also displayed coloured regions on a map of the world; European, North-West African, Mediterranean too. "Oh my god, it's so diverse," she let out with excitement as she looked at the different coloured maps.

"Wow," said El-Taco. "Let me show you mine." He took out his Helix phone and showed her his results; European, Mediterranean, South American, North American, East and Central Asian.

"That's amazing," said Penelope. "So what were you up to today?" she asked.

"I had another recording session in the studio today. I got a few more songs written up. Toby's helping me out with everything else. Can't thank him enough."

"Cool. What are your songs about?"

"Oh... you know like errr, personal stuff, like pain and loss, and struggling to get by and things like that."

"What genre do you specialise in?"

"Hispanic rock now. It's more fitting and doesn't get old. I used to specialise in grunge metal but I moved on from that."

"Wasn't that like back in the '90s or something?"

"Yeah, my mum used to listen to things like that when I was a kid. Doesn't bring back the best of memories though."

"Why?" she asked.

"Well, uh... my Dad left us, and my Mum wasn't always there for me. She was always drinking and taking drugs and... she's been with other guys too. And I would always hear this kind of music being played, it was her favourite I guess. It grew on me."

"You know," said Penelope, "if you let me, why don't I make documentary about you?"

"Why?"

"To inspire people. You see, you could have done nothing and given up when things got worse for you. But you didn't. You committed to what you were good at. And now look. You're a local star in the making."

He laughed in her face. "A star? Yeah right."

"Hey. You may be no Elvis but at least it's a start. You see, my Dad used to give young people a chance to contribute to the community. Toby is helping you get your album made. So let me help you get all the publicity you need."

"Sure," he said. "I could do with a few more followers."

"And I could do with some food. I'm hungry."

They made their orders and got themselves some freshly made sandwiches and shared a bag of potato chips to go with their coffees. More people came into the coffee shop and ordered their lunch, since it was packed, they settled for takeaways. They left the coffee house together.

***

That evening, Toby helped Adee Lee put on her coat as they left the Al Franco Italian restaurant close to the city centre. She was wearing a red dress to go with her red hair, her red lips, and her red shoes.

"That was really nice, Toby. Thank you," said Adee.

"It's nothing," said Toby. He was looking slimmer. "Come on, I want to show you something." She held Toby's arm as they walked over to Helix Tower and went to the top floor. And then they made their way onto to the roof. The air was warm, and yet there was a cool breeze that came and went.

"What a view!" said Adee. She marvelled at the view of the city. "This is incredible." The cityscape was getting darker as the sun slowly set. The sun was a long and narrow orange semi-circle on the horizon, it gave the underside of the clouds a pink and purple glow while the rest of the sky turned a darker blue after every minute.

"We're just in time," said Toby. He took out the latest prototype of his Helix Camera Drone and Helix Tablet. He turned them on and activated the app. The drone spun its propellers and began to rise. "Check this out."

Adee looked at the screen on the tablet and watched as Toby controlled the drone and the camera with the buttons on the app with his thumbs.

"That's cool," said Adee. The drone went higher and higher as he filmed the sunset and the cityscape. "That is so high," she commented, "I could never have imagined how the city would look from above like this."

"There's more," said Toby. "Here, you wanna try?"

"Oh gosh, I wouldn't know what to do," Adee said with hesitation as she looked at the tablet.

"It's easy. Hold the tablet like this and control it like a remote control car. See." He handed the tablet over to her. She held the tablet horizontally the same way Toby did. She placed her thumbs on the controls.

"Ummmm... what do I do?"

"Try turning it. Here let me show you." He stepped closer to her and placed his hands over hers, and controlled the buttons with his thumbs on top of hers. She didn't flinch. She felt the warmth in his hand and relaxed. She watched the screen on the tablet as the drone hovered and moved around in different directions.

Soon, the sun set, the sky was dark blue and the whole cityscape was a collection of black blocks covered with white lights, flickering like diamonds on black velvet. The air chilled in the sun's absence. Adee stood closer to Toby and felt warm.

"This city is beautiful," said Adee.

Toby saw the reflection of himself on the shiny surface of the tablet, he remembered the words that Eric once told him: "Don't be a chicken. You gotta look tough. Put yourself forward with confidence." He swallowed and took in a deep breath though his nose.

"Is it? I wasn't looking at the city," he said. Her eyes met his. He slowly leaned in and kissed Adee's mouth. Her scent was sweet. "I'm curious," he whispered, "what perfume is that?"

"Helix for Her," she replied. "I chose this one to impress you." She smiled. He smiled back.

"I like it. I brought you up here to impress you."

"I already am." She put her arms around him and kissed him. They embraced and kissed with passion as the drone circled around above them.

***

That night, Jodie was in the kitchen of her apartment, cooking. She had tied her blonde hair into a ponytail, bare feet, and was wearing a white apron over her light purple night dress that had little pink heart shapes dotted around in different places. On the hob she was stirring a tomato sauce in a saucepan mixed with minced turkey with chopped up onions and peppers, green, yellow, and red. In the stock pot on the hob were aubergines boiled in water. Behind her on the counter was a baking tray ready for them. Her head turned back and forth from a cookbook she was following.

Just then, the front door opened and Cactus walked in, exhausted from a workout.

"Hey babe," he said. He sniffed. "Mmmm. Something smells good."

"You're on time," she turned off the hob.

"What's this?" he asked.

"I'm making dinner. Turkey stuffed aubergines." She took out the aubergines from the hot water with tongs, placed them on the baking tray and cut them open with a knife.

"Dayum," he said, impressed. A warm smile spread across

his face. She mimicked a warm smile back and then stuffed the aubergines with the turkey from the saucepan using a tablespoon.

"Since when were you into this whole housewife thing?" He asked.

"I don't know," said Jodie. "It's something my Mum used to do. I like it. I would help her out in the kitchen, prepare meals and... she always told me that I would be good cook one day. Now, come to think of it, it's something I always wanted to do. You know. Make a home." She said with glee as she stuffed the aubergines with care. He nodded.

"You know, my mama never did anything like this. She wasn't much of a cook. But coming home to see a meal prepared like this, it feels kind of... nice."

"Yeah. I guess." She laughed. Then she put the baking tray in to the oven. "There. They'll be ready in ten minutes. You go and take a shower. I'll get the salad ready. Your bath robe is on the bed."

"Dayum, girl. You're good at this already." He said with an bigger smile, impressed.

Later, Cactus emerged from the bedroom in his black bath robe. Jodie had finished making the salad. The aubergine bakes were done. She took them out of the oven. As soon as she noticed him:

"You can put your dirty clothes into the laundry basket next to the washing machine. I'll take care of the rest."

"Baby, you ought to relax. You work too hard."

"Really? I didn't think so. Come, let's eat." She prepared the table. He watched as she put the aubergine bakes on to the plates and then put the salad next to them. He smiled at her.

"Jodie."

"What?" She stopped to look at him. He walked over to her, put his arm around her and kissed her on the lips.

"Thank you," said Cactus and gave a little stroke on her arm.

"Cactus." She paused. "Malcolm, I love you."

"I love you too," said Cactus.

They sat at the table. Then Jodie almost forgot, she took out a bottle of red wine from a cupboard and then some wine glasses. He took the bottle and pulled out the cork with his hand with a pop. He poured them the drinks, they clinked their glasses, and enjoyed their meal together.

Chapter 39

One morning, as Penelope walked down one of the hallways of Coast City University, she was more nervous than ever before. She'd initially come here for women's studies when she was eighteen, but then transferred to politics. Her degree remained incomplete. She was twenty-one years old when she was arrested during her third year in this university. "God damn it," she thought, "I'd have graduated that year. Now I've come back, not as a drop-out but as a felon. I bet everyone here thinks I'm a failure. A laughing stock."

But then she tried to reassure herself that not every successful person went to university or had a degree. And not everyone was given a second chance, not like hers, especially when she has her daddy's business to run. At the age of twenty-four she represented one of the biggest corporations in America. She'd came to do a speech. She was in her dark blue Helix blazer and skirt that went down to the knee, white blouse, black shoes to go with her black stockings. She had straightened her brown hair that that went down to her shoulders. She wore her smaller framed silver glasses. She came complete with the silver Helix Inc. pin badge on her blazer, and a briefcase.

Her heart-beat was frantic, her sweat dampening her clothes and her stomach felt bloated, like she was about to throw up any minute.

As the students walked past her in the hallways some recognised her, while others had their eyes on their smartphones, probably Horus phones. Footsteps echoed across the hallway as students made their way to lectures, chatting away and laughing. Penelope tried her best not to look at them.

She cleared her throat. "I hope the vocal classes helped," she thought to herself.

Bzzz Bzzz her phone went. She took out her phone and looked as she walked on. She received a text from El-Taco. "Good luck, baby." It gave her a weak smile. She texted back.

"Thanks, babe."

She found the doors to the symposium, and stopped in front of them. "What if it's empty?" she thought. "What if everyone laughs at me when I walk in? Am I in the wrong place?"

She paused for one moment to take in a deep breath before pushing the door open. "No. Let's get this over with."

The symposium was packed. There were still students coming in to fill the seats, putting down their bags, taking off their coats and jackets, sipping away at their paper coffee cups, chatting away and gossiping among themselves. No one among this new generation of students recognised her. Probably better that way. Even if they did, would they care?

The wooden panels on the walls were dark oak. The thin carpets were dark grey, they gave off a strong shampoo smell, they must have been cleaned during the weekend. All the seats and the tables were a lighter oak wood colour. The white ceiling held fluorescent lights that were very bright. They made every surface shine so that if you looked at them for too long it hurt your eyes. The wall at the front was painted light grey and it had a gigantic white square painted in the middle of it for the smartboard. There were a few tables at the front, also oak, with generic black office chairs behind them. And right there, in the middle of the space between the front wall and the oak seats going up to the back was the podium, also oak. It had two thin microphones attached to it. Penelope noticed the two large black speakers hanging on both sides of the white square on the front wall. She gulped. "I hope they're not too loud."

Sitting at one of the desks preparing some paperwork was the Dean Jo Williams, a balding man in his mid-fifties. He had a dark grey suit with a light blue tie to go with his white shirt, dark grey trousers and black shoes.

"Ah, Ms Helix, how nice to see you here." He walked over to her. They shook hands.

"Nice to see you too. Please, call me Penelope."

"I'd like to thank you again for your cause. Your father gave a speech here on a few occasions, many students since then have joined Helix Inc. and had successful careers ever since. We have not heard of such success stories for years. I think your speech will give these students a light of hope."

"I hope so," said Penelope. With a weak smile.

"Please take a seat, I'll call you up in a moment."

He walked over to the podium. Penelope sat at one of the black office chairs, sat up and crossed her legs. She kept her head up and her back straight. "Alright everyone, may I have your attention please," said the Dean. The students took turns to mockingly tell one another to hush. Shhhh-shhhh-shhh. "Thank you." He smiled with a nod acknowledging their humour. The Dean began his introduction:

"Good morning everyone, today we have a very special guest..." His voice suddenly faded from her mind. At least the speakers were not too loud.

She had been craving the spotlight for years. To be honoured and respected. But not in these circumstances. "Do all these students know what I've done?" she thought. "That riot. Which one? My prison sentence? My online polls? The cringy articles I wrote? Did they see my apology video? My ad campaigns? ...Oh God, I gotta get out of here before they all start booing at me!"

As these thoughts whizzed around in her mind, it had dawned on her that this wasn't some social media profile where she can just type away an argument nor a place to just record on a camera and upload to the internet. This was real life. She had to talk to her spectators face-to-face. "Shit." A realization suddenly hit her. "Why did I have such a big breakfast this morning? I thought it would give me all the energy I needed to deal with all this. Now I'm gonna puke it all out on to the symposium floor."

"So without further ado, let's give our guest a warm welcome, Penelope Helix!"

The Dean began clapping. Most of the students clapped along while a small number remained indifferent.

"Oh God," she thought. "Stay calm. Stay calm." She walked over the podium with her speech, she gritted her teeth behind a forced smile. She looked around to acknowledge the students, make some eyes contact with a few of them.

"Thank you for having me," said Penelope.

A student wolf whistled at Penelope. She turned her eyes around the symposium, and spotted the sniggering youth in a hoody, sitting at the back row with his friends. "Why that little...!"

The mantra in her head went:

"Don't feed the trolls. Don't feed the trolls. Don't feed the trolls. Don't feed the trolls."

She started her speech. She cleared her throat. The Dean shook his head at the student with disapproval.

"Some of you already know me through the press and social media. As matter of fact I run Helix Press which is a subsidiary of Helix Inc. My brothers and my sister run the other subsidiaries of Helix Inc. Helix Motors, Helix Gen, and Helix Tech. I have noticed many of you carry Helix tech already such as the phones and laptops. Heh. Which goes to show how Helix plays a role in your lives. We at Helix take immense pride in our ability to innovate and contribute to an evolving market. To serve people's needs. Many people who work at Helix Inc. studied in this university and then moved on to work for us. As you can see, we are still growing. We are growing because this is the legacy of my father, Gerald Helix, and those who came before him." The symposium remained silent.

"Before I continue, let me ask a question: Who saw the documentaries we released recently? Please raise your hand." More than half of the students raised their hands.

"Thank you," said Penelope. "Those documentaries came into being because we need to remind ourselves what we stand for and why we do the things we do. They were made by the most hard-working and talented people in Helix Inc. And we are going to need a new generation of talent. Starting with you. To continue my father's legacy, the Helix legacy. We are passing down everything our forefathers gave to us so we can give it to you, to make the world a better place for our children. For a better future." She paused for a moment to give herself a quick breather.

"So we're going to need some new talent to work with our crew. So when you finish university you can start working for Helix Inc. and get your career started with us. We offer apprenticeships and internships. I am sure you all have fresh and new ideas. You can gain experience and start your career at Helix Inc."

"I think that's it," said Penelope. "I'll take your questions now."

A small number of students raised their hands. She chose one.

"What was prison like?"

"Let's just say you don't wanna go there. Best keep out of trouble." She chuckled.

"I'm learning to become a software engineer. Does Helix Tech accept graduates too?"

"Yes, whatever skill set you have to offer I'm sure there will be a place in Helix Inc. for you."

"Yeah right," one student smirked. He had a stencil cut out of Che Guevara on his t-shirt. "You just want cheap labour. What company doesn't. Graduates have less experience, that's why you wanna pay them less. Is that why you're here?" The Dean gave the student a disapproving look.

She paused to think of a carefully worded response.

"If we did that then nobody would have stayed at Helix Inc. for long. We believe in meritocracy; we have many seniors among us at Helix Inc. who have been with us for years. As I mentioned earlier, some of them were graduates who came from this university. As a result, we have flourished. Recently, we recruited a friend of mine named Jane Saunders, she graduated from here and now she works for us. In fact, she was the one who did all the research for the documentaries you saw. We couldn't have done it without her. If she can a massive impact for Helix Inc. and for this city, then you can do too."

To that, most of the students smiled.

"Today, many young people have been tossed on to the scrap heap and left behind. My father gave young people a chance. My father believed in opportunities. That is what made Helix Inc. great. And I too believe in that. Helix Inc. offers many exciting career opportunities for young people because my father believed that young people are the future. If we invest in the future, we make a better world for our children, for the future. Whether you seek a temporary role to gain experience or a permanent career path at Helix, there is something here for everyone. It's my father's legacy. The Helix legacy. And I plan to honour that legacy. We all win."

She stood away from the podium and opened out her arms, and made her call:

"Who's with Helix?"

There was a sudden shot of hands reaching for the sky. All the students were in favour.

***

Later that day, Jodie was in Saint Luke's Cathedral. She walked along the aisle slowly to marvel at the interior design. It was a grey day, there was no sunlight to shine through the stained-glass windows. She sat in one of the vacant rows of seats and looked ahead. There was a small number of people in the cathedral. In the corner of the cathedral stood an old nun who was talking to some visitors. Jodie looked around the cathedral, hoping nobody was watching. What if someone recognised her? So what if they did? That's a not a reason to hide in the shadows. She no longer cared. She wanted solace. Regardless, she looked forward and focused her sight to the front of the cathedral, admiring the stunning artwork of the polyptic: the paintings of the saints, of Mother Mary, and of Jesus. She took in a deep breath and exhaled. There was something about this place that made her feel good. She felt liberated somehow.

Two elderly women spotted Jodie. One looked amazed in joy, dressed in dark green, the other was cynical, dressed in dark red. They began to whisper among themselves.

"I say, that young woman over there looks like Jodie Helix," said the one in dark green.

"It can't be. A woman like that has no morals."

"Don't say that, Eveline. People can change for the better, you know."

"Humph! If that is her indeed then she has a real nerve coming here. A church, of all places."

"Come now, dear. There's no need to be like that. She only recently came out of prison. Perhaps she learned her lesson."

"Oh, don't be so soft, Martha."

"Let's go and talk to her."

"No, I can't." Eveline turned away and folded her arms.

"Very well then, I shall go and talk to her myself."

And so Martha timidly approached.

"Pardon me, dear. I don't mean to disturb you. But are

you Jodie Helix?"

"Yes. I am." She blushed.

"Oh, how wonderful to see you here."

"Really?"

"Why, yes, of course. You see, I've been an admirer of your mother and father for many years. They used to come here quite often. It has been a long time since a member of the Helix family has visited or prayed in this cathedral. It felt sort of empty. Might I ask what brings you here?"

"I don't know," said Jodie. "Hope, I guess. Maybe I was feeling lost. It's hard to explain."

"I understand, dear," said Martha. "Even if you don't find God, God always finds you." Martha smiled.

"Thank you," said Jodie.

"Now I shall leave you to your day, I shall pray for your family."

"I appreciate it. Thank you."

"Have you finished, Martha?" a cold voice boomed. It was the old woman in dark red.

"Eveline, keep your voice down."

"No, Martha, I have a good reason to give her a piece of my mind." Then she turned to Jodie and soured her face. "What makes you think you have a right to be here? Especially in a house of God after what you've done?"

"That's enough, Eveline." Martha placed both of her hands on her shoulders as she shook her head in disapproval. Eveline's harsh voice was so loud it made people look in their direction. Jodie swallowed. She shuffled her feet, unable to make eye contact with the old angry face chastising her. She pulled at the collar of her blouse as she looked around. Other people watched as she sat there and took it. "What do I do?" Jodie thought. "Get up and run? No! People will think I'm a coward. But I've got to stand up for myself. Stand up and do what? What do I say? No, just sit there. Don't say anything."

"You're a spoilt little brat," Eveline went on, "That's what you are. You're just pretending. I know a liar when I SEE

ONE! Just because your father was a successful businessman doesn't mean you are any better than us. You think you're so special? Huh? Do you think the world belongs to you?"

"Let's go now. You're making a scene," Martha urged.

The old nun in the corner watched in dismay. She placed a hand on the cross that hung down from her neck. "There's something wrong. I must intervene." But her feet remained rooted to the ground, she could not move. All she could do was watch.

"Ha! Your mother was a wonderful woman. But you. You will never be like her. You're a WHORE!" Jodie's jaw dropped. Stunned by what she just heard she slowly turned to face the old woman yelling at her while the other elderly woman tugged her arm.

"Eveline!" Martha gasped. "You've gone too far! Enough! We're going. Come on!" The spectators also gasped. Other members of the church looked on in shock.

"What?" Jodie replied disgusted. Her eyes began to swell up with tears. Her mind raced with thoughts. "What did you call me?! I have a good mind to claw your face right now! You bitch!" Her inner voice intervened– "DON'T! DON'T! Whatever you do, don't respond. People are looking at you. If you misbehave in front of all these people right now the whole world will know about it. Don't respond. Bite your tongue." She pressed her ankles together so hard the joints began to ache. At first she gave an angered look at the old woman, but then she turned her head away to face the front and close her eyes. Her jaw trembled as she tried keep her mouth firmly shut in fear of saying anything stupid by mistake. She pressed her ankles against one another even tighter. She bowed her head and clasped her hands tight trying to ignore the mad woman yelling at her. This was not a place for Jodie to unleash any fury. Her primal instinct was to lash out and attack. If this was any other woman, Jodie would have unleashed a string of insults from a snake-like tongue. But...no, that Jodie was in the past, not this time. She was not going to let some elderly woman humiliate her in front of everyone in Saint Luke's Cathedral, nor was she going to let herself be provoked that easily. "I will not react." Her rebellious inner voice went on, "I will not react. It's not worth it."

The nun could sense the torment within Jodie from where she stood. She too felt her chest tighten and her stomach shrink. All she could do was watch as she shook her head.

"Now look what you've done. Everyone is looking at us. Now come on. Let's go." Martha tugged at Eveline's arm one last time.

"Let go, already. Fine." She jerked her arm away "Humph!" She marched towards the main entrance. Martha sighed, she shook her head, Jodie opened her eyes to look at them. All Martha could do was mouth "Sorry about that, dear." Then she hurried along to catch up with the friend who stormed out. One by one the onlookers in the cathedral went back to minding their own business.

Jodie clasped her hands even tighter when she closed her eyes again. She felt her stomach shrink. Exhausted by the whole ordeal, she couldn't get up. Her ankles loosened. She was out of breath with a sinking feeling in her stomach. Her breathing became frantic. All she could whisper was: "God help me."

As if the nun heard those very words, she walked over to Jodie and leaned in.

"Are you alright, child?" asked the nun in a soft tone. Jodie looked up at the nun, hoping for a bit of mercy.

"I'm fine," Jodie's voice broke. She swallowed.

"You did the right thing. You held firm. You are a lot stronger than you think."

"I didn't do anything," said Jodie. She was about to break down. "I'm beginning to think coming here was a mistake." She was out of breath.

"Not at all. You are in the right place." She noticed Jodie's hands desperately clasped together unable to let go. "And I can see you are trying to pray."

Jodie look at her hands. She gave out an awkward chuckle. She couldn't release her hands. Her jaw began to tremble.

"But... I don't know how," said Jodie. She bowed her head in shame, then shook her head. Her voice croaked fighting back her tears. All the muscles around her shoulders were tense, they began to ache.

"It's alright, child." She placed one hand on Jodie's shoulder and one on her back as she sat next to her. "It's never too late." She allowed a longer moment of silence to pass. This gave Jodie the much-needed break to inhale and then exhale. She felt weak. "Here, I will recite a prayer and you can follow me. Yes?"

Jodie nodded. The nun's soothing voice helped her relax a little, it helped loosen her hands. The world's weight was lifted off her shoulders. The nun sat next to Jodie, looked ahead and placed her hands together in front of her as she looked forward and focused her eyes on the painting of Mary. Jodie sniffed, then placed her hands together gently as the nun did. The nun recited a prayer, slowly, one sentence at a time. Jodie repeated:

Our Father, who art in heaven,
Hallowed be thy Name,
Thy kingdom come,
Thy will be done on earth as it is in Heaven.

Give us this day our daily bread,
And forgive us our debts,
as we forgive our debtors,
And lead us not into temptation,
but deliver us from evil,

For thine is the kingdom,
and the power, and the glory,
for ever. Amen.

Jodie let out a huge sigh of relief. She relaxed. All her inner demons were let out. They got up.

"There," said the nun, placing one hand one top of the other over her stomach. "Feeling better?"

"Yes. Thank you," said Jodie with a grateful smile. She wiped the tears from her eyes with her fingers. She held back her urge to put her arms around the nun to give her a big hug as a grandchild would hold her grandmother. Instead, she reached out her hand for a handshake. The nun took it with both hands. They felt warm.

"May God be with you," said the nun.

As Jodie left the Cathedral, the nun watched. She drew a cross with her fingers and whispered to herself, "God bless you, child."

***

That evening, Toby was at a Helix Fitness Gym. He was on the cardio machine. Wet with sweat.

He had his eyes on the digital counters. So far he been on the cardio machine for 38 minutes. His initial goal was 30 minutes, but something made him go on. His heart was pounding against his chest.

"Come on. Come on. Keep going." He thought to himself.

Pushing and pulling at the bars with his arms while he peddled with his legs. His joints were aching. Sweat ran down his face. His vest had dark wet patches all over it. The laces on his trainers were done up.

"Make it forty. Make it forty," he said to himself. He watched each second on the digital counter. He had his wireless headphones over his head listening to motivational rock music to give him a boost.

"Keep going." He felt the pain the in his arm and his legs, he was out of breath. "Almost there." There was immense tension in his muscles as if they had rubber bands tightly wrapped around each muscle, squeezing them tighter and tighter. "Come on! Come on! Come on!" His inner mantra went.

The counter read:

    39 minutes and 50 seconds.

    10 seconds left...

    "10... 9... 8... 7... 6... 5... 4... 3... 2... 1... 0."

    40 minutes!

"Yes!" He slammed a hand on the big red button on the the panel in front of him. He threw himself onto the panel to rest, panting, soaked in sweat. He did it. He did cardio for 40 minutes when 30 minutes was enough. Years ago his fatter self couldn't have managed two minutes. But tonight, he did twenty times that. He felt uplifted with a sense of achievement.

"This is it Toby," he said to himself. "If you want to get better you've got to raise standards. This is no time for settling for crap. You have one life. Do it now while you still can." He took off his headphones and .took out his plastic bottle from a rucksack to drink water.

A group of youths on the other side of the gym recognised Toby and approached him.

"Hey Toby," one called out. "Remember me? Of course not, you only know me by my screen name. I am BaboonBoom. From Brooks Box Live. We used to play online together."

"Oh. Huh. It's been a long time." Toby let out nervous laughter. He had almost forgotten what most of the people he played online with looked like. "What's your real name anyway?"

"It's Terrence," He was mixed-race and in his early twenties. His black and yellow cap was facing backwards and it matched his black and yellow trainers and tracksuits. He had a gold chain around his neck and came complete with black gym gloves. He'd shaven lines in his eye brows. He allowed a pause, then began his roasting. "Hey man, how come you don't play anymore?"

"I don't have time. I have a multi-billion dollar business to run. Look at me. I've been overweight for so long if I carry on like this I won't live much longer. I've got to take care of the business my dad built."

"Not even one hour for like... one match on 'E-Football Manager'?" another youth whined.

"I told you, I can't!" Toby enforced it with a frown.

"You chickening out?" asked Terrence in a mocking fashion.

"No."

"You bailed out of a game midway, dude," another youth added.

"Yeah, what was so important you had to leave so suddenly?" another youth chimed in.

"I told you, I've a business to run. It's not as easy as you think."

"Bullshit. You can sit on your fat ass playing while everyone else is doing all the work making you money."

"I can't do both," said Toby. He sighed. "My gaming days are over. This company belongs to my dad and he gave it to me. I can't let him down."

"Sure," Terrence said sarcastically. "If he cares so much then why doesn't he come back?"

"Yeah, what's he hiding for?" said another youth.

"None of your business," said Toby.

"How about one game? Huh? Come on. Just one," Terrence pushed one last time.

"No. What do you want from me?" Toby confronted Terrence.

"I just want you to know that I have beaten every single game that has come out this year. I have more trophies than you now. Where are yours?"

"I don't have any." Toby bowed his head as he shook in a sheepish manner.

"Ha! How come?"

"I don't want them."

"Why? Because you're no longer the champion? Because I am about to become what you used to be? Come on, man. You can do better than that."

"Yeah," said Toby. "I'm in a game that is a lot bigger than what's in the comfort of a living room. This is big. This is not a video game, it's real life. You lose in one video game, there's always another one. But if I fuck this up my whole life will be over. This is what matters to me. In the future I will be making the games you'll be playing. You'll be on my platform. So you better watch yourself. You keep this up, I will delete your account and all your trophies."

"Ooooooooooh!" The youths howled.

BabbonBoom had no comeback nor a threat to throw at Toby other than: "Fuck you, fat-ass. You can have all the money you want, but you ain't getting laid."

"I already have."

"HA! With who?"

"Dude, didn't you know? He's dating that Blue Eagle reporter... uh... What's her name?"

"Adee Lee," Toby answered.

"Oh yeah, that cute red head."

"No way!"

"Ha! Hell no man, that relationship won't last," mocked Terrence.

"As long as she loves me, she will stay with me."

"If," smirked Terrence. "If." He repeated it one more time before he chuckled at himself and walked away. The rest of the gang of youths joined in with his laughter.

Toby tightened his fists, gritting his teeth behind his firmly closed mouth. "If?" Toby thought, "If? I'll give him 'if'. If he doesn't shut up I will grab that little dumbbell over there and smash his face with it– DON'T!" An inner voice intervened. "Control yourself. These kids can take out their phones and film you any minute. Don't even think about doing anything stupid."

"I finally got one over on Toby Helix," Terrence thought to himself. "See ya later, fat-ass," he called out before he left the gym. The rest of the gang of youths laughed along with him as they followed him out. Toby watched as he waited for the group to disappear. His eyes burned with rage. "I could have punched the guy. Right here right now. But that would have got me into a lot of trouble. Arrested for assault. My brand would have taken a hit. My father would be very disappointed, he may not be around but he'll know about it for sure." But all he could let out was "Phew." He wiped the sweat from his forehead. The tension in his shoulders eased off, his stomach felt contracted no more. He allowed himself to stagger towards a bench and sat down. He took his fitness gloves off and threw them on the floor as he leaned his head forward for a breather. His hands were wet, giving off a stench of sweat. He felt weak, as if all the energy was sucked out of him. "I did it," he thought to himself. "I stayed out of trouble this time." He drank the remaining water in his plastic water bottle and put it in his rucksack. He picked up his gym gloves and put them in his rucksack. He got up, pulled a towel from his rucksack and wiped off the sweat from his body, then threw it over his shoulder. He picked up his rucksack and then headed for the exit. That was enough for one day.

***

That night, Eric was driving home, tired from work. It had been a long day. But he wasn't alone, Marie sat in the passenger seat next to him. Also tired from a long day. They took a glance at one another and then smiled. He breathed in the scent of the leather seats, the pine air freshener hanging from the rear-view mirror, the petrol from the car, combined with her sweet scent. Something about this made him feel complete. He took his time as he drove home from work. There was no need to rush. The traffic wasn't as busy as usual.

Down the street he noticed a pub. He thirsted for a drink. His dry mouth salivated.

"Drink. I'm thirsty," he thought. "Then how will I drive home–No! Wait! ... Nah."

He turned his head away from the pub and focused on the road.

They stopped at traffic lights. Eric's car was at the front. But he wasn't alone.

To his left, was some guy in a white Brooks Car, blasting his techno music so loud. He revved the engine. He challenged Eric to race. He revved his engine again.

VRRROOOOMMMM VRRRROOOOOMMMM

"Oh no," Eric thought. "Not now. I am not racing. No way. Especially when I'm with Marie. I am not getting in trouble with the law again." He tried not to look at the guy in the white car and focused on the road in front of him. He tried to ignore the revving engine right next to his car.

VRRRROOOMMMMM! VRRRROOOMMMMM!

But it was impossible. It was too loud to ignore. Each rev made his lungs vibrate.

"Nope," he thought. "Nope... Nope.... No! I am NOT doing this." Then his thoughts switched from himself to the world outside his car. "Are there people watching? If so, how many are there? Have they recognised me already? Are they taking pictures of my car? Are they recording me on their phones again?... Fuck!" He took in a deep breath as he briefly squeezed his eyes shut to take a quick inhale and then opened them. "Don't look at them. Just stare at the road ahead. Fuck it. I ain't doing this again." His heart was beating so fast it was doing the racing for him.

Marie watched his every move. His face. His eyes. With

anticipation. "What's he gonna do?" she thought. "Has he really changed? Is this all a facade? Is Eric lying when he tells me that he's a changed man?"

His eyes turned to look at the driver– "DAMN!" He turned his head to face the front again. He could have sworn the grinning guy at the wheel was yelling. "What's wrong? You chicken?!" Mockingly laughing at him. Next to that driver was a blonde who looked like a supermodel. Eric recognised her. "Holy shit! An ex-girlfriend. From like...what... fuck knows how many years ago." And she's with him. Laughing at him.

The couple gave off a hysterical laughter, like a couple of hyenas, challenging him to a race with their music blasting out of their car disrupting the peaceful and quiet drive Eric wanted with his girlfriend. His neck became stiff. He tried to calm himself down with another deep breath in and then out. It was almost impossible to hear oneself think with all that cacophony going on around him.

But something made Eric turn to face Marie. Marie already had her eyes on him when his eyes turned to look at her briefly before switching back to the road. Her face was compassionate, but her eyes did all the talking. No... Not talking... WARNING. Her lips didn't move. And yet she somehow telepathically spoke directly into Eric's mind: "You better not, Eric. You better not."

The lights have been red for a while now, they were about to change any second.

VRRROOOOMM VRRRROOOOMM VRRROOOOMM

The loud engine next to Eric made his lungs vibrate again. Eric looked at the lights as he lights as he gritted his teeth behind his closed mouth. "Come on, change, damn you, CHANGE! Come on! Let's get this over with."

His mind was a tornado of thoughts.

"That driver thinks I'm a chicken. He'll tell all his friends about it. Hey, I challenged Eric Helix to a race and he chickened out. HAHAHAHAHAHAHAHAHA. Ex-girlfriend will spread rumors about me. Online AND offline. Haha. He embarrassed himself in front of his girl. The cops. Jail time again. Where's Dad? Helix motors. I will not fuck this up. Endless humiliation on social media. Marie's watching you. The pub. The laughing hyenas in the other car."

His inner voice was thrashing about violently in his mind. Combatting the demons in his mind, all he could repeat to himself. "Fuck off! Fuck off! FUCK OFF! FUUUUUCK OOOOFFF!!!!"

Green!

The tires of the car emitted a loud screeching noise, desperately letting the whole city hear its screams.

But it wasn't Eric's car. It was the white car. Smoke came out of the car's exhaust pipe, burning rubber. The white car shot off with a ZOOM. Without even going a few blocks a police car burst out of an alleyway and gave chase. "Heh. Busted already. That bastard." Eric chuckled to himself. His heart thumping against his chest like a big drum. Eric moved off at a steady speed, the muscles in his shoulders ached from the tension. "I bet Marie thinks I'm a real pussy now. Now the whole world knows that I chickened out of a race. It's gonna be all over social media any minute. But god damn it, at least I still have my company. Helix Inc. My father's legacy. I'm not going to jail. I'm clean. It's over now."

But there was nobody around who recognised Eric. Instead the show was on the couple who got pulled over. A few people stood around to film them on their phones, laughing at them in a mocking way. Oblivious to Eric's presence as he drove past.

Eric's hand was on the gear stick while the other was on the steering wheel. Then he felt a warm hand place on top of his, her soft pale skin sent a soothing energy that slowed down his heart rate. He began to relax.

"I love you," said Marie.

He turned to look at her, he took her hand, and kissed the back of her hand as he looked into her blue eyes. His eyes and kiss said it all. "I love you too." He didn't need to say a word. They made their way home. Eric drove home in peace and quiet.

Eric thought of something he'd read in prison:

"Ego is man's biggest enemy. A demon that seduces men is like an enticing woman, and the Heavens will throw everything at you to put you to the test to see if you succumb. Will you stand with Godly principles or will you submit to the devil? The choice is yours."

The Heavens tested Eric to his limit. He prevailed. He wanted a peaceful drive home with his girlfriend, and to have dinner with her. As ordinary as that may seem, it was a joyous occasion. His wish was granted.

Chapter 40

One night, Eric rolled around in his bed. He turned to the left. Then to the right. And then he woke up sweating. He rubbed his eyes with his fingers.

"Damn," he whispered. And then sighed.

Sleeping next to him was Marie Baker. She was naked and so was he. She was sound asleep with a slight smile. Dreaming, no doubt. Like a peasant girl who spent the night with the prince.

Eric sat up and looked at the digital clock. It was 4:03am. He picked up the remote control and turned on the gigantic TV in front of his bed. Blue Eagle TV was reporting on Horus Inc. and its announcements of a new car, a new smart phone, and a range of other new products.

"What the fuck?" he whispered. He soured his face at the news bulletin and then changed the channel. Then the TV showed a rerun of a programme that was aired earlier that night called 'Business Talk'. A group of business experts made speculations over what Horus Inc. was planning to do. Horus Inc., Crows Cars, Brooks Inc. and other companies have proposed a project and presented it to the Mayor, to build a new city-wide monorail system as a new means of public transport. They planned to import driverless electric trains from China to make it environmentally friendly and ease congestion. They showed 3D models, concept art, and computer-generated footage of how the whole thing would look once it's complete. They aim to complete this project in less than five years. Part of this project will be funded by taxpayers, but once the construction is done both the Mayor and all companies involved will profit from commuters. The Mayor was yet to approve the project and give them the green light for construction. This whole idea was initiated by Horus Inc. The business experts continued to talk about how further ahead of the game it was compared to Helix Inc.

Eric soured his face and gritted his teeth. He changed the channel. Just before a programme was about to start, a voiceover said "This episode was sponsored by Horus Inc." Irritated, Eric changed the channel again. Every time Eric flipped through the channels, all he heard was "Horus Inc.", "Horus Inc.", "Horus Inc." He growled through his teeth. In a sudden fit of rage he turned off the TV and then threw the remote control across the room where it smashed and the batteries scattered around the floor. Marie woke up.

"Eric? What's wrong?" Asked Marie.

Eric didn't answer. He stared ahead with a sulk.

"Eric?" Marie asked again. She placed a hand on his arm. Her touch removed the cold stare from his face. His attention went back to her. It softened him somehow. He exhaled and put his hand on hers.

"It's nothing. Go back to sleep," said Eric.

He got up and made his way to the bathroom, and washed his face with cold water. He let out a deep breath. When he got out of the bathroom he looked at the cityscape, and there it was, Horus Tower in the distance, with its yellow sun symbol, it glowed like an orb in the middle of it. Eric frowned with irritation.

"You son of a bitch," he whispered as he glared at the needle tower. "I'm gonna fuck you over."

At that moment, he heard a bzzz bzzz coming from the coffee table. He walked over and picked up his phone. A message from Jodie read: "Can we talk when you're free?"

"How about now?" Eric messaged back.

She called him.

"Hey Eric."

"Hey Jodie."

"Can't you sleep either?"

"No," said Eric. "It's everywhere I go now. Horus this, Horus that." He looked out the window again to glare at the needle tower. "It's haunting me like a fucking ghost."

"I want to beat them as much as you do."

Then they heard a bleep bleep.

"Hold on a sec," said Jodie. There was brief moment of silence. "It's Penelope."

"No. Not now," said Eric.

"She wants to talk too," Jodie replied.

"I'm not having her shouting in my ear at this time of night," said Eric.

"Deal with it!" said Jodie. "She's our little sister."

Eric sighed.

"Okay fine. Put her on," said Eric.

"Hello?" a voice squeaked.

"Hey Penelope," said Jodie.

"Hey Jodie, I couldn't sleep," said Penelope.

"Tell me about it," said Eric.

"Eric? You too?" asked Penelope.

"Yeah," Eric replied.

"Listen guys, I couldn't sleep so I've been up all night on social media promoting our campaigns. No matter how hard we spread the word Horus is getting more publicity and more followers than we are. It's driving me crazy!"

"Tell me about it." Eric repeated with a chuckle.

They heard another bleep bleep.

"Hold on," said Jodie.

"Hello?" A voice mumbled.

"Hi Toby," said Jodie.

"Hey Tobeee," Penelope squeaked.

"Hey guys," said Toby. "I couldn't sleep.

"I was expecting that," Eric laughed.

"No no. Listen. I just had this bad dream. It was really bad!" Toby said as if he was out of breath.

"What did you see?" asked Jodie.

"Well, there was us, out in the middle of the city when all of a sudden there was an earthquake and then a giant skyscraper burst out of the ground. It grew so tall it reached the clouds. It was so fast. And then another skyscraper burst out. And another. And then another. Like, all of Coast City, was nothing compared to these giant towers. And that's when it happened. The earthquake got worse, the road we were standing on cracks open and right behind us was Dad's tower falling over us. We fall through the giant crack, it swallowed us. We were screaming as we fell into a deep dark pit. Helix Tower collapsed and sealed it shut. Everything went black. And all I heard was... screaming. And then I woke up."

There was a long moment of silence.

"Hello? You guys still there?" asked Toby panicked.

"That was the exact same dream I had!" said Penelope.

"Oh my god. Me too," said Jodie.

"Holy shit," said Eric.

"What? All of you?" asked Toby. "We saw the same vision?"

"Yeah," Eric replied.

"What do you think it means?" asked Toby.

"More competitors I guess," said Penelope.

"With bigger towers," said Eric. "Look at Dubai. It's one

tall skyscraper after another. It's madness over there. At this rate, we are going to need a bigger tower."

"No that's not it," said Jodie. "I have a feeling it's Dad. This dream. It's trying to tell us something. I can't make it out. I fear something awful is going to happen if we don't act now."

"But what can we do?" said Toby. "We're doing our best to keep Helix Inc. running. In Dad's absence."

"Do you think... maybe... something has happened to him?" asked Penelope.

"I don't think so," said Jodie. "My guess is we are missing him."

"I think so too," said Penelope.

"We've got to think of something," said Toby.

"We better get some sleep first," said Eric. "We can't think when we're like this."

"But it's morning," said Toby.

"It's the weekend," said Eric.

"Yeah, let's not tire ourselves out right now," said Jodie. "We'll get together on Monday and see what we can come up with. We should talk to Gosia too."

"Sure," said Penelope.

"Okay guys," said Jodie, "Goodnight." Then she chuckled. "Well, good morning."

"Yeah, bye for now," said Toby.

"See ya guys later," said Penelope.

"Bye," said Eric.

Eric let out a sigh of relief. He turned off his phone. When he looked outside, the light of dawn revealed the colours of the cityscape. They were no longer black blocks. Among them stood the Horus needle tower with its glowing yellow orb. The sky faded from navy to a lighter blue and there was a yellowish-white line that spread across the horizon. And then the sun revealed itself. Rays of sunlight burst from behind the building into Eric's eyes. Like a carefully aligned constellation, the sun was right behind the Horus needle tower, and its sun logo was aligned with the centre of the sun. Eric looked away and whispered to himself. "God damn it, Dad. Where are you?"

He exhaled once more, this time he felt relaxed. Talking to his brother and sisters seemed to have relieved him of all the stress he'd felt from the night. He went back to bed. Feeling his presence, Marie snuggled up to him. Eric held her in his arms, and then closed his eyes to get some sleep.

Chapter 41

The following Monday morning had a dark start, dark grey clouds sealed the sky. It looked as though it was about to rain. The siblings stood quietly as the elevator made its way up to the top floor of Helix Tower. They all leaned against the elevator walls, arms crossed, looking down on the floor.

"Yo Eric," Toby broke the silence. "I saw that monorail project on TV. It got me thinking. Suppose Helix Tech and Helix Motors build bigger drones that can carry people. You know, like an air-taxi. Once we get them built all we have to do is construct helipads on top of some buildings. That means we can create a private drone service for the wealthy. It may not be the most accessible, but it's the only way we can compete against the monorail project. But in order to do that we're going to need the Mayor's approval first."

"Maybe. I don't know," said Eric. "I can't think right now."

"The Mayor will approve the monorail project. I know it," said Penelope.

"I know it too," said Jodie. She placed a hand on Penelope's arm. "The only thing we can do now is find a way to beat Horus."

"But how?" asked Penelope.

"Helix Inc. was the best corporation before. We're going to make it the best again," Eric said with determination. He clenched his fist. A few moments later the elevator doors opened and they made their way down the corridor. The two bodyguards stood by the doors of the CEO office.

"Hold it," said the bodyguard with the long blonde hair.

"Huh?" Toby let out.

"We want to see her," said Eric.

"She wants to be left alone," said the guard.

"Why?" asked Jodie.

"Classified," the guard replied.

"Is she alright?" asked Eric.

"She doesn't want to speak to anybody right now. You have to wait until she's available."

"That's not like her," Toby said. "What are you hiding from us?"

"Listen up ya'll," said the black guard who stood with his arms crossed. "We're not going to debate. She doesn't want to see anyone. Those are orders!"

"But this is urgent, we have to see her!" Penelope raised her voice.

"And what is this urgent matter?" asked the blonde guard.

"Classified," Jodie parroted with a smirk. The guards looked at one another for a moment. Then sighed. The blonde one took out his walkie-talkie.

"Ma'am. The siblings are here. They want to see you."

"Let them in." Gosia's voice was heard.

The guards opened the doors with their cardkeys. The siblings walked in. The guards followed and locked the doors behind them.

Gosia was in her seat at the CEO table leaning on her hands. She didn't even raise her head to look at them. No smile. No greeting. She looked pale. The dark grey clouds outside were visible through the floor-to-ceiling windows, it made the room slightly dark despite the limited daylight.

"Take a seat," said Gosia. Her voice was cold. She didn't even gesture. The siblings obeyed. They sat down and listened carefully. First, Gosia cupped her hands over her face while she took in a deep breath and then she placed both palms in front of her like a poker player revealing her cards.

"I'm afraid I have some bad news." She wasn't bluffing. "I recently learned that I have cancer."

The siblings' mouths gaped open, they had the look of horror. There was a long moment of silence until Eric broke it.

"Uh... what kind of cancer?"

Gosia opened the desk drawer and took out a piece of paper. It was a letter from Coast City General hospital.

"To be precise," said Gosia. "it's Acute Lymphoblastic Leukemia. A-L-L for short. It says here that I have Philadelphia chromosome mutation. Apparently it's an aggressive disease." She sighed and put the paper on the desk.

"May I?" Penelope reached out her hand to read it. Gosia nodded, Penelope took the letter and read it.

"Is there a cure?" asked Eric.

"No," said Gosia. "I looked it up. Bone marrow transplants are a common treatment but they often fail. Besides, it's in its late stages already. There is no cure."

"But there must be!" said Penelope.

"If there was, we wouldn't be having this conversation." Gosia replied.

"Gosia, we're going to do everything we can to help you." Jodie said with determination.

"Please," she said. "Don't worry about me. I don't want to be a burden on you."

"You are not. It's thanks to you we have come this far. We are going to do everything we can to help you." Jodie replied.

"Thank you, but there is nothing you can do," said Gosia. Jodie was angered by that response.

"Oh yeah?" Jodie got up and marched over to where Gosia was sitting.

"What are you doing?" asked Gosia.

Jodie placed her hand under desk until she found the red button and pressed it. The panels at the back of the office opened. And then the red curtains opened up to reveal the painting of Katherine Helix.

"Our Mother died of cancer. Remember that?" said Jodie.

"We couldn't save her," said Eric.

"This is our only chance," said Penelope.

"Dad's not around," said Toby. "If we don't act now, it will be too late. You're the only family we have."

"Don't worry. We'll think of something," said Jodie.

Gosia could not help but smile as tears filled eyes and rolled down her cheeks. Her voice broke.

"Thank you." It was all she could muster. She quickly wiped her tears with her hands. "Come here," said Jodie and embraced her. She held her close.

"We don't want to lose you," said Penelope. She walked over and embraced them both. She couldn't hold back her tears. Toby didn't know what to say. He too walked over and put his arms around. And finally, Eric, not wanting to feel left out, joined in with the group hug.

Outside, the dark grey clouds could no longer hold themselves, they relieved all tension by pouring down heavy rain onto the glass windows.

Chapter 42

The sun had set. It was a long day at work. Eric drove his dark blue Helix sports car after he picked up Marie from work. He was quiet throughout the journey. He looked at the road the whole time. No smile appeared on his face. He didn't even look at her or say "Hi." This made Marie puzzled. As Eric drove along the main roads of the city, she waited for him to say something. He tried to focus on the road but then all kinds of thoughts began to whizz around in his head; it was at that time it occurred to him how cars on roads were like healthy cells in blood vessels, all part of the anatomy of a city like Coast City and how it was part of a healthy economy. Healthy economy? Healthy cells? Anatomy? Oh no. Cancer cells. And then his mind was haunted by images of his sick mother, the tragedy of how a beautiful woman like her withered away as the cancer cells ate her alive on the inside like millions of tiny monsters. Death. Time. Running out. He tightened his grip on the steering wheel. He gritted his teeth but he didn't allow them to be shown. It was the only thing he was able to control at that moment. With all these these thoughts spinning around in his head like a tornado, Horus Inc. was forgotten. He had bigger priorities. Marie frowned at Eric in puzzlement at first but then she gave a sympathetic look and tilted her head. "Maybe he had a bad day," she thought. The awkward silence lasted long enough.

"Eric, what's wrong?"

"Nothing."

"You seem to be in a bad mood," said Marie.

"No. I'm not."

"Do you realise you didn't even look at me when you picked me up? Or say hello?"

"Okay sure. Hi." He turned his head to give her a quick glance and his eyes went back on to the road.

"Something's up. I know it. Otherwise you wouldn't be so cold."

"I'm not being cold."

"Eric, whatever is bothering you, you can tell me."

"It's nothing. Really."

"Well if it's nothing, you wouldn't be like this."

"Look, Marie. What are you getting at?"

"You have a problem, Eric. You don't want to tell me? That's fine. But I'd rather walk than be driven by a zombie." She folded her arms.

"Very funny."

"Drop me off here."

"No. We're almost there."

"Please Eric, you're not being yourself right now. At least let me give you space."

"I'm fine! Okay?!" He yelled back.

"No you're not." She gave a firm reply. "If you were you wouldn't be like this."

"Shut up already!" He yelled again.

"Pull over," she commanded.

Eric finally obeyed. He swerved the car over to the pavement where he brought the car to a screeching halt. She got out of the car and closed the door without saying goodbye.

The door slam snapped Eric back into the real world. He turned his head to watch Marie walk off. He covered his face with his hands, took in a deep breath, and exhaled slowly. He punched the steering wheel. "Shit! I did it again! I'm such an idiot!" With haste he got out of the car, he left the key in the ignition and the engine running, with its bright white headlights still on. Only an idiot would do that in the middle of a big city like Coast City, it's not like it didn't have anyone who would seize such an opportunity of stealing the car like that in such a moment. Eric knew that, but he didn't care.

"Marie." She carried on walking. It was her turn to give the silent treatment. The air was cold as the wind blew. "Marie. Wait." He called out even louder. He ran over and stopped in front of her. He placed both hands on her shoulders. "Marie. I'm sorry." Her eyes looked into his. Her face was as cold as the night itself. She still had her arms folded. "I shouldn't have snapped at you like that." Her sternness vanished.

"What's wrong, Eric? Why don't you want to tell me?"

He sighed. "It's... it's Gosia, she's got cancer."

"Oh... that's terrible."

"My mother died of cancer too."

"I'm sorry."

"Gosia may not be my Mum but she has been our only support since we came out of jail. It stinks. All of it. Like a ghost out to haunt me. I watched my mother die and now it's all happening again.... and... and..." He was lost for words.

"Is there anything I can do?" asked Marie.

"No. But know this, I am going to fight tooth and nail to save her."

Marie unlocked her arms, leaned forward, placed her hands on both sides of his face and kissed him passionately on his lips. She looked into his eyes.

"I love you, Eric. I will support you no matter what happens."

Eric said nothing, he pulled her closer and they embraced as they both exhaled. It soothed them both. They felt warm in each other's arms. As Eric held Marie close to her, he smelt the sweet scent in her blonde hair which was mixed with Helix for Her perfume. He breathed her in deep. She held him tighter too. As they embraced, Eric slowly opened his eyes and saw the car he left behind.

The front headlights of the car looked into his eyes. While its engine hummed, the flares of the headlights shined into his soul as if it was talking to him. "Good move, Eric. You did well." To that, Eric could only smile. He kissed Marie again. She gave him a warm smile and took his arm as he led her back into his car. He opened the door for her, she got in, and then he closed the door for her. He ran to the other side of the car and hopped in. "Come on, let's go home," said Eric. He gently put his foot on the gas and the car resumed its journey, merging into the night traffic.

***

Jodie and Cactus were sitting at their dinner table. Jodie leaned on her hand while she stirred the peas on the plate with her fork.

"Wassup baby?" asked Cactus.

"Nothing," Jodie replied with a cold tone.

"Pfff. No need to be so moody."

"I'm NOT moody. I... I ... I'm just having a bad day, that's all."

"Maybe I can make you feel better," said Cactus.

"Don't bother."

"Man. What the fuck's your problem? Why you giving me the cold shoulder?" He leaned back in his chair and showed his palms. To that Jodie slammed her fork on the table.

"Gosia's got Cancer!" she screamed. "OKAY?!" She paused to let that sink in. Cactus's frown disappeared. "When I was a kid my mum died of cancer. We hardly saw Dad ever since. And now that he's gone and Gosia's got it too and if we lose her I'm scared we're going to lose all of Helix.... I ... I feel so lost."

She put her face into her hands and began to cry. "Jodie... I'm sorry," he said.

Her crying said it all: "Hold me." He got up and went over to her and held her in his arms. Jodie began to cried harder. She pressed her cheek onto his hard shoulder.

"I feel alone," said Jodie. Tears rolled down her cheeks. "I'm scared."

"You're not alone, baby. You got me."

He held her while she let it all out. He stroke her soft blonde hair as he breathed her in. Then kissed her forehead. He wished he could do anything to make this sadness go away.

***

Penelope was sitting on her soft couch, tapping away at her laptop. Her eyes were focused on the screen. El-Taco walked in bopping his head back and forth like a pigeon. He had his headphones on while he listened to some tunes he recorded. He paused his music and took the headphones off.

"Hey baby, when we gonna eat?"

"Not now," she replied in a cold tone. Her eyes stayed on the screen.

"Uuuuh, yeah, well I'm hungry. I don't feel like going anywhere either." He paused for moment to see if he could get a response from her. She didn't even look at him. "We can get a delivery." He said with optimism. That made Penelope roll her eyes in annoyance and she let out an irritated sigh.

"You do what you want."

"Gee, baby. No need to be so bossy."

"Look!" She took her eyes of the laptop and ignited her red eyes at him. "Can't you see that I'm busy here?!" she snapped back. "Just go away!"

"What the hell's your problem?"

"It's not ME!"

"Then what is it?" El-Taco grew annoyed.

"Gosia's got cancer you fucking idiot!" she screamed. "Can't you see I'm sad." Her voice broke. "Can't you see that I am hurting?" Tears flowed out of her eyes. She took her glasses off and put her face into cupped her hands. She cried. El-Taco watched for a moment to let a moment pass for her.

"I'm sorry," said El-Taco. She carried on crying. "Baby, you said you're hurting, but... at least let me make you feel better."

"I'm sorry. I don't know what came over me." She wiped the tears with her hands. He sat next to her and pulled her towards him. She relaxed when she felt his warmth. She sniffed.

"Cancer killed my mum, and I'm scared that I'm gonna lose Gosia too," said Penelope. She broke down into tears.

"You're not alone. I will always be there for you," said El-Taco.

He couldn't think of anything else to say. Penelope put her arms around him tightly as she continued to cry.

***

When Toby got home after work he took off his suit jacket and tossed it aside. He sat down on his new leather couch to allow a deep sigh of relief the day was over. He sat quietly in his living room for while. He looked around at the quiet place he was in.

His apartment was neat and tidy. The walls were painted dark-greyish blue. Canvas printouts of the biggest video game franchises he liked were tiled next to each other as they hung on the walls. The crown molding lights were white. The floors were oak laminated flooring. He had the glass cabinets installed. The same ones Eric had in his apartment. All of them displayed his video game trophies and his favourite video game merchandise, from plush toys to action figures. All of them seemed like a distant memory. Relics from the past. He got up to take a look at them. He ran his hand along one of the steel frames that held the glass. "It was just a hobby," he thought to himself. Former gaming champion now trying to be a CEO of Helix Inc. He chuckled at the thought. But then he thought of his mother. Had she not gone she probably would have encouraged him to do something else. But what? He could not answer. The thought saddened him. Had cancer not killed her she would have been around to guide him. At least Gosia gave him the kick in the ass he needed. Still, he blamed himself. But then, had he taken the chance his father had given him all those years ago he would never have been in prison. "Man, I'm such an idiot," he said to himself.

He went into the kitchen and looked in the fridge. It was empty. He sighed with annoyance.

"Damn. I forgot," he said to himself. He didn't feel like cooking or going out for any late-night shopping either. He went back to the couch and sat down. He looked through his phone. How about some takeaways? Nah. Not getting back into junk food. He noticed he had some unread messages when all of a sudden his phone rang. The ringtone made him jump.

"Hello?" Toby answered.

"Toby, I've been messaging you." It was Adee Lee. "I was beginning to wonder if you had gone off on me."

"No. Nothing of the sort. It's just that I didn't get a chance to respond. Or know what to say at the time.

"Are you okay?"

"Yes, well, no uhh, I, mean we, at Helix. We're in real deep shit right now."

"Why? What's happened?"

"Adee, our Vice president Gosia has got cancer."

"Oh my God, that's terrible. Vice President? Are you close?"

"Not exactly. She's the only person who has a connection to Dad. She knows the business better than we do. If we lose her we are doomed."

"I'm sorry to hear that. Can I come over?" she asked.

There was a pause.

"Sure."

A short amount of time later there was a knock at the door.

He would have jumped for joy at a sound, knowing a delivery man was bringing him food. But not this time. He didn't want any junk food. He wanted her. This time he felt a sense of relief that someone was coming to see him. To soothe him. He opened the door and there she was. Adee had the look of worry of her face, in her eyes was compassion.

"Hey," said Toby. He forced a smile.

"Toby," was all she could muster. She put her arms around him and they embraced. As they held each other, it felt as though time began to slow down. He felt better.

Chapter 43

The next day, the four siblings were already seated in the boardroom when Jane Saunders and Daniel Crawley walked in. They all had their briefcases out in front of them. The four of them had the look of determination on their faces. Eric tapped his fingers on the table while he waited, Jodie sat cross-legged and shook one of her feet, Penelope was trying hard not to bite her nails, a habit she still hadn't been able to rid herself of. Toby fidgeted with his collar and his tie. Jane and Daniel had briefcases of their own, which they placed on the table and opened them.

"Okay guys. Time is running out," Eric began.

"We need to act now," said Jodie.

"Jane, did you find anything?" asked Penelope.

"Yes, I know several people attending Coast City University right now. They gave me access to their archives. Everything they could find."

"What have you got?" Penelope asked. Jane took a folder from her briefcase and looked through some bits of paper.

"I got some good news and bad news," said Jane. "I asked about Gosia's condition in regards to Acute Lymphoblastic Leukemia and... there is a cure." The four siblings looked at Jane with immense hope. They held their breath, and listened. Frozen. "Diseases like this have been cured with Cannabis oil by administering cannabinoid extracts orally to the patient. But there are side effects, they cause nausea due to its bitter taste. But overall they fully recovered."

"Cannabis?" asked Toby.

"Yes," said Jane.

"Wait. Why would Gosia say there isn't a cure?" asked Jodie.

"Because cannabis is illegal here in Coast City. Even in medical form," Jane replied.

"Damn!" Eric slammed a fist on the table. "But where did that report come from?"

"Canada," said Jane. "Toronto to be specific."

"Then we have to take her there," said Jodie. "I propose we start a new company... Helix Pharma. We are going to find ways to raise money to open laboratories for research and develop medication for all."

"But how can you conduct research with a drug that is illegal here?" asked Daniel.

"Then we are going have to open Helix Pharma in Canada," said Jodie.

"Hell no! I ain't going near that stuff again," said Toby. "I went to jail because of that. Remember?"

"You don't have to," said Jodie. "I will. With Helix Pharma

open in Canada, Helix Gen will have to do without me for a while until we get Gosia cured."

"But even if you developed a medicine for cancer patients with cannabis, how can we bring it here without getting arrested?" asked Toby. "Like... can we not somehow get it legalised here?"

"Maybe... maybe if I talk to the Mayor," said Penelope.

"Good idea," said Eric.

"Better yet, we should all go and appeal to him," said Penelope.

"Sounds like a good plan so far," said Daniel. "Now, is this going public or are you going to keep this quiet?"

"We're going public," said Penelope. "I asked Gosia about it and she said she's okay with it. Hopefully to raise awareness about cancer and how poorly funded the research is."

"Do you guys have any ideas?" asked Daniel.

"I've got one," said Toby. "El-Taco. His online popularity has been growing lately. I think it's time we released his album. After that we can throw a charity concert."

"That sounds like a good start. What genre of music does he specialise in? Do people like it?"

"He makes Classical Rock now. With a touch of Hispanic. It sounds really cool," Toby said with excitement.

"Very good," said Daniel. "We could make merchandise of him made like t-shirts, wristbands, Limited Vinyl releases, special edition deluxe CDs, autographed merch, clothing like hoodies, vests and bandanas."

"Perfect!" said Penelope with excitement. "We can do a documentary about him too. His life. His passion for music and how he got to where he is today." She turned to Jane. "You can interview him. And make some kind of biographical documentary and we can release on Helix Live."

"Can you do the same for Cactus too?" asked Jodie. "This will show how Helix gives everyone equal opportunities and how we help these people turn their lives around.

"Yes," said Jane. "Speaking of equal opportunities, we can

show the world how diverse we are too. Then we spread the word online like a... hashtag We are diverse. This will be the biggest marketing campaign ever."

"Diversity. Of course." Penelope let out with excitement. "I will publicise our ancestry DNA results. This is proof."

"Yeah. No other company in Coast City displays theirs either. This ought to attract more customers," said Toby.

"Hmmm. But I'm not sure what I could do on my end," said Eric. "What can Helix Motors do?"

Daniel paused to think. "You can host a charity event too. Like a Car Meet. Helix Motors has been around for so long, why don't you bring out the oldest models up to the latest and let people see them. That's one idea."

"Yes. We could do that. But isn't there something people can do to participate in? You know like make them feel they are doing something?" said Eric. He put his hands on his forehead and then pulled his hair back with them. "Damn it," he exhaled.

"Eric, chill," said Jodie.

"Give me a minute," said Eric. He got up and walked over to the windows to look outside. He felt the gentle cold breeze on his face as it came through a window that was left slightly ajar.

"But is this campaign exclusive to Helix only?" asked Daniel. "After all, health concerns all of us. And I'm sure many people we know and love have died from cancer. So how about we approach other companies. Perhaps we could ask them to join us in our campaign to fund money for research. A big collaboration."

"I don't see why not," said Penelope. "I could always get in touch with Horus Inc.'s Head of PR... what was her name... Yazmeen Shaheed. Maybe we can work together."

"Go for it," said Jane.

"I'll see if I can approach Barry Brooks, see what he says," said Jodie.

"I can get Adee Lee from Blue Eagle TV to cover our story,"

said Toby. "They recently started buying our camera drones for their live broadcasts. They might as well use them for our events."

"Good plan," said Daniel nodding. "What do you think, Eric?"

Eric didn't answer. He stood by the window and stared at the traffic below. From where he stood they looked liked rows of toy cars. "Eric?"

"That's it," said Eric. He said as he turned around and looked at everyone in the boardroom. "A convoy! A cruise around the city. Anyone with a car can join us. We can do like... uh... a circuit around the city and then we drive in. To participate, they can sign up with a donation, an amount of their choice. And they could win the latest model Helix car!"

"That sounds good," said Daniel.

"Smart move," Jodie smiled.

"We can get our Helix driving students to join us too," Eric added.

"Perfect!" said Toby. "This will be perfect filming material for the drones. Blue Eagle TV will put us all over the news for sure."

"This will sure give us a publicity boost," said Daniel.

"I have an idea too," said Jane. "Why don't we create a crowd-funding platform? That way everyone can donate as much or little as frequently as they like. As long as we keep them up to date, of course."

"Jane, you're a genius!" Penelope said loudly.

"What about the press?" asked Daniel. "People are going to want to know why you want to go ahead with this initiative. I'm guessing you spoke to Gosia about this. Does she want to keep her condition private?"

"We've already spoken to Gosia. She says it's okay to broadcast her condition. That will raise awareness and will get people to join our cause," said Penelope.

"Looks like that settles it then," said Eric.

"Once we get the support of all other companies and the

Mayor's approval, there will be no stopping us," said Penelope as she held out a fist.

"We're gonna save Gosia. And we are going to kill cancer before it kills anymore." Toby stood up.

"Yeah!" everyone shouted out loud.

The agreement was mutual. One by one, everyone put all their notes and ideas into their briefcases and closed them. Eric went over to the window and closed it, the cool breeze was cut off. He looked down at the city again. "Come on, Eric." He heard a voice call out to him. Everyone else had already left the boardroom while only Toby stood by the door and held it open for him. Eric hurried over. And shut the door behind him.

Chapter 44

The Mayor sat at his desk fiddling with a small flagpole of the United States. He placed it next to his phone.

The four siblings entered his office, the Mayor gestured and then they sat in the seats opposite him. All four were looking their best, in their suits. Sitting up straight, they tried to look calm. Jodie and Penelope sat with their legs crossed tightly, a little nervous. Eric tapped his forefinger on the arm rest of his seat. Toby scratched the surface his armrest with his nails resisting the urge to bite his nails, "Don't be nervous," he thought to himself. "Not now, not in front of the Mayor." The Mayor gave them a welcoming smile as he linked his fingers on the desk.

"I have to say it's nice to see all four of you in my office at the same time," said the Mayor. "So what is this matter of great importance?"

"Mr Mayor, we need your help," said Penelope.

"With what?" asked the Mayor.

"Someone we know has cancer," said Jodie.

"Leukemia," Toby added.

"And who is this someone you know?" asked the Mayor.

"It's Gosia," said Jodie.

"Oh, I am so sorry. I've known her for years. A loyal employee of Gerald's. I know he would be upset by such news."

"But there is something else, there may be a cure," said Eric.

"Is that so?" asked the Mayor. "Then what do want you my help for?"

"We want to start a new company," said Jodie.

"Helix Pharma," said Penelope, "So we can carry out research. Research about... cannabis."

As soon as the word 'cannabis' passed her lips the Mayor unlinked his fingers and placed both hands on the desk with a stern tap, and frowned. "That is out of the question."

"But sir, wait," Eric urged, "We are talking about human lives here."

"I am not legalising any drugs in my city," said the Mayor. His voice was stern and cold. "I am aware of the many campaigns hellbent on legalising recreational drugs using the healthcare tactic. We don't make laws on a whim. These things require certainty."

"We're not talking about recreational drugs, sir," said Eric. "It's for a medical purpose."

Penelope joined in. "And there is evidence too. In Canada there is–"

"This is NOT Canada, Ms Helix. This is Coast City. Do you know what will happen if I allow marijuana to be sold on the market? Do you realise that crime will go up? Don't you know how many people's lives have been ruined by drug addicts?"

"Sir, we're not addicts, we're professionals. We–" Penelope tried again.

"I will not discuss this matter anymore," said the Mayor. "Before we conclude is there anything else?"

"What about research?" Penelope pushed one more time.

"You can by all means start your own pharmaceutical

company. As long as it complies to Coast City standards and regulations. But if you want to play with drugs, you will have to go elsewhere. Do you understand?"

The Helix siblings nodded.

"Thank you for your time Mr Mayor," said Penelope. Eric led the way out. They closed the doors behind them and walked along the hallway. Their hearts sank. They couldn't keep their heads up. It would have been completely quiet except for the sounds of their footsteps that echoed across the hallways of the Coast City Town Hall. Penelope covered her mouth with a hand.

"What's wrong?" asked Jodie.

"I don't believe it." Penelope lowered her voice. "What we are doing is for a good cause. And he didn't want it." Penelope shook her head. "I mean, doesn't he remember Mum? Did he not think for one minute what Dad went through? I thought they were friends... and... and...oh I don't know. I'm so confused." Her eyes began to fill with tears. Jodie put an arm around her and pulled her towards her.

"It don't make sense to me neither," said Toby. "If it was over recreational drugs then yeah I would understand his position. But from a business perspective the demand is pretty high and it would save the lives of more voters."

"We ought to tell the press about this," said Eric bitterly.

"No!" said Penelope. "Whatever you do, don't badmouth the Mayor. Don't tarnish his image. He will hate us even more for it."

"Then what do you suggest we do?" said Eric.

"We say nothing. We did not approach the Mayor about this. Okay? This is our safest bet right now."

"Then how are we supposed to get the people on our side?" asked Eric.

"As we discussed before, in our meeting," said Jodie. "We've got to focus on our projects and show the world what we are doing. Let our work do the talking. And then we let everyone else decide for themselves."

"Are we still going ahead with writing to executives asking them to collaborate with us?" asked Eric.

"Yes, we are," said Penelope. "We've got to try. I've got my formal letter ready for Horus Inc. I'm mailing it this afternoon."

"Good move, Penelope. I better get mine ready," said Jodie. "I'm writing to Barry Brooks"

"I'll write to the CEO of Dove Bank and Crow Cars," said Eric.

"I'll write to the CEO of Blue Eagle TV," said Toby.

"Good," said Penelope. "Until we hear from them, we finalise our plans and we keep quiet."

They emerged from the quiet Coast City Town Hall into the noisy city outside. People and vehicles went about their lives on the streets and roads. The smell of exhaust smoke from cars, the sounds of footsteps of hundreds of people, oblivious to their plans. The siblings looked up at skyscrapers that towered above them all. There was mutual feeling among themselves. A whole world was waiting for them. It was time for them to make their mark.

***

Dear Yazmeen Shaheed,

It is with great pleasure that we invite you and all at Horus Inc. to collaborate with us as we at Helix Inc. are working on a new project.

We are conducting research to find new ways of treating cancer and one possible cure we have found and want to develop further is the use of cannabis oil.

To fight this deadly disease we need to work together. I'm sure you and many others know someone who has lost someone to cancer.

Although not permitted in Coast City, we will be conducting our research in Toronto, Canada where we will open our laboratories.

We hope this is a positive step in the right direction. Once we obtain enough evidence for our new pharmaceutical drugs, we hope to get it legalised here in Coast City so that it will be accessible to anyone with a prescription from doctors.

I say with hope this will bring us all closer together and build a strong relationship. I look forward to hearing from you soon.

> *Your Sincerely*
> *Penelope Helix*
> *CEO of Helix Press.*

***

Dear Penelope Helix,

On behalf of Horus Inc. we thank you kindly for your invitation to collaborate on such a project.

We are flattered you reached out to us for support. It sounds like a noble cause therefore we congratulate you on your initiative. However, after careful consideration, we sadly have to decline for the following reasons:

Though your research may be carried out in a different location, cannabis is illegal here in Coast City. In order for it to be legalised here it would require resources for political campaigning for which there may be no guarantee.

We prefer to distance ourselves from political matters since they have the potential to damage our reputation as a business, especially regarding cannabis.

There will be unforeseen consequences not just for our business and customers but for all of Coast City. It is a risk we simply cannot take.

The location is understandable however we don't view research in Canada for a medical drug a suitable use of our time or resources.

Researching cannabis as means of finding a cure for cancer sounds like flawed concept. Even if we were to collaborate with you on such a project, there is simply no guarantee of its success.

We would like to thank you for your understanding. We wish you luck on your endeavour.

Yours Sincerely
Yazmeen Shaheed
Head of PR, Horus Inc.

***

Penelope took the letter from Horus Inc. home the day it arrived in her office. She didn't know why. Confirmation perhaps? Whatever her reason was, she stood in the living room of her apartment that evening to read it again and again. The more she read it, the more disappointed she became. She took out her phone and messaged her siblings to ask them if they had heard from the companies they sent their letters too. They all replied, they too were given the same mutual response. They all declined. No one wanted to collaborate with them.

At that moment, Penelope felt all alone. She felt a kind of pain in her chest. Thousands of thoughts spiralled in her mind. She suddenly felt weak. She loosened the grip of her phone and the letter as her arms began to drop to her sides. To her the whole world began to slow down. Another letdown. Another disappointment. The thoughts that whizzed around her head were like ghosts haunting her: Helix Inc. lagging behind Horus Inc., Gosia's condition, her missing father, the regret of not accepting his offer, the three years in the detention center, the riots she started, her mother's death.

Finally her hands fell as low as they could as they hung by her sides. She dropped the letter and her phone onto the floor. She felt weak. She bowed her head down in defeat and looked sad. Exhausted. Emotionally and physically drained, the only thing she wanted at that moment was a hot shower. She forgot all about the letter and her phone and left them on the living room floor. She dragged her feet as she made her way to the bedroom and grabbed a towel. She put her small framed glasses aside. She stripped naked and walked in. The hot water that fell on her face and the water vapour gave her some kind of soothing relief. It eased off all the tensions somehow. She leaned back against the tiles on the wall and sat down into the small pool of water at the bottom of the shower. She placed her arms over her knees, bent her head down and began to cry. It would be the longest shower she ever took.

After her long hot shower, she went back to her living room and picked up her phone and the letter. She was in a white bath robe and had a white towel wrapped around her head. She looked at the letter again, this time with a clear head she went over to her laptop on the coffee table and turned it on. She sat on her couch and called Jane.

"Hey Jane, got a minute?" asked Penelope.

"Sure. Any news?"

"The Mayor doesn't want to know. We sent letters out to companies asking them to work with our cannabis research and they declined."

"Which ones?" asked Jane.

"All of them."

"Those bastards!" Jane let out with rage. Penelope sat calm and unmoved.

"We are alone, Jane. Looks we have to do all this all by ourselves."

"Damn right we will!" Jane growled with anger. "We're gonna put them in the papers. We're gonna name them and shame them!"

"No," said Penelope in calmer tone.

"What?!" Jane exclaimed.

"We will not tell anyone we approached anyone for help. We're telling the press we are doing this whole thing ourselves. Whoever wants to help us is more than welcome. That's all," said Penelope.

"But Penelope, doesn't all this bother you? Aren't you outraged?" asked Jane. Penelope sighed.

"I don't have time or the energy to be angry or bitter anymore. All we can do is our best. That's all I can say. Our focus now is to get our projects out there and spread the word online," said Penelope as she massaged her closed eyelids with her finger tips.

"Sure. You take care, okay."

"You too," Penelope said and turned off her phone.

She forgot why she turned on her laptop, so she turned it off and sat on her couch with her knees close to her chest and put her arms around them in silence. When she tilted her head to one side she noticed her new plants on the white window sill, she took out a hand and caressed one of the leaves with her fingers as one would hold the hand of a loved one. She admired the colour and the texture of the leaf. This plant was one of several that had been with her since she came out of prison, it was like a familiar face she saw when she came home from work. And yet she felt something was missing in her life. Just then El-Taco arrived and walked in through the front door. She turned to face him. Relieved to see not just another familiar face, a lover. She no longer felt alone.

"Hey babe, wassup?" He smiled at the sight of her.

"Nothing." She looked at him with a weak smile.

"Rough day?" he asked.

She only nodded. But the rest of her said it all, "Hold me." He went over her, pulled her up from the couch, held her close and kissed her on the mouth. He pulled off the towel from her head and allowed it drop on the floor to reveal her short brown hair. And then he undressed her bath robe. She stood naked and put her arms around him and held him close as they kissed passionately. He picked her up and carried her into the bedroom where they made love.

Chapter 45

Two days later, the sky was partly cloudy, the Helix siblings dominated the papers again. The newsagent piled up the newspapers around his kiosk. All of them had pictures of the Helix siblings in their suits, while some had pictures of Gosia the Vice President. The headlines read as such:

"Helix Crusade"

"Helix vs. Cancer"

"Cancer: Helix VP Diagnosed"

"Cancer Haunts Helix Again" This one had an old photo of Katherine Helix next to a picture of Gosia.

"Read all about it." The chubby newsagent called out. "The Helix sibling are at war with Cancer. Helix Vice President is diagnosed with Cancer. Read all about it."

Kamau the black street cleaner pulled his wheelie bin along, and greeted the newsagent with a tip of his hat.

"How ya keepin?" asked the black street cleaner.

"Keeping well. Yourself?"

"Same here," the cleaner replied. Then he looked at the newspapers. "Aw man. I remember when the news broke out about Katherine dying of cancer. Poor Gerald wasn't the same since. It looked like he aged another twenty years. I don't think he ever got over it."

"Would you?"

"I don't think so, my older brother died of cancer years ago. He was my guide. To see him waste away like that..." he paused, then shook head in pity.

"I know the feeling, my sister-in-law died recently, breast cancer. My wife is devastated. She was her twin." The cleaner sighed.

"The one thing the haves and have-nots have in common is that sickness, loss and pain do not discriminate. May the lord have mercy on us."

"Amen."

"You think the siblings will succeed with their campaign?" asked the cleaner.

"I certainly hope so," said the newsagent.

"Hmm." Nodded the cleaner. "I wish them luck. Have a good day," Kamau tipped his hat again and pulled his wheelie bin.

"See ya." The newsagent then resumed his calling. "Read all about it. Read all about it."

***

Penelope did everything she could to announce all upcoming events to as many people as she could with her online presence, from advertising on billboards to TV adverts. Using her social media profile she kept everyone up to date about Gosia's health as it was carefully monitored everyday and the progress of their research for a medical drug. She set up a crowdfunding platform so that people could donate to help fund the research.

Everyone was invited to join their cause to volunteer. To enhance their invitation further, Penelope uploaded the ancestry DNA results to the Helix Inc. website. And then she created the following hashtags that trended across the internet and spread their message around the world.

#Diversity

#WeAreDiverse

#Hope

#Fightcancer

A few days later, Eric converted one of the Helix Motors showrooms into a Car Museum, mostly featuring Helix cars and vehicles. On display were old prototypes as well as failed and discontinued designs as part of the story of Helix Motors's progress. Different models of Helix cars were displayed for each decade from the 1920's until recent years. Thousands turned up to the see the older models, the launch was a huge success. Eric even had the latest Helix station wagon on display for people to sign up for a prize draw.

Toby released his drones and sold thousands, ready to fly them and film the convoy around the city along with Blue Eagle TV who also bought the drones for their channel. Many signed up to the new Helix Live channel where people uploaded recorded footage and broadcast live events. Discount points for Helix products were given to people who used Helix Tech, the popular the footage that had the highest amount of views the higher the number of points they received.

The following week, Eric lead the convoy of cars, bearing the Coast City flag and the American flag. Some of the drivers cheered with joy as they blasted their horns. Vehicles of every shape, size and colour followed Eric's blue Helix muscle car as he lead them around and through the city. Among them were the popular vloggers Bumblebee Charlie and Ladybird Linus. They sat in a Helix truck next to the driver in a cowboy hat, Charlie filmed themselves on their new Helix smartphone broadcasting their fun convoy experience while Linus filmed with his drone that hovered above the truck.

Next came El-Taco's concert. With his new band and his improved singing voice, he took Classical Rock to a new level. Somehow he made it cool again. A whole crowd of fans and new followers flooded the Coast City Arena in their thousands. But the Helix siblings had a special surprise for the crowd, a makeshift wrestling ring was built on the stage, and out came Cactus dressed in his iconic black and green wrestling costume. He had a green mask on. The crowd cheered on the famous wrestler and inspiring fitness coach. But then, out came a another wrestler, dressed in black and red, the villain. And El-Taco announced his name, Cancer. The crowd booed and hissed at the wrestler with a red mask. To that, Cactus and Cancer began their rehearsed wrestling match. The fight was exciting to watch, Cancer broke a chair on Cactus who was unfazed, he grabbed Cancer, threw him into the ropes and when he bounced back, Cactus struck him in the face with his elbow making Cancer fall flat. Cactus then conducted his next act, he climbed up one of the corner padding and threw himself into the air to perform his move, the Body Slam. Then he grabbed Cancer's leg and bent it backwards, Cancer slammed his hand on the ring in submission. *Ding Ding*. The match was over. The crowd cheered again. El-Taco ended his concert with a few more songs. His merch was sold out.

Among the crowd were members of a Canadian band named Stickleback, a bunch of guys who specialised in Post-Grunge and Hard Rock. They were dressed in black leather jackets with spikes, black jeans, and wore t-shirts bearing the symbol of their band, the Stickleback fish that had spines sticking out of their fins. The band logo resembled a cartoony blue fish. They were known for their blue mohawk hairstyles. Impressed with his music, they invited El-Taco to join them in their North American Tour to be featured as a guest performer throughout Mexico, Canada, and USA. El-Taco accepted with excitement. The band also invited Cactus to perform his wrestling act. He also accepted. This boosted Cactus's and El-Taco's popularity. Thousands more followed them on social media. The demand for Cactus and El-Taco action figures soared. The Helix siblings approached Osprey Toys to make toys for them. Again they refused to make toys of celebrities that 'glamorised drugs and violence' even though they made countless toys of action heroes and movie that did those very things in the past. So the Helix siblings approached Rebel-Print and offered them a contract to make toys for them using their latest 3D-printing technology. Once again, Osprey Toys's loss was Rebel-Print's gain. Their sales and profits sky rocketed. The sales helped boost the research for Helix Pharma.

Jane Saunders followed El-Taco and Cactus as they toured around North America, she hired a team of students from Coast City University to film their performances. They made documentaries about the lives of El-Taco and Cactus, how they went from failed nobodies who overcame their struggles, and then became greater versions of themselves. Once the documentaries were made, they were uploaded to the internet for the whole world to see. This increased their popularity across the world. Thousands more donated to the crowdfunding platform while many others bought El-Taco's music and merch as well Cactus action figures and fitness gear.

Throughout the following year, the Helix siblings fought tooth and nail to get Helix to the top of the market. But Horus Inc. was still the top corporation in Coast City. The Helix siblings did everything they could to make Helix Inc. better. Eric thought it was time to add motorcycles to Helix Motors, so they began to research and develop electric motorcycles. Toby announced and launched a new service, the Helix Cloud Service where people could store their data online and he promised absolute privacy and no information would be shared with anyone else. Penelope launched apprenticeships for young people and visited universities to inspire them to join Helix Inc. Jodie stayed in Toronto to manage all the costs and fund the research for Helix Pharma, meanwhile she monitored Gosia's health in a private hospital. After many tests, the scientists and doctors were certain that this new medicine was going to cure Gosia.

And then, one day, the scientists at Toronto finally made a breakthrough. After a few more tests, they found a cure for cancer with cannabis oil. They gave a sample to Gosia, one small dose at a time until all the cancer cells were killed off. Gosia stepped out of the hospital and returned to Coast City in good health. Jodie later followed her for a press conference in Coast City while she left the scientists and doctors to run the laboratory in her absence. The people of Coast City were stunned.

The Helix siblings did the unthinkable, not only did they find a cure for cancer, they outdid their father Gerald Helix. They'd made history.

***

The morning that came after Jodie and Gosia's Helix Pharma press conference, the Helix siblings were all over the papers again. They dominated the headlines. Their pictures were everywhere. Joy across the city was unconfined. Every citizen walked the street with hope and optimism. Everyone was in a better mood as if the whole city took a happy pill. The sky was blue and clear, the sun shined with immense brightness as though the Heavens smiled upon Coast City.

The chubby newsagent piled all his newspapers neatly around his kiosk and arranged them in a way that resembled skyscrapers in a city. There was a big smile on his face.

"They did it!" he cried out with excitement. "They did it! THEY DID IT!" He waved his arms around with joy. Today, his "read-all-about-it" script was out the window. It was all unscripted euphoria. "Helix destroyed Cancer! We're saved!" He let out at the top of his voice.

The black street cleaner arrived with a bounce in his walk whistling Vivaldi's Summer as he pulled his wheelie bin along the street. He too had a big smile on his face. He looked at the papers. His face lit up with amazement. All the newspapers had pictures of the Helix siblings in their Helix suits while some had Gosia on them. Even the front covers of magazines. The headlines read:

"Helix Victory"

"Helix Beat Cancer"

"Helix Triumph"

"Gosia Cured"

"Helix - 1, Cancer - 0"

"Cure for Cancer Found"

One newspaper had the headline "Cancer Got Pricked!" and it had a picture of Cactus the wrestler holding Cancer the wrestler in a headlock. The Helix spiral logo was on almost every page and surface. Other newspapers had pictures of El-Taco with his band, and a whole crowd that filled a landscape.

"Oh my God!" Kamau exclaimed, "This is the best news I heard in a long time! They sure put Coast City on the map." The newsagent and the street cleaner hugged as they as they jumped up and down with joy and laughed. One customer walked over to the kiosk with a smile.

At that moment a new Helix Station Wagon drove passed by with its windows rolled down. The driver threw his fist out with joy, he honked the car as he cheered. *Beep-Beep-Beep-Beep*.

"Yahoooo! I won the car! Ha ha haaaaa!" shouted the driver. He was an old man in denim overalls and a grey shirt. Probably a plumber. "Took my kids to school with this beauty. Ha ha!"

The newsagent and the street cleaner waved at the driver.

"Have a great day, sir," said the cleaner.

"That was the car Eric had for the prize draw. I signed up for that too. My donation went to that Cancer research."

"I donated too," said the street cleaner.

"I guess we all did it. The whole world knows about us now. Thanks to the siblings. Man, what a difference they've made. Well done to them. Thank the Lord."

"Indeed," said the street cleaner. "Later today I'll be going to the cathedral to praise the Lord."

"Me too. Those kids have come a long way."

"Amen to that."

"See ya later, Kamau."

"Have a good one," said the street cleaner, he tipped his hat and pulled his wheelie bin as he whistled his tune.

Big Billy was at the new Edge Hotel. He sat at the new bar in his shirt and tie, with a neatly trimmed beard. On the table he had newspapers and magazines, next to them were a few photo frames. With a pair of scissors, he was cutting out pictures of all the Helix siblings. He put them into the frames and then he hung them next to the other pictures of his opening ceremony with Barry Brooks. All four Helix siblings had a picture frame of their own. His celebrity picture collection was complete. He stood back to look at all the pictures, placed his hands on his hips, a big smile appeared on his face, and then he nodded with satisfaction.

The Helix siblings were the talk of the city and all of America for days. Radio shows and online podcasts constantly talked about the Helix siblings and how each one of them changed and how they came together and performed some kind of miracle. Along with them were mentions of El-Taco the singer and Cactus the wrestler. Despite Horus Inc.'s desperate marketing campaign online and offline, nobody even mentioned it. They were sidelined for the time being. However, Helix Inc. and Horus Inc. were neck and neck close. Their share prices became equal. Helix Inc. had finally caught up.

Chapter 46

One morning, the Mayor was in his quiet office reading through some paperwork that was laid out on his desk. He sat back in his leather chair as he held one document in his left hand while he held a pen in the other. He pressed the lid to his lower lip as he read it. The sun shined through the window and the open brown wooden shutters. It gave him and his office a little sense of warmth. After a while he put the pen down and reached out for his cup of coffee to drink. He resumed his reading, once he finished he put the paper down and signed it. He sat back and relaxed smiling to himself. He looked at the calendar hanging on the wall. The next Mayor election was months away. He nodded to himself. He brushed his grey hair back with his fingers, took a deep breath and exhaled, and then he got up to look out of the window. He marvelled at the cityscape as he smiled. He made a mental note of each building and of who lived or worked in each building. He went over the years in his mind of all the people he met, reminiscing all the political campaigns and the gatherings in his mind.

Then he turned to look at a handful of photographs on a table close to one of the windows.

"Ah yes," he whispered to himself. Each one held a memory as he picked up one photograph at a time, with him accompanied with acquaintances. One with Troy Barker, CEO of Dove Bank receiving funding for his election campaign. Another photo with Harold McKay, CEO of Crow Cars in a show room. Another photo with Barry Brooks, CEO of Brooks Inc., when they hosted a fashion show together. And then he picked up the photograph with him and Gerald Helix when they were in a charity ball for the Coast City General Hospital. He sighed, put the photo down, and went back to the paperwork on his desk.

A short while later he began to hear a noise coming from outside. He raised his head from his paperwork, got up and went to the window to look outside. His mouth gaped at what he saw. There was a massive crowd of people outside the Mayor's office.

"By God. What is it this time?" he whispered to himself.

The crowd began chanting their slogans. As more people joined, the chanting grew louder. More people gathered as time went by. Protestors of every group joined in. Each one holding banners and placards of their own. All the familiar groups returned. The gays and lesbians had their rainbow flags. The feminists were clad in pink. The anarchists wore black. The environmentalists and vegans were in green. The communists and socialists were in red. The rest of the crowd were ordinary Coast City citizens waving the blue Coast City flag and the American flag. Soon all the streets near the Coast City Town Hall were flooded with people from every walk of life. United as one. With one voice. One goal.

"Legalise Weed! Legalise Weed! Legalise Weed! Legalise Weed!" they chanted.

"What do we want? Weed! When do we want it? Now!"

The banners and placards they held read as such:

"Save our families, Mr Mayor."

"Kill Cancer before it Kills us."

"Go Green, Grow Weed!"

"Weed Power!"

"Healthcare for all! Healthcare Now!"

"Referendum Now!"

The Mayor frowned as he observed the crowd in the streets below. He spotted a Blue Eagle TV van parked at a street corner and next to that were two familiar figures. He turned away from the window, picked up the remote control, and turned on the TV. He saw Adee Lee talking to one of the members of the crowd with her microphone while they chanted their slogans. He was a built man in his late thirties, in a postal uniform. He had dark brown hair, tanned with light brown eyes. His uniform was dark red and black with a white logo on it, a flaming bird crest with its wings spread with the letters PPS, underneath was the name 'Phoenix Parcel Service'.

"Good morning, I'm Adee Lee and I am here with Jonathan Hicks who created a petition on SignMyPetition.com. As you can see behind me, there are masses of people who signed the petition and are calling on the Mayor to legalise cannabis. So Jonathan what prompted you to start this petition?"

"I wanted to send a message to all the politicians out there that drugs like cannabis can be used for something positive," said Jonathan. "I wanted to do something good for mankind. Just like the Helix family. I mean, what they did got my attention. I think they set the precedent for a bigger cause. They inspired me. They did their part. They've done all the work. They saved a life. And, I thought, well maybe I should do something. It turned out better than expected. The initial goal was 500,000 signatures. But in a single week it was signed by 2.2 million people and it's still growing. I mean, wow, when so many people sign a petition like that so quickly, that tells me this means a lot to them." He showed the petition results on his Helix phone.

"I see," said Adee. "So why does this matter to you?"

"I have a family and I am concerned for their health. God forbid if anything happens to them like getting cancer, just like what the Helix family went through, I want to be able to make sure I can get them the help they need," Jonathan replied.

"There are other states and countries where cannabis is legal. So one would ask why not go there?" Asked Adee.

"I don't have the luxury to move to wherever or whenever I want. That's too much of an inconvenience for me. I have a job here. I have family and friends here. I lived my whole life in Coast City. Why should people have to travel far just to get the treatment they need when they can get it right here? And as you can see..." He gestured with his hand to the crowd around them. "I'm not the only one who thinks that."

At that moment, their conversation was interrupted by a woman yelling nearby.

"This is a HUMAN issue!" The woman's yell sounded familiar. "Healthcare concerns ALL of us." Adee Lee looked around to see who it was and then she spotted her. It was a familiar face. "Oh... thank you Jonathan. I hope you succeed. Okay viewers let's hear what the protesters have to say." She walked over to the protestor who she spoke to years earlier. It was the old woman who dressed as a hippy from the 1970's again. This time her long hair had gone all grey but she still had her large pair of glasses, a bandana made of plastic flowers, colourful shirt, brown waistcoat with laces, dark brown miniskirt and orange boots that went up to the knee. She still had her long and colourful necklaces made of different coloured beads and the large silver 'Peace' symbol.

"Hello," said Adee, " I think I've seen you before in a different protest. A few years ago?"

"Yes, dear. You did." The hippy woman replied with smile.

"So what are you here for today?" asked Adee.

"Simple. I want to weed to be legalised."

"And why is that?"

"Since cannabis can be used to cure illnesses, then I don't see why it should be banned. I say the legalisation is long overdue. We want to get on with our lives without worrying about illnesses that can kill us." Her voice became stern and her smile vanished. "Now let me ask you something." She pointed her finger at Adee and soured her face. "Which is worse? Knowing there is a disease that can kill you? Or knowing there is a cure for a disease that can kill you but the government won't allow it? Well I say the latter is much worse than the former. What right does the government have to deny us of a medicine that can cure us? Since when do they get to decide whether we live or not? Well I say NO to that! I hate it. Something has to be done. It's NOT RIGHT!" Then she turned to the camera and pointed. "And that goes for all of you politicians out there." She began to raise her voice again. "This is a human issue. You got that? When it comes to cancer, it's a matter of life and death. You better be listening because we will not sleep until we have our voices heard!"

The Mayor turned off the TV, put down the remote, and then he closed the shutters. He sat down on his leather chair, and placed both hands over his face as he leaned on his desk to take in a deep breath, and then exhaled. He tried to ignore the crowd. But the chanting outside dominated his office. He sat there and thought for a whole minute. He looked at the black telephone on his desk, he reached for it, but his hand stopped in mid-air before he could touch it. He could call the police to disperse the crowd, but he knew that would not win the people over to his side. Especially with an election coming up. He stopped to think for a few moments, and then he called his secretary.

"Get me the Helix siblings," said the Mayor.

***

Later that day, the four siblings were escorted to the Coast City Town Hall by Helix Security in their big black Helix MPVs. The siblings were dressed in their best dark blue suits. Each of them with a silver Helix Inc. pin on their jackets. Behind them was another black Helix MPV full of bodyguards. The siblings watched through the windows as they approached.

"Wow! Who would have thought it?!" Toby exclaimed. "The Mayor called us. He needs our help. I didn't think this would ever happen." Toby chirped like an excited child.

"It looks like he takes us seriously," said Eric trying to keep his cool.

"Maybe now he see us the same way he saw Dad," said Jodie. "You know, friends as well as business partners." She turned to look at Penelope. "Hey Penelope. How come you're quiet?"

"I can't wait to give him this," said Penelope. She held a black leather folder in her arms. It had a small silver Helix Pharma logo on it. "All the work we have done. All the research we collected. All the facts and figures he needs are right here." She paused for a moment. "I always wanted to make a difference. I always wanted to influence people to get the government to do something. And this is it. Today is the day I finally get to do it." She marvelled at the black leather folder as she held it. She caressed it like it was a precious artefact. She smiled with pride. The rest of the siblings joined in with their proud smiles, lost in a world of their own.

"We're here," said the driver. The siblings gasped when they saw the huge crowd outside the Town Hall.

"Oh my god!" Toby exclaimed. "Look at them. There's so many people here."

"They're cheering us on. I can't believe it," said Jodie.

The two vehicles parked as close to the Town Hall's entrance as possible. The bodyguards of the vehicle behind them came out and formed a circle around the first vehicle to make sure the siblings were protected. Another group of bodyguards split the crowd to create a pathway for the siblings.

"I'll go out first," said Eric. He positioned himself so that he could see his reflection in the rear-view mirror. He quickly checked himself and finger combed his hair. "There. I'm ready." The sliding door was opened.

The crowd was all smiles and excitement as they called out to the siblings, calling for them to come out so they could see them.

First Eric stepped out of the car with a big smile on his face. The crowd erupted with a loud cheer. He walked slowly with regality to marvel at the crowd before him. His heart raced. He raised his hand to wave at the crowd like a prince, and smiled at them. Then Jodie emerged from the car, the crowd cheered louder. She smiled and waved at the crowd as she walked. Penelope was about to come out of the car, when she felt a hand on her shoulder.

"Wait" said Toby. "Let me go next. I'm saving the best for last." Toby winked as he nodded at her. Toby then stepped out of the car. The crowd cheered again. In his excitement he threw both hands in the air waved to greet the crowd like a birthday-boy. This was the loudest cheer he ever had. To him this was better than any video game convention he attended.

And finally, when Penelope stepped out of the Helix MPV, the crowd cheered even louder. She stood still calm, collected, and smiled. Then she gently held up the black leather folder to show them like it was an Oscar trophy. To which the crowd cheered even louder.

Jodie walked closer to Penelope to put a hand on her back. "Look, Penelope. They love you," Jodie said with glee.

"Us." Penelope replied with a quiet voice. "They love us."

"Come on. Let's go in," said Eric. "We don't want to keep the Mayor waiting."

The crowd had their Helix phones out, took pictures of the siblings, while some filmed them live on the Helix streaming app. Encircled by their bodyguards, the siblings entered the Coast City Town Hall.

***

The crowd continued to chant their slogans outside. The Mayor stood by the window as the siblings entered the office. With the shutters re-opened he watched the city outside from his window. He turned to look at them to show that his face had no emotion. His hands were held behind his back. The siblings stood tall with pride before him, smiling. Looking and feeling pleased with themselves. They tried to contain their excitement. They were filled with immense pride in their achievement. Penelope stood in front with the black leather folder in her arms. The office would have been quiet had it not been for the crowd outside urging the Mayor to change his mind. The Mayor walked in front of his desk. His eyes darted from one sibling to another. Unfazed by their joy. He took in a deep breath through his nose and spoke.

"How did you do it?" said the Mayor.

"We put our heads together and committed to a common goal," said Eric.

Jodie, Toby and Penelope nodded. The Mayor joined in with the nodding in acknowledgment.

"I know why you did it," said the Mayor. "I am absolutely thrilled to see Gosia in good spirits. I am very pleased for you."

The siblings looked at one another with joy.

"However!" he boomed. The smiles on the siblings were wiped from their faces. His voice was stern, his eyes glared,

344

and his nostrils flared. "Do not think for one second that I am going to legalise cannabis in Coast City." He paused for a moment to let that sink in. "Do you realise how that makes me look now?" asked the Mayor. "Now do you see the consequences of your actions?"

The siblings were stunned. They stood confused with their proud postures gone. Rapid blinks with slight headshakes among them. Toby swallowed.

"But..." Toby said.

"Mr Mayor–" Penelope tried to reason with him.

"And YOU! Penelope. You promised me you were going to help me win the next election. How do you plan to fix this?" said the Mayor.

"But Mr Mayor, I can assure you," said Penelope. "This is going to help you."

"How?" said the Mayor. "Those people want an illegal drug on the market. And when I refuse, I will lose votes. Which means I will lose the next election!"

The siblings were stunned again. They dropped their jaws in shock. Jodie could take no more. "You..." Jodie said with a vengeful tone. Her eyes narrowed with rage. "I can't believe you are saying such a thing."

"Jodie wait," Toby said. He was about to put a hand on her shoulder, but Jodie jerked away to march over to the Mayor.

"We just saved a LIFE!" said Jodie. "We can save more."

"And ALL you can think about is VOTES?" Eric growled. He was beginning to fume, he took it like a personal insult. He folded his arms tight as he narrowed his eyes at the Mayor. Better to lock his own hands in place before doing something stupid with them.

"You said you wanted facts and figures before you put forward any legislation," said Penelope. "Well there you have it. On a silver platter. What more can you want? You can only win!"

"It doesn't work that way," said the Mayor.

"Hold up guys. Let's not get ahead of ourselves," said Eric.

He breathed through his nose, relaxed his arms and stepped forward to confront the Mayor. "You're not the one who lost family to cancer," Eric said to the Mayor. He glared into his eyes. "But we have." He paused. "They have." Eric pointed to the windows referring to the crowd outside. Their chants and slogans could still be heard. "The fate of their loved ones is in your hands. You're the one choosing not to act." The Mayor narrowed his eyes. "These people went through pain. Loss. Like we did. We don't want them to go through all that." Eric paused hoping the Mayor would take on board what he had said.

"If I allow this," said the Mayor, "then what will be next? Legalise amphetamine? LSD? All because a bunch of kids got bored?"

"You still don't get it, do you?" said Eric. "There is a difference between a medical drug and recreational drug!"

"We're saving lives here!" Said Jodie. "All you have to do is make it a prescription drug. There are ways around this," she urged.

"If we had this cure years ago Mum would still be here," said Toby. "And Gosia wouldn't have had to suffer. We wouldn't be having this conversation either."

The Mayor looked away.

"If I lose this election, I will hold you all responsible."

"What?" Toby gasped.

Penelope stepped forward. "Mr Mayor, I thought we were friends. Why would you do this?"

"I am no longer interested. Get out!" said the Mayor. The siblings shook their heads at the Mayor with disgust.

"Mr Mayor," Penelope said sternly. She took in a deep breath. "If you lose this election, it won't be because of us. It will be your own doing." She presented the black leather folder. "Here! This is for you." She put it on his desk. Eric smirked.

"Yeah," said Eric. "When you lose your voters, we will still have our customers." He looked right into the Mayor's elderly eyes and then grinned.

"Out, I said," the Mayor growled under his breath.

Once again, the Helix siblings left the Mayor's office disappointed. Eric lead the way as they closed the doors behind them.

***

Disheartened, they walked along the hallway slowly, almost dragging their feet along the way. Their faces were sad and they had their heads bowed down. And then they stopped to collect themselves.

"I need to use the bathroom," said Penelope.

"So do I," said Jodie.

The ladies split off and went into the ladies' room.

"I gotta take a leak," said Eric.

"Me too," said Toby. He followed Eric into the gents.

After the men finished off their business Eric leaned against a wall and crossed his arms. Toby paced around next to the sinks with his hands behind his back.

"I don't get it," said Toby. "Why would he not do it?"

"Politicians... they are all the same. Corrupt. Self-serving." There was an angry tone in his voice.

"Even so, I mean... we can save people's lives. If I was him I would have grabbed this opportunity with both hands. I would have had the people on my side. Especially with the election coming up," said Toby.

Eric's eyes narrowed in thought. "We need to expand. If Coast City has to miss out on a medical drug, then so be it. We'll provide them everything else. We may not have the power to change the government, but as a corporation we adapt to the market. After all, it's the people who decide where the market goes." He put one arm around Toby and raised his other fist in the air. "And WE will go with them."

"Wow," Toby replied. He popped a smile.

"Come on, let's go."

"Wait," said Toby. He looked in the mirror to adjust his tie.

"Ah yeah, I almost forgot." Eric also adjusted his tie and

then finger combed his hair brown hair. They left the bathroom.

When Jodie and Penelope entered the ladies' room, Penelope walked over to a sink, stared at herself in the mirror for a moment before putting her face into her hands. She sniffed. Jodie walked over to her.

"Are you crying?" asked Jodie.

"No. There's just something in my eye. Mascara I think." Penelope replied. Jodie put her hands on Penelope's shoulders.

"I'm upset too," said Jodie trying to comfort her.

"It's just that... I'm trying not to let this get to me. I don't want to feel like this but I can't help it." Penelope's voice croaked, her jaw trembled.

"Come here," said Jodie. She held her little sister tight. "Let it out." She felt Penelope's chest expand and contract.

"I feel sad too," said Jodie as she caressed Penelope's short brown hair and then let go. "Hey. Don't take it personally. You did nothing wrong. We did what we thought was best for Gosia. For everyone. If the Mayor doesn't see it that way then it's his problem."

"I guess," Penelope nodded. She wiped her eyes with her fingers and then sighed.

"Gosia is still with us. We couldn't save Mum, but we saved her instead," said Jodie.

"Yeah, we did," Penelope nodded.

"And we're going to save many others. They're waiting for us. Let's pull ourselves together and get out there."

"Yeah, we will." Penelope took off her small-framed glasses, wiped them clean, and put them back on. "Let's go."

The four siblings rejoined in the hallway. Their faces had switched from sadness to hope. They looked at one another, and smiled. They changed postures, held their chests high with pride. This time they had their heads held high in defiance ready to face the crowd outside with confidence. They left the building.

The crowd let out a loud cheer as the siblings emerged from the building. They smiled and waved at the crowd. Upon hearing the noise, the Mayor turned on the TV to watch the live Blue Eagle TV broadcast. To his confusion the siblings looked as if they had won a victory. They were encircled by their bodyguards again as they slowly made their way back to their vehicles. Adee Lee approached them with her cameraman.

"Excuse me, Blue Eagle TV. You got a minute?" she called out as she waved a hand. The siblings nodded, the bodyguards allowed Adee and her cameraman to walked into their circle. "Thank you. So how did it go? What did the Mayor say?" The closest members of the crowd hushed and listened with keen ears while the rest of them took pictures and filmed on their Helix phones. Some of them shouted out questions of their own:

"Is he going to legalise weed?"

"Will cannabis oil be allowed on the market?"

Penelope stood forward and spoke in a calm soft voice. Nothing like the way she spoke all those years ago.

"We just had a fruitful meeting with the Mayor," said Penelope. "The Mayor congratulated us on our achievements. He's happy for us." The other siblings smiled and nodded.

"Will it be available to the public?"

"Only to those who live within the jurisdictions that allow cannabis as a medical drug. Here in Coast City it is still illegal to be in possession of cannabis no matter what the use. We have to keep to the rules. We must show respect to the customs of Coast City. However, we at Helix Pharma can get them mass produced elsewhere as a medical drug. We are now launching a program to give patients care in places where it is legal to do so. As long as they are prescribed by doctors."

"So what does that mean?" asked Adee Lee.

"The same way Helix Pharma took care of Gosia Kowalski

in Canada, we aim to create branches a little closer to home. Anyone diagnosed with the same illness, we will treat them at an affordable price," said Penelope. To that the crowd cheered.

"But what about the Mayor?" asked a member of the crowd. "Why won't he legalise it here?"

"The Mayor is a good man," said Penelope. "We are positive he will do what's best for the city."

"But Ms Helix, surely you could have appealed to change his mind," said Adee Lee.

"It is not for us to dictate to the Mayor what he should and should not legalise," Penelope replied. "Our work will continue, we hope our research will find a cure for all cancers. This is the beginning."

The crowd cheered again.

"Thank you, Ms Helix," said Adee Lee. She and her cameraman stepped out of the circle and then the bodyguards slowly escorted the siblings to their Helix MPV. The siblings continued to smile and wave to the crowd. The siblings and the bodyguards entered their vehicles and left the crowd outside the Town Hall.

"Well? What do we do now?" asked one crowd member.

"They may be gone but the Mayor is still in there," said another.

"I say we carry on. We've got to keep trying. Get our voices heard!" A protestor shouted out.

"Yeah!" They all shouted in agreement. The chanting resumed:

"Legalise Weed! Legalise Weed! Legalise Weed! Legalise Weed!"

The Mayor turned off the TV and sat back down in his chair. He slouched and leaned into his hands while the chanting could be heard from outside. He took his time to take a few deep breaths. Then he leaned to his right and opened one of the drawers on his desk. He took out a an old photograph of himself, and his wife who held a little baby girl in her arms. He placed two fingertips on the picture of the baby. A tear dropped onto the glass. "Maggie," he whispered to himself. He sniffed. Then he stared at the black leather folder Penelope had left on his desk.

***

The work at Helix Inc. continued. With growing revenue, Helix Motors announced the design of a new car, the Helix Hatchback. Many bought their Helix cars with Helix Car Insurance. At Helix Tech, Toby developed a Cloud Storage Service with a monthly payment that enabled people to save huge amounts of their data online, and as an app that worked with all Helix devices. He announced that unlike Taurus, they will not share customers' data with anyone, not even the police or the government to ensure security and privacy. At Helix Gen, Jodie brought out a new line of clothing for mothers and pregnant women, a more family oriented ranged. All of them were made out of animal-free clothing which grew in popularity. At Helix Press, Penelope did everything she could to boost Helix Inc.'s online profile, from writing articles to online marketing to promote their products, informing Coast City of all their activities. Jane Saunders worked alongside her, providing apprenticeships and internships for youths and university students, giving them employment opportunities and investing in new ideas and talent to keep them ahead of the game. El-Taco continued his rock performances around America, selling his music and merchandise along the way, raising awareness of cancer. Cactus continued to work at Helix Fitness as a fitness coach while running the gyms. This also promoted the Helix Gen snack bars and raised awareness of good health. Every Helix customer had discounts on other Helix products and services. Profits for Helix Inc. continued to rise. The profits were used to fund research and develop Helix Pharma further. Helix Inc.'s popularity continued to grow. But the value of Helix Inc. was still equal to Horus Inc. Their stock prices went up and down by tiny amounts everyday, like two horses in a race desperately trying to outperform the other.

***

Two weeks later, it was announced the Mayor would read out a speech which was broadcast by Blue Eagle TV. The whole city watched and listened. The employees of Helix Inc. had their radios on as they worked, but the Helix siblings sat in a boardroom to watch on the big screen.

"Good morning, Honourable Citizens of Coast City. First I want to thank you all for raising your concerns with me. As you know there is an election coming up and it is my duty as a Mayor to serve you as best as I can. It is vital that we work together to keep Coast City a safe, peaceful, and a prosperous place to live. Having looked at all the research and all the information in-depth, it is with great pleasure that I announce that cannabis oil will be a legal medical drug for all. From now on, cancer will no longer be a threat to our health, or a lingering anxiety. Medicine is not a luxury, it's a necessity. When we have the knowledge and technology, it is unthinkable to allow sickness to take away our friends and loved ones. I would also like to take this opportunity to thank the Helix siblings for carrying out the research and supplying me with all the data that was necessary to make this a reality. So starting today, we work together to rid the world of cancer one breakthrough at a time. Coast City will not only survive, but it will lead the way in medical research."

The siblings gasped and jumped with joy.

"Yeeeeeah!" Eric threw his fist in the air.

"Yes!" Jodie let out.

"Woohoooo!" cheered Toby. He jumped up and down and waved his arms in the air.

"We did it!" shouted Penelope. She threw both fists in the air like a champion. And then they all came together and

352

threw their arms around each other into a big embrace. They gave each other a big tight squeeze. They couldn't help but laugh at their success.

"Come on guys," said Eric. "Let's go see Gosia."

They then rushed over to the top floor to join Gosia. The bodyguards opened the doors. Gosia got up from her seat and smiled at them. They rushed over to her.

"Hey Gosia, did you see the Mayor's speech?" Penelope asked.

"Yes I did. Well done," said Gosia. "You should be pleased with yourselves."

"We couldn't have done it without you," said Jodie. She put her arms around Gosia and gave her big hug. All the other siblings joined with the group hug.

That did it. The whole city cheered. The Mayor's speech was shared all over the internet and it spread like wildfire. Helix Inc.'s popularity exploded. Helix Inc. delivered the final blow to Horus Inc. and knocked them out of the competition. The stock prices of Helix Inc. sky-rocketed. The ultimate corporate annihilation.

And then the siblings worked with the Mayor to promote his election campaign. Working alongside all the biggest corporations of Coast City, Dove Bank, Brooks Inc., and Crow Cars to name a few teamed up with Helix Inc. to fund the Mayor's election campaign. Election day arrived and the Mayor won. The siblings stood by the Mayor as he celebrated his victory.

The next morning after the success of his campaign, the Mayor walked into his office with excitement. In his hands he had a sealed box, he put it on the table and opened it. He took out a photograph of the Mayor himself celebrating his election victory. Standing next to him were the four Helix siblings. He put that photograph next to the photo of him with Gerald Helix. He smiled and exhaled with pride. Another photograph added to his collection of memories, another record of success. His table of photographs resembled a polyptych in a church. He stood back to marvel at his collection and crossed his arms for a moment. With the shutters opened, the sun shined its bright rays through the windows, giving the office a new sense of warmth. He nodded, went to his desk, and went back to work.

Chapter 47

One morning, Jodie and Penelope were in a boardroom together. They sat at a table where wedding magazines and catalogues were spread out displaying pages of stunning photography. Outside, it was partly cloudy yet the sun shined on the gloss finish of the pages that gave the room an extra glow. Jodie and Penelope chatted away as they sipped on coffee in between. Their eyes widened with excitement as they flipped through the pages. Almost every new design was followed by another gasp of amazement. Just then they heard a knock at the door.

"Come in," Penelope called out. Toby entered the room panting in his suit. "You run a marathon?" She teased.

"How many more pounds have you shed?" Jodie winked.

"Oh stop it," said Toby as he laughed it off. "Listen! I got some great news. I just had a meeting with Helix Tech. We now have enough funds to make a new Helix Console! We are back in the video game industry!" He yelled out with excitement as he spread out his arms. "It's a dream come true. I am finally building my own console and we'll be developing our own games too." He stopped to get his breath back. "So now, I need you to spread the word. We are about to commence the research and development phase before we announce a release date."

"Sure. That's great news," Penelope replied with a smile.

"Uhh... how come you two look so happy?" Toby asked. The wedding magazines on the table caught his attention. "Someone getting married?"

Jodie and Penelope looked at each other with an inaudible conversation. Shall we tell him? Sure. And then they turned to him.

"Yup," said Penelope. "We are." Jodie nodded with a wide smile. "El-Taco proposed to me the other day. And I said yes," said Penelope.

"Cactus proposed. I said yes."

"Wow! That's great news. Congratulations. This is unexpected. Well I, uh... speaking of weddings, I've got news of my own too. I proposed to Adee Lee. And she said Yes!"

"Wooohooo!" Penelope cheered.

"There's gonna be three weddings." Jodie let out with joy.

"I got an idea. You should invite her over here so we can plan them together," said Penelope.

"We gotta share this with Eric," said Jodie. She took out here phone and called Eric.

"Hey Eric. Come quick. We got something to show you... Oh we have some weddings to plan... how did I know what?... huh?... We're in Penelope's boardroom... Okay see you in a bit." She ended the call. "He's coming now. Hmmm. He sounded like he was caught off-guard when I mentioned weddings."

"Oh?" Penelope let out with curiosity.

"You don't think he's got wedding bells ringing in his head. Do you?"

"We'll see." Jodie replied.

The door soon opened and Eric walked in. As he shut the door behind him his eyes went from one sibling to the other like he had been caught getting up to mischief.

"Hey guys, what's going on?" asked Eric. His voice was quiet.

"Hey Eric! Check this out, we got weddings to plan." Toby put a hand on Eric's back and guided him to the table of magazines. "Look!"

"Errr... who's wedding is this?" asked Eric.

"Mine," said Jodie with a big smile.

"Mine," Penelope chimed in with a giggle.

"Mine too," said Toby.

"Come on. Is this a joke?" Eric asked with a raised eyebrow.

"Nope," Penelope squeaked. "El-Taco proposed to me and I said yes."

"Cactus asked me to marry him and I accepted."

"And I asked Adee Lee to marry me. She said yes."

"Wow," said Eric. He was out of breath in an instant. "You had me scared for a minute there."

"Why?" asked Toby.

"You thinking of marriage too?" asked Jodie.

"Well... uh," Eric began, he brushed his hair with his hand and gave his head a nervous tilt to one side. "Actually, it's as if you've read my mind." He allowed a smile to spread across his face. "I have news of my own."

"Here we go," said Jodie. She leaned in, placed her elbows on the table and rested her chin on to her hands. She listened with intent.

"Ooooooh," Penelope let out.

"What?" asked Toby.

"I asked Marie to marry me. She said yes," Said Eric.

"Eric, that's fantastic," Jodie replied.

"Oh my god that's great news!" Penelope burst out as she linked her fingers together. Jodie and Penelope jumped to their feet and gave their brothers a big hug. They held each other tightly for a moment.

"That makes four weddings!" Penelope squeaked.

"Or one with all four of us," said Jodie.

"Wow. This is going to be the biggest wedding ever!" Toby yelled. "We ought to tell the world!"

"Let's go and tell Gosia. Together," said Jodie. "Then we can spread the word."

They all left the boardroom and then walked over to the elevator at a fast pace.

As the elevator made its way up to the floor of the CEO office, none of the siblings were able to keep still since they were overjoyed with excitement. Eric tapped the heel of his shoe to the floor. Toby leaned against the wall with his arms crossed while trying to steady his breathing. He kept his eyes on the lights of the elevator as if he was being lifted into the heavens. Meanwhile Jodie and Penelope giggled among themselves as they whispered to one another.

The elevator doors opened, and they noticed the bodyguards were gone. They walked over to the double doors.

"Huh? She can't have gone out now?" said Toby.

"We'll see," said Eric. He knocked on the doors. Nothing happened. Then Eric took out his card key. "Hmmm, what if...?" He tapped the panel by the doors with it, the green light on the panel lit up, the doors clicked as they unlocked.

"How the–?" Jodie let out.

They walked into the CEO office. It was empty. The siblings looked around, puzzled.

"Where could she have gone?" asked Penelope. They walked in. Eric looked at his card key and scratched his head.

"How could my card open these doors?" Eric asked out loud.

"Maybe the card access system accidentally upgraded your card status to CEO level. A glitch in the update perhaps," said Toby. "If that's the case then... here, let me try mine." Toby left the office and closed the doors, the panel inside the room lit up green, and then Toby came back in. "Hey! Mine too. I hope no one else gains access here. I'll go check it out later."

"Hey look," said Jodie. She spotted something on the main desk and walked over to it. There was an envelope and a remote control next to it. Their names were written on the envelope. "It's for us." She picked up the envelope and opened it. The other three siblings walked over to her. Jodie took out the letter and read it out loud.

"Dear Eric, Jodie, Penelope, and Toby,

It is with deep regret that I have to leave. I will no longer be working at Helix Inc. Since I have stepped down as Vice-President, you are now the CEOs of Helix Inc. By now your cards will be updated. I have sent my bodyguards on vacation, however Helix Security is available at your command.

Thank you so much for saving my life. I didn't think I'd live to share this news with you. You have given me a second chance in life. During my treatment, I commissioned a paternal DNA test to find out who I am and where my family was before I left this earth. I know where they are now, I spoke to them. They are expecting me. So now I am going back to Poland. It's a little village north-west of Gdansk. I plan to settle down, get married, and have children.

I'm sorry to leave at such a short notice. Once you press the mark on the remote control, everything will be explained. Despite the little time we spent together, I have grown to love you. I will miss you all.

Take good care of each other.

Yours,
Gosia Kowalski"

The siblings stood in silence. Jodie put the letter down. They glanced at one another in confusion.

"She... she's gone," said Toby.

"We didn't get to tell her," said Penelope with disappointment. "She won't be at our wedding."

"Why couldn't she tell us before she left?" asked Jodie.

Jodie picked up the remote control. On one of the buttons

of the remote control was dried dot of dark blue paint to indicate what button to press. "Everything will be revealed I hope," said Jodie. She pointed it at the gigantic Helix TV screen in front of the desk, and pressed the button.

The screen switched on. First it showed the Helix Inc. logo slowly spinning with the text 'Loading' at the bottom. And then the footage began to play. The siblings gasped at what they saw. An elderly man was lying on a large comfortable bed with silk bed sheets. He was in some luxurious bedroom in a mansion with gold decorated mahogany furniture. It was Gerald Helix. He looked nothing like the way the siblings last saw him. He wasn't a strong man standing tall in a suit. He was weak, fragile, and he struggled to breathe. He took in one deep breath and then slowly let it out. His grey hair was white. His face sagged and his cheek bones stuck out. In a short space of time, he looked like he aged another twenty years. He groaned in pain. His voice was weak. He swallowed, and then he began to speak:

"My dearest children, Eric, Jodie, Penelope, Toby,

First I want to say sorry for everything I put you through. By the time you are watching this I will be gone. Resting at the family mausoleum. I have not been truthful in my last remaining days. But... let me explain.

It was me. I did it. All of it.

I knew something awful was going to happen after I left Helix. It was me who paid off the judge. It was I who made sure you got the same prison sentence. With you in prison, I executed the next part of my plan. I created Horus Inc. to knock Helix Inc. down to the bottom, but I kept it financially afloat to prevent it from going bankrupt while you were gone. It was me. I was the CEO of Horus Inc.

It was I who asked Barry Brooks, Crow Cars, and Dove Bank to work with me behind the scenes. It was I who consulted the Mayor on the aquarium and the monorail project.

It was I who told Gosia what to do. I made her Vice-

President of Helix Inc. to keep things going. Please don't be mad at them. They only did what I asked them to do.

You are probably mad at me right now, but please understand.

All I ever wanted was to see you all succeed. To continue our family's legacy. This was my last act of hope. To get you all to change. You are now magnificent, responsible adults. I am so proud of you.

As a final parting gift, Horus Inc. now belongs to you. Do with it as you will.

You have earned it.

Goodbye."

Gerald Helix used the last of his strength to smile. The screen went black. The footage stopped. And then panels began to open slowly. Jodie dropped the remote control as tears began to fill up in her eyes and her jaw trembled. Penelope covered her mouth with both hands, and began to cry. Eric and Toby bowed their heads in sadness. The red curtains opened up one last time to reveal what was hidden. The siblings gasped at what they saw.

"What the–?!" Eric exclaimed.

"Oh my God!" Penelope cried.

"How?" Toby froze.

Jodie was lost for words as she covered her mouth with a hand.

The painting of Katherine Helix had changed. Standing next to her was Gerald Helix himself in the very outfit they last saw him. He was depicted in his sharp black suit, his blackish-silver tie, and his grey hair brushed back. He was complete with a silver belt buckle, a silver pin on his suit, and the silver cufflinks with the Helix Inc. logo on them. It was as if he walked into the painting after the siblings left that evening. His eyes looked into the beholder with a serious stare. The stern look pierced through their souls. His appearance was the opposite of Katherine's compassionate smile. And yet, somehow, the painting looked complete. The Helix couple reunited in Heaven. Both were perfectly depicted.

In an instant, Jodie felt weak, unable to stand. She sat on the leather chair behind her, buried her face into her hands and began to cry.

"Dad!" Penelope cried. Her voice broke from crying.

"Is this some sick joke?" Toby cried.

Toby and Penelope sat on the chairs in front of the main desk and bowed their heads. Penelope took off her small-frame glasses, covered her eyes, and then began to cry. Toby loosened his tie and unbuttoned the collar of his shirt. But Eric stood quiet. His face went from sadness to a raging frown. He breathed through his nose like an angry bull. He seized the telephone on the desk and dialled a number.

"Is this reception? ... Get me security right now!" he commanded. There was a pause. "Security? Now listen you, I want all surveillance footage of this building. You got that?... Since the time we got back... What do you mean 'what am I looking for?' There has been a break-in!" There was a longer pause. "I want to know who's been in this office since we got back... since uh... the day you picked us up from prison. Get on it." There was another long pause. "Well?... No break-in?... All access was approved? By who? ... What? Why would you delete certain time periods? ... Who told you to do that?... What do you mean you don't know?!"

"It's no use, Eric," said Jodie. "Dad must have told them to." She wiped her eyes with her hands. She sniffed. Penelope also sniffed as he wiped her tears with her hands. Eric's breathing became frantic as he looked at Jodie. The voice on the other line could be heard.

"Yeah, I'm still here," said Eric. "No, I'm not alright! I just found out my father is dead! God damn it!" Eric slammed the phone down and leaned on the desk to steady himself. He tried to regain his breath as his chest expanded and contracted. His breathing hissed through his teeth.

"Sit down, Eric," whispered Jodie. Eric became weak. He staggered over to one of the chairs in front of the desk. He sat down, sank his head down, and sobbed. He loosened his tie and unbuttoned the collar of his shirt.

"What do we do now?" asked Penelope. "I wanted to tell him the good news. And now..." Penelope began to cry again. Jodie got up, walked over to Penelope and held her in her arms. She squeezed tightly.

"We are all we've got now," said Jodie.

There was a long moment of silence. The sky outside darkened with grey clouds that concealed the blue sky. A flash of white light was followed by a crack of thunder. Suddenly rain began to hit the glass floor-to-ceiling windows and the water ran down their surfaces. The sound of rain dominated the office. All four siblings sat in mutual sadness and grief.

"Wait a minute," said Toby, "The family mausoleum? That's where he is."

"We gotta get there right now." Eric stood up.

"Come on," said Jodie. She helped Penelope get on to her feet. They made their way through the doors, down the hallway, and then into the elevator. Jodie snapped back to reality when she noticed herself in one the mirrors in the elevator.

"We can't go out like this," said Jodie. She sniffed again and wiped her eyes with her hands. And then she wiped Penelope's tears with her hands. She too sniffed. Eric and Toby looked at themselves in the mirrors, they buttoned up their collars and adjusted their ties. "We act as if nothing happened. Okay?" The rest of the siblings nodded in agreement. They reached the ground floor and made their way to reception. Their request was met immediately, two bodyguards appeared from behind the reception desk, and then they escorted the siblings to the car park below. The black Helix MPV emerged from the underground car park into the stormy weather outside where the rain continued to drizzle onto the city.

The family mausoleum was a marble building in the grand garden of Helix Manor. It was shaped like an ancient Greek temple with ionic columns on the outside of it that held up the roof. The marble was a white prosecco colour with waves of pale white lines along the surface. The walls had diamond shaped stained glass windows placed in between each column. The building itself was on a large marble platform with four steps that led to the doorway with a black metal gate. The whole exterior of the mansion was well maintained despite Gerald's absence. The MPV slowly drove along the cobbled road that lead to the grand garden and stopped. The four siblings emerged from the vehicle, and rushed into the mausoleum while the bodyguards waited in the car.

The interior of the mausoleum was also a white prosecco colour. The sound of their footsteps echoed all around them as they walked on the marble floor. This was where everyone bearing the Helix family name was put to rest. It felt cold inside. The siblings took their time as they scanned every name on every golden plaque as they looked around. And then they spotted the brand new golden plaque with his name on it, 'Gerald Helix' which was next to Katherine Helix's plaque.

"He died quite recently," said Toby. His voice was beginning to break.

Penelope walked up to the plaque and began to cry again. Jodie walked over to the plaque and placed her hand on it, after feeling the cold metal for a moment she stepped back. Eric did the same, but then he turned away with his eyes firmly shut. He shook his head before opening his eyes as they began to fill with tears.

"Eric? Are you alright?" asked Jodie.

"I didn't get to say goodbye to him," said Eric. He sniffed. His breathing became unsteady. "I just remembered the last thing I said to him."

The other siblings froze in silence. Stunned. The memory

of their last confrontation was replayed in their heads. Each voice echoed within.

"Screw you man!" Eric's voice echoed.

"Fuck you asshole!" Jodie's voice echoed.

"Drop dead you misogynist pig!" Penelope's voice echoed.

"You're a fuckin' lunatic," Toby's voice echoed.

Although the voices were in their heads, they felt like they were shouted inside the mausoleum right where they were standing. Echoing, loud, and clear, haunting them like ghosts.

"Oh God... Daddy, I'm so sorry." Penelope broke down again. She walked over to Gerald's plaque, placed both hands on it, pressed her face to it, and cried uncontrollably. She tightened her eyes shut. Struck with grief. "I wish I could hug you right now." Her throat struggled as she swallowed hard through her crying. Tears ran down her cheeks like the rain that ran down the stained glass windows of the mausoleum. She hyperventilated until Toby came over to her and held her in his arms.

"Don't worry, Penelope," Toby whispered. "I've got you." Somehow his arms and warm chest soothed her, her breathing became steady again. Eric turned back to face the golden plaque and placed a hand above it as he looked closely at it.

"Dad, I'm sorry," he whispered. "I wish you were here right now... so I can tell you that." He leaned his forehead on the back of his hand. Jodie walked over to Eric and leaned on him as she placed a hand on the plaque.

"So do I," she sobbed. "So do I."

They huddled together as they leaned against the cold marble bearing the gold plaque. Tears rolled down their cheeks as the rain continued outside. There was a flash of lightning followed by a roaring crack of thunder. It rained heavier. The siblings were unmoved by it. They allowed time to pass by as the heavy rain came down. There was something in the sound of the rain that eased the pain.

After a while, they slowly pulled themselves together and

made their way to the mausoleum's doorway where the gate was ajar.

"I can't bear to look at this place," said Penelope. Her voice croaked from all the crying. She dried her tears.

"You know, I never felt the need to come here until now. Maybe I should visit more often." Toby said as he looked at the other plaques. "To pay my respects. After all, these people are our ancestors. There's still much about them we don't know. But I want to learn."

"All in good time," said Jodie.

"We have to tell the world about Dad," said Eric.

"Not now, Eric," said Jodie. "We need time."

"If not now, when?" asked Toby.

"You guys go home," said Penelope. "I'll tell everyone at Helix what's going on. We'll spread the word later. I'll take care of the rest."

The rain softened a bit. The four siblings made their way back to the Helix MPV that awaited them. They didn't care about the rain soaking them. They walked at such a slow pace that they almost dragged their feet along the way. They got into the vehicle, closed the door, and then the MPV made its way out of the manor, back to the city.

***

Penelope came back into the boardroom where all the magazines and catalogues were laid on the table. Her hair and blazer were soaked in the rain. She sneezed, sniffed, and then wiped her nose with a wet handkerchief. She walked over to the table to look at the pictures of wedding dresses, wedding cakes, flowers and decorations. She sighed as she gathered the magazines to tidy the table.

As she closed the pages of each magazine and catalogue, she made a pile on one end of the table. She stopped when she saw the sight of the cityscape outside. She went over to the window and observed the cityscape under the grey sky. The buildings themselves looked depressed with the rain pouring down on them, it looked as if they were crying at their loss too. Penelope went back to the table to finish tidying the table until she made one big pile of magazines stacked on top of one another.

"The wedding will have to wait," she said to herself. She picked up the pile and put it on a small table in the corner of the boardroom where a small plant stood. She took out a little paper cup from the water cooler, filled half of it with water and watered the plant. She crushed the paper cup with her hand and threw it into the blue 'Recycle' bin.

She made her way to the door to leave before she heard a knock, she opened it. It was Jane Saunders looking all excited.

"Heeyyy." She gave a little wave with her hand. "I do hope I'm not too late to join in on the wedding plans." Her smile faded when she saw Penelope's face. "Penelope? What's wrong? Where's Jodie?" Penelope waved her in, Jane entered the boardroom, and then closed the door. Penelope had her head titled to one side as she looked down on the floor.

"We'll have to talk about the wedding some other time," said Penelope. Her voice was beginning to break again.

"What's happened?" Asked Jane who looked worried.

"It's my Dad. I just found out he's dead."

"No!" Jane gasped. In shock she covered her mouth with a hand for a moment before taking it away. "How?"

"Natural causes I guess. He said goodbye to us in a video before he died."

"But... where is he now?"

"He's resting at the family mausoleum. I just came back from there."

"Oh Penelope, I am so sorry. ... come here." She held her arms out and embraced her. "I feel awful," said Jane.

"So do I," Penelope croaked. She tried not to cry again, holding back tears. "There's something else too. Gosia's gone. She has left the company for good."

"Then... Who's in charge now?"

"I am. And so are my brothers and sister. We are the CEOs of Helix Inc. now."

"Oh my god. Penelope, I don't what to say. But what about Jodie? Eric? Toby? Where are they?"

"They know. They've gone home."

"You should take the day off too." Jane urged, she placed a hand on Penelope's shoulder.

"Maybe. But I need Helix Press to start getting ready to spread the word. That's why I came back here. We decided to do this tomorrow. Hopefully by then I'll be in the right state of mind."

"You go home, Penelope. I'll take care of the rest."

Penelope nodded. "Okay."

"Come on, I'll walk you down. How are you getting home?"

"Cab."

"Okay."

The rain continued to pour outside. Jane accompanied Penelope to the front door, she hailed a yellow cab not caring about getting wet in the rain. Penelope went into the cab and Jane ran back indoors.

***

The next day, it was all over the news that Gerald Helix was dead. The citizens of Coast City went about their lives at a slower pace than usual, but with saddened faces. Many read the news on their Helix phones. Heaven sealed the sky with dark grey clouds and brought forth the rain that soaked the city that needed a good shower to ease the pain. The rain was steady, it came down and splashed on their umbrellas as people walked.

The newspaper kiosk was overwhelmed with customers. They all had pictures of Gerald Helix on them, in his suit with a smile. The headlines read:

"Gerald Helix Dead"

"Legend Lost"

"RIP Gerald Helix"

As the clerk arranged the papers in his kiosk, the black street cleaner pulled along his wheeled bin and stopped to look at the newspapers. He was also quiet. There was no whistling from him that day. The clerk and the cleaner looked at each other for a moment but said nothing. Their sad faces did all the talking. The black street cleaner tipped his hat at the clerk, the clerk nodded and resumed his work, and the street cleaner walked along pulling his wheelie bin.

Chapter 48

The city was at a standstill that day. The sky was concealed with dark grey clouds. A vast crowd gathered in a small park down the road from the park where the Jeffery Irons statue stood. The crowd was made up of students who took time out of their lectures to pensioners who risked the cold, wet weather, but there were no banners, no colours to identify with anything. They were all united with a mutual emotion– sadness and grief. Only silence, except in between the speeches.

This was the commemoration ceremony of Gerald Helix. On the stage was a podium with two flags that stood next to it, the dark blue Coast City flag and the American flag. Next to the stage where the podium stood was a structure of equal size to the Jeffery Irons statue that was covered with a large dark blue piece of cloth. Cameramen and reporters from different TV channels including Blue Eagle TV surrounded the stage and the concealed structure for live broadcasts. On the stage stood the Mayor, behind him sat the four Helix siblings in their black suits. They sat up straight, shoulders back with their heads held high, with no emotion on their faces; the tears can wait. They took their turns to read out a speech, each one telling a funny story reminiscing some childhood memories with their father, at least that somehow eased the pain. The sound that came out of the speakers echoed across the open park. The crowd remained silent while some wiped tears from their eyes, either with their fingers or with a handkerchief.

Once the speeches were over, the Mayor and the siblings made their way down from the stage to the ground, and then they walked over to the great concealed structure. The siblings reached out to the cloth and pulled it down to reveal a new black statue on a pedestal. It was of Gerald Helix in his suit just as he looked in the painting in his office. Unlike the serious face of Jeffery Irons, his face was smiling. The crowd clapped as they marvelled at the new black statue. On the pedestal was a huge gold plaque with Gerald Helix's name engraved into it. And underneath his name was the quote "Freedom, Prosperity, and Peace." Eric stepped forward and placed his hand on the gold plaque. Just as his fingertips touched the cold piece of metal, rain drops landed on his hand and on the plaque. He looked up and he saw that it was about to rain. The ceremony was coming to an end. As though the Heavens wanted to participate in its closure by relieving itself with tears of its own.

The crowd gathered around the statue to take a closer look and offer their condolences to the siblings. Each person shook their hands and offered words of comfort. The siblings were only able to force a smile back, nod in acknowledgment and to express gratitude for them for coming. Among the crowd were their fiancés. Marie Baker walked over to Eric and kissed him on his cheek. Cactus walked over to Jodie and held her in his arms. El-Taco followed suit as he held Penelope in his arms. Adee Lee took the day off from Blue Eagle TV to comfort Toby, she held on to his arm. The couples looked up at the statue together. They could not hold back their sadness any longer. The one person they wanted most at their weddings was not coming. That fact had not yet sunk in. The collective sadness among the city's crowd was too much to bear. It's as if all the citizens of Coast City were saying, "It's okay. Let it out. We feel your pain."

Jodie turned, placed her head on Cactus's chest and began to cry. Tears rolled down her eyes. He held her closer.

"I want my Dad back," said Jodie. Her voice was breaking.

"I know," said Cactus. He placed a hand on her cheek.

"Who's going to walk me down the aisle on our wedding day?" Jodie asked.

"I will," said a familiar voice. Jodie turned to look. It was Barry Brooks. He stood strong with his cane and a stoic look on his face. "That is, if you'd like me to." Jodie nodded, wiped her tears with her fingers, forced a smile and then embraced Barry. And then she introduced Barry to Cactus, they shook hands.

Penelope cried on El-Taco's shoulder. "I have no Daddy to walk me down the aisle," she said. And then someone placed a hand on the back of her shoulder, she turned to see who it was. It was the Mayor.

"Penelope, would you allow me to accompany you on your wedding day?" said the Mayor. Penelope was stunned, she too forced a smile.

"Yes sir, I'd like that very much." She couldn't hold herself. She embraced the Mayor. He held her as if he would have held his own daughter.

The sadness of the crowd was taking its toll on Toby. If he stood there any longer, he feared, he may break down. "Let's just get this over with," he thought.

As if Adee had read his mind. She held on to his arm with both hands and tightened her grip. "This will pass. It will be water under the bridge in no time." She kissed him on his cheek. "Trust me." She embraced him. And then he held her tight.

Eric held his stoic facade, he hadn't blinked for a while. His mind was whizzing with all kinds of thoughts. Marie felt a raging fire in his stomach.

"Eric, look at me," said Marie. She held his head with both hands as she looked into his eyes. "He may not be at our wedding in person, but he'll be there in spirit." She kissed him on the lips, finger-combed his hair to the right, and smiled at him. The fire in his stomach was extinguished. He embraced her and held her tight.

The rain began to intensify. The organisers began to pack up the stage and put away the chairs, the flags and the podium. The reporters accompanied their cameramen as they stopped filming and packed up their cameras and equipment, and then they left. The crowd slowly dispersed as they opened up their umbrellas and disappeared back into the streets of the city. All except one person who walked into the park. The black street cleaner stood in front of the statue and looked up as it rained. He didn't care about the water tapping on his hat, either to discourage him from getting wet before catching a cold, or maybe trying to remind him to get back to work. This would be the only time alone with the statue of his idol before the city resumed its lively routine.

"Oh Gerry," he whispered. He tried to think of something to say out loud. A farewell message perhaps? He sighed as he reminisced all the good times the city had with him. He stood there silently for a few more moments as he leaned on his broom like a walking stick. But all he could muster was "Goodbye Gerry." He tipped his hat and walked away.

Chapter 49

The following spring arrived, Saint Luke's Cathedral was illuminated by the brightest of sunlight that shined through the stained glass windows as though the Heavens had smiled upon the City that day. It was the wedding day of the Helix siblings.

The cathedral was of pure divinity. Almost every surface was made of silver white marble. So clean and shiny. The gothic windows were made of elaborate tracery designs filled with multi-coloured stained glass. When the sunlight beamed through stained glass, it shined the colours onto the silver white marble which made the floors look like a heavenly garden of multi-coloured flowers. The floral designs were mixtures of green, blue, yellow, and red. Some of the windows depicted the saints, among them Saint Luke himself.

The repetition of pointed arches joined together like they were a forest of neatly arranged tall trees held up by large marble pillars. There was a gentle scent of incense that hung in the air that gave the place a sense of relaxation. The polyptych at the front of the cathedral had paintings of Mary, Jesus, and of Saint Luke the Physician, with golden frames. The nave was decorated with tall white vases that had a mixture of pink and white roses. The white vases had dark blue ribbons that spiralled around them from the top to the bottom. The rows of seats were filled with the biggest names of Coast City, and celebrities from around the United States. It was as if Coast City was having a royal wedding of its own. The front seats were filled with the closest and distant relatives of the Helix family who had travelled miles to be here. They chatted among themselves as they waited eagerly to see the brides.

At the front by the altar stood the priest who held a large leather-bound bible with solid gold corners. Eric, Toby, Cactus, and El-Taco were in black suits that were decorated with a white rose each. They had dark blue ties. They all had silver Helix jewellery on them; tie pins, cufflinks, watches, and belt buckles. Next to them stood their best men.

The music of the organ began playing the bridal chorus. It made the hairs on everyone's body stand on end. The cathedral came to life with the divine echo coming from the wind instrument. Hearing it gave everyone a jolt of excitement as everyone got up onto their feet and stood. Many had their phones out to film and take pictures. It brought tears to many women who had their handkerchiefs out to wipe their tears of joy. Excitement filled the air.

Inspired by the painting of Katherine Helix, Jodie and Penelope decided to use the exact same colours she wore.

Her dress was ivory and the four roses she held were pink for her daughters and white for her sons. And so the brides wore ivory wedding dresses and the bouquets they held were of pink roses. They each wore a silver tiara with spirals that resembled the Helix logo surrounded by silver flowery designs. Jodie had her long blonde hair straightened as if she had a head of gold silk that went down to her bust. Penelope had her short brown hair cut down to the shoulder. She wore her specs with small thin silver frames. Marie Baker's long blonde hair was all wavy that also went down to her bust. Adee Lee was the only redhead, long and straight hair that went down to the bust. All jewellery were made of silver, with swirls, spirals, and diamonds. There were smiles all around.

First Marie Baker's father walked her down the aisle over to Eric. And then Jodie took Barry Brooks' arm and he walked her down the aisle over to Cactus. She gave him the look of thank you as if to thank her own father. Barry Brooks smiled back. Then Penelope took the Mayor's arm and he walked her down the aisle over to El-Taco as if she was his own daughter. And finally, Adee Lee's father walked her down the aisle over to Toby Helix. Each bride was accompanied by two brides-maids in pink dresses. The couples looked at one another with immense joy before turning to the priest who then opened his bible and began to read passages from it. The organ stopped playing, and then everyone sat down in silence. The priest read out the following verses from the bible:

Genesis, Chapter 1, Verses 26-28

And God said, Let us make man in our image, after our likeness:
and let them have dominion over the fish of the sea, and over the birds of the air,
and over the cattle, and over all the earth,
and over every creeping thing that creepeth upon the earth.

So God created man in his own image,
in the image of God he created him; male and female he
created them.

And God blessed them, and God said unto them,
Be fruitful and multiply, and replenish the earth, and
subdue it:
and have dominion over the fish of the sea, and over the
birds of the air,
and over every living thing that moveth upon the earth.

Then the priest asked each of the couples if they would love, comfort, honour, and support each other through hard times for as long they lived, and they all agreed to their vows. The bridesmaids and best men produced the rings, the couples put them on, each followed by a loving kiss. The cathedral came to life again with the organ playing the wedding march. The newlywed couples made their way down the aisle towards the main doors to make their exit.

The sky was clear and the sun beamed its warm light onto the city. Birds flew around the cathedral as the wedding bells rang. The doors opened and the crowd outside let out loud cheers of joy as they threw confetti at the couples. The Helix drones hovered above the crowds as they filmed to broadcast live on the Helix app. The vast majority of the crowd filmed and took pictures with their Helix phones.

In the distance down the road from the cathedral was the newsagent at his kiosk and the black street cleaner. They watched as the couples exited the cathedral. The black street cleaner took off his hat and waved it with celebration, he let out a laughter of joy. The newsagent had a little party tooter in hand, he blew it, and then laughed it off.

In front of the main doorways of the cathedral stood four white Helix Classic cars from the 1940s decorated with ribbons of dark blue, pink, and ivory. Just before the couples entered the vehicles, the brides tossed their bouquets into the air, and then the lucky ladies in the crowd caught them, each one letting out a laughter of joy. The couples got into their cars and were driven off to their honeymoons.

Chapter 50

Daniel Crawley was on the subway train earlier than usual. When the subway train arrived at the platform, it seemed to have moved faster that day. A briefcase in one hand, he checked his watch with the other arm, it was 8:38 am. "Good," he thought.

The doors opened, the commuters took their time as they went on to the platform and made their way towards the exits or onto other conjoining platforms. Daniel followed his familiar path towards the stairs that led to the outside world. As he walked along with the commuters he spotted new adverts on LED screens on the walls along the walkways, almost all of them displayed Helix products: The upcoming Helix Video Game console with games available for pre-order, the new Helix Tablet to accompany the Helix smart phone, Helix perfumes and aftershaves, The Helix Hatchback Car that came with reduced Helix Car Insurance, and the new Helix Fridge that was larger and used less electricity. This made Daniel smile in satisfaction. Knowing that he worked for the biggest and most successful corporation in the whole city, and that he played a role in many of their projects. He looked around and noticed among the commuters that the vast majority of them were using the Helix phone, either to read the latest news, play a game, listen to music, or watch the latest TV show. He also noticed a lot of people were wearing the Helix brand of clothing for all kinds of occasions, be it casual or for work. This inflated his chest with pride. "Yup, I work there," he thought. He made his way up the stairs to the ground level.

It was a bright and sunny spring day in Coast City. The

city was alive with the usual sound of people's footsteps on the pavement and the traffic on the roads. He breathed in a sigh of relief to be out into the city. He was still early so he took his time to look up at the skyscrapers and marvelled at their architecture. When he saw the Helix tower, he felt a pleasant surge go through his mind. "Work, here I come," he thought.

"Good morning, Daniel," he heard a familiar voice.

"Good morning, Kamau," replied Daniel.

"Have a good day." The black street cleaner tipped his hat and smiled as he swept the pavement with his broom. He whistled the familiar Vivaldi Spring tune. Daniel saw the familiar portable coffee stall and decided to treat himself to a latte. But there was a different girl at the stall, she looked young, possibly a college or a university student. He approached the stall took a look at the menu and noticed it was updated.

"Hmmm." Daniel let out intrigued.

"Good morning, sir. What can I get you?" said the barista. She had long curly brown hair, blue eyes, and a sweet smile.

"I think I'll try the Japanese Matcha Latte," said Daniel.

"Coming right up."

He read her name tag.

"Say, Ellen, where's Edwina?" he asked.

"Oh, she's a Supply Chain Manager now. She's the one who hired me," Ellen replied.

"You a student?"

"Yeah."

"In what field?"

"Medicine."

"That's good," said Daniel. "You see, I work for Helix Inc."

"Wow! Really?" Her face lit up with excitement.

"Yeah." He took out a business card and gave it to her. "Maybe in future we can get you into an internship at Helix Pharma. If you're interested."

"Oh definitely!" She took the card and looked at it. "I'll keep this for sure. Here's your latte Mr, Crawley. Have a nice day."

"Thank you, you may call me Daniel. Cheers."

He took his time as he walked towards the Helix tower taking one sip at a time. He threw the paper cup into a bin and went into the tower. He walked past the reception desk.

"Good morning, Esha," he greeted a young Indian woman, long black hair and an Indian tan behind the reception desk; she wore a dark blue blazer.

"Good morning, Mr Crawley." She greeted him with a smile.

Daniel made his way to the staff elevator. He tapped his ID card on to the panel next to the doors. It bleeped and the light on it went green. Then he pressed the button to call the elevator. As he waited for the elevator to come down, he heard hasty footsteps coming towards him. He turned to see who it was.

"Jane? Jane Saunders?"

"Oh Daniel, uh yeah." She was panting.

"Are you alright?"

"I'm fine. I thought I was running late. That's all. What are you doing here?" she asked.

"I have a meeting with the Helixes," Daniel replied.

"Me too," said Jane.

"Same time? 9am?"

"Yeah."

"Do you know what it's about?

"No. But it must be important since they want to see us first thing in the morning."

A gentle hum descended to the ground floor, the elevator doors opened.

"Come on, let's go up."

***

At the top floor, Eric Helix stood by his gigantic mahogany desk in the CEO office. He was in a black suit to go with his shiny black shoes. His brown hair was brushed back.

"Are all taxes paid?... Excellent... Thank you. Good day."
He put the phone down. However, Eric was not alone. Next
to his desk were three other desks that were also large and
mahogany. Next to Eric sat Jodie. Next to her sat Penelope.
And at the table on the end stood Toby.

Each desk had the name of the Helix CEO on a gold
plaque. The other siblings were talking on their phones. Jodie
was talking about a new fashion line to get it ready for spring
with a theme based on Easter. Penelope was talking on the
phone to an orphan charity she was hoping to raise money
for. Toby was on the phone talking to his colleagues about the
new Helix video game console, the Helix Dome II and how
they should get some more games ready for its release date.
Eric took his time to look out the window to enjoy the view of
the cityscape. The bright sunny day made him smile. Then he
leaned on his desk as he took a look around the office.

The painting of Katherine and Gerald Helix was on display in front of them, there was no need to hide it. Surrounding it were monochrome photographs of all their successful
projects and campaigns; Helix Pharma, El-Taco's concert,
Cactus in a Helix Fitness Gym, the Helix Motors Show room
with the new station wagon, the unveiling of the new Helix
phone, the Mayor's election victory etc. Next to them were
photos of their wedding with the Mayor and Barry Brooks.
Eric breathed a sigh of relief. He looked at his silver Helix
watch. He gestured to his siblings to remind them a meeting
was about to commence. One by one, they put their phones
down.

There was a knock at the double doors.

"Come in." Toby called out and in walked Daniel Crawley
and Jane Saunders.

"Hey Jane," Penelope waved with glee.

"Good morning to you all," said Daniel.

"Take a seat," Jodie gestured.

There were leather seats arranged in the form of a semi
circle in front of two of the middle desks. Eric and Toby got

hold of their leather desk chairs and brought them over to the table next to theirs. Eric sat next to Jodie at her desk. And Toby sat next to Penelope at her desk. That way they weren't so far apart and they wouldn't need to yell across the room.

"First, I– I mean WE would like to say a big thank you to you both for your hard work." All the siblings chuckled at the first line.

"Smashing start, Eric," Penelope giggled.

"Anyway, your dedication and commitment have brought Helix Inc. to the top. Once again we are the leaders of the market. We even beat Horus Inc. which is now a subsidiary of ours."

"Amazing," said Jane.

"I don't know what to say. Other than congratulations," said Daniel.

"Now let's talk about you," said Toby. "When we came out of prison, we were in a tight little corner but we stood our ground and fought."

"You guys did a fantastic job," said Jodie. "Daniel Crawley, you handled every project well. And Jane Saunders, you gave us the best marketing we needed. Without your contribution we wouldn't be here today."

"So we have come to the mutual decision that you both get a promotion and a pay rise," said Eric.

Daniel and Jane's face lit up. The news took their breath away.

"Jane, you are now Head of Marketing," said Penelope.

"Daniel Crawley, you are now Senior Project Director," said Jodie.

Daniel and Jane could not suppress a smile. They were almost out of breath in an instant. The siblings gave them a moment for the news to sink in.

"So what do you think?" asked Penelope.

"Thank you so much guys, I am... oh god, I'm delighted," said Jane with joy.

"I don't know what to say other then thank you very much." He tried to stay as humble as possible.

"We thought we keep it brief and to the point," said Eric. "Besides we got a lot of work to do. We have a lot of projects lined up for this year and the next. So we're going to need the best project manager and marketing team to work with us."

"Before we finish, is there anything you'd like to say?" asked Toby.

"Nope," Jane answered.

"Not at all," replied Daniel.

The meeting concluded when Jodie said with a smile, "Great. Let's get to work."

THE END

Acknowledgements

I would like to give special thanks to the editors for their efforts and for their support.

Dr. Stephen Carver at the Literary Consultancy and Dr Katie Isbester, Petya Tsankova, book designer, and Frances the proofreader at Clapham Publishing Services.

Without them I could never have achieved this novel and for that I am eternally grateful.

Franck Reporter for his amazing photograph for the cover.

Other stories from the Author

Just Business...

School Shooter

Trevor

The Forest

Lightning Source UK Ltd.
Milton Keynes UK
UKHW020634110722
405680UK00009B/718